THE
DAWNING
OF SCARLETT

JENNIFER OSBORN

First Edition
Indescribable Publishing
ISBN-13: 978-0692675649
ISBN-10: 0692675647

Cover photo – © 2016 Jennifer Osborn
Photography by christinaMarieThomas Photography

Cover design by Soxie Weston for Soxsational Cover
Art. www.soxsationalcoverart.com

Edited by KLH CreateWorks

Formatting by Max Effect, www.formaxeffect.com

Bramstall Logo © 2016 Jennifer Osborn
Artwork by Jerome Sayers

Revenant alphabet © 2016 Jennifer Osborn
Artwork by Jerome Sayers

For Kierdan

ONE
THE BIRTH

Sixteen years ago...

BRICE ELLIS DROVE SLOWLY IN A TORRENTIAL DOWN-pour as the car's wipers struggled to keep up with the onslaught of water. The radio blared *Burning Down the House* in a thrumming beat, but it did little to drown out the pounding on the roof of his car. It was dark and he cursed himself for going out so late. The rain would have been easier to handle in daylight. But that was him, constantly avoiding any type of contact with the world at large.

Although he wasn't far from home, the slow pace made him impatient. The lines on the road were hard to see and the occasional streetlights did almost nothing to help his vision along the deserted street.

The circuitous path to his house typically didn't bother him. His home was nestled far up in the mountains of northern New York, and he liked his cabin with all its books and isolation. He didn't have to deal with people and all the frustrations they brought. Sure, it was hard to be away from a good grocery store and he was forced to have propane brought to his home monthly. But he had electricity and running water, and that was enough for him. His only concession he granted himself in living so far away was the internet he just had installed. It was pricey but worth it.

It was grief that had pushed him to move out of society's reach. His new wife had died in childbirth, something for which he had been completely unprepared. That kind of thing was unheard of in this world of modern medicine and progress, so when Elaine had died, and the baby boy along with her, Brice's life changed forever. He quit the university as one of their youngest professors and dropped out of life altogether.

He gripped the steering wheel and cursed under his breath. He wanted to be home and tucked away safe from this rain. He had waited as long as he could to make a run for supplies, and now that he was out, he was trapped in one of the worst storms in recorded New York history.

Well, it's my own fault, he thought. He shouldn't have been so adverse to people that he would allow his supplies to get so low.

The first thing he was going to do when he got home was turn up the heat, have a hot shower, and go to bed. This cold, damp feeling was unbearable. He had a new, deeper appreciation for babies and nappies now. That thought made him wince as memories of Elaine and the baby came unbidden to his mind.

He reached down to the cup holder to get a drink of coffee when suddenly a dark specter rushed before the car in a blur. Slamming on the breaks, his head slammed into the steering wheel and his vision went white. He groaned as he leaned back, blinking until his vision cleared. Had he hit something? He hadn't heard a bang, but it had been so close.

What kind of animal had that been?

His eyes shot around in a panic looking for it, but he could only see the yellow of his headlights breaking through the oppressive darkness and the silver bullets of water as they sailed to the ground. He threw the car into park and got out.

He searched for what he might have hit. Nothing was there. No animal of any kind. Well, if it had been an animal, it would have to have been a bear; it had been so big. Brice spun around and looked toward the ditch to see if anything had landed there. But it was empty.

He stood stunned, not really knowing what to do. His heart pounded hard, and he looked around again to take a second sweep. Still, there was nothing.

Shaking his head, he got back into his car. He turned on the dome light to get a look at his forehead. He had an angry welt the size of an egg.

Tonight was just not his night. Perfect. Great.

He reached for his seatbelt and put it on. If any more rabid bears, or whatever it was, ran in front of him again, he'd be a little more restrained—with a killer headache and a nasty attitude.

He drove the rest of the way without incident. Thank God. He couldn't take anything else going wrong. His cabin stood as a shadow against the dark night, the front door illuminated by a single light. He pulled up to the front, rushed out of the car, and removed the bags from the trunk. Bounding into the cabin, he dropped the first set of bags on the floor and went out for the next.

It was on his third trip that he saw her. A woman lay outside his door, grasping her belly in pain. His heart thudded. What was a woman doing here? She was drenched, and the rain pelted her face without mercy. Even with her dark hair plastered to her forehead, she was so beautiful it momentarily stunned him.

"Help me," she ground out.

Her voice was like music, and it succeeded in moving him to action. He rushed to her and slid in the wet mud as he attempted to stop. He gathered her into his arms and started to take her into the cabin. Her hand shot out to grasp the doorjamb.

"Wait," she begged. "Are you alone?"

"Yes, why?"

Her hand went limp with the rest of her body. Brice carried her inside and deposited her on his bed. He turned to dig out his emergency cell phone from the drawer in his desk. It was a phone he never used but always kept charged, just in case. He began to dial as he spun back around to face the woman.

"No!" she screamed, her wide eyes with terror.

Brice stopped. "I have to get you some help." His finger was poised over the buttons to finish the last number on the keypad.

"No! Do not call anyone, do you understand?"

He couldn't understand her hesitation. "Look, I can tell you're in pain. I have to get help here, now." His voice trailed off as she dropped her hands to reveal a rather large belly. Oh, God. She was pregnant. And not just pregnant, but ready to deliver. His mind immediately went to Elaine and her last moments on this earth. His feet felt anchored to the floor as his mind saw Elaine crying out in pain. His past and present warped into a single, ghostly image. He blinked hard and tried to focus on the here and now.

The woman drew up her knees and screamed in pain. All the glass in the house exploded into tiny pieces and sailed on the air. Brice instinctively dropped to the floor to cover his head. He looked up to see her panting, and that was when he saw her eyes glowing green, her canines growing longer. He scrambled back as far as he could, the broken glass biting into his hands as he moved.

She screamed again, and he realized she was about to give birth. But to what? What was she? She turned to look at him, profound agony written on her face. She reached out to him. "Please help me. But only you," she forced out.

"What are you?" Brice slowly asked. She was something straight out of a Stephen King novel, but at the same time the most beautiful woman he had ever seen.

"Please," she begged, still reaching for him.

He realized it didn't matter. She needed his help and he would have to act right now. Dropping the phone on the floor, he went to her and took her hand. Her eyes showed fear as she glanced down to their embracing hands.

"You're bleeding," she said in a panic.

He tried to pull his hand away but couldn't loosen it from her grip. She stared at him and her face took on a predatory look. She licked her lips, and he could see the fangs pushing down on her bottom lip.

Eventually, she let go of his hand and grasped the blankets. She threw her head back and screamed again. "Please help me. My baby is coming now!"

"Let me call someone. I don't know how to deliver a baby," Brice pleaded, and watched her arch her back as if she were pushing.

"It must be only you," she cried. "Please, only you. No one must know about this. No one. They will kill this child, do you understand?"

"Who will?"

Another scream, another push, and she grabbed his shirt. "He is coming. He will find me and kill us both. Please. Please help me." The woman shoved him away and motioned to the foot of the bed. "The baby is coming now. Help!"

Brice mechanically moved to her feet and watched as the baby's head began to crown. Icy fear poured over him. He was going to deliver a baby. Right now.

"Okay, okay. I got this, I got this," he said to himself. As the woman cried out again, the house shook. Brice didn't have time to think about it as the baby's shoulders made it out of the woman.

The woman rose up and stared at him in fear. Brice gazed at her odd green eyes. "It's okay. You're doing fine," he reassured. She panted and nodded quickly. "One more push and I think this baby will be out," he said, surprising himself at how confident he sounded. "You ready?" The rain was so loud it almost drowned out his voice. But the woman nodded.

She leaned back and then pushed forward one last time. Brice reached down just in time to catch the baby as it slid out of her body. Then the lights went out.

Brice felt the wet mess in his hands and the umbilical cord still attached like a tether. It needed to be cut, but he couldn't see anything in the darkness. He didn't know what to do. He needed to put down the silent baby so he could get to his generator, but he was afraid it would slip off the bed. The wind howled through the open windows and he instinctively pulled the small bundle against him.

"What is it?" the woman weakly asked.

"I don't know. I can't see anything," Brice replied, and was torn over what to do.

"It's not crying. Something's wrong," the woman observed in almost inaudible whisper.

The lights came back on and the sight horrified Brice. A puddle of blood grew quickly all around the woman's body like a grotesque halo. He glanced down to the still babe. "It's a girl," he said blankly.

He didn't know what to do. The child should be crying but wasn't, and the woman was bleeding out before his eyes. He had to save them. He lay the baby down and cleaned out her mouth as quickly as possible, then breathed a gentle breath into her mouth to see if the lungs moved. He was relieved when they did. Lifting the baby again, he turned her over and tapped on her back once, twice, and then again, and a small, mewing cry escaped her lips.

Relief washed over him and he laid her down and turned to the mother. He wasn't sure how to stop her bleeding. It poured out of her now in a rush. Even if he called for help, no one would reach her in time to save her.

She took his arm. "Protect her. They will come for her. You

must hide her. Promise me."

He nodded involuntarily. "I will protect her. I promise." He wasn't sure what he was promising to protect her from, but he would do anything this dying woman asked.

"Let her feed," the woman demanded quietly.

"Feed?" Brice asked, confused.

"Yes, blood. She needs blood. For now, she can have what is left of mine. Bring her to me. Quickly." The woman's voice faded, her arms reaching up weakly for the babe.

Brice hesitated for a brief moment, and then brought the child closer. The woman embraced her, then lay the babe's mouth to her neck. The child paused for a moment, then latched onto her mother's skin. Brice stood back and watched as the child began to suck hard.

The woman whispered, "I love you, Scarlett." Then she hummed brokenly through her obvious pain. Her eyes grew dark, then closed; her lifeless arm dropped by her side.

Brice knew she had died. On his bed, here in the cabin in the woods. It was just like Elaine all over again. He wanted to rush out of here and away from the grisly scene. He was just about to when the baby let out a helpless cry.

He shook his head to wake himself up and reached down to pick up the slimy infant. She instantly quieted and burrowed into his clothes. He saw the small canines in her gums and knew this child wasn't normal—just like her mother.

Grabbing one of his shirts hanging on the chair next to the bed, he wrapped the baby girl up in it. Holding her close, he knew he would do whatever it took to protect her.

TWO

THE MEETING

Present day
Two months until my Dawning

I SIT WITH MY HANDS AROUND MY COFFEE CUP, TAP-ping my fingernails against it in eager anticipation for the sun to set. It's Friday night, and I'm excited to begin my weekend. It means a lot of good things for me—Snyder Blood Bank, or SBB, Perkalicious, and seeing my dad. Not necessarily in that order, but you get the idea. A routine I hold onto, because soon it could all be gone.

I take a sip of coffee and glance at the clock. Another five minutes and the sun will be down, then I can get to the coffee shop to begin my shift. My apartment feels too small when I'm like this. It's cloistered, like the walls will close in on me if I don't get out. Part of it is just knowing I'm going to be around packets and packets of blood soon, and that's such a weird sort of comfort. It means I won't hurt anyone and I won't starve—two very important things for a pale revenant.

Three minutes. Three minutes and I can head out the door. I get up and wash out my coffee cup, then grab my small shoulder purse and sling it over my head. Not long now and I can be on my way. I decide I can stand one more look in the mirror.

I walk to my bathroom and turn on the light to look myself

over. My blond hair is pulled tightly back into a ponytail and my light brown eyes are clear and without makeup. Missi always tries to get me to wear some, but I find it's a waste of my time. I press down my clothing and confirm I look fine. I really didn't need to look myself over, but I'm so anxious to get out, I have to do something.

My fingers find their way to my necklace, and I close my eyes and breathe in slowly to calm the building frustration. I have short patience when I feel trapped. Thinking of my mother wearing this exact necklace when she was alive seems to help center me. It's the only connection to her besides a few random other things my father found on her. I wonder, were she alive, if she would be proud of me. I feel like I can almost hear her sometimes, telling me to be kind and more patient. I honestly try.

Her necklace is an odd design and one I've never seen anywhere else. The pendant is a gold triangle with a hawk and a raven both holding tightly to a squirming, two-headed snake. Each head is trained on a bird, ready to strike. It's a weird, fierce sort of battle to put on a medallion. My father has no idea as to its meaning, but just knowing it was my mother's is enough.

If my Uncle Chasem were here, he would tell me to recite my lineage and oaths of my kind that I'd be required to say during the rite of Dawning, should I ever be given the opportunity. I've said it so many times it's ingrained in me. But I know I won't be able to, so the memorization is pointless. Still, it's something he wants me to know.

I've grown up knowing I won't get to go through the rite of Dawning, because that depends on my blood father, and it's pretty clear he won't let it happen. He wants me dead, after all. So I'm faced with the choices of fighting or being a renegade. I know I won't be a renegade. I won't prey on the weaker of my kind, but I also won't be food for them, either. So I'll have to fight. I can do that, I think...I hope. That's why Chasem trains me so hard. He wants me prepared for the renegades who he says will come for me.

I glance at my clock and breathe a sigh of relief. I can go out now. The sun should be completely down. I grab my keys and cell phone and dash out the door.

The hot evening air hits my face like a slap as I make my way onto the city sidewalk. I love New York City on evenings likes this. Frenetic energy radiates from the bustle of activity, and it feeds my soul unlike anything else. People and cars dash by to get to their destinations, unconcerned with anything around them. Cars honk, people yell, and it's intoxicating.

Ms. Beatty waves to me from across the street as she sits on the steps of her apartment building. She waves a fan to cool herself and smiles. I've sat over on those uneven stairs many evenings just to chat with her about life. She's what I imagine a human grandmother must be—all gray hair and deep wrinkles, but soft and non-judgmental about people. I think she senses I'm different but doesn't seem to mind or even ask questions about it. I'm glad, because I wouldn't know what to say.

I reach the meat-packing district and realize I need to hold my breath as much as possible. The coppery tang in the air from the blood hits me hard. I feel my fangs wanting to drop down in response, but I resist and just focus on really unappealing stuff. Like how my skin would feel burning in sunlight, or how hard Chasem hits when I don't dodge one of his blows in training. I strain to keep my mind off the taste in the air, but it's like trying to stop the beating of your own heart.

I pick up the pace, but I have to keep it at a human speed or else someone would notice and get curious. I don't need that kind of attention. So, I count numbers in my head, recite vocabulary words from school like decomposition, biocatalysis, and ectotherm. Before I know it, I'm past that part of the city and closer to my destination.

Perkalicious is a small coffee shop not far from a branch of NYU and has been my weekend employment for the last year. It's a small shop nestled between an electronics store and a tax preparation office. It's not very wide but incredibly long and only has windows in the front.

The doorbell chimes as I walk in, and I'm immediately assaulted with the rich smell of freshly ground coffee. Eddie Maxwell looks up from the counter and barely takes notice. He owns the store and is one of the easiest guys to work for despite his surly demeanor. Eddie's hair is almost nonexistent on the top, and the rest is reduced to a thin patch circling his head. He's pudgy and as round as the shape of his head. But he has a good heart and gives me a lot of leeway. Chasem knows him and was able to get me the job here. I'm not sure if Eddie knows what I am, but Chasem trusts him, so I do, too.

"He's in rare form tonight. Watch out," Emma Burton says as she brushes by me holding a tray. Her dark hair flows behind her like a wedding train. Emma is my coworker, and one of my best friends. Chasem never explained how he knew her, but she's human, knows what Chasem and I both are, and is unaffected by it. With her, I can just be me.

"Yeah, I can see that. He honestly looks like he has a stick up his butt," I remark.

"And that's different from any other time how?" Emma asks with a giggle, then walks away.

As I head back toward the employee room, I pass a table and see a boy about seventeen with ear buds in. The scent of his blood reaches me first, sweet and intoxicating. I'm so used to ignoring the scent of human blood that it surprises me how strongly it gets my attention. The boy's chestnut hair is long and curly on the top but trimmed close around his temples and in the back. He looks down, and just as I pass him, he gazes up and everything slows. His eyes are a clear gray with flecks of hazel, and they seem to stare straight into my soul. I can't hear anything but my own breathing. His chiseled jaw leads to two blushed, full lips. They turn up into a slight smile as he regards me. I almost run into a table because I'm staring at him, but I avoid disaster at the last moment.

I tear my eyes away and flee toward the back room to put my stuff away and grab an apron. I stand at the open locker and try to figure out what just happened. Shaking my head to clear it, I tell myself he's only a boy—nothing to be enamored with. Some part of me isn't listening to that logic, but I can't be distracted by anyone or anything right now. My birthday is coming up, and with it, my Dawning.

I rush out past the table, taking care not to look at the boy or breathe. Friday night is bustling with activity at the coffee shop, and Eddie looks happily annoyed. Even though he has to manage waiting on so many people, it will mean a good night in sales.

"You're early. Trying to brown-nose me?" Eddie asks as he sets a coffee for a "Tina" on the counter.

I laugh and tie my apron. "I had nothing better to do. Want me to go back home?" I point behind myself with my thumb and wait for his reply, which comes in the form of a frown. "Well, okay then." I smile at him and grab a tray to go clean up a few tables.

I glance at the boy and notice he's reading a book on ancient archeology of Eastern Europe. Not light reading by any stretch, and certainly not something I would expect a boy of his age to dig into. I think I might have read that same book when I was ten.

I force myself to stoically ignore him when I hear a faint conversation from the back of the shop.

"He's an easy mark," a male voice hisses.

"He might not have much cash on him," another observes.

"But his backpack is a leather Jansport, so he isn't poor."

I gaze back to see three men huddled around a table, gazing at the boy in question. I can feel the menace rolling off them. They're going to mug the boy if they get a chance.

I do not need to be involved. I certainly don't need to care. But I realize I want to—on both counts. God, this is so messed up. The boy continues to read and is oblivious to the attention he's gained from the men in the back.

When he gathers up his belongings and shoves them into his backpack, I panic. I want him to stay longer until I can figure out what to do. I saunter over to the table. "Hi," I say to get his attention.

He stops, glances up to me with a friendly grin, and pulls out his ear buds. "Hi yourself."

"Would you like another coffee, or whatever it is you're drinking?"

He shakes his head. "No, thank you. I've got to be heading out."

I try not to look back to the men, who I'm sure are watching us. "Well, it's on the house. Anything you want."

A confused look crosses his face. "On the house? What, did I win something?" He regards me with a devastatingly handsome face, and it momentarily stuns me.

I force myself to find my voice. "Yes, on the house. No, you didn't win anything. We just do random giveaways. What would you like?" I move the tray around in my hands and wait for him to pick something.

He stands and I realize he's about six feet tall, which has me looking up at him. He's trim but not skinny, and I can see the muscles through his shirt. "No, thanks. I really have to go," he utters. "But I appreciate the offer. A rain check?" he asks sincerely, then waits for my reply as he adjusts his pack on his shoulder.

"Oh, yeah, sure. Another time." I try to smile, to seem

relaxed, but in reality I'm trying to figure out what I can do to keep him from being hurt.

The boy winks at me. "Thanks..." He glances at my nametag. "Scarlett. I'm Nick. See you later." He grabs his jacket and heads out the door.

I find myself watching as he walks out into the fading twilight and out of my sight. Before I move, I feel the air whoosh past me as the men follow him out. I look over to Eddie, who's busy waiting on a customer, and decide I don't have time to explain it to him.

I rush out the back of the building in a moment and inhale deeply. I can taste the boy's scent in the air and realize he's somewhere in the back part of the block. Propelling myself up, I catch the rusty fire escape on the side of the crumbling building and scurry up. It protests for a brief moment as I scale it. Once on top of the flat tar roof, I dash across, gaze down over the edge, and find what I'm looking for.

The men have caught up with Nick and have cornered him in the alley on the other side of our building. The largest of them has a knife to Nick's throat. Nick has his hands raised while one of the other men rifles through his pockets.

I feel my fangs drop involuntarily, more out of excitement than a desire to feed. My vision sharpens like radar. The men's images become heat signatures, and I can make them out easily against the dead asphalt and stone all around them, regardless of the receding light.

The man holding the knife punches Nick hard in the stomach, and the boy doubles over and lands on his hands, gasping for air.

I drop behind the one who's going through Nick's backpack and strike him, sending him flying through the air to collide with the dumpster at the front of the alley. Before he sees me, I speed over to the man with the knife and take his legs out from underneath him. I bring my foot down hard on his wrist and hear the bones break with a satisfying crunch.

The man howls in pain and jumps up. I growl and jump the distance back to the first man, who's still gasping for air. I pick him up and hurl him toward the third man, who has now come back from keeping watch to investigate the commotion. They collide in a puddle of arms and legs. They help each other up and rush out of the alley in fear. The man with the broken wrist follows closely behind, cradling his arm but not looking back.

I jump up to one of the window ledges on the side of the building and rush up like a spider to the top. I watch as Nick stands and looks around, confused and panting. His eyes dart around, looking for the men and the danger, but he finds himself alone. He picks up his bag and rubs his neck.

"Go home," I say from the top of the building, and duck back as he looks up to find the source of the command. I wait and listen closely. It's quiet for a moment, but finally I hear him walking out of the alley.

"Thank you," he says hoarsely. The patter of his feet gets softer until I can no longer hear him.

"You're welcome," I whisper, feeling like I've done well by my pale revenant side. My mother would have been proud of me today.

THREE
ALL WORK AND NO PLAY

WHEN I GET BACK TO PERKALICIOUS, I TRY TO EX-plain to Eddie where I've been. He silences me with a raised hand and goes on about his work. He seems distracted, but about what, I'm not sure. With him it could be about anything. He can be as moody as any of the human girls who go to my school.

"So, you checking out that handsome piece of meat sitting there when you came in? I saw you talking to him," Emma says as she casually leans on the counter.

"Piece of meat? God, Em." I push past her and grab a wet cloth to wipe off the tables. I brush by her, ignoring her comment. I don't really want to explain what I did and how interested I actually am in him.

She follows me. "So, you never answered."

"Was there a question?" I say, evading her as much as I can. I hear Emma chuckle.

"Estas en lujuria," she mutters under her breath. I have no idea what she said, but she shakes her head and smiles.

"Don't you have work to do, Em?"

Emma laughs. "It's okay, Scarlett. You can appreciate a fine-looking boy. Doesn't mean you're committed or anything."

"Hmm." I keep working and stoically ignore her. She walks away, whistling an Elvis tune.

The rest of the evening goes on without incident, but I find my mind wandering to Nick and whether or not he made it home okay. I hope he did. A small part of me starts to consider the fact that he might show up here again, and I find I like that idea, even though it's the worst idea ever. If Emma knew...jeez.

It finally reaches 11:00 pm, and I'm relieved that my time at the coffee shop is over. Since I have to be at Snyder Blood Bank at Tremont Memorial Hospital by 11:30 on Fridays, Eddie gives me a pass on closing. So I grab my bag and head into the crisp night air.

The sky is clear tonight, and despite the bright glow from the city I can make out most of the constellations far above me. The stars wink down at me against their onyx backdrop, and it makes me remember Dad, sitting with me and an astronomy book when I was four, showing me how to discern the seasons and time by their position in the sky. He made me giggle with all the stories and names of each constellation. They were my version of fairytales.

He would be proud that I took the time to look at the stars and appreciate them. He thinks I hurry too much through my life, barreling on towards my seventeenth birthday with no thought of anything else. He might be right. I pull my focus away from the stars and start down the street towards Tremont. It's six blocks away, but I can make it with no problem.

I'm two blocks into my walk when I glance down a side street and see Chasem standing there, watching me outside a small grocery store. He's illuminated by the store's interior light bleeding through the window. He stands still and stares intently at me. A car passes by, obstructing my vision, and after it passes Chasem is gone. I search all around but don't see him. Was I dreaming? Was he really there?

After a few minutes, I convince myself I have imagined the whole thing and start walking again. But I feel the hair on my neck standing on end. It's not like me to imagine things like that. But I have had a lot on my mind lately, and I haven't been sleeping well due to some rather bizarre dreams. Maybe it's just wishful thinking that he'd been there. I make a mental note to ask him about it tomorrow when we train.

When I finally make it to Tremont, I pull out my badge and show the bored security guard, who buzzes me in. The hallway leading back to Snyder Blood bank is illuminated by harsh florescent lights, making everything look washed out. The floor is shiny and slick, and my Converse squeak loudly as I go, making it painfully obvious that I'm there.

The second shift employee is an unpleasant woman by the name of Rita. Her name doesn't fit her at all. Rita reminds me of someone who should have dark hair and a snappy wit, but instead, this Rita is short, graying, and abrasive. I tend to avoid her at all costs.

When Rita sees me, she tosses her keys on the counter and simply walks away to clock out, even though she has ten minutes left until I start.

"Well, good night to you, too," I huff under my breath. I wonder what in her life could be so bad as to make her constantly so horrible to people. I dismiss the thought as soon as I have it because I don't want to waste any time on her wondering why she is the way she is. I honestly don't care.

I grab the white jacket from my locker and clip on my ID that proudly proclaims "Scarlett Ellis" and has one of the worst pictures of me I've ever seen. I think the guy who took my photo hated his job so much he wanted to prove it in the pictures he took.

When I'm all put together, I walk up to the front desk and see my partner for the evening, Andre Parker, walking inside.

"Good evening, Scarlett," he says with a smile, and winks at me. His mocha eyes almost twinkle like he has a secret.

"Hey, Andre," I reply, and sit down.

"What? Rita's gone already?" he asks, looking around.

I shrug. "Who knows? She left her keys and walked away."

Andre smiles and brushes his hands over his closely trimmed afro. "Her loss. What woman wouldn't want to watch me enter a room?" He laughs and makes a tsk sound.

I laugh as well. "Ego much?"

"Hell no. It's not ego when it's true. Just ask the ladies."

"Okay, Jason Derulo. Go get your stuff and clock in," I say dismissively.

Andre dances off dramatically to get his things and I laugh. With him around, our very boring job becomes more interesting. Because we monitor and fill requests for the available blood supply, it can be very cumbersome stuff, but Andre makes it easier.

I have to admit, working this job has a certain amount of irony. I can't survive without blood, and revenants would do anything to get it. Yet, here I sit, monitoring and doling out blood to humans when it should be the other way around. Another high mark for Chasem in getting me this job, too.

The rest of the evening is quiet, so we decide to play a game of basketball using a garbage can and a wad of paper. I let Andre win. I wouldn't want him to see my true speed and wonder about me; therefore, I fake the inexperienced player. Andre sashays and moves like he's a dancer, and it makes me giggle.

When Andre leaves to deliver blood to the respective departments in the hospital, I pull out the paperwork for two pints of A+ blood to be delivered to Neville Treatment Center. Chasem had the fake organization set up years ago, and it's the perfect foil to cover the pints I take. I scan them out and put them into a cold pack to deliver them straight to my bag. By the time Andre comes back, I'm sitting back with my feet up on the counter and playing with my phone.

5:30 am comes around before we know it, and we hand off the keys to our relieving shift.

"See you tonight?" Andre asks, inching toward the door.

"Yep," I agree and smile. "Try not to get into trouble."

He flashes a grin. "No promises. See you later." And like that, he's gone.

I head out into the early morning and start to walk. The one thing I love about New York City is that it's always active no matter what time of day or night. So, traffic is still moving and people are walking around.

I head out to the bus stop to wait for the one that will take me to Chasem's place to keep up our weekly schedule of epic training. Chasem is an ascended vampire warrior, has never been defeated in battle, and is a tough trainer. He pushes me really hard, and there are times I find myself swearing at him under my breath. He doesn't treat me like a girl but like an equal most of the time. I've left his place bruised more times than I care to count, and with a bloody noise or skinned knuckles more times than not. But Chasem believes I need to be ready. My seventeenth birthday is coming, and renegades with it.

A man is sleeping at the bus stop with his head leaning against the fiberglass wall, unkempt and mouth agape. A slight snoring sound comes from him.

"Great," I say to myself as I sit to wait.

I stare out into the darkness and look forward to my Sunday afternoon, when I'll get to see my Dad. Sundays are our days to catch up and have a meal. He comes into the city from his cabin, and we watch movies or play games—anything I want. Lately, it's been a matter of my father quizzing me on what Chasem teaches me, and whether or not I'm ready to be a rogue. Chasem pushes me extra hard to be able to protect myself.

I feel the man before I see him. A sudden whisper of incoherent voices assails my head, and as I gaze out, I see two glowing eyes staring back at me from an alley. I jump up to prepare to fight, but just like that he's gone, and I can't see where he went. Maybe it's only a transient revenant passing through, and not a renegade or enforcer. I shudder hard at either possibility.

This is the first time I've ever heard another revenant in my mind. It's a sign of my impending deadline to Dawn. I shake my head to clear out the feeling of residue the voices leave in my head as I look for him.

If a renegade is here, maybe my blood father, Apollo, will know how to find me, too. My life could truly be in danger. I search everywhere for him but can't find him, and I no longer feel his presence. I contemplate going out into the darkness, and then the bus arrives. The sleeping man wakes up and gives me an uninterested look, then boards the bus. I don't move for a moment, and right before the bus driver shuts his door, I yell for him to wait and step inside. As the bus pulls away, I can't be sure, but I think I see a flash of eyes rapidly fading in the distance.

I always hate the briny smell in the air as I walk to Chasem's building in the shipping district on the Hudson River. The area isn't meant to be lived in, as indicated by uneven sidewalks—when there's even a side walk present—and the various warehouses surrounding it. I'm always on high alert in the deserted, early-morning streets, but I never pass another soul.

His building rises ten stories high, and from the outside, it looks like it's seen better days. The inside, though, is a master-piece. I'm not sure exactly how much money Chasem has, but it's sizable, and he's spared no expense on the interior of this building. The first floor houses a kitchen, a gym, and the sparring area, and the second floor is a running track, open in the middle so I can gaze down on the first floor. The tenth floor is the living quarters. Floors three through nine are a complete mystery to me. Chasem says he uses it for storage—storage of what, I'm not sure.

It's pitch black when I arrive, which isn't unusual. With a touch of a button, all the windows have the ability to turn opaque one moment, and clear the next. It's a really cool effect I wish I had on my apartment windows. Chasem leaves his windows darkened most of the time on the lower levels, and clear on the upper levels at night.

I disarm the beeping alarm and walk into the still air of first floor entrance. He hasn't been home for a while. I reset the alarm and walk in toward the kitchen area off to the right, dropping my keys and bag on the table where I see a hand-written note.

Gone out. Dinner is the refrigerator - C

"Figures," I mumble and walk to the fridge to place the blood packets from my bag in there. A plate of cold fried chicken sits on a white plate beside a bottle of blood. It makes me wonder what kind of blood it will be this time. Chasem believes various kinds of blood feed our bodies differently, like vitamins to a human. Deer blood might make our sight better, or beef blood might assist hearing, but even he concedes that human blood is the ultimate revenant food. Still, he tries to get me used to animal blood. He'd rather I know I can survive on animal blood if I choose it.

I valiantly grab the chicken and the blood and slam the door closed with my foot. I'm so hungry that I stand leaning against the sink, eating a leg and not bothering with a plate or manners. I can hear Chasem's voice in my head, chiding me. I ignore it and continue to eat. I toss the bones into the garbage can and retrieve the bottle of blood, heading to the elevator to go up to the living quarters on the top level.

The elevator opens to a large, spacious living room. A kitchen area is on the left, while on the right the floor is recessed and holds several couches centered around a clear gas fireplace. All the furniture is pure white, which I often wonder how he can keep so clean. The windows are floor-to-ceiling and turn on a hinge in the center to open. A few are opened slightly to let in a breeze, and they're clear now so I can see the lights glowing from across the Hudson.

I turn on the lights and head back to my room. Having my own space here makes this place feel as much like my home as his. He really tries hard to make it that way. His sister was my mother, and her death when I was a baby weighs heavily on him. After all, I'm the only family he has left. I think that's why he trains and pushes me so hard; he wants me to make it—and not only make it, but thrive.

I kick off my shoes and crawl onto the bed with my bottle of blood, leaning against the headboard. I hit the remote on the bed stand to turn on Rob Zombie and try to wind down from the night. As I do, I take a drink of the blood, then I smack my lips together and frown. Something's off about it; it has a taste I can't place. I take another drink.

Suddenly, I'm standing in a field, illuminated by sunlight, but I'm not burning. It's warm and relaxing. I look down to the translucent skin of my hands and can see the blood coursing through my veins. I turn my hand over, staring at it.

A movement catches my eye and I look up. Before me is a beautiful woman with dark hair and clear eyes. At first, her gaze is loving, adoring almost, and then it fades into a bone-chilling shriek as she turns to run away in horror. I try to reassure her that it's okay, but the words get stuck in my throat. Her skin burns and flakes away, and before I know it, her scream fades to a muffled shriek, abruptly cut off as she becomes a pile of ash. A maniacal laugh sounds beside me, and I turn to see a dark-headed man with a deviant grin.

"Wasn't that lovely?" he asks me, laughing right as I feel my skin start to burn.

FOUR

TRAINING

I **AWAKE TO THE SOUND OF A KNOCK ON MY DOOR. I** jerk up and try to figure out where I am. I quickly realize I'm at Chasem's and immediately relax. Everything looks exactly the same as when I fell asleep. Did I fall asleep? Something creeps around the periphery of my brain like maybe it was something more, but I can't remember what happened when I fell asleep. It must just be exhaustion.

I grab my phone by the bed and see the time as 2:00 pm. Wow, I slept a long time.

Another knock sounds on my door. "Scar?" Chasem asks through the closed door.

"I'm up! I'm up!" I yell and jump to my feet. "Be right there."

I hear Chasem's footsteps as he moves down the hall. I lean over my bed and wipe my face. Even though I should be energized from all that sleep, I'm still groggy. I get up and wash my face, then change into my workout clothes. By the time I'm out in the living area, Chasem is moving around the kitchen, and a plate and glass are waiting for me at the bar. Chasem glances over and sees me but keeps moving around the kitchen without a word.

I sit down to eat my eggs and bacon, looking at the glass to see it's full of blood. I frown, trying to remember something my brain's saying I should know. But what?

I shrug and take a sip. The salty-iron taste almost makes me groan it's so good. I find I can't stop and finish off the whole glass. When I put it down, I see Chasem leaning against the counter with his arms folded.

"Want more?" he asks plainly.

"Yes, please," I respond. My body feels parched, and the only thing I can think about it getting more blood. "What kind is this anyway?"

"Does it taste strange?" he asks, not turning around as he opens the fridge and pulls out a dark container. He turns to me, fills my glass, and watches with raised eyebrows.

"No, it tastes really good." I down the next glass just as quick, then feel some left on the side of my mouth and reflexively wipe it away with my wrist.

"You could use a napkin, you know," Chasem quips, a hint of a smile playing around the edge of his mouth.

"Sorry. So?"

"So what?" Chase answers, suddenly serious.

"What kind was that?" I hold the empty glass and wish I had more.

Chasem takes my glass and puts it into the sink, then turns back around with orange juice and a clean glass. He pours it and stares at me. "Shark. Good for mental function." He says it like it's a lie. I say nothing for a moment but gaze intently at him. There's no reason it's a lie, so I nod and keep eating.

"Hurry up and finish. We have a lot to practice," Chasem demands as he walks out of the kitchen.

"Again!" Chasem screams as I lay on the ground, grasping onto my Kali sticks. He stands over me, barely exerted, and I'm sweating up a storm. I lift myself up on my arms and legs and stand again, posed for his next attack. He advances, swinging steadily, and I block most of the shots. A few times, he hits my fingers, and I grit my teeth through the pain. Before I know it, he sweeps my feet out from under me, and I'm on my back again, and when he strikes down at my head, I roll out of the way just in time.

I jump up and rush backward on the mat, finding my footing immediately, but Chasem is already on me, striking at me relentlessly. His pace towards me is deliberate and controlled, forcing me back time and time again. I feel like I will lose this sparring session when I recognize a small vulnerability on his left side every few moves he makes. I watch for my moment, then spin and strike, catching him in the side. He winces, but it doesn't bring him down. It actually seems to push him faster towards me.

He moves so fast it's almost a blur. I force myself to quit thinking, quit reacting to every action and strike, but I do succeed in keeping him from hitting my body. After a few minutes of the blistering attack, I find my strength flagging. I become slower, and Chasem takes advantage of it, hitting me hard on the shoulder, and I drop one of my Kali sticks. Chasem drops both of his and reaches out, lifting me by the neck toward the wall, pinning me hard against it.

"Never, ever give up! Do you hear me? Never!" he screams, his hot breath on my face. I squirm and struggle to get free of his grip but find I'm stuck.

His gaze is fierce, his lip curled up in a snarl. "Fight!" he screams again, but it's as if I can't convince myself that I can get free. My visions starts to darken from the lack of oxygen, and Chasem releases me. I collapse in a puddle, heaving hard and coughing, trying to suck air into my lungs though my burning throat.

I see Chasem pace for a few moments with his hands on his hips, like he doesn't know what to do. All around him, the mirrors tremble slightly, as if they'll shatter at any moment. Chasem reaches for his water, takes a quick drink, then hurls the bottle toward the wall. I've never seen him like this. He's usually so contained—tough, but contained. Now, he seems like a caged lion.

He turns towards me and leans down. "You can't be like this, Scar. You can't. You have to keep fighting, no matter what. Do you understand? It *will* be a matter of life or death. Never surrender, do you understand?"

His light-brown eyes are wild, his face flushed. He looks at me with a question. Then I see it, a weakness—his face is exposed. I kick up my leg and catch him in the chin, and he staggers back. A few cuss words escape him and then he starts to laugh. "That's what I'm talking about. Good job. Hold onto that."

He walks back to me, still holding his face, and offers a hand. I surprise myself by not wanting to take it because, truthfully, I'm pissed. I know he only has my best interest in mind, but he'd choked me.

He shoves his hand towards me again to convince me to take it. I soften some and grab a hold. When he pulls me up, he gives me a slight pat on the shoulder as if to say, "There, everything's okay now." But it isn't okay. My shoulder aches and my throat burns. I want to pout, but I won't give into the desire because I don't want him to see any defeat in me.

Chasem walks out of the sparring room, rubbing his chin, not offering me a look or word. At first, I'm not sure what to do. I'm frustrated and in pain, and I want him to explain what just happened. But his walking away effectively ended the opportunity for that. I see a boxing dummy, cast in the likeness of a torso and head of a man, and I rush over to it.

I slam it with my fists over and over again, kicking it for all I'm worth. I won't lie and say I didn't see Chasem's face as I struck the dummy, because I did. I don't want to tell him how angry he's made me, so this is the next best thing. I keep hitting until I have nothing left, which doesn't take long. My fight with Chasem was enough to do that. I heave hard, the air hitting my lungs like daggers.

When I feel a little more in control of myself, I walk out to confront Chasem. It doesn't take long to find him. He sits in the small sitting area just beyond the kitchenette with his feet up on an ottoman, like he doesn't have a care in the world. His sweat-soaked shirt clings to his muscular frame, his warrior tattoos visible on his arms. By his feet sits another glass of blood. His eyes flicker up, and a conciliatory look crosses his face.

"Here," he says before I've had a chance to reply. He pushes the glass towards me. I've never had this much blood in such a short amount of time in my whole life. It seems out of place and really weird.

"More blood?" I challenge. "What's going on, Chasem?" I realize I'm clenching my fists, but I don't care. I'm mad and I want answers.

Chasem sits up and leans on his knees. "You need this. Drink it." His voice is softly demanding. We stare at each other for a few moments, saying nothing. Chasem breaks first and sighs. "Please, Scarlett, drink the blood."

I relax my hands and drop into a chair, but I still don't take the glass. "Why? You know as well as I do that I only need about two pints a week to be healthy."

"But more will make you strong, and you need to be strong. Drink it."

"I don't understand what's going on, Chasem. My birthday is two months away. Nothing's going to happen before then. So why ply me with blood?" A part of me idly thinks about how I really want the blood. I always want blood. It's like breathing, a need that never goes away. But I can endure on two pints just fine, and I have. It takes the edge off and keeps temptation at bay. But still, I don't like how Chasem pushes this on me, like a desperate attempt at something I don't understand. But why now? Why is he making this an issue?

Chasem regards me coolly, but there's an undercurrent of something I can't quiet name. Frustration? Worry? Anger? I just can't tell.

Chasem leans back in his seat. "You know, you keep asking me what's wrong. I could ask you the same thing. Why are you questioning me? Haven't I always looked out for you? You've always trusted me before, so what's changed?"

"You've never been this hair-trigger crazy before," I remark, letting my annoyance show.

"Well, you've never been this close to your Dawning before. Can you understand how critical this will be?"

Do I understand? Hell yeah, I do. Every moment is a study on what will happen when I hit my dawning—remembering who will be out to kill me and claim my power, not the least of whom is my father. There's never a moment I'm not thinking about it.

"I get it, okay? You've drilled it into my head enough times," I snip. I wish I can speed up time and be there to get it over with.

"Good. Because Apollo won't rest until he finds you and destroys you. I don't want Jasmine's death to be for nothing. Ever." A look of grief crosses his face. "I miss her. I wish she could be here to see you, now." He stares down at his hands, studying the lines like he might find the cure to cancer there.

I feel myself feeling guilty for his uncharacteristic vulnerability. My uncle is always hard and contained. He can be loving, but rarely does he allow softness to show. So to watch it now is really difficult. I made him think about my mother. Before I even consider it, I reach for the blood and down it as quickly as I can. When I set the glass down, Chasem stares at me with a pleased look, a slight grin playing around the edges of his mouth.

"Good girl." Chasem stands and slaps his legs. "Well, you better go get a shower and change so you can make it to work on time. I don't want Eddie to accuse me again of not taking your job there seriously."

I glance at the clock and realize he's right. I rush off to my room to get ready, all the while thinking that there's something more Chasem's keeping from me.

FIVE

NICK

RIDING ON THE BACK OF CHASEM'S HARLEY THROUGH the streets of New York at night is always exhilarating. The air is cool and alive, pulling my hair back in a caress as we go. Chasem has on his leather jacket, and with his longer, chestnut, wavy hair, he looks like something straight out of a biker magazine. His Dawning mark peeks out from the top of his collar like an exotic red tattoo. No one ever messes with us, which is good. Even if he looked like a priest, he'd be the most dangerous predator to come across; no one would even realize that fact until they were dead.

Chasem is a fully ascended revenant warrior, and my mother's twin, which is incredibly unusual in that community. Revenants tend to only have one child, if at all, because of the vulnerable responsibility of handling the next generation's Dawning.

One result of Dawning is that the child becomes physically stronger than the parents, and normally this isn't a problem if there has been a healthy relationship between parent and child. But in the worst cases, children have been known to slaughter abusive parents upon Dawning.

Because of this, it isn't unheard of for parents to kill an infant immediately after its birth. Revenants don't have laws again infanticide within the first week. But the propitiation of race is essential for the survival of our kind, so it's a dichotomy every revenant couple tries to balance. Most couples abandon their children, where those children are placed in pods to be looked after by the government. By doing this, those children who can never Dawn become fodder for the renegades—or they become renegades themselves. Scary stuff.

My grandparents had given in to having one child and, to their surprise, two appeared. My grandparents were loving and kind, and when both Chasem and my mother Jasmine Dawned, it was as it was supposed to have been. They received their strength and memories from the generations before, allowing my grandparents to live in protected peace.

Chasem then moved on to what can only be considered a revenant army. It's the elite guard for our race, and Chasem moved up the ranks quickly. He'd been recognized by the ruling house as an asset to be used in their service. So, he became a warrior in service to the king.

My mother was another story. She remained at home in service to her parents. From all accounts, my mother was beautiful but painfully shy. When she visited Chasem at the royal house one unfortunate day, it sealed her fate. The revenant prince, Apollo Bramstall, took one look at her and was smitten. Apollo pursued her, but she wouldn't give in for the longest time. Then Apollo eventually won her heart, and that was how I came to be here.

Chasem doesn't talk much about what happened after that, except to say my mother tried to hide being pregnant as long as she could. When she couldn't any longer, she fled to the human world to hide. That's where my human father came in. Brice Ellis took her in and delivered me. My mother died a few minutes after I was born and is buried behind our house in the woods.

I've spent many days sitting by her grave, talking to her, asking her questions that I'll never get to hear her answer. I feel her absence like I feel the presence of the Chasem and Brice. I'll never get to hug her, or tell her I love her, but I will have her memories when I turn seventeen. For that very fact, I'm anxious for it to arrive.

Chasem drops me off in front of Perkalicious but doesn't seem to want to leave. "Do you have your phone?" he asks tensely.

"Yes," I reply suspiciously. "Don't I always?"

Chasem eyes me. "Are you armed?"

I pat my thigh. "Never without it, per your nagging."

Chasem doesn't grin at my barb. Instead, he revs the motorcycle and stares at me like he's torn between leaving and staying. "See you later, okay?"

"Yes, sir. Right after SBB." We stare at each other. He still guns the motor but doesn't move, and his face is etched with apprehension. "Chasem?" I ask, furrowing my brows.

"Be careful," he finally says, then pulls away. I watch him disappear into the tail-light traffic until I can no longer discern him.

I adjust my bag on my shoulder and turn to go into Perkalicious. The Rolling Stones are barely heard above the loud conversation within the cafe. Eddie runs back and forth between the espresso machine and the counter. He sees me but only offers a glance, then goes back to making drinks. Emma works at the counter, and as she sees me, a large smile breaks across her face.

I frown. What?

A couple has decided to block the isle back to the employee room with their PDA. I force my way around them, nudging them to let them know they're really in my way, but they don't seem to want to move. When I finally get around them, I'm staring at the most handsome face I've ever seen. It's Nick.

Oh. That's what.

He smiles warmly. "Hey," he says, and steps back for me to

have room on the other side of the enamored couple. Do they really not see me trying to get around them? I'm worried that I'm being super awkward in front of Nick, although I'm not sure why I'm worried about that.

"Hey, Nick," I say and adjust my bag, not wanting to make eye contact with him.

"You remembered my name." He chuckles. "You're Scarlett, right?"

I nod and then look up at his gorgeous eyes. He smiles again. It's breathtaking, to be sure, and I try to steady myself. "Seems you remembered mine, too. You okay after last night?" I ask.

His eyes narrow. "How do you know what happened last night? Was that your voice I heard?"

I realize my mistake. Damn.

"Nope," I reply and start to walk around him.

"To bad," he adds, and I keep walking. "It was kind of sexy."

I all but run back to the employee room. My heart's beating hard and I feel squirrelly excitement pounding through me like a hammer. All I can see in my mind are his eyes, regarding me with laughter. I shift my weight and shake my hands, trying to refocus my brain. He's just so damned handsome. But I've seen handsome boys before and managed then to appreciate them in a purely detached way. Not Nick. He's like an accelerant to some sort of spark inside me. Well, I'll just have to put out that spark. I don't have the time or the ability to be involved with anyone, not that I ever have been. I learned early in life to keep people at arm's length.

I breathe in and bring my arms down by my side. Calm. Just calm. It'll be fine.

Sexy.

He called my voice sexy.

The squirrels run around my insides again. I throw my stuff in my locker and slam it closed, then put the lock on, complaining under my breath the entire time. What is wrong with me?

I put on my apron and see Nick leaning against the wall with his arms folded, looking toward the front of the store. He turns in time to see me walking out, and his smile almost brings me to my knees. There's a small dimple in his right cheek. I avert my eyes and start to walk past him, but his arm shoots out as if to stop me. He doesn't touch me, though.

"Hey again, Scarlett. I was wondering when you go on break."

Stunned I look up. "My break?"

"Yes, your break. Do you get one?" His gaze is intense but open, and he brushes his curly hair off of his forehead and waits. His eyes flicker to my neck for a moment and then back to my eyes, but he doesn't say anything.

"I do, but not for about an hour and half."

"Okay," he agrees. "I'll wait. Can I spend it with you?"

"Wait," I say, incredulous. "That's a long time to wait. I'm sure you have better things to do." I want to dissuade him from this, although another part of me jumps up and down with excitement over spending some time with him.

"Easy, shmeesy. I have homework that will more than keep me busy."

"Did you just say shmeesy? Is that a word?" I laugh and realize that's not how I should act if I'm trying to reject his interest. I try to make myself look serious again.

"It is now." He smirks and winks at me. "I'll talk to you then." He doesn't give me time to respond as he walks past me to a table in the corner. He sees me still standing there, then makes a "go on" motion. I look away and rush so quickly behind the counter that I almost run into Emma.

"Whoa, watch it!" she half-snaps as she dances with two coffees to place on the counter. "Tall, dark, and caffeinated has you distracted."

"Sorry," I mutter and see her wink at me. I go to the cash register to take an order, and my eyes catch Nick staring at me with a smile.

The first part of my night flies by. It's so hard to concentrate, knowing I've agreed to sit with Nick on my break. Well, I technically didn't agree to sit with him, but at this point it's a given. He's true to his word and seems to keep his nose stuck in a book the entire time. Occasionally, I catch him glancing my way and I quickly look somewhere else. When he doesn't catch me looking, I study his face.

His skin is so smooth, not even a blemish or mark, and it's the color of pale copper. Dark eyebrows and long lashes conceal his eyes as he glances down. Intently reading, he rests his hand against his face and lightly taps, as if it helps him keep a rhythm. I can't help but chuckle.

Eddie catches me staring at Nick every so often and frowns at me. That's all the reprimand I need to get my head in the game. I try never to glance at Emma, who's decided it's in my best interest to give me grief. Before long, my first break arrives.

"I'm taking a break now," I throw Eddie's way, and he frowns. We never announce our breaks or ask permission. Usually, if we see a moment to take our break, we just go ahead and take it.

He scowls. "Yeah, so?"

"Have fun," Emma interjects.

"Don't you have a couple tables to clean up out front?" Eddie chides Emma, and she raises her hand in surrender.

I shrug and reach into the cooler behind the counter to grab a Coke Zero, then slowly walk over to Nick's table.

He sees me coming and leans back to stretch, reaching high with his arms. A big smile crosses his face, and my heart skips. "Break time?" he asks.

"Yeah. You waited," I observe.

"Yep, I said I would."

"Do you always do what you say?" My voice comes out slightly annoyed.

"Always," he confirms. "Sit." He indicates a chair in front of him and I obey, trying not to look at him. "So," he begins, closing his book after putting his pencil in to mark his place. He studies me for a moment, then frowns. "What happened to your neck?"

"What?" I ask and realize he sees the effects of my sparing with Chasem. I involuntarily respond by raising my hand to cover it. "Oh, this? It's nothing." I have to think fast. "My scarf got caught in an elevator door. Almost choked me to death." I add a small, embarrassed laugh to make it believable.

"Wrong," he counters. "I can see the outline of fingers." He leans over his book. "Is someone abusing you?"

I want to jump up and run away, but I can't. So I try to play it cool. "No one is abusing me." Truth. "This is nothing." Lie. It actually is something. Chasem has never, ever done that to me before. He's pushed me, come at me with all his might to make me stronger—but he's never almost choked me unconscious. That's new and unexpected, and very much out of his character. I look at Nick, who appears not to have believed a word I said.

His brow furrows. "Look, I know we don't know each other, but I can help you if you need it. I can be a good ear if you want to talk about it."

I stand up. "Look, I've got to be getting back to work," I say, pointing behind me.

"Wait, no. Please. Sit back down. You just got here." He seems to struggle for a moment. "Okay, I'll be quiet...for now. But don't go. Please? Don't go."

His eyes plead with me and I find myself sitting back down. I'm not sure where to go from here. But he saves me from having to decide.

"My last name is Lightener and I'm a senior at Rockefeller High. Do you go there? I haven't seen you before, and believe me, I'd notice." His face is alight with amusement.

"No, I don't. I go to Excelsior Academy."

His eyebrows raise. "Oh, a private school. You must be smart." He fingers the book in front of him. "What's your last name?"

"Ellis," I answer and wonder why I'm even answering any of his questions. I typically am not this open.

"Nice to officially meet you." He holds out his hand to me and I take it. His hand is larger than mine and warm. I realize I'm holding it a little too long and jerk it back.

He smiles kindly at me, then picks at his book again. "So, sophomore or junior?"

"Junior. No offense, but this feels like twenty questions," I snap automatically. But another part of me wants to know him, and him me. I can almost hear Chasem's warning voice in my head, but I try ignore it.

His face drops and he looks down. "Sorry. You just fascinate me."

I immediately regret it. "No, look, sorry. I just don't meet a lot of people and I guess I've forgotten how to be polite."

Nick chuckles. "In this busy place, you don't meet many people? How is that possible?"

"Well, I don't exactly take my breaks with customers," I add pointedly. "You're the first, actually."

He leans back in his chair. "Well, good. And to be fair, I don't exactly ask baristas to join me on their breaks."

"Well, I guess we're both doing something we don't normally do." I see him smile again and he leans forward.

"Would it be too forward of me to ask if you have a boyfriend?"

Now it's my turn to smile. And blush. A lot. "No. I don't have a boyfriend," I stammer and look around, thinking I've spoken a little too loudly. "What about you?" I say conspiratorially.

He looks down. "Ah, no. No girlfriend." He glances up with something that looks remotely like pain. There's a story there, and I want to push for more details, but I hold my tongue. We aren't at the point where I can ask him anything I want. Not that we're going to head toward that point in the first place. But still.

"Do you live with your Dad or brothers?" he asks casually.

What?

"Um, no. I'm an only child and I live alone," I say before I mean to let all that slip. It's not normal for a sixteen-year-old girl to live alone, but I have for a year. Brice and Chasem agreed I'm mature enough, and it keeps me hidden from anyone seeking me out. If I ever got in trouble, Chasem would be at my door in a matter of minutes. Plus, I'm responsible enough to go to school on my own and work my own jobs.

"Alone?" he says with a raised voice. "But you're—"

"Too young, I know," I finish for him. "I'm emancipated."

"Oh. Then..."

"Then what?" I demand.

He shakes his head and looks in my eyes. "So. Emancipated Scarlett Ellis, would you like to go out sometime?" His voice sounds so unsure as he asks me.

The bats beat around in my stomach again and I know I'm gaping at him. I can't say yes. I can't. I can't get involved with anyone because I'm close to my Dawning and will be a target before long. I gaze into his gray eyes and feel lost. Before I can stop myself, the one word I never mean to say drops out. "Sure."

SIX

BRICE

I LOVE SUNDAY NIGHTS WITH MY DAD. CHASEM BRINGS me home and Brice is always waiting for me in my apartment, usually with dinner and a couple DVDs or the chest board set up for an epic battle. We spend the night eating and laughing and talking about how my week has been and how work is going. Brice never asks me about Chasem, and I suspect it's because they speak regularly and probably about me. It's a little annoying, because I wish I knew what they discussed.

I walk into my apartment and inhale the most delicious aroma of fried chicken. Brice has jazz playing and moves around my kitchen with ease. I shut the door and walk past him to put the blood away in the fridge. Brice smiles at me. I notice his blond hair has been recently cut short and styled. He usually doesn't give much thought to his appearance, so this is a new occurrence.

"Hey, Dad."

"Hey, kiddo!" He side-hugs me while his other hand holds the spatula. "Almost done here. You ready to eat?" The chicken pops and hisses.

I nod. "Absolutely. It smells great."

Brice winks and returns to cooking. I sit at the bar, watching him while he checks the mashed potatoes. In a fluid move, he sets the small bar with plates and glasses before pulling out the iced tea from the fridge.

"So, how's school coming?" he asks, pouring the tea.

I shrug. "Okay, I guess. I'm taking junior college courses right now, and it's a little boring, but at least I'm acing it."

Brice nods. "I spoke with Ms. Prenov. She said you're distracted."

Ms. Prenov is my music teacher. She takes me to task on the violin and piano whenever she gets the chance. As much as I love music, I hate having to take a class and get graded on something so...creative. How can you judge creativity? But Ms. Prenov sits back in her chair and makes remarks in her clipped Russian accent about how my playing lacks emotion. I assure you, I have a lot of emotion when I'm irritated with her. She just doesn't see it.

"Ms. Prenov just wants me to try the cello next. I don't want to, so I just play the piano mainly. I don't know, Dad. I wish she'd just get off my case. I'm the top of the class, so how can she ride me over something so ambiguous?"

Brice smiles. "She just wants you to be the best you can. Music is what she does. If she says it's lacking something, can't you at least believe she might be right?"

I watch him put the chicken onto our plates and then spoon some mash potatoes and gravy beside it. Is my music missing something? I don't think it is; it feels pretty complete to me.

"Yeah, okay," I acquiesce. I don't like disagreeing with him, and if he asks me to consider something, I'll certainly try. We eat in silence for a minute and Brice gets a faraway look in his eye.

"So," he begins. "I wanted to tell you something." He sits back and wipes his mouth. "I've...well. I've met someone."

I stare blankly at him. "So? I meet people all the time."

A look of apprehension crosses his face. "No. No, I mean I've—I've met someone. A woman."

I blink a few times and then it dawns on me. He's met someone he likes. "*Oh*," I say, drawing out the word.

"But it's nothing serious right now. Just going to the movies and out to eat. Just as friends. I haven't even kissed her yet," he adds defensively, avoiding my gaze.

I feel my eyebrows raise. "What's her name? Where did you meet her?"

"Well," he begins, moving his mashed potatoes around with his fork. "Her name is Sarah Boll, and we met at the small grocery store I go to once a week. She happened to be there when I was, and she accidentally ran into my cart." He looks up, apologetic.

"So, where does this Sarah Boll live?" I cross my arms. I really want to interrogate him, but I try to find a middle ground with not pushing too hard. He's my father, after all, and no one is worthy of him in my estimation.

"She just moved to Amherst Ridge." He smiles. Amherst Ridge is the small town fifteen miles away from where Brice lives. So, little Miss Sarah Boll just moved there.

"What does she do?" I don't relax my stance. I will find out everything I can about her if she's going to be around my dad.

"She's a nurse, as a matter of fact," he assures. Then he stands abruptly. "I brought some cookies for dessert while we watch a movie. Want some?" He reaches to the box of cookies and holds them out. I refuse the cookies and realize our conversation is effectively over. He's nervous, so he doesn't want to share anything more. I decide to quit asking about her, but I'm going to find out all I can about Sarah Boll, Nurse, of Amherst Ridge.

It's early morning when we both go to sleep. It's my normal time, but not for Brice. When I was little, Brice used to adjust his sleep to mine and we'd have whole nights of reading and games. Since I moved out, he learned to sleep at night again. But I have to say, I miss my time with him, running through the cabin playing hide-and-go-seek.

I'm out almost as soon as I hit the pillow.

I stand in the bright field, reveling in the sun and gazing at its brightness. I run a little and find I almost want to dance in celebration of the warmth. My skin is whole and untouched by the exposure. I giggle at how good it feels. As I run, I realize my feet are bare, and the feeling of the grass beneath tickles my toes.

I look up and stop in my tracks. A woman stands before me, smiling. She reaches out to me, and suddenly her look of joy turns to fear, and she runs away. I want to tell her I won't hurt her, but she doesn't listen. A moment before she begins to burn in the sunlight, she utters one word. "Why?" Then she disintegrates into a pile of ash. The laughter starts again from beside me, and I see a man with shadowed eyes regarding me.

"Oh, well. We keep trying."

Brice shakes me awake. It takes me a moment to realize I'm in my own bed, in my apartment—safe.

He utters, "Scarlett, baby. You're okay, you're okay. It was only a dream. Wake up."

I sit up suddenly. "Oh!"

Brice sits down beside me. "You were screaming. You want to talk about it?"

I shake my head and rub my face. What a strange dream. I make a mental note to buy a book on dream interpretation. "No, it wasn't important."

Brice looks at me skeptically. "You sure? Talking would help."

"I'm sure." I glance at my clock. It's ten in the morning. I hadn't been asleep very long. I glance at Brice and see he's dressed. "You heading home now?"

"Yeah," he agrees. "I'm supposed to catch up with Sarah this afternoon. So, I figured I'd get going and get a few hours of sleep at home. But I can stay if you need me." He eyes me warily.

I shake my head. "No, you go on. I'm fine. I probably just had some bad blood or something. You go on ahead."

He looks relieved, and I want to kill Sarah Boll for taking my place in his life. "You sure? 'Cause I can stay."

"No, Dad, really. Go," I say selflessly. I really want him to stay, but I can't do that to him. He needs to live his life regardless of how much I need him. "I'm going to try to go back to sleep before school."

Brice smiles and leans in to kiss my forehead. "I love you, baby. Always."

"Love you, too," I reply softly. I watch as he tells me he'll call me later and disappears out my door. A few moments later, the slamming of my apartment door tells me he's gone.

I lay back on my bed and think about the woman in the dream—and the man. This is the second time I've dreamed about being in daylight with people. It's funny, but in the dream, I don't feel like myself. I feel like I'm someone else. How can I dream about being someone else? Weird.

I throw the pillow over my head and recite *Hamlet* in my head to go back to sleep. It works immediately.

SEVEN

EXCELSIOR ACADEMY

EXCELSIOR ACADEMY IS A NON-TRADITIONAL PRIVATE school in upper Manhattan, housed in a three-story brownstone and bordered by plastic surgeons' offices on both sides. The school boasts that their attendees are children of diplomats, famous musicians, and actors. It's very exclusive, and I'm not sure how Brice got me in, but he had some connections with some professor friends of his who gladly helped. Chasem, of course, pays the fees.

I attend classes four days a week from three in the afternoon to ten at night. I hate that I have to get there during the day, because it makes avoiding sunlight tricky. Typically, I wear a special hoodie and jeans to make it from my apartment to the subway and then from the subway to the building. I'm pretty successful in that I haven't fried yet.

Humans have it so lucky; if I get exposed to the sun, I'll be reduced to ash. Oddly enough, when we burn, it produces a sweet smell instead of the ghastly odor of burning human flesh. In fact, that's how the whole urban lore of spontaneous combustion came about. When humans couldn't explain why some people had been reduced to ash in the sunlight, smelling oh-so-sweet, it became this odd legend that somehow humans must have been the victims. They've never given any thought to my kind actually existing. But their ignorance is our protection.

It's a sunny day today, so I'm jittery and anxious about not making it. But Chasem told me the hoodie will protect with its special UV-protectant lining and that sunlight can't get through. I have a mask to completely cover my face if I need it. That stays buttoned on the inside of the hood, but thankfully I've never had to use it. I do wear gloves as well, and when I get the stupid questions from people about why I'm so covered on sunny days, I give them the same answer—xeroderma pigmentosum. The term is so technical that I don't get many questions after that, but every now and again, I have to explain to a super curious soul all the ins and outs of it. The Academy believes I have it as well, and they make adjustments to suit my needs. So, avoidance of sunlight is never a question.

I rush up the stairs and into the Academy, then shut the heavy door, thankful to be inside and in the safety of shade. I sling my book bag over my shoulder and stroll to the set of lockers along the wall, taking my gloves off as I go. A few students have arrived as well and huddle in small groups, talking. Most avoid me, and I them.

I have two friends here who I hang with—Misaki Brophy, or Missi, as she likes to be called, and Trevor Petrey. They both approached me my first day here freshman year, right after Haley Kent decided to "accidentally" knock me down. They came to my rescue that day, and we've been friends ever since. Although they know I tend to not share much with them in the way of my home life, they've still never pried. I love them for it.

As I get to my locker, I see Missi walk in the door in a huff, trying to balance her book bag and her lunch bag. Her mother believes American diets are too fatty and makes sure to send her with enough healthy food to feed an army. What her mother considers to be a good thing only succeeds in making Missi more of a target for bullies. She is already, because of her biracial status and her shy demeanor, not to mention that her best friend is gay. She's always been a walking target. But Missi valiantly withstands all the pressure.

She's really beautiful in an elegant way. Her hair is straight and shimmery black, hanging in a thick curtain down her back. Her face is creamy smooth, without a hint of a blemish, and accented by almond-shaped eyes the color of moss. I might be a little envious of her beauty. Her mother is a famous model in Japan, and her father's a fight promoter in the US. But her famous parentage does nothing to endear her to anyone here, because so many students at this school are the products of the same sort of infamous coupling.

She arrives at her locker, which is right beside mine, and frowns. Then she crams her things into the locker with the type of strength her father would envy. I watch her for a moment with a slight smile on my face.

"Care to share?" I ask, watching her continue her brutal assault on the innocent books.

"No." Another book flies into her locker from her bag. "Maybe." Another one gets tossed and the door slams. "Well, okay. My Father wants me to take boxing lessons and work with a trainer." She leans back against the locker wall and closes her eyes. "He thinks I'm too thin and too frail. Far be it for me to just be me."

I cross my arms and lean against my own locker. "And he's just now deciding this why?"

She looks at me and starts to say something, then changes her mind about whatever it was. "God, Scar, what happened to your throat?"

Her hand raises to the collar of my jacket to pull it back. I swat her away and zip up my jacket, which I'm sure doesn't do anything to cover it.

"Nothing. My jacket got caught in the elevator door at home. It about killed me. But I'm okay."

"That looks horrendous. I bet I have some press powder

that would help cover that." She digs through her bag, having completely bought my story. She never waivers in trusting what I tell her is true. She pulls out a compact and a scarf with skulls on it. "You can use this, and maybe this?" She holds them out to me and I take both.

"Thanks, Missi," I say, and immediately wrap the scarf around my neck. I like that it has skulls—it's my style completely.

We walk down the hall in relative quiet. After a few steps, Missi sighs heavily. "I don't want to take boxing lessons. I'll probably break a bone or something. My dad has such a hard time accepting that I'd rather read a book and listen to classical music than do something physical and play hard rock."

"Have you tried telling him this?" I prod, hoping it might offer her something useful.

She nods. "Lots of times. But since I'm his only child and not the boy he hoped for, he keeps trying to groom me to be tougher."

"What does your mom say? She has to be on your side." I glance up to see Trevor waiting by our first class with his pink backpack on. He smiles when he sees us.

"My mom just wants me to work out, although she thought something a little less brutal like Pilates or Yoga. But she won't interfere. I think it's the Asian female upbringing in her. But Dad is so intent on making me a tough little Irish girl. Both of their cultures leave me completely confused. I wished they would just let me be myself."

"Hey there, girls," Trevor says, syrupy-sweet. He's large for a teenage boy—heck, even for a full-grown man. He's at least six-four and two hundred-thirty pounds. His size would be impressive if he didn't have a metrosexual haircut and insist on wearing pink. Due to that, he lessens any threat his size might have presented.

Missi offers a half-wave and walks past us into the classroom.

"What's up with her?" Trevor snips. "Did she break a nail or something?"

I laugh. "Hardly. Her Dad wants to toughen her up. Wants her to take boxing lessons."

Trevor's face tightens up in mock horror. He throws his hands up to his neck. "What? Oh my god, that poor thing."

I smile at him and we both walk inside, he running a trot to catch up to Missi so he can put his arm around her in moral support.

Our first class of the day is Math. As this is a non-traditional school, we're all in the same class but at different levels. I'm a junior by high school definition, but some of my subjects are at the PhD level because I got tired of pretending I couldn't do the work. My teachers struggle to keep up with me, but I can't act dumb and do the regular collage work. I'm just driven by a challenge.

I glance up to see Haley Kent sneering at me. I naturally give her the middle finger. She *hmpfs* and turns around. I open my newest book, *Level Sets and Extrema of Random Processes and Field*, and start reading. My mind isn't into it as instead I wonder about two things at once—the date I agreed to go on with Nick, and what's going on with Chasem.

The date part is going to be easy. I'll play hooky from school on Wednesday and go to dinner with Nick. Well, the hooky is the easiest part, but the actual date probably won't be.

The Chasem issue is different. I can't figure out why he's being so paranoid and why he was so reluctant to let me go to work on Saturday. Strange.

My phone vibrates and I take it out to find a text from Nick. *Hey*, it reads.

Hey back, I shoot off, and try to appear like I'm paying attention. I see Missi look over at me, as does Trevor, who's just on the other side of her. I shrug as if to say "what?"

My phone vibrates again, but I don't immediately look at it. I glance around to find Ms. Crawford diligently working with Sebastian Jordan on his work. Her back is to me, so I'm safe.

I glance down discreetly and see, *You at school?* I roll my eyes. He knows I go to night school, so for him to ask is slightly insulting.

Yes, of course, where else would I be?

I wait a few minutes and there's no reply. For whatever reason, this bothers me. How long could it take to text me back? I finally resolve to put down my phone when it vibrates again. I glance over to Missi, who studiously tries not to pay attention to what's going on.

Out saving random guys from muggings? it reads.

I almost want to laugh out loud. How he could know it was me, I don't know. But to put it out there is so very...bold. I smile.

I don't do crap like that. I might hurt myself. I hit send, wondering what he'll think of it. I look up to see Ms. Crawford turning around and glancing about the room. I try my best to appear busy reading.

In my peripheral vision, I see her approach me. I glance up with my hands folded over my book. Ms. Crawford is such a friendly teacher, with short, curly hair and large glasses much too big for her face. She smiles at me. "How's it coming, Scarlett?"

"Okay," I immediately answer. My phone vibrates and I jump, but I don't take my eyes off Ms. Crawford. I pat my chest and remark, "Hiccups".

She nods and smiles again. "Well, if you need to go get some water, let me know."

I smile back. "No, I'm fine, I think. They should go away soon."

"Well, okay," she says slowly. "I wanted to tell you that Dr.

Shah from NYU has agreed to come and sit with you next week to go over the book and discuss the theories there. Okay?"

I nod. "Sure. That sounds interesting," I agree, and try to appear as humble as possible.

Seemingly convinced, she smiles at me and turns. "I'll let you know."

As soon as she's far enough away, I grab my phone. Looking down I read what he texted.

Or you might get a date.

I laugh and then I start to fake a cough as everyone looks at me.

Trevor and Missi both lean forward with looks of wonder. I shake my head and try to brush them off, but I know the questions are coming.

The rest of the day is uneventful and I avoid most of the questions from Trevor and Missi, but I know they know something's up. I'm relieved when the final bell rings and we're free to leave.

Missi heads out, and Trevor puts his arm around her, trying to comfort her as they walk out to the waiting limos. I wave to them and start toward the subway.

The smell of urine and mechanic's oil fills my nose as I make my way to the harshly lit platform to wait for my train. As I stand there, I feel the hairs on my neck prickle, and a million whispers suddenly echo in my head. I look around and I see him.

He stands at the end of the platform, a hoodie drawn up tight around his head, his hands in his pockets. The light shines down on him, but he looks down, his face obscured in shadow. I don't know who he is, but I have a feeling *what* he is. He's a renegade, and he's hunting.

The train powers down the tracks and the brakes squeal as it stops. I try to keep my eyes on him, but he disappears in a burst of people exiting the train. I can't see where he went and finally give up, letting the crowd push me inside the train.

The rest of my trip, I keep one hand on my knives and my head over my shoulder. Not until I make it home do I finally relax.

EIGHT

FIRST DATE

WEDNESDAY ARRIVES AND I FIND MYSELF STANDING in front of my mirror, looking myself over. I feel like no matter what I do, I'm not good enough. My bed is strewn with a large pile of clothes. Nothing I put on works. I sigh and decide I'll go with something I wear normally. I throw on a Misfits t-shirt and tie the sides, then put on a sleeveless denim vest over the top. The sides of my jeans are lined with knives, and I have more at my ankles. I'll be ready.

The last thing I put on is my mother's necklace, and I stare at it. I wish I had a picture of her. Chasem tells me all the time how much I look like her, but still, I wish I can look at her myself.

My phone dings and I grab it.

Have fun tonight and please do anything I would do! Please give me details! It's a text from Emma.

It will probably be boring, I text back.

Doubtful. You better text me when it's over. Don't make me come over there.

Shush.Ttyl.

A knock sounds at the door and I take a deep breath. I know Chasem won't approve of a date, but really, what can it hurt? It's not like I'm about to have a boyfriend or anything. It's a date. Just an innocent, innocuous date. I can have those, right?

I reach my door and look around my living room one more time. Everything is in order. I never have anyone here beyond Chasem and Brice, so I'm never really prepared for company. This is a new thing. I've never been on a date, either, so it's an evening of firsts.

I turn the nob and open the door. Nick's tall frame fills my doorway. His curly hair is stylishly messy and he's dressed in a blue button-down with the sleeves rolled up. He smiles and my heart stops.

"Hi there," he says and hands me a single red rose.

I slowly take it and stand back to invite him in. His presence in my personal space makes everything seem so small. I walk toward the kitchen counter and lean on it, finding myself feeling unsure of everything. He ambles around the apartment, glancing around casually, but it still feels like there's a purpose to it, as if he's looking for something. Before I know it, he glances into my bedroom, then returns to me with a big smile.

"Ready to go?" he asks genteelly.

I nod and grab my keys off the counter, noticing that he's still looking around the walls and such. We head out the door and to the elevator. On our way to the ground floor, I can feel the warmth of his body next to mine. I want to sneak a look to him but decide to look stoically ahead at the numbers as they tick off in our descent.

Clearing my throat, I find courage to speak. "What were you looking for?" I glance up to him and his eyebrows are raised in a question.

"Excuse me?"

"Back there, in my apartment. You acted like you were looking for something."

"Did I?" he answers cryptically.

"Yes. You did."

"Hmm. Why are you irritable?"

"I'm not," I reply a little too loudly. His answering smile

makes me feel caught. "Well, maybe I don't like it when people dodge my questions."

"Oh," he says. "Like when someone obviously saves you and then denies it and won't explain why? You mean that kind of dodge?" His eyes bore into mine with a glint of amusement. I tear my gaze away and burst out into the lobby in a huff. I keep going right out the door into the fresh night air. After a few minutes, Nick catches up to me.

"Where you going?" he asks with a laugh.

"I thought we were going to get dinner." I'm so mad I don't want to look at him.

"We are, but it's the other way." He chuckles. I stop and glare at him. He lifts his hands in surrender. "Friend here." He points to himself.

I realize I'm letting him get under my skin. Why had I even agreed to this date? My internal voice reminds me he's incredibly handsome, and I wanted to go on a date with him. That's why. I want to slap my internal voice. I think of Chasem's words about not letting my temper get the best of me, because when I do, my opponent can also get the better of me.

I force myself to breathe in and breathe out, then I smile. "Sorry. That way?" I point toward the other direction.

Nick smiles and nods, and I force myself to walk more calmly. His long legs allow him to seem like he's not making much effort at all to move forward. "Do you like sushi?" he asks hesitantly.

I nod. "I love sushi."

"Love is a strong word, don't you think?"

I consider that. "Well, maybe, but what other term could I use for something I like a lot?"

"Hmm. How about, 'I fancy sushi'?" he says, and we both laugh. A slight blush steals over his cheeks. "Okay, so 'fancy' isn't the right word. But I just think 'love' is used too often and for too many things."

"There are different kinds of love, you know. Different origins of the word translated into 'love'. In Greek, there are four different words related to it, and there are five in Italian and Hindi. So, really I could say I love sushi and be completely right, depending on which version of love it is."

Nick stared down at me. "Thanks, smarty pants. But I still think it's a word that should be used for something really special."

"Okay. Point taken. I'll try to refrain from using that word around you."

We arrive at the restaurant and Nick opens the door for me. We get a small table toward the back of the restaurant. The waitress is old, with deep lines on her face and gray hair tied in a loose bun at the back of her head. She frowns at me when she lays down my menu and mutters under her breath, "Kyuuketsuki."

"What?" Nick says, leaning forward, but the woman just walks away.

I know the word, but I don't want to think about it. She knows what I am. How? I'm not sure, but it's a word specifically for my kind.

We look down at our menus in silence for a minute, making our choices. Our waitress returns to take our order but glares at me the whole time before going off in a huff.

"What's her problem?" Nick asks angrily.

"I don't know, but don't let her ruin our dinner."

"Okay," Nick agrees. He smiles, and it's so beautiful. I've never seen such a perfect human boy in my life. Even his fingers are perfect as he folds them on top of the table.

"So, you've been dying to know about me," he begins.

"Oh, have I?" I sputter. "Pray tell, what gave you that idea?"

He leans back in his chair and smiles again. "I just know." He fakes regaining his composure and starts talking again. "My full name is Nicholas Thomas Lightener, I'm seventeen, I have a baby sister named Abigail—she's ten—and I live with my father and mother in Midtown East. I'm on the rowing team at school and just joined the debate team. My favorite color is green and I listen to hard rock." He leans forward and smiles at me, waiting.

"Wow," I remark, drawing out the word. "Those are some deets, Mr. Nicholas Thomas Lightener."

"They are," he confirms and stares at me, obviously waiting for me to reciprocate. His gray eyes regard me with an unwavering stare. "So?"

"I don't have much to tell," I mutter, picking at the paper napkin on the chipped table.

"I doubt that. Just tell me anything." He leans back in his chair again, waiting. He is so frustrating.

"Well, my favorite color is red," I allow, and then I stop.

"Okay. So, favorite color is established. What's your middle name?"

"Elaine." And I watch his face. It's like he's discovered something important.

"So, Scarlett Elaine Ellis, what kind of music do you like?"

"Oh, I listen to everything," I reply, and it's true. I listen to classical, rock, country, rap. I just like music in general.

"Okay. Do you have a hobby besides saving guys being mugged in a back alley?"

My temper flares. "Why do you keep asking me about that? I told you, it wasn't me."

"And I told you, I don't believe you. I know it was you. I just don't understand why you won't admit it." His smile drops slightly then grows into a goofy grin. "You were a hero, and I'm glad you helped me out. Can't I just be allowed to thank you?"

No amount of arguing is going to sway him from the truth. My carefully placed emotional wall gives a little.

Chasem has pushed me my entire life to never share anything about who I am. It gets really lonely at times, and if I didn't at least have Emma knowing about me, I think I'd lose my mind. Staring into Nick's beautiful gray eyes, I realized I want to get to know him. But I also know the risks and understand Chasem's carefully crafted warnings to me about friendships and intimacy. Damn it, though. I want this boy to know me.

"You're welcome," I whisper, and with that I know I'm crossing a line. This boy knows where I work, and now where I live. "But if you ever tell anyone, I'll deny it. No one would believe you anyway," I add sharply.

He nods and smiles. "I'm not going to tell anyone. Man, you were so fast I couldn't even see you clearly, and you took those guys out so easily. How are you that strong and that fast?"

The waitress returns with two sushi rolls and edamame. I try to smile at her, but she rushes away again, obviously bothered. Nick eyes her wearily and then looks back at me. "You know why she doesn't like you, don't you?"

It bothers me that he's so perceptive. I should lie, but I shrug instead. "She just knows I'm different is all."

Nick leans in and whispers conspiratorially, "Different how?"

I mimic his stance and smile. "Just different. Now, are you going to eat your sushi, or do I have to do it for you?"

Nick laughs and it's like music. I smile at him, in awe of this human boy. He picks up his chopsticks and dips a piece of sushi into the soy sauce, then in a show he makes a loud "mmm" noise. I sit there and just watch him, mesmerized by how he moves, how his hands hold the chopsticks, and how his eyes dart down and back up to me. This all has me feeling a little high.

Nick stops and leans over our plates, looking at me and mimicking me. "Now, are you going to eat your sushi, or do I have to do it for you?" His face is so close to mine I can make out every single speck of hazel in his eyes. I glance down at this lips and watch him lick them, just a little. I'm not sure why, but I lean over and kiss him.

His lips freeze in surprise for a moment, warm and tasting like salt, but they quickly yield to mine. Before I know it, his surprise melts into participation, and he kisses me back. It's all pleasantly confusing, and I feel dizzy. My blood pounds wildly in my veins and I'm worried my eyes are going to change out of excitement. But before I can pull back, he does first, and his breath is hot on my cheek.

I keep my eyes down, for fear of what they might show. I glance up at the artery in his neck, veiled by the paper-thin skin of a human. The blood moves in thick shots and I hear his heart pounding. I feel the urge to let my canines drop and lean over to bite him. I've learned to control myself so much around humans that I'm able to push the desire down. But he gives off the most intoxicating smell. I find myself wondering what his blood would taste like. It's odd to even think about, because I don't even need blood right now, but he's somehow attracting me in a way I don't understand. It's a strange desire to bite— not to hurt, not even to drink, but to bite. I can't make sense of it.

"Was that to keep me from taking some of your sushi?" He laughs and reaches over, grabbing a piece of my roll with his chopsticks. I find I'm laughing with him, and I start eating, trying to calm the rapid beating of my heart. I keep my head down, really worried that my eyes have already turned.

I wait a moment and then look up, but Nick only stares into my eyes. He says nothing. He doesn't appear scared or con- fused, so everything must look like it should.

We talk and laugh through the rest of our dinner, ignoring the other patrons who come and go. Our waitress never comes back to check on us, but at some point a waiter walks by and deposits the bill on the table. Nick pays, and we start the slow walk back to my apartment.

NINE
RENEGADES

WE AMBLE ALONG IN THE COOL EVENING, NOT SAY-ing much to each other. I find that, as much as I'm trying to steal looks from him, he's doing the same to me.

At one point, his hand brushes mine, but I don't move away. Before I know it, he's holding my hand. His is large and warm and feels strangely comforting. I feel him firmly holding my hand, and then he seems to realize this and relaxes his grip.

"Is this okay?" he asks as we walk.

"Yes," I sigh, and it is. A fluttering takes off in my stomach and I try to make myself breathe slowly. My eyes are still incredibly close to turning out of excitement.

I see his head turn towards me as we walk, warmth filling me like nothing else in my entire life. It feels like I'm being drawn into an intoxicating spell, and I don't want out. I want to be a human girl with a human boy, just enjoying the night.

A buzz sounds from Nick's pocket and he releases my hand to take his phone out. His brow furrows as he reads it.

"I...ah. I have to go." His troubled eyes meet mine.

"Is everything okay?" I ask, watching a war take place on his face.

"Yes, fine. Um. I hate to bail on you. Here, let me get you a cab," he offers, raising his hand to flag a taxi. I pull down his arm.

"No, don't. I'm only a few blocks from my apartment. Seriously, I walk further than this all the time."

He frowns and gazes intently at me. "You sure? I mean, I could—"

"I'm sure. I'm good. Go."

He gives me a forced smile. "Okay. I'll text you later." I can tell from the look on his face that something's wrong, but what? Before I can even respond, he dashes off down the street.

I turn and head to my apartment. I find myself smiling at how it felt to kiss him and hold his hand. Is this what it feels like to start falling in love? It feels kind of like eating your favorite food—or in my case, human blood—to satisfaction. Like the stuff it gives you bleeds out of your fingers and toes and you can almost levitate because all is right in the world. Yeah, he's done that for me, and this was only our first date.

I'm about a block from my apartment building when a light catches my attention in one of the dark side-alleys. It flashes once, and a thousand voices fill my head in a rush. A cackling laugh ricochets off the walls like a bullet.

My senses swing up on high alert. A renegade is here, and I'm startled to find there are actually two as they step out into the partly illuminated alley. One has long hair falling into his face, while the other has a hoodie over his head.

"Scarlett," the one with the long hair sneers. "We've been looking for you."

I glance around to make sure no one sees me and pull out the daggers concealed in my jeans. I walk slowly toward them into the depth of the alley. "What do you mean, 'you've been looking for me'? I don't Dawn for another two months, so hunting me now seems pointless. Don't you agree?"

The one with the hood drops it from his face, and I see a shaved head, covered in intricate tattoos in vampiric script. They give a warning of his abilities. "No, it isn't pointless.

Rather, it's quite profitable for us to find you before you Dawn."

Still moving toward them, I assess the area around them as Chasem taught me. Can they use anything as a weapon? No, there's nothing to grab. But I don't wonder for long, as they both pull out their own knives and start toward me.

"You know, if you kill me now, you won't get anything from me. No power and no memories, and my blood will be bitter on your tongue. So, why don't you take your bad selves back to whatever hole you crawled out of? And I'll be willing to forget this whole matter."

The one with the longer hair lets out the same frenzied laugh as before. "You think we mean to kill you?"

I felt my eyebrows draw down. "Why else would renegades be after me? Don't you prey on the unbound? Hoping to steal from them? Oh, I know how you operate. But I'm warning you, I won't be the one losing this fight. I hope you both are prepared to lose your lives." I stop walking and hold my blades in both hands, waiting for them to get close enough.

"Well, little girl, it won't be any of us losing anything, tonight."

"Famous last words," I yell, then rush forward, catapulting myself off the wall and slicing down at the neck of the renegade with long hair. He crumples, holding onto his neck as streams of blood shoot out of a nicked artery.

The second one catches me as my momentum flings me and slams me down. I land hard on my back and kick up, catching the bald one in the chin. Just like I'd done to Chasem. But this one isn't nearly as trained or honed as Chasem is, and he staggers back, knocking the other one over who still tries to stem the blood loss by grasping onto his neck.

I flip up and lick the blood off the knife. "Hmm. I've had better."

The bald one rushes at me and I spin in time to kick him

forward. He lands hard on all fours. Before I can reach him, something bashes into my head and light explodes in my vision. I fall to the ground but instinctively roll away. I blink hard and hear the bleeding renegade begging his friend to help him. The bald one grabs a hold of my shirt and drags me toward the end of the alley. I slide out of his grip, to his surprise, and as he turns to look, I hurl my blade and catch him in the heart. He gasps and falls to his knees, then topples onto his side.

"That's for getting my favorite shirt dirty," I huff, and walk toward him, lightheaded, to retrieve my blade from where it impales his chest. Right as I reach it, he grips my wrist and whispers, "Apollo."

I stagger more than walk home. Every step hurts my head as I move, like someone's punching me in the back of the neck with every jarring move I make. I want to pull out my phone to text Chasem, but I honestly can't focus clearly enough to type anything. So, I resolve to do it when I get home.

I can't think very clearly as I make it into my building and up to my floor. The elevator doors open with a ding and I step out. My feet feel heavy and my vision turns sideways. The pain radiates from the back of my head like a bulldozer, and I consider the fact that I may not make it to my door.

A few more feet and I'll be there. My keys. I have keys somewhere in my pocket. I fumble and dig for them, and finally find them. Navigating that little key into the slit of the lock is rather challenging, but I eventually slide it in and disengage the lock. I'm in my apartment. Right as I walk inside and start to close the door, everything goes black.

I'm stiff and can tell I've been lying on the floor when I feel hands moving me. Nick places me on the couch and dials a number on his phone. How did he get here, and how long have

I been out?

He almost chides me under his breath in a panic, and I notice he's got a rather large, red mark on the side of his face. He keeps asking me what happened, and I can't clear my head enough to try to figure out a way to explain it. Eventually, I hear him say he's going to call an ambulance.

"Don't," I rasp to him. "Don't call anyone."

"You're bleeding! I need to call 9-1-1." He's almost angry. "Why did I leave you? I should have stayed with you 'til you got home."

I reach out to him. "Stop, Nick. I'll be okay."

"How do you know?" he yells, and I wince from the pain it sends through my ears.

"Stop yelling, please. Bring me my phone."

Nick complies and I try to dial Chasem's number, but just can't do it. I finally give up and hand the phone to Nick. "Please dial this number for me." He complies and hands the phone back to me.

The line rings a few moments and then goes straight to voicemail. "Chase, it's me. I had a couple renegades jump me tonight. I'm hurt and could use a little help. It's not bad, so don't freak out. I just think I need a few stitches in my head. I might have a concussion. I don't know. Call me or come by. Bye." And I hang up.

Nick is immediately beside me with a cold cloth. He presses it gently to the back of my head and I wince. "Keep it there," he demands and sits on my coffee table, looking at me.

"Who's Chase?" he asks with tight lips.

"My uncle." That's all I can say and then I'm out again.

"Scarlett!" Nick yells, and I hear angry growling in it. I try to open my eyes, but it takes a moment. When I do, I see Chasem holding Nick against the wall, a knife to his throat.

"Who are you?" Chasem demands hotly.

"Nick Lightener," he forces out through gritted teeth, his

hands held high.

"Chasem, stop. He's a friend," I beg.

"He's a human!" Chasem retorts. He turns back to Nick with such malice I think for sure he's going to cut his throat.

Nick tries to shove Chasem back, but he isn't strong enough. I make it to wobbly legs and rush to Chasem, trying to pull his knifed hand from Nick's neck. Chasem's eyes flicker to me for a second and then he relents, lowers his hand, and steps back.

Nick angrily rubs his neck. "Uncle or not, you're a psycho," he yells. He glances at me and a strange look crosses his face. Then he catches me right before I hit the floor. To my surprise, Chasem's also beside me, and they've both become unwilling teammates in helping me back to the couch.

"Steady there," Nick whispers as he sets me down. "You shouldn't be up." He sits beside me on the couch. Chasem sits down on my coffee table in front of me. "What happened, Scarlett? Who attacked you?" Nick asks.

I shake my head at Nick and glance to his worried eyes. He wants answers, and I can't think clearly enough to make something up.

Chasem steadfastly ignores the volley of questions from Nick. "You need a few stitches. And some—" He stops and eyes Nick angrily. I finish it for him in my head. *Blood.*

Chasem stands and walks to my kitchen cabinets to return with a kit. He'll do what needs to be done.

Nick looks pale. "Why aren't you taking her to the hospital or calling the police? She got attacked tonight." His voice is high and loud, and I wince again at the pain. "And why the hell are you calling me 'human'? Aren't we all human?"

Chasem ignores him. He sits on the couch and turns me to face away from him. Then he cleans the back of my head and I feel a small pinch on my skin. "He needs to go, Scar," he says harshly. "Like, now."

The tugging of the skin at the back of my head makes me

dizzy, so much so that I close my eyes to breathe in through my nose and out through my mouth. It takes just a few seconds, but I manage to calm my head some.

Reluctantly, I say with my eyes closed, "Maybe you should go, Nick." But I hear nothing, so I open my eyes. He stares at me with the most unfathomable look, then crosses his arms.

"What is going on here, Scarlett? Is he the one who put those bruises on your neck?"

I feel the tugging at the back of my neck come to an abrupt stop. *Oh boy.*

Chasem growls low. "Are you going to leave on your own, or am I going to have to throw you out? 'Cause I can tell you, I will be tempted to use the window and the not the door. Your choice."

The tugging returns to my neck.

Nick stares at me. He reaches out and grabs my hand, giving it a reassuring squeeze. He leans over and speaks gently, almost like I'm a wounded animal. "I'm not sure what's going on here, but I'll go ahead and leave. If you're sure."

He looks so reluctant, like he would have stayed and dared fight Chasem in the meantime to be here. I think it's gallant and chivalrous and it actually makes me feel a little giddy. Even though Chasem would eat him for lunch, it's still a noble thought that he wants to attempt it.

"I'm sure. I'll text you, okay?"

He nods once and stands. Before he leaves, he does the bravest thing I've ever seen anyone do. He stops and stands over Chasem. "And if you hurt her again, you will answer to me. I promise."

The tugging stops again and I think I should be jumping up to get between them. Then I hear Chasem chuckle.

"You know, I like you. You have more brawn than brain, although that brawn would only get you about two seconds tops in a battle with me. So you best be on your way before I decide to finish what I started earlier."

"I mean it," Nick repeats, then tacks on, "Scarlett, I'll talk to you soon."

I hear the door open and then close.

"What was that all about, Scarlett?"

I close my eyes as I hear him breathe deeply. "Nothing, Chase. He's harmless."

"Oh yeah? You exposed yourself to him in the worst way imaginable. Does he know what you are?"

"No, he doesn't know anything. He's just a friend."

"You can't have friends like that. It exposes you to too much risk."

I don't know how to argue with him. He's right, of course, but I want Nick in my life, like a moth wants the flame. The thought of him not being in my life makes me wince. I consider what would have happened to Nick had he not left when I asked him to; he likely would have been killed. I replay the quick fight over in my head.

"Chase, one of the renegades mentioned a name."

"Oh?" he says, and just sews and pulls at my skin.

"He said 'Apollo'."

Chasem stops. "What else?"

"Nothing else. But do you think he really sent them after me? I mean, what use can I be right now?"

Chasem starts the sewing again. "With Apollo, anything is possible. He wants you dead, after all. You can't ever forget that. To let your guard down would be catastrophic for you."

I nod. I understand the why of Apollo wanting me dead, but the other side of me thinks of my grandparents. They were what revenant parents should be, and they loved their children so much, they were willing to sacrifice themselves for their children's wellbeing. Not Apollo Bramstall. No, as a father, he failed.

Chase gets up and walks to the kitchen to wash his hands

and throw away all the bloody bandages.

I gently lean my head back on the couch and close my eyes again. "I'm tired of being so careful all the time. I want to just be normal for a change."

His voice is suddenly beside me. "Well, you're not. So let that fuzzy pipe dream go. Here." I open my eyes and he hands me a couple pills and a glass of blood. I take them and down the blood. "You need to rest and let that heal. And I meant what I said. You need to let boy go before he gets caught in the crossfire, or worse, killed. If not by a renegade, by me."

I don't have the heart to tell Chasem he almost killed Nick tonight and that I'd felt helpless to stop it.

TEN
REJECTION

BRICE MANAGES TO GET ME OUT OF SCHOOL FOR THE rest of the week, saying I have a stomach bug. I'm thankful for that. I feel like crap the next day and don't want to do anything but sleep.

Chasem has called Emma over to stay the rest of the night with me to check in on me from time to time as I sleep. But it's hard to get much rest because my phone keeps dinging with texts from Missi and Trevor, checking in on how I'm doing. As much as I'm glad to know they care enough to ask, it bothers me to no end that Nick hasn't sent me anything. I mean, I'd kissed him, for goodness sake. I hope he might want to follow up with a text or something. But I get nada, nothing, zilch. I'm lying if I say it doesn't bother me. Because it does.

Laying in the darkness of my apartment, I hear a knock at my door. I start to get up, but Emma answers it first. I know it's not Chasem, because it's daylight outside. Maybe Brice came by to see how I'm doing. I throw on my robe without much care and look out my bedroom door.

"Well hello, Mr. Epic first date," Emma says.

Nick stands there, holding a bag of magazines and fast food. He stares at her, confused, then glances past her to me.

Emma grabs her bag and turns to me. "Scar, I'm heading out. Call me later, okay?"

I nod and walk out into the living room. "Thanks, Em."

She winks at me and shifts her body around Nick as he stands there looking a little lost. Once she's gone, he turns to face me, lifts up the bags, and smiles. "Hey. I thought you could use some care packages while you recuperate. Can I come in?" Humor lights his grey eyes.

I consider his request and don't speak for a moment because I'm so stunned that he's actually standing at my door. His eyebrows raise in a question and it dawns on me that I need to say something.

I step aside. "Yes, please come in."

He walks in and over to the bar to lay the bags down. He turns to me, suddenly serious. "How's the head?"

"Fine," I automatically reply.

Nick reaches out to me and turns me around. "Let me see."

I comply and look down to give him easier access to my wound. I feel the goose bumps rising as he lightly traces a finger around the cut on the back of my head, and I shudder at his soft touch.

"Your uncle does good work. I can't believe how healed it looks."

I turn around and smile. "Yeah, he's good that way."

We both stand awkwardly for a moment. I realize my robe is a little cock-eyed and adjust it to be neater. I haven't even brushed my teeth. I just need to be careful in not getting to close. Don't want him to get a whiff of what was bound to be rank breath.

"So hey, aren't you supposed to be in school?" I ask and leave the kitchen to sit down.

He smirks. "Yeah, well, skipping one day isn't a big deal."

"You skipped? Why?"

"I would think the answer's obvious, considering I'm standing in your living room." He chuckles.

"You didn't need to, really. I'm fine. If the only thing you needed to know was if my head was okay, you could have texted me. It would have saved you a trip."

Nick sits down beside me, then reaches out and takes my hand. It's warm and strong, and I like how we fit—my smaller hand in his larger one. His touching me is a connection I realize I've been craving in spite of myself. I know I shouldn't want it, but I do. It feels almost as strong as craving blood. I'm not sure why; no one in my life has ever garnered such a reaction from me. Yes, I am powerless to stop my feelings—Chasem be damned.

"I had to see you. A text wouldn't have cut it. I hope you don't mind."

"No, I don't mind," I say with a small voice. I hate how it comes out so needy-sounding. I clear my throat and pull my hand away. "But still, it was unnecessary."

"Not for me. I promise, seeing you was very necessary." His voice is low and seductive, and I immediately find my heart in my throat. I get up from the couch to move away from him and I sway a little.

His hands come up to my back, sending jolts of electricity through me. "Whoa there. How about you sit down and let me get up for you? What were you going for?"

He's so close, I smell his scent. It's clean, like fresh laundry, and a scent to which I can't put words. But it's delicious. I want to bury my nose in his neck and inhale, but I resist.

"I was going to check out the bags you brought," I lie. I'm not going to say, *I'm running away from you because right now I want to jump on you and that would be the wrong thing by a lot.*

Chasem's words roll around in my head about how this relationship is doomed and I shouldn't be pursuing it. Nick can't know about me, or anything about my world. But I don't want to send him away. Not for anything. To hell with my future. I'm either going to be fodder for renegades or dead in two months, so why not live for now?

After sitting me down, he retrieves the things he brought and comes back to the couch. He makes a fake show of it. "Okay, so I brought you the appropriate rag magazines and Skybaby Burgers. A surefire cure for whatever ails you." He spreads out the stash before us and I realize he has food for two.

"Just for me? I see two helpings there, Dr. Lightener." I laugh.

"Yeah, well, a boy's got to eat." He winks as he eats a fry.

"Oh, that's a little presumptuous of you, don't you think? I mean, I might have taken the food and sent you away."

He grinned. "Nope. Not presumption. Not when you know the outcome."

"Oh, yeah? And that is?"

He leans conspiratorially toward me. "That you want me here as much as I want to be here. Now, doctor's orders. Eat."

We eat in relative silence, but he seems distracted, like there's something else on his mind. I catch him glancing over at me like he wants to say something, but he holds back. He's so contained. I study his face and see that the red mark on the side of his face is barely visible now.

"What happened to your face the other night?" I gaze up at him, and his expression turns blank.

"I could ask you the same thing. You got attacked or something, and you won't tell me what happened. And instead of calling the police or go to the hospital, you call your uncle. So, do you want to explain that?"

"No," I offer with a quiet voice. How can I explain renegades and Dawning and the fact that I'm a revenant?

"Yeah, me neither," he says, surrendering the topic.

We eat the rest of the meal in silence. When we finish, he cleans up and comes to sit down beside me. He reaches over and takes my hand again, almost naturally, like we've been doing it forever. His thumb lazily strokes the top of my hand.

"So, spit it out," I push.

His eyes shoot to mine in surprise. "What?"

"Whatever is rolling around in that head of yours."

He sighs. "Am I that obvious?"

I nod. He sits up straighter and turns to face me. "I...well. I know there's something different about you. And your uncle. I know you don't know me enough to trust me yet, but I just wanted you to know...whatever it is...it doesn't matter to me."

"What?" I ask incredulously. "What gives you that idea?"

He smiles wryly. "Your eyes. They changed color last night when your uncle was sewing up your neck. They were the most beautiful light green. His flashed that color for a split second when he came in and saw you passed out on the couch. He's freakishly strong, too. He had me up against the wall in seconds. I couldn't budge."

"Yeah, well, maybe you're just weak," I counter, trying not to address the eye-color change. That's something I can't explain with any type of made-up excuse to pass the sniff test.

He wrinkles his nose and shakes his head. "Yeah, not so much. I'm pretty strong."

"Maybe not as much as you'd like to think." I try to sound convincing, but he's right. Chasem is incredibly strong. So am I. Much stronger than a human.

"You can trust me, you know. It might take some time for you to realize it, but I won't betray your trust. You can keep denying it, but you won't convince me otherwise."

I look away. He's right again. I know I need to try to convince him he's wrong and that it's just a trick of the light with my eyes, or something else. But I don't have it in me to be illusive, so I remain silent.

"There's one thing that does still bug me, though," he says carefully.

"What's that?" I turn back to him.

His face is wary and nervous. "Well, I don't understand why your uncle is abusive toward you and why you don't let me help you."

I snort. "Abusive? Towards me? You have to be kidding."

He purses his lips and frowns. "I know it was him. The handprint you had on your neck before was about his size. Again, I know you don't trust me, but if he's harming you, I want to be here for you."

I sigh. This again. I wish he isn't so observant. He's right on the money about the who, but I can't tell him the why. Chasem is never abusive towards me. He just got carried away in my training.

I figure I can tell him only enough to answer the question— to put him at ease and still not tell him anything too revealing.

"Chasem trains me. We work out on the weekends. Those bruises were from a sparring session. He grabbed a hold of me a little too hard, but it wasn't abuse."

He stares at me. "Sparring." Not a question.

I lean my head back and close my eyes. "Yes. I promise. It was only working out and it was completely accidental."

He frowns, clearly not convinced. I reach out to him and take his hand. He glances down at it and back up to me, and before I know it he leans in and kisses me. It starts off very carefully, and then it changes to needy, hot, and hungry. I pull him close to me, grasping at his hair and yanking him down on top of me. We're all hands and panting, like two starving people.

But as soon as my head hits the sofa, pain lances through me. I wince and jerk away, my back arching up. Nick pulls back and whispers, "I'm sorry." Then I open my eyes and see his eyes widen. I know what he's seeing. My eyes must have flashed.

I turn away and pull myself up. "Go, Nick. Okay? Please."

He comes close and kneels in front of me. I won't look at

him. He reaches up and turns my face to force me to look at him.

"Please. Don't send me away," he whispers in a low, guttural voice.

His eyes plead with me. I want to drown in their depths and never be rescued. I want to reach over and touch his face, but I resist. I have to find a way to push him away before it's too late.

"I—"

He interrupts me. "I looked up the word the waitress used when we went out."

My mouth shuts with an audible snap.

Oh. My. God.

"Nick—"

His grip tightens on my hand. "Vampire. It meant vampire. And I told you before, I don't care."

I jerk my hand away easily and stand. I'm unsteady but I make it to the bar and grab a hold of the edge. I want to run away but there's nowhere to go. He knows. Oh God, he knows. Part of me considers going to the restaurant and killing the waitress for the whole debacle.

Keeping my back to him, I say carefully, "You need to go, Nick. I mean it. Just go and don't look back."

"No," he yells, and I jump but don't turn around. "I want to be with you. Don't you understand? I don't care what you are."

I start to think of how his blood would taste if I bite him, and I feel my canines dropping. I know my eyes have changed. I whirl around to him and step close, exposing my fangs.

"You. Need. To go. Now."

He draws back with a look of apprehension, and I hear his heartbeat speeding up. Holding onto my resolve, I open the door for him and stand there, glaring at him. I'm glad I frightened him. He needs to see who I really am. This cannot work, no matter how much I want it. It just can't.

I watch him clench his fists and release them, then he quietly walks out the door. I slam it shut, latch it, and let myself slid down the inside of the door to collapse into a bundle of tears.

ELEVEN
THE BEATING

"**H**IT ME, ALREADY!" CHASEM YELLS, AND I HURL another throwing star at him, only for him to dodge it easily.

My moves are sloppy today. I chalk it up to staying in bed for as long as I did, partly to heal and partly because I'm so depressed. The wrong part of me had hoped Nick would text me or something to try to get me to reconsider. The right part of me hopes he won't, and that part of me feels validated when the hours tick by and he just hasn't contacted me. I just try to sleep and not think about the separation.

I fling a star towards Chasem and it goes so wide he doesn't even have to move. He gives me a droll stare. "Come on, Scar. Focus."

I throw up my hands and walk off the mats. Chasem catches up and turns me toward him. "What's going on? Why are you stopping?"

"I'm tired, Chase, and my head hurts. I just need a minute." For once, Chasem doesn't argue and walks with me to the small kitchenette. I let my weight drop in one of the chairs and lay my head back. My head doesn't really hurt. Only my stomach does from the knots thinking about Nick.

Chasem stands over me and hands me a glass of blood. "Here. This will help."

I take it without enthusiasm and rest it on my knee. More blood. I should be thrilled at the amount of blood I'm getting lately, but I just can't seem to care. The glass reminds me of the differences separating me from Nick, and I don't like it. I find myself wishing I could just be a normal human girl who only has to worry about school and chores. Not blood and Dawning and the constant worry of renegades right around the corner.

Chasem senses my hesitation and sits down beside me. "Come on, Scarlett. What's going on? You seem really distract-ed today. Even more than you are normally. So talk to me. What is it? Another renegade chase you or something like that?"

I shake my head but don't answer. I know what his response will be, and I'm not ready to hear a lecture. I stare at his face and wish he was Jasmine. I need a mother's per-spective, not a male warrior's view on things. So, I push down my feelings and just try to divert Chasem's worry.

"School is just getting difficult," I lie, hoping he believes me.

His eyebrows shoot up. "Oh. Well, you know, I was thinking of talking to Brice about having you withdraw for this semester, anyway. You need to focus all your energy on training."

"No!" I yell. I don't want that. I want some part of normal to stay in my life, regardless of what's expected of me or what's coming. The thought of not being in school makes me ill.

He purses his lips. "Why, might I ask? I mean, you know what's coming. You know how critical this is."

I get up and pace around because I have to get away from all of this. At least for a few moments. Chasem never relents and always pushes me to keep going. I want to run away, but I know I can't. I know he means well, and he truly *is* trying to save my life.

So I stop and let out a big sigh. I pick the glass of blood back up and down it. As I wipe my mouth, I utter, "Sorry. It's not important. Let's get back to work."

Chasem smiles like it's the best thing I've said all day. "Let's go."

I walk back into my room and I just want to collapse. Chasem was so excited about my enthusiasm that he put me through so many relentless paces. I drop onto the bed, my head lulling forward.

I see my phone on the night stand and wonder if I have any texts. I grab it and enter my code. My heart sinks when there's nothing from Nick.

I rub my face and wonder what he's doing. He knows what I am now, and I hope he keeps it secret. Jeez, Chasem would throw a clot if he knew Nick knows what I am.

I hear Nick's voice echo in my head, telling me he doesn't care. He just doesn't. I feel the adrenaline thrumming through my body at the prospect. The fact that he knows is liberating. But he's gone, and that depresses me all over again.

I glance at my phone and make a split-second decision. I jump up and grab my jacket, then run down the hallway. Chasem stands in the kitchen, holding a sandwich mid-bite, his mouth hanging open.

"What are you doing?"

"I'll be back," I yell as I dash out the door. I hear Chasem starting to say something but I cut him off when I slam the door.

I rush down the stairs as quickly as I can and down to the street below. The night air is cool as it hits my face and the cars whiz by to unknown destinations.

I run around to the back side of the building, where I can scale it all the way up and make quick time along the rooftops. I love letting my true nature out, pushing and running with all my might. It's like stretching after sitting still for a long time. It feels so refreshing.

Passing windows obscured by the darkness, blocking out the bits of conversation I hear and actions I see, I only have one goal—one aim—and don't want anything to stop me. The tall buildings give way to elegant brownstones, and I hit the ground with a soft thud a few blocks from his house. I hear small rodents scurrying away from me. I can track their bodies like heat signatures, and I feel their blood like a fragrance reaching out to me. It doesn't particularly attract me, but if I ever needed their blood in a pinch, it would do.

I turn away and stroll out of the alley to the empty side-walk. The lights along the street punch through the darkness like beams, and I feel them land on my head and then fade as I pass them by. I see my destination—Nick's house, settled neatly in the middle of the block.

He doesn't want to see me, I know. But it doesn't mean I can't see him. I walk to the back side of the row of houses, then duck through the pockets of darkness until I'm directly behind his house. Sheltered by the black, I stand and glance up the walls of his house to see an illuminated window. Watching carefully, I hope I catch a glance of him so I know where he is.

It takes ten minutes, but I finally see him passing the window on the second floor. I glance around in case anyone's there; the backyards are quiet except for the occasional dog barking on the next block over.

I move along the shadows until I make it to his house, then scale the solitary tree growing high above the roof. I stop at eye level with his open window. Nick sits on his bed with his face in his hands, bathed in the room's bright light. His stance is weary, weighted down, and it makes me curious.

His bedroom door opens and a man in his late forties enters. Nick jumps up and I notice the man holds a belt stretched between his hands. He steps into the room and closes the door, glaring at Nick.

Nick is taller than him and has his back to me, but I can see he's clenching his fists. He stands but doesn't release the tension.

"You knew this would happen. So turn around," his dad says calmly.

"Dad, I—"

His dad explodes and swings the belt hard. It lands on Nick's arm with a sickening smack. I see Nick's arm go up to protect his face from any more blows.

"Turn around, or so help me, I will beat you anywhere I can," his father screams, and swings again. This time, the belt lands on Nick's back.

"Dad, please!" Nick begs, but obediently turns around and grips the desk with his face to me, waiting with a grimace.

His father whips Nick furiously. Tears stream from his eyes, and even though each blow makes his face flinch, he doesn't cry out. The only noises he makes are a few scattered grunts. His gaze hovers on me, but I'm hidden in the darkness so I know he can't see me.

I'm so livid I feel my fangs drop and my eyes change. I want to rush in there and tear his father apart, bit by bit. The man gives no mercy, and after several hard blows, finally stops. Nick shakes but never turns around to face his father. His face is red, and an involuntary tear runs down his face.

His dad leans in and says, "Now. If you ever disrespect me like that again, I will not stop until either you collapse from the beating or I do. Understand?"

Nick's lips are pressed tightly together and the tears still roll down his face as he breathes hard through his nose. But he says nothing, still glaring in my direction and grasping the edge of his desk for dear life.

His father yells, "I said, do you understand?"

"Yes." The word grinds out of Nick's mouth.

"Yes, what?"

"Yes, sir," he spits.

"Good. Now do your homework."

His father walks calmly out. As soon as the door shuts, Nick falls to his knees and I can't see him any longer. But I hear him. He sobs, and my heart breaks. I want to go to him and pull him into my arms, tell him everything will be okay. But I can't. I stay there and watch him eventually get up, turn his light off, and gingerly lay down on his bed.

I drop from the tree and scurry up the side of his building to wait outside his window. After a time, his gasps slow from shuttering to soft breathing. I realize he's fallen asleep. In that moment, I don't listen to the voice of warning, and I crawl into his window as softly as I can.

He lays drawn up in a fetal position, and although he's asleep, no part of him looks peaceful. Even asleep, he's all tension. I lean close to him and let my fingers brush over his curls, but he doesn't stir.

Gazing down at him, I realize something in me has turned completely regarding Nick. I no longer want him to stay away. In fact, I resolve to make up the mistake I made in sending him away. It isn't just the beating I witnessed, but all the feelings I have about thinking he was better off without me are suddenly pushed down. The beating just made me see that Nick deserves to be happy and protected. Even if I'm not the one he's meant to be with, I can at least make sure that he's safe, somehow. I'm just not sure how to accomplish that. I do know that I'm not going to push him away. If he wants me, he can have me.

I sit in a chair and watch him sleep for the longest time, trying in vain to see how this beautiful boy could have deserved anything like what his father dished out to him. The cruelty of it had been intense. How could a parent do that to a child? Brice would have never lifted a finger to me, even when I did misbehave.

When I think of Chasem, my heart clenches. He had

strangled me, but only trying to get me to fight back. When I think of Nick's concern about those marks, his words take on a whole new meaning in the context of his father's abuse.

I walk to his bedside and lean in to kiss him gently on the cheek. He turns over on his stomach and a thrill shoots through me as he whispers my name in his sleep.

In that moment, he's captured my heart forever.

TWELVE

CONFESSIONS

IT'S MORNING WHEN A KNOCK SOUNDS AT MY DOOR. I adjust my clothes and brush back my hair before I answer. Taking in a cleansing breath, I open the door.

Nick stands there with his backpack dangling from one arm, wearing a long-sleeved shirt. My heart skitters as I take in his handsome face.

"Hi," I awkwardly say.

"Hey," he replies without smiling.

"Thanks for coming by. Come on in." I stand back and let him enter.

He walks in and sighs, then turns to me. "What do want?" he coolly asks as I shut the door.

"Well," I begin, "I wanted to apologize."

His eyebrows raise. "Oh yeah? What for?"

I invade his personal space and glance up at him. "For being an ass."

Nick's eyes flicker down to mine for a moment, then he steps away from me. "Well, no worries. Apology accepted." He looks agitated and strolls towards the door.

"Wait," I stammer. "I didn't mean it."

He turns and glares at me. "What? The apology? Fine." He reaches for the doorknob.

"No. I mean I don't want you to go away. Please wait." I step close to him. "Can we just forget about the other morning?"

Nick drops his bag by my couch and sits on the arm, rubbing his eyes. "What part? The throwing me out of your house? Or the part where you basically rejected me?"

I walk into the gap between his long legs and put my arms around his neck. He doesn't touch me but warily gazes up at me. I lean in and whisper against his lips, "All of it. Please say you forgive me." I press my lips softly against his and he responds for a moment, but then pulls away and walks out of my reach.

"I can't do this, Scarlett. I can't. Either you want me or you don't. I don't want to play games." His back is to me and I reach out to him, pressing my body to his back. He sucks in a sharp breath and I realize I'm hurting the places where he'd been beaten.

"Sorry," I whisper as I pull away.

"It's okay. Just pulled some muscles at practice yesterday."

My heart feels sick knowing what had really happened. He turns around and moves painfully to the couch, then gently sits down. I sit beside him and take his hand. He cautiously looks at me.

"Please, Nick. Give me another chance. Please? Do over?"

His face remains unchanged for a moment, then he lets out a deep breath. Before I know it, he draws me close to him and holds me tenderly. "Okay," he concedes against the top of my head.

I feel my body relaxing, and I wrap my arms around him gently. Suddenly, the vision of him griping his desk as his father beat him comes to my mind and I desperately try to not think about it. But it's hard. I literally want to rip his father's throat out with my teeth. I imagine the man slowly bleeding out at my feet, and it's a satisfying thought. The angry fury licks up the inside of my body and I just want to kill him. The part of myself I normally keep quiet perks up. Typically, I can keep the violent revenant nature down, but it now lurks around, eager for me to meet Nick's father when it's dark. I shake my head, forcing myself not to give into that side of me and trying to calm down.

Nick catches the change. "What are you thinking about?"

"Nothing," I respond automatically.

He pulls me back and studies my eyes. "That's not true. Your eyes are green." I automatically look down, not wanting to meet his gaze. He firmly lifts my chin. His eyes bore into mine. "What is it? Remember, you can tell me anything. Anything."

I struggle with what to say under his attention. "I just feel bad for what I put you through is all."

Nick regards me for a moment. "You sure that's all it is?"

I nod and lean into him. His warm hand comes down and brushes my arm. I gaze at his neck and lean in to kiss it. I hear a small gasp, and his heart rate speeds up. This somehow causes my own pulse to mirror his. It's exciting to know I affect him as much as he does me.

His skin smells sweet like sugar, and I resist the urge to lick up his neck. But I do inhale. I make out the scent of his blood beneath his skin, and it's mouthwatering. I pull back and keep looking down. Nick stays tethered to me by holding my hand.

"You...thinking about biting me?" he asks with a small quaver in his voice.

At that, I let go of his hands and walk toward the kitchen. "Well, yes. But I won't do it, so you don't have to worry."

I hear him move and suddenly feel his body heat behind me. "I'm not worried. But I do have questions, if that's okay."

I turn around, and he's so close, looking down at me with those beautiful eyes of his. He offers a small smile. "Will you be honest with me? If I ask a hard question?"

I want to tell him everything, but I worry my complete transparency will be harmful. Maybe he'll run away from me screaming if I truly let him into my weird world. Before I can second-guess anything, I hear myself saying, "Yes. What do you want to know?"

He speaks slowly. "Do you drink blood?"

"Okay, you know I'm a revenant...a vampire...and you just asked me if I drink blood?"

He takes a deep breath. "Well, I mean, do you drink human blood?"

I move away from him, walk to the couch, and sit down. "Yes."

I hear his heart rate increase, but he steadies his shoulders and sits down beside me. "Do you kill people?"

My eyes flicker to his hands, where he's grasping onto the seam of his jeans. His knuckles are white. I lift my eyes to meet his. "No," I firmly answer. "I drink donated blood, and some-times animal blood. But I've never killed a human in my life. I'm what we call a *pale revenant*."

His shoulders relax and he lets out a breath. "Okay. What is a pale revenant?"

"Well, there are two factions of my kind—pale revenants and dark revenants. Pale revenants do not kill humans. We live under the philosophy that all life has value. A dark revenant thinks all life is here to serve us. They kill indiscriminately."

"And you're pale?"

"I just said I was. Were you worried I was going to kill you? If that's the case, why did you come back here?"

"Because you asked me to," he replies with a little laugh. "But I knew you wouldn't kill me. Even if you did, it wouldn't really matter all that much."

His words break my heart. "What? Do you have a death wish or something? Of course it matters. You matter." I get up to walk around, feeling like my apartment is suddenly smaller. I find myself pacing in a small circle. "You still came here, knowing I was a revenant and what that meant. You had to know it was a real possibility I was going to want to bite you, and still, here you are."

"I wasn't worried about you harming me. I know that sounds crazy, but I'm not afraid of you."

"Yeah, well, your heartrate tells me something different."

He gets up and steps close to me, holding my shoulders. "Look at me," he commands, and I lift my eyes. "I know you won't harm me because of how you look at me. You have care and concern in your eyes, which tells me a lot. But I won't lie— the thought of you biting me is a little bit of a turn on." He grins.

I laugh. "A turn on? Really?"

"God, yes," he admits with a slight chuckle. "Can I ask you another thing?"

"Sure," I answer hesitantly, my heart now going a million miles a minute.

"You can't be in the sunlight, can you?"

"No," I say sadly. "None of my kind can. There are always rumors that someone has found a cure, but so far, no one has."

We walk to the couch and sit back down. "A cure?"

I nod. "Yes. Since we're born revenants, some think our issues are genetic mutations that can be fixed."

"Huh," he utters and sits back. "So, you were born a revenant and not bitten?"

I nod. "Yep. A bite from my kind won't make anyone like us. It will make you feel euphoric and you won't want to pull away from it, but in the end it can leave you only dead."

"Euphoric, huh?"

"Yes. It makes prey enjoy their death. They won't fight." I see Nick shutter slightly. "I said I'm pale. I won't kill you."

"I know that," he replies. "I was just thinking of those who the dark have probably killed. It seems perverse for someone to welcome that kind of death." He eyes me. "Although, if you were my agent of death, I'd probably enjoy it, too."

I laugh nervously. His hand finds mine and it's reassuring. We sit in the quiet for a few moments. No doubt Nick's considering what I just told him.

"So, is Chasem a pale revenant?" he asks, his thumb rubbing small circles on the back of my hand.

"Yep. He wasn't always pale, but he changed his way of thinking right after he and my mother Dawned."

"Dawned?"

I glance down at my shirt and finger the hem. "Dawning is when a revenant moves into full adulthood. A revenant's history is kept in their blood. When they turn seventeen, they inherit the history and strength from their parents through drinking their blood. It makes us exponentially stronger, too, because in essence we're inheriting the blood from our entire lineage."

"Freaky," Nick whispers. "Where are your parents? You said you're sixteen, so you aren't far from your Dawning, right?"

"Would you like something to drink?" I abruptly get up and head to the kitchen. "I have coke or water."

"Stop," he interrupts. "What's wrong?"

"Nothing," I deflect. "So, do you want anything?"

He gets up and follows me into the kitchen. "Scarlett, what is it? Why does the question about your parents bother you so much?"

"I really don't want to talk about it, okay? Probably no more than you want to talk about yours," I snap without meaning to.

He steps back. "What does that mean?"

"Nothing. I'm sorry." I walk over to him and put my head on his shoulder. "Look, I know you want to know about my parents, but I can only tell you my mother is dead and my father wishes I were." Nick tries to get me to look to him but I won't. "Can we not talk about parents?" I ask. "Please? I really just want to not think about them. I'll explain later, but can we talk about something else?

"Sure," he breathes and lifts my head. Leaning in, he gives me a soft kiss. Then it deepens and I find myself holding onto him, trailing my hands up the expanse of his muscular back. When I do, he immediately lets out a little yelp.

I quickly release him. "God, I'm sorry. I forgot about your injury."

"It's okay," he grits out. "It's just going to take a few days to heal."

I lean in and kiss him without touching his back. "I hope it gets better soon. I don't like seeing you in pain."

"Believe me," he concedes, "neither do I."

THIRTEEN
CAPTURED

"**SO, YOU MUST HAVE A BOYFRIEND,**" **ANDRE SAYS AS** he leans over me. I jump and hide my phone.

"What makes you think that?" I shoot back, annoyed.

Andre bends his lanky form into a chair at SBB and folds his arms. His eyes are bright with mirth. "Well, it could be the fact that you're texting like crazy and are hiding your phone every time I come near you. So, either you're planning to overthrow the government, or you're in it deep with someone. Am I right?"

"No," I shoot back. He gives me a droll stare. "Well...maybe."

Andre laughs hard and then leans forward. "I knew it. I know all the symptoms of that disease. Girl, you need to have a man in your life. I'm surprised you haven't had one before now."

I playfully punch him. "No one could compare to you, so I just gave up."

He gets up and adjusts his clothing. "Good thing you settled, because no one could ever match me." He sniffs. "Feel me?"

"Yeah, yeah," I say, laughing. He makes a show of removing invisible lint off his clothing. He grins at me, and his teeth are brilliantly white against his mahogany skin.

"You so need help," I observe. "If your ego gets much bigger, you won't fit through the doors!"

He laughs easily and sits down. "It's my cross to bear. Everyone has one. So," he begins as he pushes on my chair with his foot, "does loverboy have a name?"

I pause and consider whether or not I should tell him. But he's already guessed that Nick exists, so what's the point of playing coy?

"His name is Nick," I begrudgingly offer. "He's a senior at Rockefeller."

"Ah. A senior, huh? And you're slumming it, too. Won't your snooty friends at Excelsior have a problem with that?"

I get up and take my paperwork to the scanner to make images of it for the document management system. "My friends at Excelsior have nothing to say about who I date and why."

"That's because you've never dated before. At least, you haven't shared that you have in the last year of working here." Andre puts his feet up on the counter.

"I don't tell you everything," I retort.

"You hardly tell me anything about your personal life," he clarifies.

"Exactly."

Andre doesn't say anything right off the bat but just waves his crossed feet back and forth on the counter. I come back to the computer to import the documents I just scanned, and the night continues on as normal. Well, as much as normal can be with Andre. He jokes his way through everything.

The time comes for him to leave to make the blood deliveries to the different floors, and while he's gone, I retrieve my normal pints of blood and store them in the bag in my locker.

I come back to the desk and wish I can text Nick. I know he's sleeping right now, so I resist the urge to send him anything. Instead, I scroll through some of our conversation already, mainly about the rowing team and his classes, but very little about his family beyond his mom and sister. He never talks about his dad. I know why and don't push, but just like he asked me about my family, I wish he would let me ask about his dad. I'll just have to be patient, and he'll tell me when he's ready.

"Excuse me," an unfamiliar voice says. I look up to see two police officers standing at the counter. One casually rests his hand on the butt of his gun in its holster.

"Can I help you?" I ask.

"Can you open the door to let us in?" the first officer asks, and I nod and buzz them into our office area. Only then do I see Marjorie Stamper behind them. She's the night staff supervisor for the Tremont Hospital. I stand up as they close the door.

"What's going on?" I look to each man, and then Marjorie comes forward.

"Scarlett, these men have a warrant to search your locker." She seems almost apologetic as she looks at me. "Can you take them back there?"

My locker? What's going on? This seems incredibly weird. I turn back toward the small employee room with our break area and a few lockers in it and point to mine. The silent officer steps forward and pulls it open to retrieve my bag.

"Hey!" I protest as he opens it up. "You never said anything about my bag."

He pulls out two pints of blood and stares at Marjorie. She shakes her head at me. "Why are you holding blood in your personal bag?"

"I, ah—" I stammer. The blood is accounted for. It's logged to Neville Treatment Center, but I realize in this moment that I shouldn't be holding it in my bag as far as they're concerned. It looks like I'm stealing it.

"We had a report that blood is being stolen out of here for a Satanic Cult. Care to share why these are in your bag?"

I shake my head. The first officer grabs me and turns me around. "Scarlett Bramstall, you are under arrest for theft." Then he reads me my rights.

"Her last name is Ellis," Marjorie corrects, but the officer ignores her as he continues to Mirandize me. I'm spun around and led out the door and through the hallway to the back entrance. We exit into the dark night right as I catch sight of Andre coming up behind Marjorie. His eyebrows are up and he looks really surprised.

"Call my father!" I shout to him as I'm thrown into the back seat of an unmarked car.

One officer gets in the back with me. He pulls out his gun and holds it to my head as the other jumps in the front to drive us away. The lights of the hospital quickly fade.

"Got you, you little bitch!" the one holding a gun to me mocks. "That was easier than I thought it was going to be."

"Told you, Cal. Like taking candy from a baby," the driver says. "You better unarm her quickly."

"What's going on here?" I ask as Cal lifts my pant legs to pull out the blades hidden on my ankles.

"She wants to know what we're doing here, John. You want to tell her, or shall I?" The gun barrel wobbles against my temple as Cal pats me down. He discovers the weapons on my thighs and says, "John, we'll need to stop and get her out because I can't get to the blades on the inside of her pants."

"Goody. We get to undress her," John says as he leers into the rearview mirror at me.

"We can't hurt her, though. Ryker said," Cal remarks, still feeling around my waist.

"Yeah, well, having a little fun won't hurt her. It might just make this worthwhile."

My heart pounds at the thought of them actually considering this. If I can get to the weapons at my back before they discover them, I might have a fighting chance.

"You aren't cops, are you?" I ask.

"Nope. I'm afraid to inform you we're helots," Cal offers and smiles at me. "Surprise."

Helots are human slaves to dark revenants, both renegades and Dawned. "Who are you working for?" I ask as Cal gropes me while executing a poor search for weapons. He has no idea how many I actually have. The fact that they're helots offers me hope that I can overpower them easily.

Neither one answers me. "We can do a thorough search when we get there. Just keep the gun on her," John says while looking back at us.

We drive for what seems like hours, arriving at an old farmhouse outside of town. Cal gets out and reaches in to grab me. When he does, I kick him square in the chin and he drops like a rock. I scoot out and run as quickly as I can. Before I get very far at all, something pinches my back in two spots and my vision lights up. I lose all control over my arms and legs and fall to the ground, hearing a sort of crackling noise in my ears.

John comes into my vision with a stun gun in his hand. Cal staggers behind him to gaze at me, and then John brings his boot down on my face.

A voice echoes around me, but I can't make it out. The light is a harsh spotlight on me and the voices come from the dark periphery. My vision is blurry and I try to focus, but it's hard. My head lulls back and forth as I try to control its movement.

"She's awake," someone pronounces. "I'll call Ryker." Steps move away from me and a door closes. A visage comes in close to me as he squats down.

"Good to see there's no permanent damage," John says, hunkering beside me. I'm finally able to focus on him. "You better play nice, or we'll have to take drastic measures."

I try to ascertain where I am, but the room is shadowed and I can't make out anything familiar. "Where am I?"

"Oh, just somewhere we can hold you for a while. Hope you didn't have plans." He smirks as he gets up.

"Who is your ceannard?" I ask, hoping I can figure out what's going on. Renegades will definitely hunt me and drink me dry, but not until I've Dawned. If a renegade wants me now, I'll only be a source of sport or some blood, but of no value until after I've moved past my Dawning—whether I drink my parents' blood or not.

"It doesn't matter who it is, does it? I mean, whether you know now or not won't change the outcome of what's about to happen." John paces. "No, it doesn't matter who we report to. You're going to starve here. Hope you're ready."

He leans in with a syringe in his hand. I try to scoot back, but it's pointless. The needle pierces my skin and everything goes fuzzy.

FOURTEEN
STARVED

DAYS PASS AND BLEND INTO WEIRD MOMENTS OF A drug-induced haze. There are flashes of Cal and John looming over me and giving me shots. It's dark and quiet, and I'm only awake long enough to see them come in. I can tell time passes, but I can't tell how much.

I have foggy, intense dreams about burning revenants in sunlight and a man with pale green eyes. Pain radiates through me constantly. I'm hungry, thirsty, and I feel like my skin is crumbling away.

I hear Nick calling to me from somewhere. I want to answer, but I can't. The fevered dream is followed by warped images of John and Cal and pinpricks to the inside of my arm.

When I finally come to full awareness, my mind buzzes oddly. The dark, musky room smells strongly of soil. The air is cold and slightly moist. At the end of the room, I see some light streaming in through a small square window in the door. The floor and the walls are both made of dirt. A very perfect hole dug into the side of the earth. I lift my body and my head throbs. In fact, every part of me seems steeped in intense pain.

It's quiet, and nothing moves outside the door. I rub my teeth with my tongue and discover my fangs are down. *What?* That only means one thing; I'm thirsty. Like, profoundly thirsty. If my body is acting of its own accord, then I must actually be starving. The realization doesn't disturb me. I feel like I'm standing far back in my head and someone else is there up front, controlling me.

I try to sit up, and my head swims. My muscles are weak and scream in pain every time I move. My vision goes in out of heat-sensor mode, looking for anything with blood. I shake my head to stop it, and that works for a moment as I see correctly. Then it goes right back to heat senor.

My mind growls in uncontrollable anger, needing to feed. The revenant part of me is dark, searching, looking. Painful cramps rack my stomach and I clench myself tightly.

I pull at my shirt; it feels too big for me. It's an odd, fleeting thought. My mind is obsessed with the thirst. Feed, I need to feed. My brain latches onto the memory of the metallic taste and how it's so much better when it's from a living host—not the cold blood from bags. Warm means alive, and alive means a beating heart full of satiating nourishment. Cramps hit me again, forcing me to lay down on my side to pull my legs up to my chest.

The smell of Nick's blood comes to my mind and I howl in pain. The eager revenant inside me feels like it's punching through my gut. I'm not sure what compels me, but I rush to the window in the door and reach out, growling loud. I want to stop what I'm doing but I feel crazed, unhinged, and out of control.

Two men sit at a table playing cards. My vision turns to an odd sort of heat sensor and I make out the heavy points that allow me the easiest access to their blood, lit up in a pattern of reds and yellows. Neck, wrist, leg. I see their heads turn towards me as they show up in a crimson glow, painting them like macabre artwork. I can hear their hearts pulsating, and I want to kill them. They are not revenants but humans, and I want to drain them completely.

"Damn," one of them whispers. Something inside me tells

me his name is John. I force myself to calm. "That is one scary girl."

I feel the sudden need to compose myself. "John," I begin softly. "I need to talk to you. Can you come here?"

Yes, my revenant side urges. *Get him close. Very close.*

John shakes his head. "Nope. Sorry, chicky." He returns to playing cards again.

Get him close. Bite him. Drain him. Kill.

"Please, John. I'm weak and I can't speak any louder. Please come over here. I have something to tell you."

"You were just howling. So I know you can speak louder than that. I'm not stupid."

"She looks bizarre," Cal says, alarmed. "Like a serious freak show. Those eyes make me want to shutter."

"Ryker said it would only take ten days or so. Looks like he was right. What is this, day nine?" John questions.

"Please, Cal, will you come here? I'll make it worth your while." I lick my lips in a show.

Must kill them both.

"Screw you," Cal screams. "Now be quiet."

"I know you want me, Cal. Come in here and I'll be your dream. I promise. You'll enjoy it." I can't stop what I'm saying. It's like someone else is talking but I don't have the capability to stop it.

The thoughts of me at his throat, pulling the complete volume of blood out of him, almost overwhelms my brain.

"Do you have any more tranqs to hit her with?" Cal asks John.

"No. Ryker said she would only need them for the first five days, and that after that she'd go into a coma. I can't explain why she's up and walking around right now. It should be physically impossible. Just ignore her. He'll be here soon to take her to the Alabaster City," John warns, still playing cards. "I win!" he yells as he throws down a card.

"You cheated!" Cal screams, and their voices are a jumble of argument.

I let myself slide down the door and pull my legs up to my body.

I awaken again to a voice at the door. I'm not sure how much time has passed, but it feels like hours. My memories of late have been flashes of nightmares, of John and Cal leaning over me and sticking needles in my arms. This time, I feel fully awake.

Blood, my mind screams. My revenant side tells me Cal is at the door, speaking to me.

"...'cause I could come in there, if you promise," he whispers.

Promise anything.

"Yes, I promise," I assure him, but I don't know what I am assuring him of. I force myself up and hear the jangle of the lock being disengaged.

Maniacal laughter echoes through my head.

No, stay away. Run away, Cal. Please. I want to say this to him, but my lips won't move. It's as if someone else entirely controls me now.

"Stand back against the wall," Cal orders as he holds a stun gun.

Somehow, I find the power to move back until the dirt wall bites into my back. My fingers dig into the soil in anticipation. I want to stop what my mind is planning, but I can't.

Cal slowly opens the door and peeks in, holding a camping lantern. He closes the door but doesn't lock it. My eyes watch every move he makes with intense curiosity. I'm going to drink him dry, and there's nothing I can do to stop myself. His heat glows like a torch in the darkness. I can make out every line on him in high contrast. I want him now. My heart thuds loudly in my ears.

"So, did you mean what you said? You'd make it worth my while?" Cal's eyebrows raise in a question.

I slowly nod.

"Good. I've always wanted to know what it would be like to be with a real-life princess and all. Never been with a revenant, either, so looks like I hit the jackpot. Take your clothes off," he orders.

I shake my head. "You first."

Cal lays down the stun gun next to his feet and strips off his shirt. He unbuckles his pants and pauses. "Come here," he orders.

Okay.

The monster inside me catapults me across the room and I descend upon Cal in one swift move. I pin him to the floor and bite down hard, cutting off the beginning of a yell. His blood shoots into my mouth like water from a strong hose, and I drag hard on his vein.

Cal relaxes and whispers, "Oh, yeah, oh...yeah." His hands embrace me and rub down my back as if he's comforting me, but he doesn't struggle to get away. My brain tells me this is how my prey is supposed to respond. I drink deeply, sucking hard against his throat. After a time, his hand stops rubbing and eventually drops limply to the ground.

Finally, I can get no more blood from him and release him. Looking down, I see his empty eyes still regarding me. I'm filled with a sudden disgust for what I've just done. The monster inside me is quiet now, and I feel like I've woken up from a dream. I just killed someone.

I scurry backward and the wall hits my back hard. Tears fall from my eyes. I have become dark. I just killed someone. How can I ever forgive myself?

"Oh God, oh God, oh God," I whisper, more than horrified.

I shake my head to stop my panic and see the light flooding in through the open door. I force myself up and can tell I'm stronger than I was. I'm not better, but I'm stronger. I rush through the open door into the outer room and it's bright—so bright it hurts my eyes. To my left is a set of stairs, and I take them two by two.

I make out light coming in through the bottom of the door and hear two male voices. One belongs to John, but I can't identify the other one.

John reassures the other man that I'm weak and caged. They move towards the door, and I run down the stairs to hide behind them as I hear the door open. Footsteps make their way down the stairs in a laborious walk.

"That's funny," John says. "Cal was down here, I thought." The man stands behind him, watching as John rushes towards the open prison door. John is in the room in an instant with the man behind him. I see this as my chance and rush up the stairs. I hear the yelling behind me.

"Get her!" the man orders, and I ignore it as I burst into what can only be described as a kitchen. A few revenants sit in a living room to the right, and they jump up as soon as they see me. I run to the left and drive through a window.

The glass cuts my arms and face but I don't stop. I run as hard as I can, rushing through the forest, dodging trees and rocks. I have no idea which way the city is, but I just keep running. It's like running through mud. My limbs don't want to respond like they are supposed to.

I'm yanked to the ground as someone tackles me. A revenant man holds me down, his eyes fiery, and he easily pins me. I reach up and punch him in the side of his face, but it doesn't do anything but make him angry. He pulls out a blade and holds it to my throat.

"Try that again and I will gut you. Make no mistake," he growls low. "Now stand up."

I comply while he has me by the hair. After a few minutes, John catches up to us, breathing heavily and flanked by revenants and humans. "I'm sorry, Ryker. She hasn't had any food or blood in ten days. I swear."

"Well, she has now. Looks like she made a meal out of Calvin," Ryker quips. He does not loosen his grip on his blade but holds it tight against my throat. "Now walk, you bitch, and you better not make a move to run, or so help me, I will cut off your feet, understand?"

I nod. My scalp protests as he leads me by hair in the direction of the farmhouse. My mind races with how to get free of this man. He's incredibly strong compared to my weakened state. I start to devise a plan to break free when I see a bullet rip through John's chest and he drops to the ground. The men around us follow, dropping like flies.

Ryker pulls my body close to his, the knife pressed so hard against my throat that I feel it break the skin. He turns, searching for the source of the shots, but he can't find them.

"I will kill her!" Ryker screams. "Do not test my resolve! She will be a puddle of flesh at my feet."

The bullets keep coming and finally stop after no one is left standing but Ryker and me. He turns with me in tow like a rag doll. Finally, he stops as three images come out of the shadows. I see Eddie, Chasem, and, bringing up the rear, Nick.

My heart leaps for joy at what I see. Nick aims a gun at Ryker's head, and he looks glorious. His face is bruised, but still the best thing I've laid eyes on in a very long time.

"Better tell your helot to aim that gun elsewhere before I forget and cut her head off," Ryker growls to Chasem.

Chasem is ice-cold and dressed in leather gear, weapons hanging off every part of him. He's completely calm as he walks closer.

"You okay, baby?" Nick asks as he walks forward with the gun still leveled at Ryker. It shakes almost imperceptibly. His eyes flicker to mine, and I nod quickly.

"She won't be if you don't put down that gun. Now, lower

it!" Ryker demands.

Nick seems to think for a moment, then complies, as does Eddie. Chasem keeps walking until he's about fifteen feet from us.

"That's far enough," Ryker warns. "I'm not sure how you found us, but if you don't want me to kill her, I suggest you leave, now."

"I can't do that. Not without her," Chasem says mildly.

"Well, you are out of luck, my friend. You can't have her," Ryker growls.

"We stopped being friends a long time ago. Now, release the girl," Chasem demands.

"You can't make any demands of me anymore. You are a traitor, and if you were back in the Alabaster City you'd be killed as such. Turn around and go back where you came from."

"I'm sorry. I just can't." As the last word leaves his mouth, Chasem flings a knife which impales Ryker's hand. Ryker yells in frustration but releases me. My last view is of him disappearing into the woods. I scurry as far away from him as I can get. But Ryker's gone, Chasem and Eddie in hot pursuit.

Nick is at my side in a matter of seconds, holding me tight. "Oh God, Scarlett, are you okay?" He scans me for any injury and, as he does, I notice how transparent his skin is. I gaze at his neck and can see the vein below, full and perfect, just waiting for a puncture. My body prepares to strike, and I wonder if the monster will start to speak.

"Let me go!" I shout and rush to get away from him, holding out my hands. "Don't touch me!"

Nick glances at me, confused, but drops his hands. "Why?"

"I want to bite you. I can't control myself. I don't want to hurt you."

"You won't," he reassures. "Please." He reaches out his hand to me.

"No! It's all I can do to hold onto my self-control. Please, Nick. I don't want to harm you and I'm afraid of myself right now. I killed someone!" I finally admit and want to vomit.

Chasem is at my side immediately. "Here." He rips open a plastic bag of blood with his teeth and hands it to me. "This should help."

I fumble to get it to my mouth and drink so hard and fast that Chasem tries to pull it back from me. I find myself growling in response.

"Well, okay, but slow down. You're going to choke," he commands.

"She looks like hell. How much weight do you think she's lost?" Eddie asks.

"Twenty pounds, maybe," Chasem says as he hands me another bag. "It looks like they were starving her."

Nick keeps his distance while I drink and watches me warily. I feel really bad about snapping at him, but I don't want to lose control with him, ever.

"But why?" Nick asks, and Chasem shrugs.

"I'm not sure. I have my suspicions, but I don't want to voice those right now. Let's just take care of her and get her home."

FIFTEEN
ROAD TO RECOVERY

THE RIDE BACK TO TOWN IS QUIET. CHASEM AND Eddie sit in the front while Nick and I ride in the back. We both hug the doors, as far apart physically as we are emotionally.

I don't want to look at him. My guilt over having killed someone overwhelms me, as does my having snapped at him. I can't live with what I've done to Cal, bad guy or not. I violated what I feel is central to my being a pale revenant. I killed a living human being. I'm guilty of murder.

The car is painfully silent.

I look over at Nick as he leans against the door and keeps his gaze turned away from me. I want to snuggle up to him and have him hold me, but I'm so guilt-stricken I can barely move. I remember how it felt to have Cal's blood rushing down my throat, how Cal tried to comfort me like it was what he wanted, when I knew the truth. My bite is like a drug to a human—it makes them high. He had enjoyed his death, but it doesn't make it any less wrong.

I gaze out the window and think about our conversation, when I said I'd never killed anyone before. Now I have. It's not a nameless plastic bag full of blood. Cal had been a living, breathing human, regardless of being a helot.

We make our way into the city and pull up to Perkalicious.

Eddie shakes Chasem's hand and gets out. I watch him go into the doorway leading up to his apartment over the shop. Chasem looks in the rearview mirror at Nick.

"So. You want to be dropped at home, or you crashing at my place again? Personally, I think you need to just stay at my place for now. 'Til things cool down."

Nick shrugs. "Your place it is then."

"Wait, what? He's been staying at your place?" I demand of Chasem.

Chasem shakes his head at me in the mirror. "We can talk about it later."

"I want to talk about it now." I sit up and glare at them.

"Of course you do," Chasem retorts and starts driving. "But we will talk about it later." He eyes me furiously. I turn to Nick, who says nothing and stares out the window.

My stomach cramps up and I lean forward, clutching onto myself. I'm still so hungry, so thirsty. It doesn't make sense. I drained a human of all his blood. Plus, I had two more pints when they rescued me.

I feel Nick's hand on my back and I jerk away. "Don't touch me," I hiss, and he immediately pulls back. I'm afraid of how tenuous my hold on controlling my urges feels.

"You know what, Chasem? Go ahead and take me home," Nick says tightly.

"I don't think that's a good idea. Listen to me. I think coming back to my place is the safest bet. Okay?"

"Sure, whatever."

I glance at Nick and see his jaw working harshly as he stares out the window again. I feel Chasem reach behind his seat and pat my leg. "There's more blood coming. Hang on."

We pull into the underground garage, and before Chasem has even parked the vehicle, Nick sprints to the elevator. Chasem pulls open my door to let me out and puts his arm around me. He leans into me as we walk. "His dad beat him up pretty badly the day after you went missing. He broke into your apartment where Brice and Emma were trying to figure out what had happened to you. Brice called me and we got him some medical attention. It didn't take much to figure out who had done it, though Nick hasn't come right out and told me exactly what happened. I did pay his father a visit and told him I'd beat the living crap out of him if he hit Nick again. Needless to say, he allowed Nick to stay with me as long as he went to school. So how about you cut him some slack?"

My heart aches at the thought of Nick being beaten by his dad. I nod. "I'm just too afraid to be around him right now. I'm afraid I'll hurt him."

"I understand the concern, I do, but if you were going to attack him, you would have already. I have faith in you that you won't. So how about giving yourself a break too? Okay?"

"Okay," I agree, and we top behind Nick to wait for the elevator. Nick never makes eye contact with me. He stands ramrod-straight, and as soon as the elevator reaches the top floor, he bolts out of it.

"Yo, Nick, don't forget to call your mom, okay?" Chasem suggests.

"Fine," Nick says as he disappears down the hallway.

Chasem deposits me on the couch. "Lay down and don't move. I'll be right back."

I nod and feel relief for the first time in a long time. I close my eyes and place my arm over my eyes. I try breathing deeper and getting my body to relax, but I feel hollow.

Chasem returns with the medical kit and a glass of blood. "Okay, sit up now and drink this." I comply and suck down the blood, watching as he listens to my heart and examines every part of me with care. He asks me a few questions about what hurts and what doesn't. He hands me a couple of pills that I take without question.

"How long have I been gone, Chase?"

He doesn't look at me but presses his fingers around the soft tissue under my jaw. "Nine days."

Nine days?

"How did you find me?"

"Well, I have a couple of spies in that camp of Ryker's. They found out when you were taken and let me know what had happened. It took a lot of digging to find that farmhouse, but I eventually located it. Glad we got there when we did. You had just about gone to your baser self."

"I killed someone," I blurt out.

Chasem stops moving. "I heard you say that earlier. A human?"

Tears involuntarily stream down my face. "Yes. His name was Cal. He was one of the ones who kidnapped me." I reach out and grasp his arm. "I couldn't help it, I swear. It was like something took over and I couldn't stop."

Chasem squeezes my hand. "It's going to be okay. I promise."

"But he's dead," I counter. "There's nothing about it that makes it okay."

"And he was Ryker's helot. One of many. I've met Cal. He is...was a greasy sob. So, believe me, you did the world a favor."

"But I drank his blood. I drank him 'til his heart stopped! I committed murder!" I feel the hysteria bubbling below the surface and my sanity feels like it slips.

Chasem grabs my face and forces me to look at him. "Listen very carefully to me, Scar. What you did, you did to survive. You didn't murder anyone. This is a war. A war for you and your soul. They put you in that situation, and what you did was survive. Do you hear me?"

I want to look away but can't. His light brown eyes bore into mine. I nod, and something breaks inside me—I start sobbing uncontrollably.

Chasem gathers me in his arms and holds me. "You're safe, now. I've got you. I won't let anyone hurt you, I promise. As long as I have breath, I will protect you." He doesn't pull away the entire time I cry, holding me and gently stroking my arms.

I don't know how long I cry, but at some point, there's nothing left and I give out in exhaustion. I'm vaguely aware of him lifting me from the couch and carrying me to my room, then covering me with a blanket. He kisses my cheek and tells me to rest. I must have complied because that's the last thing I remember.

SIXTEEN

THE LIGHTENERS

I **OPEN MY EYES TO THE CLOCK READING 5:40 PM, AND I**
feel like a new person. The aches and pains are gone, and I
move with a lot more fluidity. I stretch and feel the muscles
give. I almost feel like a new me. I stand up and examine
myself in the mirror. I'm gaunt and still wearing the same
clothing from the day before. I decide a shower is what I need.
The warmth of the water washes over me like a baptism,
renewing me.

When I walk down the hall to kitchen and living room, I
hear the muffled voices of Chasem and Nick as they talk. I
watch them for a moment in amazement. A few weeks ago,
Chasem was ready to kill him, but something has shifted
between them and now they seem thick as thieves. I watch
Chasem put a reassuring hand on Nick's shoulder, then he lifts
his eyes to me and smiles.

"Good! You're awake," he says and walks towards the stove.

"Hey," I reply. "How long was I out?" Nick makes no move
to turn around to face me. I need to try to repair this, but I'm
not really sure how. I awkwardly sit down on the bar stools
beside him, but he still doesn't look my way.

"About eighteen hours or so." Chasem puts a plate in front
of me with a tall glass of blood.

"I don't want that," I say, feeling slightly self-conscious of

Nick watching me drink it. Last night, I was so panicked that I didn't care, but today is a different story.

"You sure? You've lost a lot of weight. You need to try to rebuild some—"

"I'm sure."

Chasem studies me for a moment, then nods, putting the glass in the refrigerator. "I'll be back." Before I can say anything, he disappears in the elevator.

I eat in silence, the only sound being my fork hitting the plate. Nick wipes his mouth and turns to leave. "Wait," I say with a mouthful of food. "Please."

Nick turns, sits back down, and stares at me. "It's okay. Whatever you're going to say, I get it. You need space. I'm trying to give it to you."

"What? You think I need space?" I stammer.

He looks at me and his eyebrows raise. "Yeah, I do. Last night, you were so freaked out. I heard what you were saying and what you weren't. You needed me to leave you alone. I'm human, you're revenant. I get it. I'm not what you need."

"That's not it at all," I counter.

His lips draw tight. "Oh, isn't it? You mean to tell me if I had been a revenant, you still wouldn't have let me help you like Chasem did?" Nick glowers at me.

"No. I mean, yes. I mean, it wasn't about you." I toss my fork on my plate.

He huffs in disgust. "Could have fooled me." He rubs his face. "Look, I don't want to fight. I'm just trying to process what's happening here, and I want to give you what you need. But I obviously don't have a clue."

I turn to face him. "Look, Nick, I promise you that last night, my reaction was not about what I needed as much as it was about..."

He gazes at me. "About?"

I try to figure out how to say it. How to admit I killed

someone and how afraid I am that I might kill him, too. I want to tell him so badly, but I don't want to hurt him. I don't want to see the look of abhorrence I'm sure will appear there if I do.

"Nothing," I quietly say. "Look, Nick, maybe we should be friends, okay? It will be easier all the way around."

"Easier," he repeats with an air of loathing.

"Yes." I turn away and look down at my plate.

"Huh. Yeah, okay. I hear you loud and clear. Friends it is." I hear him walk away and down the hallway. I sit there and fight the urge to run after him. It's for the best. If we're friends, I won't be close enough to bite him. He doesn't understand that, but maybe that's okay.

After texting Emma a million times that I'm okay, I force myself to call Brice. Everything happened so quickly the night before that I hadn't had a chance to call him. Chasem had let him know I'd been found, but Brice insisted on talking with me.

I hang up the phone with Brice and shake my head at how freaked out he was. I had to reassure him too many times that I'm okay and that he doesn't need to worry. I sit staring at my phone long after the light on its face fades. Brice had sounded profoundly relieved, and at one point his voice cracked. My heart breaks at the pain the whole thing caused him.

A knock sounds at my door. I look up to see Chasem there. "So, how was Brice?"

"Beside himself. Freaked out. Worried. Take your pick."

Chasem walks in and sit down beside me. "So, I thought I'd tell you. Nick wants to go back home. He's leaving tonight."

My heart thuds. "Is that wise? I mean, with his dad and all?"

Chasem shakes his head. "I don't know. I can't talk him out of it. I wanted to know if you want to come along."

"Yes, of course."

"We're leaving in ten minutes." Chasem pats my leg and

closes the door softly as he leaves.

I jump up, throw on some different clothes, and brush my hair. I rush out of my door so quickly that I almost knock Nick down. He throws out his arms to catch me.

"Slow down, there," he cautions, and I jerk away quickly to straighten myself out. But his scent is caught in my nose and it's all I can do not to lean in and inhale.

He watches me for a second to see if I'm okay, then heads off down the hallway. I watch him move and think how graceful he is with his backpack slung over his shoulder like he doesn't have a care in the world. He leans up against the wall and taps his fingers on his leg, marking the time like he did reading that night in Perkalicious. He's so handsome it makes my heart hurt.

Chasem grabs his keys to the Lexus GS and we head to Nick's house. The ride is as quiet as it was the night before, except this time Nick doesn't seem like he's actively ignoring me. This time, I sense he's thinking about something else.

We pull up to his house and double-park. Getting out, I notice Nick hovering by the car, staring up to the entrance to his house. Chasem comes around the car and nods toward the door. They scale the stairs and I lean against the car, crossing my arms.

Chasem straightens out his clothes and knocks on the door. It takes a few minutes, but eventually a woman answers. She's beautiful. Her hair is dark like Nick's, pulled into a loose ponytail, and she's shorter than both Nick and Chasem. She clutches a dish towel like it'll protect her. When she sees Nick, she rushes to him and hugs him tightly.

"Oh, thank God you're okay. I've been so worried," she says as her voice cracks. She kisses him and then pulls back to examine his face.

"I'm okay, Mom. This is—"

"Chasem Black," she finishes. "We met the other night."

Chasem nods to her with a kind look on his face.

Nick frowns. "You did?"

"Yes," she says quickly. "He's called every day to let me know how you were doing." She faces Chasem. "Thank you for taking care of my boy."

Chasem smiles. "My pleasure, Hannah."

Hannah smiles at him and then pulls Nick in. "Abby will be glad to see you. She's doing the dishes. Go say hi."

Nick nods but turns to look at me. I want to say something meaningful, but all I end up saying is, "I'll text you." He nods and waves, then disappears into his house.

Chasem and Hannah linger awkwardly by the door for moment. "Is Tim home? I'd like to talk to him, if he is."

"No," Hannah quickly offers. "He hasn't made it home from work yet."

Chasem's lips tighten and he steps closer to her. "Okay, probably for the best. You have my number. Call me if any-thing happens, okay? Anything, night or day, and I'll be here."

Hannah's lips tremble for a moment, then she seems to recover herself. "Okay. Thank you again. For everything."

"No need to thank me. You just take care of yourself and those kids in there, okay?" He leans closer to her like he's going to hug her at any moment, but he doesn't.

She smiles weakly. "I will. Goodnight, Chasem." She steps back and closes the door.

Chasem stands like the door is still open. He sighs, then turns to walk down the stairs towards me. He rounds the car and glances at me. "Get in."

I jump in and Chasem throws the car in gear and takes off. He grips the steering wheel tightly. "I have to make a quick stop." An angry menace rolls off him like something's really wrong.

"Okay. What's wrong?"

He doesn't answer for a second, and his jaw clenches.

"Nothing. I just need to send a message is all."

We drive for a bit and pull up to a small neighborhood bar called *The Place*. We park and walk up to the glass door covered by layers of older and newer advertisements. The door is indicative of the rest of the bar, which looks run-down and smells strongly of stale beer.

I follow Chasem in and am assailed by loud music and laughter. The bar to the right is crowded with cheaply dressed women and blue-collar workers. A small array of tables sit to my right and there's a pool table in the back. Chasem stands there for a moment, glancing around. Finally, he sees what he's looking for. His stride is quick and sure as he makes his way to the end of the bar.

Nick's dad nurses a drink while he complains to the bartender. Chasem walks up to him and nods to the bartender before turning to Nick's dad.

"Tim?" Chasem asks.

Tim seems to already know Chasem is there and glances at him defiantly. "What the hell do you want?" His words are slightly slurred, and he throws back another drink. His tie is cockeyed and his dark hair is messy, like he just got up out of bed.

The man sitting beside Tim turns and gives Chasem a once-over. "You know this guy, Tim?" he asks, spinning on his stool to face Chasem. His lips are so thin they're almost non-existent. His skin is pock-marked from bad acne, and he's in sore need of a haircut. His blue shirt, which proclaims "Mike" on one side, is open to a white, dirty t-shirt.

Chasem ignores Mike and leans in toward Tim. "Look, can we go outside and talk for a minute?"

Tim shakes his head and smiles as he turns. He glances to Mike and back to Chasem. "Nope. How about you say what you came to say, right here?"

Mike crosses his arms and smiles. He lifts his eyebrows and

winks at Chasem.

Chasem's lips tighten slightly. "Look, it would be better if we discussed this outside."

"Friend, if you want to take it outside, I'll join you," Mike huffs eagerly.

Chasem acts like Mike hasn't even spoken. "I just dropped Nick off at home. I wanted to let you know that if you lay one hand on him, or anyone else in your family, you'll answer to me, and it won't be as easy as last time. Do I make myself clear?"

Last time?

Tim glares up at Chasem, his jaw clenched tight, but he says nothing. Mike stands up and gets close to Chasem's face. "How about you stay away from this man's family? Or you'll answer to me." Mike's face is red and his nose almost touches Chasem's cheek.

I see Chasem clench his fists. "You should mind your own business. This is between Tim and myself. *Friend.*" Chasem slowly turns to face Mike, anger rolling off him so thickly it's like a cloak. A few of the patrons sitting beside the duo quickly get up and move away. Chasem stares at Mike for a moment, then turns to look at Tim. "You've been warned, and if you step out of line, I'll know." Chasem moves to leave, and as he does, Mike swipes a beer bottle off the bar and turns, aiming it at Chasem's head.

I scream, "Watch out, Chase!" He spins around in a blur and catches Mike's wrist. I hear an audible, sickening snap.

Mike yelps and drops to the floor. "You broke my arm! You idiot!" he bellows as he clenches his arm to his chest, rolling around on the ground.

A few men get up to approach Chasem, but he holds his hands up in surrender and backs away. Then he turns towards the door with me hot on his trail. When we get outside, Chasem pauses and takes a deep breath, trying to calm himself.

"Get in the car," he commands and walks around to the driver's side. As he sits down in the car, he grips the steering wheel and yells, letting his fangs drop and his eyes change to an eerie green. He closes his eyes and breathes deeply, one breath after another, then finally opens his eyes. They're back to normal.

"What was that about?" I demand as we pull out to leave. "How is it you know Nick's dad and his mom, for that fact?"

"Let's just say I had a come-to-Jesus talk with Tim after we took Nick to the hospital when you turned up missing."

"I don't understand how you got involved," I say, half to myself.

"No one deserves what happened to Nick, especially from his own father. Hannah doesn't deserve it either. Before long, he'll set his sights on Abby, and she'll be a punching bag just like them. I've seen it too many times."

"I'm not saying I'm not glad you threatened his dad, but I just didn't think you liked Nick all that much," I shoot back.

"Yeah, well, you didn't see him that night. He was severely beaten and all he wanted to do was find you. It was all we could do to get him treated. Brice even wanted to go find his father to make him pay, and you know how Brice would have fared in that fight. So I went instead," Chasem says almost apologetically.

I sit there and think about Brice in a physical altercation. I can't imagine he would have done well, so I feel suddenly grateful for Chasem keeping him safe.

"Thank you," I offer. "But how did you meet Nick's mom?"

"She came to the hospital after we called her. She asked if Nick could stay with me. I said he could," he says plainly.

"Poor Nick." I wish I'd been a little bit easier on him when they rescued me, but it just didn't happen that way. I make a promise to myself to try to be kinder to Nick the next time I see him.

SEVENTEEN
CRIMINAL

NICK AND HIS FAMILY ARE ALL I CAN THINK ABOUT the next day. I know Nick's dad had beaten him once with a belt, but I had no idea his father could be *that* cruel. I imagine a perverse way in which to kill him and dwell on it until I think of another equally terrible, if not worse, way to make him pay.

"Earth to Scarlett," Trevor's soft voice says over the top of my open locker door. I slam it shut to see him smiling, wearing a pink tie with male mermaids and sparkly fins on it. Missi stands beside him, waiting like she's just asked me something.

"What? I'm sorry. What did you ask?"

"I asked how you were feeling. You're so thin! Let me know what you got, so maybe I can find a way to get it, too. Lord knows I could lose some weight," Trevor crows.

"Yeah, are you better? You were out for a long time." Missi's dark eyes view me with concern.

"I'm feeling much better. And Trevor, you don't want what I had. I almost died," I warn and hope it's enough to keep him from asking more questions.

"Girl, I'd risk death if it meant I could drop some weight off my fat frame." He looks down at his body in disgust.

Missi frowns. "You look fine, Trevor. Your weight is perfect."

Trevor's face lights up and a wide smile appears. "You

really think so?"

"Yes," she agrees. She glances at me and rolls her eyes. I laugh. It feels good to be in the presence of normal people.

Human people, my subconscious reminds me, but I don't care. If I could make myself human, I would in a minute.

They are food, a strange part of my brain says, and I shudder. Visions of Trevor and Missi laid out, ghastly pale from blood loss and death, come to mind. I shake my head and rush ahead to the bathroom, leaving Trevor and Missi yelling after me.

I make it to the stall just in time, where all the contents of my stomach come up. I stand there until my body feels calm enough to stand upright. I see Cal's face in my mind and hear his voice in my head, *Oh, yeah...oh...yeah,* as he slowly died in my arms. This brings on a new wave of nausea and I dry-heave over the toilet.

I hear a knock on the stall door. "Scarlett? Are you okay?" Missi's voice is thick with concern.

"I'm fine," I grit out between heaves.

"I can go get the school nurse. Maybe you're still sick."

"No," I say a little too strongly. "I just ate something that didn't agree with me."

Killer, my conscience yells, and I want to die.

"Are you sure?" Missi asks tentatively.

"Yes. I'll be right out," I say and let my body slide down the cold metal wall of the stall. I draw my knees up and lay my head on my arms. I shouldn't be here. I should just disappear to Siberia or someplace where no humans are and live a nomad life. I could live off the blood of animals, not enough to hurt them, but just enough to keep my monster down. I'll never risk hurting someone else again.

Renegades won't find me in Siberia, and neither will Apollo. I can do that. Somehow, in my head, I decide it'll be worth it to get away. I need to devise a plan to disappear without Chasem knowing.

The nausea disappears and I stand up to open the stall door. Missi's head snaps up as I come out. Worry is etched on her face in deep lines, but she stays silent.

I rinse my mouth out and try to arrange my hair in a suitable array, but it's pointless. I pull it out of its ponytail and pull it back again. "You didn't need to wait. You're going to be late, too," I observe softly.

"Well, you know," she begins, "I can't exactly leave you by yourself if you're sick." She adjusts the bag on her shoulder and watches me intently. "Feeling better?"

"Yeah, I am. Thanks for waiting on me," I say sheepishly.

"No problem." Her eyes shine proudly.

We make our way into Math, which proceeds on as normal. Ms. Crawford looks up, startled, as does the rest of the class. She eyes us suspiciously.

"You're both late. I hope you have an excuse." She stands and folds her arms.

I reach into my pocket and present her with my excused absence note from the office. "I just got a little ill, and Missi stayed with me," I offer as contritely as I can. Missi nods beside me.

Ms. Crawford takes my note and studies it for a second. "I'm glad to see you back. I heard you had a rather nasty case of pneumonia."

I nod to confirm the cover story as she hands my excuse back.

"Do you need to have another day? Are you okay?"

"I'm fine," I say and glance to the other students, who regard me with curious interest. "I'm fine," I say to them, waiving my note.

"Go ahead and have a seat. I'll excuse you both this time."

"Thanks," Missi says and pulls me back towards a chair. Ms. Crawford keeps her eyes on me as we walk.

"Satanist," Haley Kent says with a cough as I pass her.

I scoot into my chair and glare at her. "What?" I say quietly.

She leans over, her blond, wavy hair flowing like a lion's mane around her face. "Oh, I heard all about the arrest for stealing blood to perform some sort of satanic ritual. My mother is going to Mr. Prentiss to see about having you expelled." She looks absolutely smug.

I draw back. "What? I'm no Satanist."

"Oh yeah? You didn't get arrested for stealing blood? Come on, admit it. You were really in jail and not sick." I want to punch her square in the face. She smiles like she knows she's hit her mark. Then she casually sits back in her chair. "I always knew you were a freak."

"Shut up, Haley," Trevor says a little too loudly. I raise my hand and shake my head at him to let him know I don't want him to say anything to her. He gives me a shrug.

"Oh, yeah, you getting into this? King of the freaks?"

"Girl, I wouldn't be accusing anyone of being a freak. The train wreck you've made of that top with that skirt. Tsk. You'd be more attractive playing up the male side of you than trying to be a girl."

Haley's face turns red and she starts to say something when I jump in. "Look," I growl, leaning closer to her. "I wasn't arrested, all right? And I *was* ill. So just stay out of my business."

"This doesn't look like not being arrested." She pulls out a grainy color photo that looks like it was lifted straight off the closed-circuit cameras at the hospital and holds it up like a prize. It shows me being lead down the hall by Cal and John in handcuffs. It most certainly looks like an arrest.

I feel the blood drain from my face as I look at the photo. "I wasn't arrested," I repeat as calmly as I can. "It was a joke played on me by some friends."

"Liar," Haley counters as she pulls the photo out my reach

and puts it in her pocket. "Believe me, my mother has the whole tape. The arrest, the leading you out, the shame. Why, Scarlett, your face resembles your name," Haley coos. I'm three seconds from whacking her smug face.

"Do we have a problem here?" Ms. Crawford is between us with her arms crossed, trying to ascertain what's going on. She glances back and forth. "Well?"

"Nothing, Ms. Crawford. Just girl talk." Haley smiles her megawatt smile and blinks innocently.

"Euphemistic wish, Haley?" Trevor says under his breath.

Haley glares at him, but I can tell Ms. Crawford didn't hear that.

"Scarlett?" she asks me.

"It's nothing," I reply and turn my face away from Haley.

"Well, if I hear you two talking again, you both are going to get detention. Understand?"

"Of course, Ms. Crawford," Haley smoothly says.

"Yes, ma'am," I add.

For the rest of the class, I try to think about how I can explain it. Feeling slightly panicked, I text Brice. No doubt he'll get a call from the school.

It isn't long before I'm called to the office. I get a quick hug from both Trevor and Missi as I head down the hall. Haley blows me a kiss as I walk by her. It takes everything I have not to turn around and kick her. I keep reminding myself to keep walking and not get too upset.

I open the door to the office and am greeted by the smell of glue and copier toner. There's a long counter at the front and a singular pale, wooden desk piled high with papers and file bins. In the middle of the room sits a desk with a flat computer screen, and I can barely make out Miss Horn's overly colored black hair bobbing back and forth as she types.

She glances down her nose where her glasses perch

precariously to see me walk in. She inclines her head. "Go on in, Scarlett."

I walk past her desk to the glassed office. It's small and claustrophobic, with large filing cabinets and too many things hung on the walls. The desk is immense and takes up the majority of the space. As I open the door, I see Brice and Chasem waiting. Brice sits straight and neat while Chasem sits on the edge of the radiator in front of the large window with his arms folded over his black leather jacket.

Mr. Prentiss sits back in his chair, his hands joined over his belly. He always reminds me of what a Ken doll would have looked like had he aged badly. He frowns. "Have a seat, Scarlett," he commands, and I slowly close the door to sit beside Brice. He offers a strained smile that does nothing to reassure me. Mr. Prentiss leans forward. "So, it was reported that you were arrested for—of all things—stealing blood. Patricia Kent was in here first thing this afternoon with pictures of the incident. I've called the precinct, however, and they advise there's no report of such an arrest. So, I've called your father in and your—" He inclines his head to Chasem.

"Uncle," he affirms.

"Uncle, to explain what this is about." Mr. Prentiss leans back and waits.

Brice sits up. "This was apparently a bad practical joke played on Scarlett. A couple of her friends hired actors to come and fake arrest her. That's why there was no police report."

"A practical joke?" Mr. Prentiss looks incredulous. "These are grown men who have her in cuffs. They searched her things and found blood in her bag. Kind of odd, don't you think? Why did she have blood in her possession?"

How did Mrs. Kent know all these things? There were only three people there, and two of them were helots. One of them was now dead. I involuntarily cringe.

Chasem catches it but says nothing to me. He stands and

turns to Mr. Prentiss. "She was delivering it to the Neville Treatment Center. Since I own it and Scarlett is an agent for the company, she was authorized by me to deliver it."

"Oh? And who are you to be able to do that?" Mr. Prentiss' voice is demeaning.

"I own it. So, by default, she does as well," Chasem remarks in a sharp tone as he lays a business card in front of Mr. Prentiss. "So you see, she wasn't in violation of anything." Chasem leans back smugly.

Mr. Prentiss frowns, holding the business card, and glances over to me then back to Chasem. "You had her deliver the blood?"

"Yes," he confirms. "Her bag is a specially designed bag so no one can tell what she's transporting. It's fully certified. She was set to deliver it after her shift at the blood bank had ended." Chasem pulls out a document and hands it casually to Mr. Prentiss. "Here's the original order."

Mr. Prentiss looks it over and is quiet for a long time. Finally, he says, "Well, it looks like everything is in order. It appears Mrs. Kent might have overreacted."

"Yes, she did," Chasem assures. "Next time, she might want to mind her own business, or I will sue her and this school. Do you understand?"

"Chasem..." Brice interrupts.

Chasem lifts his hand to silence Brice but watches Mr. Prentiss shift uncomfortably. "Am I clear?"

I hear Brice let out a small sigh of exasperation, but he says nothing.

Mr. Prentiss sits up and hands everything back to Chasem. "I'm sure there is no issue, Mr. Black. I appreciate you explaining it so clearly."

Chasem takes back the papers and motions for me to get up. Brice reluctantly stands as well. "Thank you, Mr. Prentiss." He pushes me out the door with Chasem directly behind us.

Once out of the building and in the night air, Brice turns on Chasem. "What the hell was that?"

Chasem stiffens. "He needed to be put in his place."

Brice purses his lips. "And you thought you'd be the one to do that? I thought we had an agreement. I handle all the educational issues and living issues, and you handle the training. Did I misunderstand that?"

There's an agreement?

Brice stands with his hands on his hips, watching Chasem shift and fold his arms.

"Guys like him think they're big dogs, and they only understand one thing. A bigger dog."

Brice rubs his hands through his hair. "Christ. I could have handled this."

Chasem mocks, "Well, no need to now, is there? I took care of it. What are you more upset about? The fact that I handled it or the fact that you couldn't?"

Brice takes a step towards Chasem and I step between them. I've never seen Brice this angry before and I'm not sure if he means to hit him or just step in to make a point. But I don't want to take a chance. I pat his chest to get his attention, but it doesn't work. He glares fiercely at Chasem. I love Brice, but if he were ever to fight with Chasem, I know who would win.

"This is unacceptable," Brice swears under his breath.

"Stop it. Both of you," I scream, and they look at me. Brice winces in apology and Chasem sighs.

Brice reaches out and hugs me. "Sorry, baby. We didn't mean to upset you. We'll stop." His arm goes around me and Chasem pats my back. "No more fighting," Brice assures. "Let's get you home."

EIGHTEEN

DISAGREE

WHEN WE GET TO MY APARTMENT BUILDING, CHASEM parks the car and he and Brice follow me up. An unspoken tension surrounds them as we ride in the small elevator. I chalk it up to residual emotions from the argument at school.

When the doors open, I bolt out and run to my door, eager to get inside and away from them. But they amble up behind me, talking in low, agitated tones. I disengage the lock and go inside, throwing my bag on the couch.

They enter and Chasem closes the door. He leans against it and folds his arms. Brice comes to me and offers a wary smile. "I know it was a tough day, but you got through it. Hopefully, this will be put to rest once and for all."

"Yeah? I hope so. Do you know if I still have a job with SBB?" I want to know, and it occurs to me that Andre might have been a tad freaked out about what happened. I know I would have been if he was arrested during a shift.

"I spoke to the hospital administrator," Chasem offers. "She was very accommodating once she discovered it was a prank gone badly. I had to offer a rather large donation to the hospital in order for her to overlook it, so you should be able to go back on Friday."

What a relief. I sit down on one of the stools at the small bar and look at the two of them. They radiate underlying tension. "Was Apollo behind this?" I ask, and Chasem's eyes flicker to me. Brice glances at him nervously.

"I'm not sure, but he could have been," Chasem remarks and steps closer.

"But why? Why have me held for days, almost starving me? It doesn't make any sense." I remember Cal's face in my mind and how he tasted. I try to shake my head and focus on something else.

"I just don't know, but I have some feelers out, trying to see if anyone has any information." Chasem drops his body onto one of the stools.

"Who is Ryker, anyway?"

Chasem stiffens and Brice glances at him again. "He was my right hand when I was in the revenant guard."

"Your right hand?" Suddenly, I can hear Ryker's gravelly voice echo in my head. *Try that again and I will gut you.* My head swims, but I force myself to focus on Chasem's face. His lips move, but there's a strange buzz in my ears and I can't understand him.

I feel Brice's hand on my arm. "Scarlett, you okay?"

I blink a few times to clear my brain. "Yeah, sorry. Just a little hungry," I say weakly.

"Well, let me make you something." Brice starts to beat around in my kitchen.

"Right hand?" I question again.

"When I was the commander of the guard, he was my second. He's a fierce solider, but I don't know if he was acting under Apollo's commands or not."

"I just don't understand why they were starving her. It doesn't make sense," Brice says as he reaches into my fridge.

Chasem plays with the magazine laying on my bar. He bends back the corners and nervously picks at it. "I think they were trying to weaken her."

"Well, it didn't completely work," I say. "It made me crazy. My revenant side lit up like a Christmas tree."

"Yeah, they just had no idea you were prepared and not as weak as they thought," Chasem says with an air of knowing. He smiles slightly. "You've become so strong."

I start to say something when Brice sets a plate in front of me and a glass of blood. Staring at the blood, I think about the temperature. Cold. Not like Cal's. I remember how the warmth of Cal's blood felt so good as it went down my throat, and how satisfying it was. I recall how his heart sounded as it pounded, weaker and weaker, until it eventually stopped. I'm suddenly disgusted and push the blood away to start eating the sandwich.

They don't seem to catch my change in thoughts, and just keep talking.

I hear a knock on the door and feel relieved at being able to get away from the conversation. When I open it, Emma stands there with a bag on her shoulder and her hair pulled back. She glances over to Chasem and Brice.

"Hola, Mr. E. Chasem. Was there a party I wasn't invited to?" I close the door behind her and she smiles at them.

"No, they just had to talk to my principal is all," I say and head back to the table.

"Bad ass. What did you do? Finally take out Haley Kent? Drain her right there in the middle of school?" She laughs and Chasem gives her a sideways look.

My stomach drops at the thought of killing...no. I'm not going to think about it.

"Want something to eat?" Brice says as he gets up and moves towards the stove.

"Nah, I ate earlier, but thanks, Mr. E," she offers with a gentle smile. She nudges me. "You feeling okay? You look a little whiter than your normal white self."

"I'm okay," I reassure.

I watch as Emma falls into an easy conversation with Chasem and Brice. She tells them about her recent adventures with her science teacher, and Brice seems all too willing to offer advice. Emma's presence allows me to stay low-key and not engage in too much conversation.

Brice and Chasem end up leaving in the early morning hours. I try to get Brice to stay here with me, but he's anxious to get to the cabin. Apparently, Sarah Boll is going to meet him in the afternoon, and he wants to get home.

Gag.

I still don't know much about her. Grabbing my phone, I shoot a text to Chasem to see if he can dig anything up on the Little Miss Nightingale.

Emma drifts off to sleep on the couch, having eaten her weight in Cheetos and chocolate. Who knew one teen girl could eat so much and stay so thin? I put a throw over her and hear her say, "I love you, Harry Styles," as she turns over.

I hear my phone ding and grab it off the coffee table. My heart races when I see it's from Nick.

Hey, it reads.

Hey back. What are you doing awake?

Couldn't sleep.

He couldn't sleep. Hmm. I don't like the sound of that. It's four in the morning; he should be unconscious.

Is everything okay? The question's instinctual. I really want to ask more than that, but I can't bring myself to. He needs to stay away from me, and I from him.

Yeah. Just had you on my mind and wanted to see how you were.

He's been thinking about me. This shoots a thrill through me, and I find myself smiling as I glance down at the phone.

Oh, you know me. Fine as frog hair.

Frog hair? I didn't know frogs had hair.

I grin. *Of course they do. But it's so fine you can't see it.*

LOL! That's pretty fine.

I bite my lip, thinking about what I want to ask. *How are things with the family?*

I wait and he doesn't reply. I walk into the kitchen and grab something to drink, and still nothing. I'm about to text again when my phone finally dings.

As good as can be expected.

It makes my heart ache. I have such great people in my life, but Nick isn't as lucky, although it really only boils down to one person for him—the ominous father. But I resist the urge. I'm about to send something else when I get another text from him.

You know, I'd still like to hang out sometime.

My heart thuds hard. I want it so badly I can hardly stand it. My hand hovers over the phone. I'm not sure what to say or how to explain that I'm afraid of being with him, afraid of myself. I never have been before, and though I know I was starving when I attacked Cal, I can still remember the monster that took over my thoughts and actions.   What if I ever did that with Nick? I care about him and I don't feel safe.

But I feel safe with Brice. I don't think I'd ever bite him. Well, Brice said I did once, when I was three, by accident. Still, I don't feel the same sort of temptation to bite like I do with Nick. Could it be that it's because I find Nick so appealing on so many levels? Physically, he makes me nervous in a fiery way, but could that be the difference?

I'm making my own head hurt. So I say the only thing I can think of to placate him.

I'd like that too. I'm sorry I was such a jerk before. I shouldn't be allowed around people. I think I was born without the socially acceptable conversation gene.

I'm going to Hell. I'm going to die and go to Hell for this, I just know it. I'm going to let him into my world and hurt him, for sure. But I can't reconcile that with the part of me that wants him so badly I can taste it. It's that deep wanting that scares me even more. What if the liking, desiring part flips the switch to wanting to drain him dry? What if I can't help myself? I'm ashamed of myself for not being able to resist him.

My phone dings. *I'm going to go to bed now I think. I'm glad I texted you. Don't leave me hanging too long, okay? :)*

A smiley face. Such an innocent symbol. If I return how I'm feeling, it would be nowhere near that. No, it would be a symbol between smut and devil. Somehow, I doubt that symbol exists.

Okay. Now go to sleep.

Night.

Night.

NINETEEN
GIVE ME SHELTER

NICK AND I EXCHANGE TEXT MESSAGES EVERY DAY but never meet up to hang out. When he suggests it, I find a reason to be busy. He never pushes, though. Instead, he just seems to take me at my word. Texting with him keeps us connected without having actual contact, and I like that. It makes me feel like I'm keeping him safe.

But during the day, my dreams are haunted by his face and the feeling of his lips on mine, demanding, hungry, needing. I put my arms around him and hold his taut body close to mine, inhaling the sweet scent of him. He whispers in my ear and makes me shiver in delight. But then, I wake up forlorn at the realization that it's only a dream.

Everything blends into a peculiar sort of march towards an impending meeting. My birth father looms over everything I do like an omen. I've tried to press Chasem into telling more about my dark father, but he always resists. He says, when I'm ready, he'll tell me. I feel ready now, but no amount of talking is going to convince him of that.

It's a hot Tuesday evening when I make my way up to my apartment. I've been feeling uneasy; maybe it's the lack of sleep or the feverish training regimen Chasem's adopted that has me snapping at everyone. Even Missi and Trevor notice how foul of a mood I'm in.

I've just dropped my books on my chair when my phone dings. I look down and see a cryptic message from Nick.

Find Chasem.

I frown and text him back. *Find Chasem? What's wrong?*

No reply. I pace and text again. *Nick, what's wrong?*

When I get no reply, I call him, but it goes right to voicemail. Hanging up, I immediately dial Chasem. He doesn't answer, either. My heart pounds hard. Something's up, but I'm not sure what. I decide to go to Nick's house to figure out what's wrong. With his father, it could be anything.

Instead of using the street, I go up to the top of the building and hurl myself over to the next one. Roof-hopping is the best way to go when I need to get somewhere quickly. Typically, no one watches the roofs.

I'm halfway there when my phone dings again. I stop to look down. It's from Chasem.

I need you to go to my apartment and wait.

Why?

Just do it and don't ask questions.

I curse and stare out across the illuminated city. The street activity swells below me, and the illuminated windows of the buildings before me are like accusing eyes, telling me that I have to do as I'm told. I've always trusted Chasem, and I need to do as he says. Changing course, I head towards his place.

I wait at his apartment for what seems like an hour. When he doesn't appear, I run the track on the second floor to burn some energy. But it's almost a wasted effort because I have to stop every few moments to check my phone. There's still nothing.

After my fifth time around, I hear the door open from the elevator. I jump over the railing to the floor below and watch as Chasem enters, holding a badly beaten Nick.

"Oh, God!" I yell and go to Nick's side. He's barely holding his weight in walking and leans heavily on me as I wrap my arm around him. He never looks at me. Not that he can; his one eye is almost completely swollen shut.

"Get him to the couch," Chasem commands, and we maneuver him there and lay him back.

I sit on the table and hold Nick's hand. "What happened?" I ask, but I already know the answer. It had to be Nick's dad.

Nick won't look at me, nor does he answer. He lays there with his arm held tightly to his side.

"Nick, what happened," I ask, attempting to stroke his cheek. His hand bats me away, but he still doesn't say anything.

"His father," Chasem pronounces like a curse. He pushes me away from Nick and assesses his wounds. As Chasem's hands travel down Nick's side, Nick winces. "Broken ribs, I think." Chasem lifts Nick's shirt, and I want to kill his father. A large bloom of an angry bruise in the shape of a shoe is imprinted on his side.

"Oh, God," I breathe.

"Leave me alone," Nick says and turns his face from me to the inside of the couch.

Chasem gently turns Nick's head back around. "I need to see how damaged that eye is."

Nick reluctantly turns back, but his good eye refuses to look at me. He breathes hard through gritted teeth as Chasem gently probes around his swollen eye.

"He might have a hairline fracture, but nothing major." Chasem sits back with his hands on his lap. "You really need a hospital."

"I already told you no," Nick grunts. "I won't go. If you insist on it, I'm out of here." He tries to rise up off the couch, but Chasem gently pushes him down.

"Easy, now. Okay. No hospital," Chasem surrenders. "You can stay here." Chasem looks up at me and his eyes glow green. "Can you take care of him? I have to go out, and I'll come back with a doc."

I nod quickly. "Of course. Whatever you need."

"I don't want her here," Nick pronounces but never looks at me.

"Well, too bad. She's here and she's all you got right now, so deal with it," Chasem says sharply. He easily gathers Nick up in his arms and starts towards the elevator. I rush ahead and push the button.

As we go up, Nick seems to relax a little in Chasem's arms. His head rests against Chasem's shoulder, his breathing staggered.

I feel my teeth drop as I clench my fists. I want to make his father pay. In my mind, I see myself dispatching him a million different ways: a knife, biting out his throat, throwing him from a tall building, plunging my hand into his chest and showing him his own beating heart. I want him dead for this.

Exiting the elevator into Chasem's living quarters, we go to the spare room just past mine. It's a bare room, holding a chest of drawers and a king-sized bed. Chasem lays Nick down carefully, who rolls over to his good side away from us and draws up his legs to his chest. Chasem paternally brushes back Nick's hair as he looks at him. His eyes meet mine and he pulls me out of the room.

"I need you to watch over him and make sure he doesn't try to get up, okay?"

I nod.

Chasem sighs heavily. "I have to go get Hannah and Abigail settled." He turns to go, but I catch his arm.

"Hannah and Abigail settled? What happened?"

Chasem's lips draw thin. "It seems Tim lost his job today, got a little drunk, and came home to take it out on his family."

"Are they okay?" I can see little Abigail in my mind and shiver at what an angry man could do to one so small.

Chasem's eyes seem to glow brighter. "They're roughed up

but otherwise okay. I think Nick got the worst of it. Seems he tried to protect his mother and sister. But I have to go get them settled in a shelter, okay?" Chasem presses his hand to my arm. "Take care of him. I'll be back soon."

I nod and watch him disappear down the shadowed hall. Then I turn back to Nick's doorway and watch him. His good eye is closed and his breathing labored. I want so badly to do something, but I'm not sure what. My insides boil with a fierce war between the need to avenge him and the need to comfort him. Walking inside the room, I stop to take off his shoes.

When I touch him, he jerks. "I just want to make you more comfortable," I whisper softly.

"Go away, Scarlett," he says against his pillow. "I don't want you to see me like this."

"Like what? Like you tried to save your sister and mother and paid a heavy price for it?" I shoot back as I try to untie his shoe.

"Like a victim," he whispers, so softly, like he doesn't want me to hear it. I stop what I'm doing and move to the side of the bed. I brush his sweaty, dark hair away from his forehead.

"I don't see you as a victim. I see you as a brave boy who tried to do the most valiant thing possible. I can't imagine what it took to fight your own father."

A single tear rolls out of his good eye. "I didn't fight him. I...just stood there and took what he wanted to give my mother so they could get away."

I stroke his cheek. "And that was valiant," I say.

"No, it wasn't being a man. If I had been stronger, I would have fought him and dished back what he gave them. But I just...couldn't. I couldn't bring myself to hit him. I don't know why." His voice cracks at the last word and he turns his face away.

I take off my shoes and crawl onto the bed with him, spooning him and wrapping my arm around his shoulder. I kiss his neck and whisper, "You were being a man by not hitting your own father."

As I hold him, I realize we're both so lost, so messed up by the people who are supposed to protect us—our fathers. Nick doesn't respond, but one of his hands finds mine and we lay wrapped up in each other in the quiet room.

Emma arrives shortly before the doctor does. When she looks in on Nick, she breathes, "Jesús dulce bebé . What happened to him?"

"His father," I remark.

"Is he related to your father?" she says quietly. "Oh, wait. No, that would make you guys cousins and, yeah, that's all kinds of wrong."

Chasem finally arrives with a doctor in tow. He stands like a caged animal with his arms crossed, watching at the end of the bed while the white-haired doctor examines Nick. At one point, I leave while they undress Nick so the doctor can look him over easily. I stand in the hallway as Nick cries out in pain, each time followed by the doctor's apology.

Each moan hits me like a knife. I want him to stop hurting Nick. It's all I can do not to go in there and bite the doctor, but I have to keep telling myself he's only doing his job. Emma stands close by with her arms crossed, trying to reassure me with placating looks.

The doctor steps out and speaks to Chasem in low tones, then leaves. I start towards Nick's door, but Chasem stops me. "The doc gave him something to sleep. Let him rest," he demands and points towards the living room. I reluctantly comply.

"Are they safe?" I ask him as he lets his weight collapse onto the sofa.

He rubs his stubbled face. "Yes. For now."

"What happened to his dad?"

"I hope you found him and killed him," Emma offers as she

leans over the kitchen counter.

Chasem eyes her for a second. "I have no idea. When I got there, Tim took one look at me and fled. I couldn't chase after him because I thought they might be fatally hurt, so I let him go." Chasem raises his elbows to his knees, the friction causing the sofa to squeak. "I will find him. And when I do..." His voice trails off.

"Kill," Emma says with a defiant glare. I give her a sideways look.

"Nick said he let his dad beat him. Did you know that?" I volunteer to Chasem as the blue flames of the fire reflect in his eyes.

Chasem's gaze shoots up in surprise and then he nods. "Yes, Hannah told me. She said he saved them. Tim was out of his mind and had hit her a couple of times when Abigail came in. She was sure he was going to go after her when Nick came home. She said Nick goaded Tim until he unleashed everything he had on the kid."

I swallow hard. What had it taken for Nick not to strike back? More than I have, I know that much.

Chasem sits back against the sofa. "What an absolute mess."

I sit down across from him and smile. "I'm actually surprised that you're involved with humans. I mean, besides helots. And speaking of that, by the way, when were you going to tell me that Eddie was yours?"

Chasem glances at me and then up to Emma. He waves his hand dismissively. "It wasn't important. I don't have many. I don't have the time nor the energy for it."

"You mean you have more than just Eddie?" I ask, incredulous.

"Drop it!" Chasem snaps.

"Okay, okay," I relent and throw up my hands. When Chasem doesn't want to talk about something, nothing can pull it out of him, no matter what.

I stand and see the sky outside beginning to lighten. The clock reads 6:00 am. "I'm going to try to get some sleep. The sun will be up soon."

Emma walks around to the couch across from Chasem's and stretches out. "Me too. Today feels like a good day to skip school," she says with a stretch and yawn.

"Yeah, you both should get some sleep," Chasem agrees and grabs the remote to turn on the opaqueness of the windows. "I'm going to head down to the gym for a while. Will you be able to listen out for Nick if he should need something?" he asks as he turns to me.

"Consider it done," I agree.

Chasem nods and, as he walks by me, kisses my forehead. "I love you."

"Love you, too."

"Oh, me too," Emma says, raising her hand.

"Yes, you too, you irritating little human," Chase says and grasps her upraised hand in a gesture of shaking it. Then he heads down the elevator.

Once he's gone, I go to my room and change into some sweats and a t-shirt, sitting on the edge of my bed. I don't want to sleep here, in my room. My heart pounds as I consider what I really want.

Slipping out into the hallway, I make my way to Nick's room. I slowly open the door and gaze in. Nick lays sleeping, shirtless, with a blanket up to his midsection. The bruises stands out starkly even against his darker skin. I quietly step in and shut the door.

I hear my own breathing as I walk to the bed and lift the sheet. He wears only his boxers. Before I think better of it, I slide in beside him and lay my head on his shoulder. His arm reaches out and rests possessively on my thigh as he nuzzles into me. His scent fills up my senses and I have the urge to bite. The fear of hurting him is dull. I want to mark him as mine in a weird sort of revenant way with a bite. I've never heard Chasem speak of it being normal, but, then again, he barely speaks of anything beyond my coming Dawning. To talk about physical attraction and romance would be bizarre. I try not to let it bear too much weight in the current moment, because I'm going to stay here, urge to bite or not.

I place my arm across his chest and lean in to kiss his forehead. I whisper, "I won't let anything hurt you again." I close my eyes and let the sleep claim me.

TWENTY

HELOT

DAYS PASS BY AND NICK IS IMPATIENT TO BE UP AND about. I offer to get him something to eat, and before I know it, he's up behind me doing it himself. I want to discourage him from it, but Chasem told me to leave him alone.

His bruises have lightened to a faded yellow, and the swelling around his eye goes away. But something sinister seems to have taken a hold of his soul. He speaks very little about anything, and never mind trying to talk to him about what happened. The only one who seems to get anything out of him is Chasem.

They sit and talk quietly with each other, and when I enter, they abruptly stop. It makes me uncomfortable. As soon as I leave the room, their conversation continues.

One afternoon, I walk into the gym to train and am surprised to see Nick there. He's wearing boxing gloves and sparring with Chasem. Chasem's tone is instructional, telling Nick "good" or "more to the left". I cross my arms and watch for a while, not really sure what I'm looking at. Why is Nick training with Chasem? Once, Nick strikes out then grabs his side, wincing in pain.

"Let's take a break. Easy workout, remember?" Chasem says, but Nick shakes his head.

"No, I'm okay. Let's keep going," he protests with heavy breathing. He wipes his face on his arm and raises his fists to strike again.

Chasem reluctantly nods and holds up his air mitts to continue. Nick swings out again and doubles over in pain.

"That's it. We're done here." Chasem takes off his gloves and pats Nick on the back.

Nick heaves in air. "But I want to be ready." Chasem ignores him and keeps walking.

"Ready for what?" I ask as I approach. Both turn to me with a surprised look.

Chasem shakes his head and glances between Nick and myself. He furrows his brows and leaves the room. I approach a sweat-drenched Nick, who stands bracing himself on his knees.

"Ready for what?" I repeat. "You aren't going after your dad, are you?"

He stands up and pulls off his gloves. "No." Brushing past me, he grabs some water but keeps his back to me.

"Then what are you getting ready for?" I cross my arms impatiently.

"I want to help defend you when you don't Dawn. I know you'll be hunted and I want to help protect you with Chasem."

"What?" I can't believe what he just said. "How do you know about any of that?"

Nick spins around to face me. "Chase told me. It should have been you, but he told me as my ceannard."

I gaze at him. Did he just say 'ceannard'? Yes, my brain tells me. He did.

"Ceannard," I say, inching closer. "As in, you're now his—"

"Helot," Nick finishes and crosses his arms, gazing at me with unfathomable eyes.

"No! Oh, no, no, no. You can't be his helot. Do you even know what that means?"

"Yes," he affirms. "I know exactly what it means. It means he can command me any way he wants."

"For life," I clarify. "Why would you do that?" He stares blankly at me. I rush to him and push him back. "Why? I don't get it. To be a helot is being indebted forever. You can't ever not be one. I don't know why you did that." I push him again and he takes a step back. "You're in the revenant world forever!"

Nick doesn't say anything and I feel tears come up in my eyes. His human life will never be the same. He'll have to keep the world of revenants a secret, but not only that, he won't be able to live a life Chasem doesn't agree to. Nick will now serve Chasem first and foremost, and as much as I love my uncle, I don't want Nick to be indebted to anyone in that way.

He inches closer to me. "I want to help protect you from renegades. I don't want to be left out like I'm not part of this equation. And I didn't exactly give Chasem a choice. If he hadn't accepted me, I would have found another way in."

I turn on Nick like a villain. "Why? I don't understand! If you know about my father, then you know he caused my mother's death when I was born and he wants to kill me for no other reason than the fact that I exist. I am *not* going to be able to Dawn, or live a peaceful life, ever. I will have to live the life of a rogue and will have to be on guard ever moment of my life. Why would you want to be a part of that chaos?"

"Because I'm in love with you!" he screams. Everything goes deathly quiet.

I stare into his gray eyes, stunned. He didn't really just say that, did he? "What?" I whisper.

His face softens and he steps closer. "I'm in love with you, and every moment we're together tells me how much I don't ever want to be without you. Not ever. Don't you get that?" His fingers trail down my arms slowly, and his eyes bore into mine. "Having you near me all day for the last week has been painful. I've wanted to tell you so many times, but I knew what you'd say. You'd be like you were after you accidentally killed that man. You'd push me away."

I wince at the thought of Cal. "It wasn't an accident," I say quietly and turn away.

"It was. I know you, Scarlett, and there's no way you killed him on purpose." Nick brings his arms around me and pulls me back against him. I feel a little dizzy as his scent fills my senses. "God, I've wanted to touch you like this for weeks now."

He's so close, like an addiction I can't resist. I hear his heart pounding and his scent calls me like a siren. I can't think straight. The carefully crafted wall I put up to push him away is almost down in a pile around my feet. In that moment, I realize I want him too much to turn away.

"Me too," I admit and turn around to face him. I gaze into his molten eyes and pull his head down. His lips are soft against mine at first, gentle, careful. Then everything explodes. His tongue plunges into my mouth and the kiss deepens. I feel a fire start in the pit of my belly and all I want is more of him, closer to me.

His hand trails down to the small of my back, he backs me up, and I don't resist. Before I know what he's doing, he lowers me to the mats, keeping contact with me. His hands hungrily explore as he hovers over me.

I can't think clearly. I can only taste him, smell him, feel him. My fangs drop involuntarily and I want so badly to bite him. I'm panting and pulling him closer. I open my eyes and he appears a mix of heat signature and color. I can see and hear his heart pounding wildly. My revenant side identifies him as something different than prey; he is...mine. That side owns him, and I want to bite him so bad I can hardly keep control. It feels heady and wild, and I'm lit up inside like an inferno.

"God, your eyes are so beautiful," Nick breathes and kisses down my neck. I find myself flipping him over and lay possessively over him. He winces slightly and I pull back, realizing I've pushed too hard on his ribs. But he sits up and pulls me back onto him. "Don't stop," he breathes against me.

"I...want to bite you," I pant. His hands reach hungrily under my shirt to my bare skin. We're a tangled mess of arms and legs, my hands running up his muscled chest and he holding me so close I shouldn't be able to breathe.

"Then do it," he commands, and I pull back, preparing to strike. Something in me is incredibly happy over what I'm about to do.

"Scarlett!" Chasem screams from somewhere in the room. At first, I ignore it, and then it becomes louder and closer. "Get off him!" My revenant side wants to make Chasem go away so I can latch onto Nick. A small shock registers inside me because I want to growl at Chasem to go away.

Finally, my brain kicks in and I jump back from Nick, panting. Nick scurries up to stand and faces Chasem. He looks only a little embarrassed.

When I look up at Chasem, he just looks angry. "I don't want to think where this was going when I came in. And you looked like you were about to bite him!"

I look away, horrified by myself. I'm not sure how to explain why I was doing what I was. I was lost in the moment and could have drained Nick of his blood if I'd also lost control. My heart thuds hard. I could have killed the one and only boy I love.

"It's okay, Chase. I told her she could," Nick says, attempting to placate Chasem. He looks almost apologetic, but it does nothing to remove the look of anger from Chasem's face.

Chasem stands there, looking between us with his hands on his hips. "Nick, go get cleaned up. And you," he points at me, "get up. We have some work to do." He stomps out of the room, leaving Nick and me staring at each other. Nick winks and reaches over to take my hand.

I briefly smile, then jump up. "Better get moving before your ceannard orders you," I remind him, slightly bitter, and head off to the equipment to get ready to train. I feel Nick's arms come around me, and he kisses my temple.

"I would gladly risk death for what just happened," he says and lets me go to walk out.

I stand there, realizing I never told him I was as much in love with him as he'd declared to me. I'm not sure what to do with that realization, because it doesn't really help, knowing how I feel. Soon, I'll either Dawn or not, and I'll be fighting every moment of every day.

I'm glad I hadn't said what I really feel out loud. I know that if I tell him, we can never go back to being friends again. Not once those words are spoken.

TWENTY-ONE

BIRDS AND BEES

"THE LIGHT IS ABSOLUTELY STUNNING ON YOUR SKIN," *he breathes. His face is close to mine and his pale green eyes regard me with a pleased smile. I glance down at my exposed arm. The warm, buttery sun shines directly on me and it doesn't burn. The majority of my body is protected in the shadow of the doorway as he watches me.*

"Is this what it's like for the humans all the time?" I hear my unfamiliar voice ask. I turn my hand over and look at the pale skin. "Good God, this is fantastic."

The man takes my hand in his and brings it up to his lips. It's a soft, endearing kiss. He keeps linked to me and pulls me from the shelter of the building's doorway. "It's safe. Come, Jasmine." He urges me forward, and I feel the complete weight of the sun on my face. I breathe in and take in the smell of the heat, laced with the scent of wax myrtle on the air, the molecules excited by the intense rays from the sun.

I step out a few more steps and something pinches my hand. I gaze down and a faint ash starts to bloom. Panic takes hold, and I rip my hand from his and dash back towards the door, where I dive towards the shadow.

I jerk awake in the darkness. Sitting up, I rub my chest because my heart is galloping and I feel like I can't breathe.

Stumbling out of bed, I try to take in a breath but the air hardly makes it in. Doubling over, I pant, trying to steady myself. It was only a dream. A dream. But I can almost smell the sweet, burning flesh.

When I finally realize that I'm okay and not burning in the sun, I walk to my bed and drop onto it. The mattress squeaks and I draw up my legs. Why do I keep dreaming about this? It occurs to me that the name spoken was "Jasmine". My heart races even more, if possible; Jasmine was my mother. But why am I dreaming of being her? I shake my head to clear out the memory.

Glancing at the clock, I see it's 1:30. I change into some jeans and head out of my room to the hallway. I listen and hear nothing from Chasem's room or Nick's. They must already be up.

My bare feet skim across the floor as I enter the great room. It's quiet and I can tell from the taste in the air that they've been gone for a while. A piece of white paper on the kitchen counter catches my eye. I reach it and see:

Training room - C

I hop on the elevator and take it to the ground floor. When the doors open, I see a shirtless Chasem sparring the dummy with blistering speed. Well, not exactly sparring—more like trying to destroy it. He's covered in sweat as his large muscles bunch and release with each merciless strike. In a sharp move, he ferociously kicks the dummy. It skitters noisily across the floor. Chasem breathes hard and turns to me with clenched fists, then motions me over.

"What did that thing ever do to you?" I joke, walking across the cold mats.

Chasem grabs a towel from a nearby table and lifts a glass of blood to his lips. "Very funny."

"Where's Nick?"

Chasem looks down for a second and then downs the entire

glass. "He went home."

My heart skips a beat. "Went home? What do you mean?"

Chasem raises his hand. "It's okay, Scar. He's just getting some more clothes."

"Oh," I say, relieved.

Chasem sits down on the table and lets his feet rest on the chair in front of it. "So. You want to explain to me your intentions with him?"

I cross my arms. "I could ask you the same thing... ceannard."

He shakes his head and looks away, then back to me. "I didn't have much of a choice. He wouldn't be swayed from it."

"How the hell did he even know about being a helot?" I demand angrily and rush toward him.

"Eddie. It was when we came to save you. Eddie thought he knew about our world, and I was so distracted in wanting to find you that I didn't even catch it when he explained it to Nick."

"Now he's chained to you forever." I feel my lips tighten. "How could you do that to him?"

Chasem gets up and approaches me. "I've never misused my position as a ceannard, ever. I respect anyone who wants to enter into that agreement with me, and I've turned many a human away who knows about us. Believe me, I tried to talk him out of it."

"Not hard enough, apparently, because you still did it," I huff, and turn to see him glaring at me.

Chasem's face reddens and he points at me. "I don't think you understand something, here. Your boy wants to be in your world. So badly, in fact, that he was determined to be a helot. If I hadn't agreed to it, he would have found another way in and I don't want to think about who he might have linked to or what he would have done."

"He's not my boy," I correct childishly.

"Oh, yes he is. Whether you want to admit it or not, that boy is in love with you. So you better decide what it is that you're doing with him. Because, correct me if I'm wrong, you almost claimed him."

I start to squirm. "I don't know what I was about to do. I just felt compelled to bite him and almost couldn't help myself. I'm glad you came in when you did. I wouldn't want to do to him what I did to Cal." I don't look at him. I don't want to think what would happen if I were to bite Nick. That can't ever happen.

He rubs his eyes and glares at me. "You. Tried. To. Claim. Him," Chasem says. "You're too young to do that, but you were going to do it anyway." He pauses and his eyes soften as some sort of thought occurs to him. "You think you'd drain him like you did Cal?" he says, disbelieving.

"Yes. Why else would I want to bite him other than to drink him dry?" I feel nauseous and want to quit talking about what a monster I can become.

"I guess I've never explained that side of our nature as revenants." He sighs hard and then throws his towel to the side. "I'll be damned if I'm going to have to explain the revenant birds and bees to you. If only your mother was here."

"But she's not!" I scream. "She's dead!"

I turn to Chasem and his face looks horrified for a brief moment, then he recovers himself. "Don't you think I know that? Don't you think I've done everything I could in her place? I miss her every day. You don't consider the fact that I lost the other half of me when she died, do you? No, you're too busy thinking about yourself to even consider anyone else."

He storms out, and even though I want to stop him, I do nothing but watch him go. I feel as terrible as he looks. I don't know why I said what I did; it was just this involuntary, knee-jerk thing.

I sit down on the cold mats and stare at my feet. I don't like arguing with Chasem. When I do, everything feels wrong. All his words bounce around in my head, a tangled mess. He misses my mother, his twin. He says I've claimed Nick, whatever that means, and that he'll do right by Nick as his ceannard. God, what a mess.

I think about the only other person who makes sense in my life and pull out my phone. I shoot off a text to Brice. *Hey, Dad, thinking of you. Just wanted to say hey.*

I wait for a while and finally I get a ding. *"Hey, honey. How are things?"*

A million different ways I could answer go through my head. Instead, I avoid them all. *I know we'll see each other on Sunday, but any chance you could come by Chasem's before then?*

I find myself playing with my jeans, running my fingernail along the seam. It seems like forever, and I finally get a reply back. *I'm with Sarah right now, but maybe tomorrow?"*

Ugh! Sarah.

Sure, dad. Love you.

Love you too, honey.

I sit staring at my phone. I want Brice to give me words of wisdom and wipe away all the grief with a strong arm around my shoulder.

TWENTY-TWO
BOYFRIENDS AND MURDER

"**SO, GUESS WHO WILL BE GOING TO EXCELSIOR** Academy?" Nick asks me as he pops a grape into his mouth. He leans over the kitchen counter and smiles like he's on TV. The bruising around his eye is almost gone.

"Um, I don't know. Who?" I ask as I reach into the fridge for a new packet of blood. The blood is unmarked, which isn't normal, but I try not to think too much about it.

Nick smiles wider. "Yours truly. Looks like your boyfriend will be going to school with you."

I spin around, not sure which thing to question first—either the school part or the boyfriend part. "What did you say?"

"You heard me. We'll be going to class together. Doesn't that rock?" He stands up and watches me.

"No, not that part, even though I want to ask 'what the hell?' The other part you said." I hold onto the packet of blood like it can protect me from any answer he might give.

"Boyfriend?" His eyes become wary.

"That's the part," I confirm.

Nick taps his finger nervously on the counter. "Well, I figured I was."

"Oh," I say and empty the blood into a glass. I actually just want to suck it straight from the pack, but that might not be ladylike. After all, I want to be ladylike sucking down my blood.

I realize I don't want to look at him. "I've never had a boy-friend before," I whisper. "But aren't you suppose to actually ask me if I want to be your girlfriend?" I hear Nick shifting nervously and I turn to him, taking a drink of my blood.

He stares at me with his gray eyes, then clears his throat and begins hesitantly. "Well, I thought since...you know...the other day, we established that there were feelings there. I mean, I told you I loved you." He stops and stares at me.

I want to go to him and wrap my arms around him, but I feel suddenly very unsure of myself. I haven't declared myself to him, but Chasem made it sound like I had some weird revenant vibe happening with the biting. I just wish he would have explained it a little more. "You did tell me you loved me," I confirm almost apologetically.

He pales. "Are you going to tell me you don't love me?" A determined look crosses his face and he rushes to me. I turn my body away and his arms are on my shoulders. "I won't believe it if you do. I know you love me. You might not have said the words, but you love me. I know it like I know I have curly hair."

I hold onto my glass. I do love him, but I have no idea what's going to happen. He's too vulnerable as a human in my world, and I will have to battle every moment of every day. How fair is that to him? I'll be fodder for renegades and I'll have to hide for the rest of my life. I know he's tied to Chasem, but I don't want to tie him to me.

I turn to face him. "Nick, I—"

Chasem interrupts me as he walks into the room. "Nick, you got a minute?" He looks incredibly grim as he glances at us. Nick releases me and walks over to Chasem, who says nothing but leads him further into the great room to speak to him. I watch as I sip my blood. Nick intently regards Chasem as he talks, and then a furious look crosses his face.

"When?" Nick demands fiercely. Chasem says something so soft I can't make it out. Nick nods and then says, "How?"

Chasem squeezes Nick's shoulder and Nick knocks it away, then he leaves in the direction of his room.

I rush over to Chasem. "What happened?" I demand.

Chasem sits on the back of the couch and crosses his arms. His shoulders hunch before letting out a heavy breath. "Nick's dad is dead," he pronounces blandly. He rubs his eyes like he is trying to clean something out of his vision..

"What happened?" My heart breaks for Nick and I want to go to him and tell him it's going to be okay.

"He drowned in the Hudson last night. I'm not sure what happened, but Hannah and Abigail are headed back to their house. The police want to speak to them, and Nick is supposed to be there, too. I'm going to go with him." Chasem's whiskey-colored eyes stare at me, waiting for a reply.

"I want to go."

He sighs, resigned. "Of course you do. We leave in ten minutes."

I stand at the door of Nick's room as he sits on the side of his bed, putting on his shoes. His shoulders are slightly hunched, and when he's done, he leans on his elbows, staring at the ground.

I walk in, crawl across his bed, and pull him back against me with my arms around his shoulders. He shakes against me, and I realize he's crying. I lay my head against his and hold him tighter. I kiss his head. "I'm so sorry, Nick," I whisper. "I love you and I'm so sorry."

He reaches up to grab my hand, then he starts to weep completely. I rock him and stroke his hair while he breaks. My strong, beautiful boy holds onto me and sobs in my arms.

"So, Mrs. Lightener, when was the last time you saw your husband?" Detective Samuel Tripp asks. He's a small man with thinning blond hair and anemic-looking skin. His partner, a younger man, well-built with caramel-colored skin, is named Joel Martinez. Joel stands back with his arms folded and tries not to be too obvious as he takes us in and looks around. We all stand in the small Lightener dining room, which feels even smaller with seven us there.

Abigail holds onto her mother and eyes the detectives warily. She lays her blond head on her mother's shoulder. Hannah gently rubs circles on her back.

"Two weeks ago," she says, and her eyes flicker to Nick. He stands beside me with his arms folded. The detective's eyes follow hers and he gazes at Nick.

"What about you?" Detective Tripp asks.

"Same. Two weeks ago." Nick's voice is hard and almost angry.

"What happened two weeks ago to push his entire family away for that amount of time?" Detective Tripp asks as Detective Martinez wanders into the kitchen.

Nick looks toward his mother and then at Chasem but doesn't immediately answer.

Tripp's eyebrows come up. "Excuse me. Who are you, exactly?" he asks Chasem.

"A friend of the family," Chasem answers confidently.

Tripp gives a cold smile. "Okay. When was the last time you saw Mr. Lightener?"

"A week ago," he answers without looking at anyone. I see Nick glance at Chasem with curiosity.

"Where was that, Mister..."

"Black. Chasem Black. I saw him at The Place. It's a small bar down on tenth." Chasem's voice is strong and unwavering.

"And what were you doing?" Detective Tripp asks.

"What else do you do in a bar?" Chasem asks sharply.

"I found something," Joel announces from the kitchen.

We all turn to see Detective Tripp get up and approach Joel, who looks over the sink. They speak quietly to each other and Joel bags some burned pieces of paper.

"What were you burning, Mrs. Lightener?" Tripp asks as he comes back into the dining room. He eyes her speculatively and sits down.

"I, uh, nothing. I haven't been home for two weeks." She glances up at Chasem and then at Nick.

"Which was the last time anyone saw him, except for Mr. Black here. What happened two weeks ago? And why haven't you been home?"

It's quiet, like pin-drop quiet. My hand finds Nick's and I squeeze. He gives me a gentle squeeze back.

"My father beat me up," Nick grinds out. I can tell it took a lot for him to admit that. He keeps his chin lifted defiantly.

A bit of a frown flashes across the detective's face, but only for a moment, and then it's gone. "Was this reported to the police?" Tripp is poised to write the answer on his pad, waiting.

Chasem answers him. "No. It wasn't. We didn't want to get Tim arrested, so I took Nick to my house and Hannah and Abigail were placed in a women's shelter."

Tripp nods and smiles arrogantly for a moment. "And why didn't anyone notify the police?"

"Look, Detective. I loved my husband. He could be a real ass sometimes and he was abusive, but I loved him. I didn't want to get him in trouble, and so we handled it ourselves," Hannah says with a strong voice.

"Do you know, then, why he was drowned?" Joel says as he walks back into the room with the bag's contents of charred paper in his hand.

"You think someone killed him?" Nick asks with slight panic.

Detective Tripp gets up. "Well, he had a lot of bruising on his neck, so maybe. We won't know until the coroner's report and autopsy are finished." He smiles at Chasem. "Mr. Black, I'm going to need your address." Chasem provides it and Tripp gives everyone an intense stare. "No one leaves town, okay? We will keep you updated. We'll show ourselves out."

The detectives walk out; we stay rooted in place until we hear the door shut, then Hannah hangs her head and begins to cry. Nick is immediately in front of her and puts his arms around his sister and his mother, consoling them. Chasem joins them for what becomes a sort of group hug, and I see Nick's hand reach behind towards me. I immediately go to him, take his hand, and instinctively put my hand on top of Abigail's head as she cries into her brother.

We're an odd sort of family, standing here in the Lightener's kitchen. I gaze over to Chasem, and he has the oddest look of compassion on his face.

Chasem sits waiting in the car as I stand on the porch with Nick. He holds me close and we don't move. Finally, Nick pulls back and gazes into my eyes.

"I'm going to miss you," he says softly, then kisses my cheek. "I got used to having you so close."

"I know," I allow. "But your mom and your sister need you right now."

His gaze on me is intense. "You know, you admitted you loved me tonight."

I nod. It was the most natural thing to say in that moment, and I wonder why it took me so long to admit it. "I did. And I do. Love you, that is. I'm sorry I had such a hard time telling you that."

"It's okay. At least you told me. So, can I take that to mean that I am, in fact, your boyfriend?"

I smile. "Leave it to you to think of something inappropriate at a time like this."

"Nothing inappropriate about it. I just know what's important to me. And that's you." He looks at me, trying hard at seriousness. "So? Are you completely mine?"

I pull him close for a last kiss. "Yes, you wild, crazy human boy. I'm yours."

On the drive to Chasem's, I consider what the police had said, that Tim had drowned and it might have been murder. I glance at Chasem and try to think if he would be capable of that. He could be, it's true, but it isn't likely. Chasem is a pale revenant like me, so human life is sacred to him. But what if he had been pushed to it? I recall him telling Tim he would have to deal with him if he hurt Nick and his mother again. But it just seems unlikely that Chasem would actually drown him.

He catches me staring at him. "What?" he asks.

"Nothing," I breathe and hope I'm right.

TWENTY-THREE

SARAH BOLL

THE POLICE COME BY TO TALK TO CHASEM THE NEXT day at his building. I watch from the railings on the second-floor track and listen intently. They suspect him and ask him how he knows Hannah and Tim and why Nick had been staying with us. Chasem provides the same explanation, and I can tell from Detective Tripp's reaction that he has doubts.

They ask him why he had seen Tim a week ago, and Chasem tells them it was only to give him an update on Nick. All the while, Chasem answers calmly and confidently to everything Martinez and Tripp throw at him. While they talk, a uniformed officer walks around the space and eventually makes his way to the training area.

His eyes grow large at all the weapons amassed there. It's a pretty good assortment. However, there are no guns visible, so that helps keep suspicion down.

They grill Chasem about what he does and how he came to own a medical facility in Manhattan. Martinez even remarks on the red Dawning tattoo visible on Chasem's neck as it peeks out from his collar. Chasem smiles and lets them know it's the privilege of ownership that allows him to control his appearance.

Martinez hands Chasem his card and leaves with the others.

Chasem puts the card on the counter, then glances up at me. He shakes his head.

"So, did you have anything to do with it?" I ask suddenly, surprising myself.

"You think I would kill him?"

I try to appear casual as I shrug. "You were pretty angry with him."

"I get pretty angry with you too, Scar, but I'd never hurt you," he huffs.

"Yeah, well, I'm your niece."

"And he is a sentient being. I wouldn't just kill him." Chasem rubs his wavy hair and looks up at me again. "Don't you have to be at school soon?"

I realize he's deflecting. I think about what he says, that he wouldn't just kill Tim. But if he were provoked...maybe.

"Fine. I'm going," I say and head up to my room.

Perkalicious is busy when I arrive later that evening, and Eddie frowns at me. He inclines his head towards a table. Sitting there is a petite blond woman with her hair swept up in a neat ponytail. She sips daintily on a coffee, casually reading a magazine. I see Emma at a table in the back. When she sees me, she shakes her head. I look to Eddie in question.

He motions me over. "She said her name is Sarah Boll and she's a friend of your father's," he gruffly explains. "She's been here for an hour to see you and only ordered a small black coffee," he complains.

I turn to see her manicured fingers turning the pages. I look back at Eddie. "Did she say what she wanted?"

"Do I look like a priest? Now go talk to her so I can get that table open for people who might actually spend money," he growls, then turns around to wait on someone.

I take a breath and walk over. She doesn't look up until I'm right at her table. She glances impassively at me. "Yes?" she breathes with a soft voice.

"Hi, I'm Scarlett Ellis," I say and adjust the bag on my shoulder.

Her face turns up in an excited smile. "Oh, good God, you're as beautiful as Brice said you were! Oh, here. Have a seat." The chair rubs loudly against the floor as she pulls it out for me. I let my weight drop into it. She regards me with an overly sweet smile.

"So. You're Sarah."

She beams. "Yes, I am. You know about me?"

"My father told me he had a friend," I say blandly.

She gently closes the magazine and gives a condescending smile. "Well, we're just a tad more than friends."

My face feels hot and I want to get up and walk away from her, but I force myself to stare into her hazel eyes. "He never said that," I contradict.

"Well, he wouldn't. He wasn't sure how you'd react," she shoots back and glares at me a little. "So, I thought I'd come here and—"

"Tell me yourself," I interrupt. And I want to say, 'Nice. Do you want to cut up his food for him too like a baby?'

She grins genteelly and taps the magazine. "Yes. I wanted to make this as easy on him as possible. He's a good man, and I'm lucky I found him."

"How is it that you came to move to Amherst Ridge, anyway? You seem a little upscale to be in a small town like that." I sit back and cross my arms.

Her face folds into a frown for a moment, then she smiles again. "Well, I was looking for someplace quiet. Amherst Ridge seemed like a good place to be."

I chuckle. "Right. There's nothing there but some grain mills and pig farms. You mean to tell me that was appealing to you?" I frown at her. Something about her makes me suspicious of everything she says.

She leans up on her arms and gives me a serious look. "Look, Scarlett, how I ended up there isn't important. But what is important is that your father and I are in love. I want to continue the relationship, but he seems to have a wall up and I think it has to do with what he thinks your reaction will be. I thought it might help if we met and you understood how serious this is for us."

I want to punch her in the face. It takes everything in me to keep my eyes from changing and not react like my body begs me to. I don't want this woman in my father's life. I don't want her in mine. She has an air of complete falseness to her.

I abruptly rise. "I'll understand it once he tells me about it. I don't need you to come here and explain it to me."

She beams. "Of course, and I'm sorry. I'm not trying to over-step here, and I certainly don't want to come between you two. I know you'll be seeing Brice on Sunday. I hope that my coming here will have primed the pump, so to speak." She stands and extends her hand to me. "I really hope we can be friends."

Not even if my life depended on it.

I stare at her hand for a moment and then begrudgingly take it. She covers my hand with her other one and almost giggles. "I'll be seeing you soon." She picks up a flat purse and walks out in her Jimmy Choos. Relief washes over me.

I glance over at Eddie, who mouths, "Thank God," and I turn back to the locker room to get ready for my shift. Emma's hot on my tracks.

"She looked like a biatch," she says with an exaggerated air. She leans against the wall. "Tell me that isn't who Brice is hooking up with."

"One and the same," I confirm without looking at her.

"Isn't that like a contradiction? She looks like a cool million and, well...he's McDonald's. I can't see those two together to save my life."

I shake my head. "Well, they're together. Like a bad dream."

I see her shift around. "Sorry, Scar. The thought of that being a potential step-monster is enough to give me chills."

"Thanks for bringing that up," I shoot back to her with a frown, then slam my small locker closed.

"It's my gift." She smirks, then offers an apologetic smile. "But really, though, they probably won't last."

I try to convince myself that what she says might be right.

I surf the net at SBB, trying to find out anything on Nurse Sarah Boll, who, by the way, was way too nicely dressed for a nurse. But maybe that's a big assumption on my part. Everything about her screamed "money".

I'm on all the social networks, searching and finding nothing about her. Not even one profile. I tap my finger by the mouse when Andre walks in.

"You look a little crazy right now. Something wrong?" He sits down beside me and spins in his chair.

"I'm trying to find someone and I think it's pretty weird that they don't have any social media profiles anywhere." I click on another search engine and enter her name again.

Andre pulls his chair closer to me and watches what I'm doing. "Some people just don't trust social media. Maybe she's one of them."

"How do you know it's a she?" I ask suspiciously. He laughs and points to the screen. "Um, Sarah Boll would be a weird name for a dude."

Oh, yeah. Right.

"Who is she, anyway?" he asks as he leans in.

"Just a woman my dad knows," I concede and turn back to the screen. The florescent light above me flickers and I glance up at it, annoyed.

"Oh, a would-be step-mom." Andre nods knowingly. "Been there before. Scar, baby, let me give you a word of friendly advice," he begins.

"She is not a would-be step-mom," I correct and click enter

on my search.

"Well, whatever. But if your dad is interested in someone, I suggest you accept that and don't make it an issue. If you do, it could put a big wedge between you and him."

I turn my chair to face him. "My dad and I are pretty close. I think if I told him I didn't like her, he might be inclined to listen to me." I trust my dad and I almost believe what I'm saying to Andre. Still, I have to admit I have a small doubt building in my head. My father has never been interested in anyone before, so it's hard to know for sure.

"Trust me. No matter how close you think you are to someone, a love interest will most certainly put that to the test. The best thing to do, no matter how badly you hate her, is to simply pretend like you don't."

"Thank you, Doctor Phil," I mutter under my breath.

"You're welcome," he replies with a Texas twang.

TWENTY-FOUR
VIEWING

ON SATURDAY, WE HEAD TO THE FUNERAL HOME IN A specially made, intensely tinted limousine that blocks the sunlight. We drive in silence. Chasem wears a Tom Ford suit and looks rather handsome with his hair combed back. I want to compliment him, but somehow that would spoil the silence, and I feel safe in the quiet. I keep replaying in my head the dreams of being in the sun, and then Chasem's talk about me trying to "claim" Nick. I'm afraid to ask what that means. I want to, but what could he say that would actually make me feel better? If "claiming" is a euphemistic phrase for killing, I don't want to know.

I think about how Chasem had been very reassuring when it came to Cal. He told me I wasn't guilty of being a dark revenant, that my starvation had pushed me into something more primal, and it wasn't my fault. He told me that a million times. Yet, when it came to Nick, he was angry and weird. Was it because Nick is now his helot?

We arrive at the funeral home and walk in under a shaded portico. The building is an old house that has been converted to a funeral home, so there are odd rooms decked out in stiff, floral couches and high-backed chairs, surrounded by dark wood tables with mounds of Kleenex boxes. The scent of lilies hangs heavy in the air, and I almost feel like I can't breathe.

We find the Lighteners waiting in a small receiving room. Hannah stands, wearing a simple black dress, her chestnut hair swept up into a loose chignon. She plays nervously with her tissue, folding it and refolding it. She sees us and a look of relief settles there. Before I know it, she immediately hugs Chasem and takes his hand. Chasem's eyes flicker to their clasped hands and then back up to her eyes, but he doesn't release her grip.

Nick stands beside her, wearing in a simple blue suit that causes his gray eyes to shine. His grim demeanor does not detract from how handsome he is. His curly hair has been parted on the side and tamed flatter than normal. He stands straight, holding his hands in front of himself. Abby huddles close to him. Nick opens his arms for me, and I embrace him. He smells heavenly, like soap and aftershave. His face is smooth, and I involuntarily caress it with my hand.

"Are you my brother's girlfriend?" Abigail asks in a small voice. I grin down at her. Her hair is the same color as Nick and Hannah's, but is naturally highlighted with streaks of caramel brown. Her eyes are clear gray and wide as she regards me.

I lean over. "I am. My name's Scarlett. Nice to meet you." I extend my hand and she shakes it.

"That's a pretty name," she offers.

"So is Abigail," I reply, and she smiles shyly at me, a small flush showing on her cheeks.

A short, balding man with round glasses greets us. "Hello, Mrs. Lightener. Mr. Black." *He knows Chasem?* He shakes both of their hands. "Mr. Lightener is right in here, if you are ready to go in," he offers in a soft, musical voice, indicating a set of sliding doors to our left.

Hannah purses her lips and takes Abigail's hand. The double doors open, revealing a large room lined with neat rows of cushioned chairs. At the front of the room is the coffin. It's opened, and Tim lays there as if he's sleeping, his hands resting peacefully on his stomach.

Hannah stifles a cry and Nick puts his arm around her. "I got you, mom," he whispers to her.

I start to walk up with them when I see Cal's body resting there instead. I release Nick's hand as he walks up with his mom. He turns to me and I shake my head. I glance back up, and Tim's body has returned to the coffin, but I can't get Cal out of my mind. I start to walk out and Chasem gives me a worried look.

"I'm okay. I just...I need air," I say, and run to the front vestibule. I find a high-backed chair and sit. Cal's body comes back into my mind, laying in a pile on the dirt floor of the farmhouse, drained completely of his blood. I killed him. I took a man's life. Did he have kids? Or maybe a significant other who's wondering where he is right now? I know he was a helot, but did he really deserve to die? I know he was holding me captive and starving me, but was that worthy of dying by my hands? I make it to the bathroom just in time to throw up.

I rinse out my mouth and try to calm the nausea. I have a sudden need for blood and think of Nick. I rush to the toilet again to lose what little is left in my stomach.

It takes a moment, but I finally make it back to the sink again and rinse out a second time. My head is buzzing and I don't think I can make it back into that room. I decide the best course of action is to find a quiet room and try to gather myself.

I pull out my phone and text Chasem and then Nick, then slip out of the bathroom. I walk down a long hallway with light wood paneling and spot a small room with a single couch and chair. A part of me starts to think I just want to run away from everything, including Nick, for his own good. What if I lose control and kill him? For the first time in my life, I hate what I am.

It's quiet here in the room, and all I can hear is my

breathing, but my thoughts are loud. I lean down into my hands and push down the tears threatening to come.

I'm sorry, Cal.

I feel a hand on my shoulder and jerk back. Chasem stands there, looking down at me. "Hey, you okay?"

I look back down at my feet. "Yeah, fine."

Chasem sits down beside me and gazes intently at me. "Come on, what's wrong?"

I lean back and meet his eyes. "Did you ever kill anyone? I mean, as a warrior in King Lucian's guard?"

Chasem's eyebrows come down slightly and his eyes flicker. "That's an odd question."

"Well, did you?"

He takes a breath. "Yes," he admits matter-of-factly. "What brought on that question?"

I stare down at the palm of my hand as if I can find some answers there, but there's nothing there but pale skin and destiny lines.

Chasem takes my hand. "Come on, Scarlett, what's going on in your head?"

"Were any of them innocent?"

He frowns. "Innocent? You mean, did I kill innocent people in service to the King? No, never."

"You mean there was never a time when you questioned if what you were doing was right or not?"

"It wasn't my place to question anything, but I never felt like I was asked to do anything questionable under Lucian."

I study his face; his tone catches my attention. "Under Apollo?"

Chasem jumps up and impatiently says, "Come on, Scarlett, this conversation won't get us anywhere. Let's go back."

I stand and let him usher me out. He radiates an odd sort of tension and I want to find out what he's avoiding.

When we make it back to the visitation area, the Lighteners

stand in the vestibule outside. Hannah is blurry-eyed and her cheeks are blotchy. Abby holds onto her mother but her face is dry. Nick sees me and immediately steps up to hug me.

"How are you feeling? Any better?" he asks, gazing intently into my eyes. His lips are pulled tight.

"Yeah, I'm better, thanks." I smile to make it more convincing.

Hannah smiles weakly at me and Chasem. "Thank you again for helping with this, Chasem. Tim looks...almost at peace."

Chasem gives a small smile. "It was nothing, really. Just glad to assist. Hey, people will be here soon. Are you ready?" He approaches her and gently rubs her arm.

"Yes, I think so." She brushes Abby's hair back and takes her hand. "Right, baby?"

Abby nods but doesn't make eye contact.

The doors to the funeral home open and in walk Detectives Tripp and Martinez. They pause and take us all in.

"Good afternoon, Mrs. Lightener. Mr. Black," Martinez says in a cordial tone.

"Detectives," Chasem says. Hannah smiles mildly and nods.

"Any news on my dad's case?" Nick asks.

"Yes," Tripp begins. "The coroner made the determination that it was murder. He didn't accidentally drown."

It's silent for a second and then Nick says, "No way. Someone killed him?"

"That's what it looks like. Mrs. Lightener, can you think of anyone who would want to hurt him?"

Hannah looks taken aback. "No. I mean, he had been gambling, but I couldn't imagine that would cause someone to kill him."

"You'd be surprised," Martinez says. "What kind of gambling was he involved in? Was it with a bookie or at a track?"

"I have no idea. He generally kept those details to himself," Hannah says.

"Do we really have to do this now? Can't you talk to the family later? They are burying a husband and father, for God's sake," Chasem replies sharply.

Tripp seems to look at Chasem for the first time. "It's nice of you to be here with them, Mr. Black."

"I told you before, I'm a close friend of the family," Chasem replies calmly.

"Do you happen to know a," Tripp pulls out a small pad of paper from his inside jacket pocket and glances at it, "Mike Vincent? He says you threatened Mr. Lightener a few weeks ago and also broke his arm. Do you recall that?"

All eyes turn to Chasem. I can tell from Nick and Hannah's reaction that they're surprised by this little bit of news.

Chasem chortles. "I do. But I didn't threaten him. We simply had a conversation. Now, if you have any more questions of me, you can direct them to my attorney. Would you like his name?" Chasem is defiant and unwavering as he gazes at Martinez and Tripp.

"Do you need an attorney, Mr. Black?" Martinez asks.

"No. I've nothing to hide, but if you're going to come to the funeral home and harass the family and accuse me of something outrageous, then we're done doing this the easy way. Now, if you'll excuse me, Mrs. Lightener needs to mourn her husband."

They glare at each other like they're sizing each other up. Finally, Tripp huffs with a strained smile. "Send us your attorney's info then." He nods to Hannah. "Mrs. Lightener. Son." They leave slowly out the door, all the while glancing back at us.

Chasem looks over to Hannah and Nick. "I'm sorry about that."

"Did you really threaten Tim?" Hannah asks quietly.

Chasem blinks a few times. "No. I just talked to him about Nick is all."

"Me?" Nick huffs.

"Yes," Chasem confirms. "It wasn't anything major. Scarlett was with me."

Nick turns on me with an angry look. "Why didn't you tell me?"

What?

"It wasn't anything important," I say, attempting to defend myself.

"Wasn't important?" Nick says incredulously. "I should have been told."

"Stop," Chasem orders. "We can talk about this later, after we've gotten through all of this. So, for the sake of getting through the next few days, can we discuss this later?" He looks around at all of us.

Nick begrudgingly nods. "Fine." But he won't look at me. A sense of dread runs over me.

The rest of the viewing goes off without a hitch, although there's a tense moment when Mike Vincent comes in to show his respects. Chasem stands stoically beside Hannah as Mike says some strained, pleasant words to her. His arm is in a sling, and he must have thought it isn't wise to challenge Chasem in his current condition. Before he leaves, he leans in to say something to Chasem in menace. Chasem only chuckles and nods.

Nick doesn't say much to me the rest of the evening, which feels like the calm before the storm.

TWENTY-FIVE
CHANGES

WE DON'T ATTEND THE GRAVESIDE SERVICE. CHASEM explains that we're both allergic to the sun, a genetic family abnormality. Hannah is so swept up in the ten-sion of what's going on that she doesn't question it.

When I try to talk to Nick about it, he's aloof and simply says it isn't a problem. When we hang up, I stare at my phone and wish things felt different. But they don't.

I arrange to meet up with Brice later in the evening. I can't wait to see my father, but my conversation with Ms. Sarah Boll still sticks heavily in my mind.

Chasem sits in the great room with his foot propped up on the coffee table, staring at the gas fire pit in the middle and dressed in a black t-shirt and jeans. He has a glass of bourbon in his hand and just stares into the flames.

"Hey," I say as I sit down, drawing my legs up to myself.

"Hey," he responds and drinks the remains of his glass. We sit there, watching the flames dance from sapphire to brilliant amber. Chasem leans forward to the bottle resting on the fire pit ledge and pours more bourbon into his glass. He sits back and downs it in one gulp, then taps absently on the glass.

"Did you talk to Hannah or Nick? Is it all over?"

Chasem nods but doesn't look at me. "An hour ago. They're home now. Apparently, they have a bunch of neighbors over there." He waves his hand. "Human stuff."

I glance down at my phone and there's still nothing from Nick. It has me worried, but I try to push it back in my head.

"You know," Chasem begins, "we need to talk about the Alabaster City."

I study his blank face, but he waits for me to reply. "What about it? You said it was too dangerous of a place to ever go, so what is there to talk about?"

Chasem leans up on his knees. "I think we should go there and try."

"Try what? You said yourself Apollo wants me dead and he won't let me Dawn. So why go? You've been preparing me to defend myself against renegades for years now. Why the change of heart?"

It doesn't seem right that he's shifting on me. His sole purpose in my training is defense, not confronting Apollo. My father wants to kill me. It's because of him my mother died in the first place. She fled the Alabaster City to the human world to hide so I could be born. Had she not done that, she most certainly would not have died after I was brought into the world.

"It wasn't only for defense that I've been training you," he pronounces. "I always knew the possibility existed that you might actually stand before Apollo to Dawn. I wasn't sure how it could happen. But I've had some intel from the city and I think maybe I need to reconsider."

I stand up angrily. "He won't just stand there and let me take his blood. He wants me dead!" I scream, and it feels good to let my anger out.

Chasem gazes at me as he laces his fingers together. "He won't have a choice. Brute force is certainly a way to insure it happens."

I look at him sideways. "What are you not telling me? Because, correct me if I'm wrong, Apollo's protected by the best ascended revenant army that's ever existed. Even if we get past them, he'll still be a formidable foe."

"You know, your lack of faith in me is rather offensive," he quips. "I know that city, and that army. I know Apollo even more. I think it would be better to figure out a way to have you Dawn than to have you run for the rest of your life. I don't want that for you," he clarifies, and pours another glass of bourbon.

"But Chase, you've known my entire life I was going to have to run and hide. I have prepared for that for a lifetime. What's changed?" I sit back down and stare at him.

"Just trust me, Scarlett. When it comes to weighing out the risks, this seems the best way to go. Your life would be yours, not subject to any renegade who might happen upon you. Dawned is certainly preferable over being a rogue."

"Say I agree to go, which I'm not saying I do, but if I do, promise me you'll command Nick to stay here."

"I'll consider it."

"Do more than consider it. Do it. I don't want him anywhere near there," I demand.

"I said I'll consider it," he replies with a final tone, his whiskey-colored eyes regarding me harshly.

"Fine. I'm going to sleep," I huff and walk out to my room.

As I lay there trying to go to sleep, I think about the Alabaster City. It's the revenant capital deep in the mountains of Bulgaria. Chasem's told me some stories about what it looked like and how it operates. It actually sounds rather beautiful. There are a few exclusive revenant cities throughout the world, but none rival the Alabaster City.

I try to wrap my mind around the fact that Chasem has changed his mind and that he wants me to confront Apollo. Something's changed for Chasem, and I can't figure out why. Nothing fits in that equation. I need to try to figure out what it is and how to keep Nick from going.

I make it to my apartment later that evening, and Brice isn't there. It concerns me that he isn't waiting on me like always, dinner ready, chess board set up and movies lined up to watch. The air is stale, so I know he hasn't been there yet.

I walk in and close the door, then check out my place. It's been such a long time since I've stayed there, it feels a little foreign. I glance at a small plant on my kitchen counter and frown. It's brown. I summarily drop it into the garbage can.

A knock sounds at the door and I run to open it. I feel as if all the blood has pooled in my feet when I see who it is. Not only Brice stands there, but he has Sarah in tow.

"Hey, baby," Brice says and leans in to kiss me. He holds a bag of Chinese carryout. Nervously, he turns to her. "Honey, this is Sarah Boll, the woman I told you I was seeing."

She looks innocently at me. Her face is a mask of joy. "Oh, Scarlett, I've heard so much about you from your father. I feel as if we know each other already." She takes my hand.

I look up at my father and he's absolutely beaming. "Come in," I say and stand back for them to enter. Sarah is dressed casually this time in jeans and a plain knit top. Much different than the last time I saw her.

I watch as my father ushers her into the apartment and motions for her to sit, but he turns to put the food on the counter. He turns to me, a little pale, and then leans closer. "I hope you don't mind that I asked her to come with me. I really wanted you two to meet. She only knows you're my daughter, nothing else." His brows are pulled down tightly as he purses his lips.

"Just don't let her look in the fridge," I quietly remind him.

"You don't mind, do you, honey?" He's almost apologetic in his tone.

I instinctively hug him, taking in the scent of his aftershave. His arms come around me and I feel safe for a split second. I pull back and regard him. I want so badly to discuss the happenings with Chasem and Nick and the murder of Nick's father. But all of that will have to wait. Now, we'll have only the most benign conversation.

"No, it's okay, Dad. Let me get us some plates."

We eat huddled around my kitchen bar, and Brice talks nonstop about things he and Sarah have been doing and that he's considering teaching again.

My eyebrows shoot up. "Really? You're thinking about going back to NYU?"

Brice stammers, "I am. I should try to do something constructive with my life."

I push around my kung pao chicken with my fork. "But won't you have to move into the city for that?"

Sarah smiles at Brice and he looks sick for a split second. "Well, Sarah—"

"He's going to stay with me. I have an apartment not far from the campus that I don't use unless I'm in town, and it has enough space. Why make him lease an apartment when he can stay there?" She smiles slyly at me, and her blue eyes seem to sparkle.

Everything is moving too fast. My father is moving in with her. I want to scream at them both. There's something serious-ly off about Sarah, or at least, I tell myself that. I wonder if I simply don't like her because she's taking my mother's place in his life. Although, they only knew each other for ten minutes before she died. But he always told me he loved her for the gift of me with which she entrusted him.

"Oh. I see." I find myself getting up to scrape off my plate in the garbage. My stomach is turning and I have to fight down the furious urge for my eyes to change.

"It's a generous offer. Plus, I'd be closer to you. Wouldn't that be nice?" Brice offers behind me.

"Sure...generous." I turn back to them and force a smile. "That was really nice of you, Sarah. Thanks for being so kind to him."

"Oh, that's me, kind to a fault." She beams and reaches over to take Brice's hand.

I sit back down at the counter and let Sarah prattle on about her job as a nurse and how she really doesn't have to work, but choses to. She's rich, apparently. Well, woohoo for her.

Brice hangs on her every word, almost breathlessly waiting for her to say something more. Clearly, he's in love, and I feel a certain sense of guilt over not wanting him to be with someone. Well, honestly, not so much someone, but her. I don't want him with her.

Instead of chess, we end up playing Monopoly. Brice relaxes and starts being playful with her as we go along. She seems almost carefree, but occasionally she stares at me with a fleeting, menacing look, and as soon as it appears, it's gone.

When it hits eleven, Brice stands up. "Well, honey, we have to be heading back to Amherst Ridge."

I nod. I understand that he won't be staying the night, not with her in tow. I have a moment of hatred for her. She's taken some of the few moments I have with him and I almost can't forgive that.

Sarah stands and takes my hand. "It was lovely to meet you, and thank you for letting me join in your time together. Brice and I had been discussing this for quite some time, and I'm glad to see it finally happen."

I walk them to the door when Sarah hugs me. I let my arms dangle, half out of surprise and half out of there is no way in hell I'm going to hug this woman. She finally relents and heads out the open door.

Brice leans into me and holds me close. "I love you, baby girl. More than my own life."

"I love you too, daddy."

He kisses me on the forehead and slips out the door. I watch as they walk down the hall. Brice waves and smiles to me. I watch them get on the elevator and don't stop until the door shuts. Strangely, a part of me wants to sit and sob at saying goodbye to him.

TWENTY-SIX

FORGIVEN

A KNOCK SOUNDS AT MY DOOR AS I SIT AT MY KIT-chen counter, catching up on my homework. I glance over to the clock and it's 3:00 am. I frown. Who would be at my door? I grab a longsword from behind my couch and glance in the peephole to see the back of Nick's head.

I open the door and stare blankly at him. "Do you know what time it is?"

He turns to me and his eyes flicker to the blade in my hand then back up to me. "Worried about something?" He walks past me to come into the apartment. I close the door, latch it, then put away the sword in its sheath behind the couch.

"Hello? Close to Dawning, here," I remind him. "What are you doing up at this time of the morning?"

He walks in a small circle and brushes his hand through his hair. "Of course I know what time it is. I just...I...I don't know." Nick sits sloppily down in a chair and rubs his eyes. "Do you have anything to drink?"

"Sure." I retrieve a water bottle for him and come to sit across from him on the couch. "I've been wondering how you're doing," I say absently.

He takes a drink of his water and puts the cap back on. "I'm not sure how I'm doing. Things are blurry around the edges right now. I couldn't sleep, so I decided to take a walk. Somehow my feet led here."

I reach out and take his hand, and he doesn't pull away. "I'm sorry I didn't tell you about Chasem going to visit your dad at that bar. I wasn't trying to keep it from you, exactly."

His brow furrows and he stares at me. "You didn't volunteer it, either," he reminds. "Why?"

I pick at the couch fabric with my free hand. "I don't know. Your dad had beaten the crap out of you and Chasem just wanted to let Tim know he couldn't keep doing that."

Nick considers it. "Do you think he killed my dad?"

"No," I immediately answer. "He might have wanted to kick his ass, but he wouldn't just kill him. Human life means too much to him."

"Because he's pale," Nick clarifies.

I think about that. It's true, Chasem is a pale revenant, but it's so much more than that. I don't think Chasem would have killed Tim. Beating him is another issue altogether, but I decide not to voice that. "Yes, that has something to do with it. But it has more to do with the fact that he's a decent guy and he just wouldn't do that."

Nick squeezes my hand. "I'm sorry I got mad at you for not telling me. My emotions are all over the place right now. I don't know what made me think Chasem would be capable of that."

He pulls me up and over to him and I willingly sit in his lap. His arms come around me and he buries his head into my shoulder. I start to comb my fingers through his hair gently. He makes a small noise of approval.

"Forgiven?" he asks against me.

"Forgiven," I whisper.

We stay locked in each other's embrace. His strong arms are around me in such a protective way that it starts to settle me. I lay my cheek on his head and continue to comb through his curls.

We don't speak, and after a time, Nick whispers, "I love you, Scarlett. So much it scares me." He turns his gray eyes up to look at me. "You're the only thing that makes sense to me right now."

I let my finger trail down his cheek and I smile at him. "You're going to get through this. They're going to find out who killed your father, and your life will start to take on a routine again."

"Doubtful. Helot, remember?" he reminds me, pointing to himself.

I tighten my lips. "I know, and believe me, I'm so angry that Chasem did that. But I know he won't lord it over you. So you can live a normal human life."

Nick shakes his head. "No, I won't let you face this alone. If you're going to be hunted by renegades, I'm going to help protect you. I promise that you won't be alone."

I get up out of his lap and gaze out the dark window. I turn to him and try to find the words to explain. "Chasem wants to go to the Alabaster City," I say so quickly my words almost jumble together.

"What?" Nick asks. "I thought your blood father wanted you dead and wasn't going to let you Dawn."

"Well," I begin, "that's true. But Chase seems to think that, somehow, we'll be able to confront Apollo and somehow it will happen. I will Dawn." I feel a panic settle in over the thought, and my apartment feels entirely too small. I have so much doubt. I've grown up with the warnings from my mother, echoed through Brice and Chasem's own warnings, about Apollo wanting to kill me. How Chasem figures we'll get him to agree to let me drink his blood seems an impossibility.

"When?" Nick asks and he's right beside me. His hands caress down my arms.

My breath hitches and I lean back into his strong body. "My birthday is in a week. So, I need to be there on that day. I don't know, I'm not convinced this is the right thing. This is just such a one-eighty from where we've been heading. I think it's too dangerous for me to go."

Nick's lips are at my neck and he kisses me softly. Goosebumps rise up on my skin and his warm breath tickles as he speaks. "I won't let anything hurt you, I promise. I'll do everything in my power to protect you."

I turn my body around to stare up into his unbelievably handsome face. His eyes bore into mine, the soft light from the lamp's reflection giving his face a soft glow. "I know you would. But I'm going into a revenant world, and we're much stronger than humans. I don't want you to be in harm's way facing one and being forced to fight. A revenant could easily crush you."

His eyebrows raise and he half smiles. "Strength doesn't always win in a fight. Haven't you been listening to your uncle in training? I mean, I'm a human, and even I get that."

"But still. No human can stand against a revenant and win. Humans are fragile."

"Listen to me, Scar. I'm going. If you head to that city, you have to take me, period. No argument, no question. Understand?"

I nod, but I honestly know that I won't let him go and will have Chasem order him as his ceannard to stay. Nick leans in slowly and kisses me. "Good. Glad we settled that."

He just doesn't realize how settled it is.

The next day, I text Brice as I ride the subway to school. I've been thinking about the evil Sarah Boll. God, I never saw this coming. I want my dad to be happy, but I think I feel that way in the abstract way, not the specific 'woman all over him' way.

I consider what Andre told me a few days ago, to just act like you like them and go on. But I hate that option. I need to know my father is okay and that no one is going to hurt him.

The subway lights flash off and on as we speed off through the dark tunnels. I hate the smell of mechanical grease and body odor I sometimes encounter when I ride. Rush hour makes it even worse. I get crammed into every space, one inch away from someone else, who may or may not have showered that day.

I stand grasping onto a sticky metal pole, wishing for cool air to breathe. I happen to glance over to the guy next to me and he grins. He feels too close for comfort, but I need to live with it. Everyone is too close for comfort. The small Hispanic woman in front of me stares off into space, trying hard not to pay attention to us. Then I feel it.

A hand caresses my backside. I turn to see the guy leering at me with a sick grin. I reach down, grab his hand, and squeeze, just enough to break a few fingers. He lets out a stream of curses and tries to back away from me, but the jostling of the train and the close quarters of the passengers send him sprawling onto the floor in a heap.

He holds his hand for a minute, desperately trying to keep from being stepped on. Someone takes pity on him and helps him up to standing, but he makes sure to stay well away from me.

After a few moments, the train comes to a halt and the lights flicker, but we're not yet at our stop. There's a collective groan from the passengers as the engineer's voice comes on the overhead speakers. "Sorry, folks, there seems to be a mechanical problem. We're working as quickly as possible to get this fixed. Try to bear with us until we can get moving again."

I sigh and look down at my phone. Thank God for train wifi. I send a quick text to Missi to tell the school that the train broke down and that I'll be there as soon as I can. Scrolling back through my messages, I see that Brice has still not replied to me, which is very odd for him. He's typically pretty quick to hit back.

I glance around the train and am met with the hateful eyes of the guy whose fingers I broke. I offer him an equally hateful grin. See? Keep your hands to yourself and nothing like that will happen again. Something catches my attention in the darkness outside the train—glowing eyes.

My heart stops. I hear voices in my head again, urging me to come out. Oh God, renegades are in the tunnels. I glance around and no one else sees them except a small girl with long brown hair. She burrows her face into her mother's side in fear.

A loud bang sounds from the top of the train and everyone shrieks. We all look up to the ceiling of the car when the lights go out. Someone screams, and then it sounds like someone's running claws down the exterior metal of the car.

I have to get off this train. If they attempt to come in here, they'll be desperate enough to get to me that they'll kill everyone in this car.

I start pushing to get through the crowd to the end of the car. I make it out the door right as the emergency lighting engages.

I glance out into the dark tunnel before me and see yellow-ish light illuminating a section about a yard away. To my right is a completely black offshoot. I step down the train stairs and instinctively pull out my blades, holding them to my side as I walk. My backpack gets discarded quickly to free myself up as I go.

The ground is moist and makes a squishing sound as I walk. The ambient noise of the subway tunnels masks most of it, but the element of surprise is gone. Glowing eyes appear deep back into the darkness. I hear a rumbling laugh to my left.

"Why are you guys hunting me? I haven't Dawned," I yell as I walk towards them. I listen to the density of the air, trying to figure out how many of them there are. It feels like three. I will my eyes to change and the tunnel lights up in odd heat signatures. My count was right. There are three—two men and one woman. And, much to my chagrin, multiple rats as they scurry along the edge of the tunnel. As one of the men shifts, I see a fourth man deep in the cavern, standing with his arms folded. His heart beats steady and sure, not rattled by the potential battle. The other three nervously shift and their hearts pound hard and fast.

"Attack," a deep, familiar voice shouts from far back in the tunnel. "But do not kill her."

TWENTY-SEVEN
ATTEMPT

THE THREE RUSH ME. THE WOMAN SPORTS A WHIP and keeps testing it against the air in loud, snapping menace. One man has a net in his hand, and the other has a long cattle prod.

They surround me, and I realize from their scent they're not revenants, but humans. Helots, no doubt. But who do they belong to? I glance back to the shadowed figure at the end of the tunnel. He doesn't move but stands with his arms folded. The humans walk around me, circling.

For a moment, I stop and breathe slowly to center myself as Chasem's taught me. Then, engage the immediate threat and use whatever momentum I can to get to the next.

Net, whip, cattle prod.

Net, whip, cattle prod.

I choose the net, because if he gets me down, I'm captured. I rush him, and as he lifts the net to cover me, his movements are slow like all humans' are. I duck low, slice the tendon behind his knee, and he buckles to the ground. I rise up and hurl a knife towards the woman with the whip, and it embeds itself in her chest. She crumples to the ground.

"Come on, make this a challenge, would you?" I taunt.

Cattle prod picks up the whip the girl dropped and stares at me, holding a weapon in both hands. I watch him so closely that I don't see the first attacker reach up to me and sweep my feet out from under me. I land hard and lose sight of the other human man, but I feel him. The prod catches, and my back arches painfully away from the source.

I roll right before the whip would have made contact with me. I'm up on my feet and I steal a glance to see if the man in the back has moved, but he hasn't. He watches like a sick voyeur.

The first man makes it to his feet, hopping on his one good leg. He moves sloppily and tries hard to hold the net up. He glances back in fear at the man in the back of the tunnel. Either that is his ceannard, or someone who will punish him with death if he fails. The fact that the dark figure's eyes are glowing tells me he's a revenant.

"Let's just take you out of the equation," I whisper, and hurl my blade towards hopping man's good leg. It lands firmly in his thigh. That's all it takes. He cries out loudly and lays in a puddle beside the dead woman.

Me and cow prod stare each other down. Sweat drips from his thick hair, running in trails down his face. I step back to create some distance between us and to keep out of the crumpled man's reach.

I feel in my belt behind me and locate a throwing star and another blade. I need to make quick work of the last human so I can get out of here. I rear back to throw the star when the man rushes me in a burst. It's enough to distract me that I don't release my weapon. I've just enough time to push the prod away and land a hard punch to his face. Blood rushes out in a burst. As he grabs his face, I bring my knee up into his midsection and he bends over, trying to get air into his lungs. I come down on the back of his neck with my elbow and knock him out.

Standing among the pile of humans, I look back to the glowing eyes of the revenant. "Chasem Black taught you well," he remarks and walks slowly towards me.

"You must not be too bright. I haven't Dawned yet. It's illegal to kill me and of no benefit whatsoever." I breathe in, trying to catch my breath, and my fingers find my next set of blades. I step backwards to keep the distance between me and the man.

"To use your own phrase, you must not be too bright, either. I don't want to kill you." He eventually makes it into the light and my heart flutters.

Ryker.

"I need you alive." He grins wide, then runs towards me. My reaction is to run as well. I don't get far. His arms are around me, tightly embracing me in an iron grip.

I bring my foot down on his and at the same time slam my head back hard into his face. He staggers back, and I turn to land a windmill kick into his face. He catches my leg before I make contact and jerks up hard. I find myself suddenly flat on my back. I bring my other leg up hard into his manly parts. He crumples. I scurry up and run. I'm not far from the train when I feel something hit me in the shoulder. The most excruciating pain radiates through me.

The train starts up and slowly moves again. I force my legs to move faster, catching my bag on the way, and jump onto the train's stairs. I'm at the top of the stairs when the train picks up speed. Ryker staggers out from the tunnel and stops, leaning over on his hands and knees, to see me speed away on the train.

I close my eyes and lay my head back against the cold metal door for just a second. I have to figure out how to get the blade out of my shoulder. I reach back and try to work it free. Each tug sends so much pain through me I have to fight the desire to throw up. It takes a few tries, but I eventually get it out.

Blood rushes down my arm and forms a pool at the bottom of my hand. I find my phone and call for help.

"Stay still," Chasem orders as he prods around on my shoulder. "If you don't, I'll sedate you," he warns in a low voice.

"Testy, testy," I remark. "But stop pushing around on it. It hurts."

"I don't expect it to be painless. Stop being so mouthy." Chasem pushes on my back. Nick stands beside him like a dutiful nurse.

I close my eyes and grit through the pain. Eventually, he stops.

"I don't think it hit anything important." The familiar prick of the numbing medicine hits my shoulders.

"It was Ryker," I say calmly. "He didn't want to kill me. It was all about capture, for sure."

"He was the same one as before, right?" Nick asks.

Chasem's breath is on my bare shoulder as he sews up the wound. "Yes," he replies and says nothing more.

Nick comes around to stand in front of me and holds my hand. "I wish we knew what he wanted besides kidnapping you." He kisses my hand, then traces small circles on the back of it.

"Can you hand me my phone?" I ask Nick, and he obliges. I take it and scroll through my messages. Still nothing from Brice. "Chasem? Have you heard anything from Brice today?"

"No, but that's not unusual. It isn't like we chat all the time. Only if you're involved."

"Well, did you call him yet about this?" My heart flutters slightly as I wonder why Brice hasn't texted or called me.

"Not yet. I wanted to make sure just how badly you were hurt, and then I was going to call him. Better to have all the info before I do. Otherwise, he gets incredibly freaked out."

I nod. It's true. For all of Brice's calmness, he has an inherent need to know every fact of a situation, and he doesn't take vagueness well.

"He's moving in with someone," I blurt out. I'm not sure

why I think that's important.

"Oh?" Chasem asks, detached.

"Yep. Some nurse he met in Amherst Ridge. Apparently, Brice is going to be teaching again at NYU, and she has a place close by in the city."

I know how my voice sounds; it's laced with anger and frustration. But honestly, Brice dating anyone feels wrong. Do all kids feel like this? I consider whether I would feel any differently had it been Chasem. I conclude that I would probably feel just as frustrated and protective. But they can't be alone forever. A pang of guilt runs through me. They both have been so focused on getting me past my Dawning that they've probably given up on a life of their own.

"What's her name?" Chase asks as he cuts the string from the last stitch.

"Sarah Boll. And don't try to find her online, because she doesn't even have a social media account."

"Hmm." Chasem tapes padding to my shoulder. "I'll get you a sling." I hear him move away and I pull my shirt back over that shoulder.

Nick stares at me and smiles weakly. "You sound really upset about Brice moving in with someone."

"I know. I'm trying not to be, Nick, I really am. But that's my dad, you know?"

Nick looks down at his hands. "Yeah, I know. Parents mean so much, good or bad."

We sit in the quiet of the training room, just holding hands and comforting each other. I study Nick's face; his square jaw and full lips are set as he concentrates on something. His brows are slightly pulled down, and the light dances off his gray eyes.

Chasem drops something into my lap. "Here, put that on."

I struggle to figure out how to get the brace around me, and Chase and Nick both work to get it on just right. I feel almost tied up and I don't like the feeling. There's a prick on my shoulder, and I see Chasem giving me a shot. "Antibiotic," he says by way of an explanation. "Come on, let's go find out about Sarah Boll." He motions for us to follow him into the elevator and I feel almost excited.

"You don't feel like we're invading his space by finding out about her?"

"Hell no," he says, entering a code on the elevator, then hitting the ninth floor.

Ninth floor?

"He's family, like you, and I have to protect you. If she isn't on social media, that sends a warning signal to me. Plus, I know she came to see you."

My mouth drops open. Eddie. Of course. "Does Eddie tell you everything?"

"Anything important that involves you. Of course, I draw the line at him complaining about disappearing to save a human." He eyes Nick and almost smiles. "But yeah, Eddie's my helot and you're my niece. Do the math."

Why I thought Chasem wouldn't be watching everything I do seems like a stupid thought. He probably even has a tracking device on me.

"You haven't chipped me, have you?" I demand.

He seems taken aback. "Even I have standards. Besides, they don't work all that great, anyway."

TWENTY-EIGHT

FIONA

WE STOP ON THE NINTH FLOOR, WHICH IS ONE I'VE never been on. It opens to a long hallway with several locked doors. Chasem leads the way to the end, enters a code on a keypad, and scans his hand on a large wall scanner. The lock disengages. When he opens the door, my mouth drops open. It's like we've entered NASA territory. Rows of black-encased server farms are lined up on either side of us.

"Hells bells," Nick breathes as he looks around.

Chasem walks to a large desk facing a wall of huge flat-screen monitors. He sits and enters a password, holding his thumb over a fingerprint scanner.

"So, let's find out who this Sarah Boll is." Several of the monitors come to life. "Hello, Fiona," Chasem says.

"Hello, sir. Are you well today?" a female voice replies.

"I am, Fiona. I'm in need of some assistance, please." Chasem sits back in his chair.

"Of course, sir. What can I do for you?" Fiona asks.

"I'm looking for an individual named Sarah Boll, a nurse who currently resides in Amherst Ridge, New York, and also owns property in New York City. Please pull up anything you can."

"Any middle initial?" Fiona asks pleasantly.

"Unknown," he replies.

"I feel like I'm in the matrix," Nick says to no one in particular.

"Sir, would you like me to hold the results until you are alone? I see Scarlett Ellis and Nicholas Lightener are with you."

"No, Fiona, you can tell me with them present."

"Very good, sir. Please give me a moment to conduct my search."

Chasem turns to me. "It won't take her long. Fiona will find out anything that exists on the woman."

"I had no idea this was here. You told me that floors three through nine were storage." I motion around me. "Were you ever going to tell me about this?"

"There wasn't a need to before now. But technically, this is storage. This is where I store Fiona."

"Sir, you don't store me. I believe we established I live here. Floor nine is mine."

"You're right, Fiona. Sorry about that," Chasem corrects. He looks at me apologetically. "She is the best in artificial intelligence right now. She runs this building and monitors various interests of mine."

"Like Neville Treatment Center?" I ask.

"Yes," he confirms.

"What's Neville Treatment Center?" Nick asks as he looks between me and Chasem.

"Sir? I have the results," Fiona interrupts.

"Go," he commands.

"There is no individual by the name of Sarah Boll either in the metropolitan New York city area or New York State. I was unable to locate medical licensing or driving records as well. Do you want me to expand my search beyond the state of New York?"

"Oh, God," I breathe.

Chasem rubs his lips and leans forward in his chair. "No. But can you locate the security footage for Perkalicious on

Friday night around seven in the evening?"

"Yes, sir. One moment," she answers.

Chasem looks to me. "It doesn't mean anything yet."

"But you have to admit it's really weird. Like really weird." I pull out my phone and check my messages. Still nothing.

Dad, please call me right away, I text him.

"Are you ready to review the footage, sir? Would you like me to begin with Scarlett entering the premises?" Fiona asks.

Chasem glances at me and shrugs. "Yes, go ahead." The footage starts with me walking in and Eddie motioning me to the back table. The view changes to another camera, and Sarah sits there, demurely watching me. "Fiona, freeze that and run facial recognition against it."

"Yes, sir."

"God, she wanted me to accept them having a relationship. I wish now I would have punched her in the face like I wanted to before."

"I know her," Nick offers.

We both turn to him and he shrugs. "I don't know her name, but I swear I've seen her outside my house a few times. I thought she lived close by. She might have even talked to my mom once."

My heart pounds hard. This was not an innocent meeting for her and Brice in that grocery store. She's injected herself into his life, but why? I can't understand why. Unless... I stop my thinking there. I won't accept where my mind's going.

"Sir?" Fiona says.

"Yes?"

"I located an old record from fifteen years ago that appears to be a younger version of her. Would you like that possible hit? It is a 95 percent probability match."

"Yes, go ahead and bring it up."

Before us appears the records of a Hartlyn Jane McKee, a sixteen-year-old runaway juvenile record. One monitor has her mug shot and one of the other monitors has a list of her committed crimes. The list includes prostitution, theft, and various other petty crimes.

"That's her," I say and point to the screen. "That's Sarah Boll."

"You're sure?" Chasem asks.

"Yes, absolutely." I hold tighter to Nick's hand. My heart feels like it's going to pound out of my chest. I have to remind myself to breathe.

"Fiona, is there anything more on her in the public record?"

"No, sir. She has no more records after that one. Would you like me to search elsewhere?"

He pauses for a moment. "Yes, search all revenant helot records for anything that has her in it."

"Yes, sir," Fiona replies pleasantly.

"There are helot records?" Nick asks before I have a chance to do the same.

"Yes, helots are required to be registered to enter a reve-nant city, almost like second-class citizens," Chasem confirms. "But none of my helots are registered because I have never had any intentions of legally going back into a revenant city. I don't want anyone I'm connected with to be on their radar."

Nick lets out a heavy breath. "Good."

"Sir?" Fiona asks.

"Go," he answers.

"I have found a helot record that matches Hartlyn McKee to a Ryker Grier. She is on the helot registry for all revenant cities. Would you like me to look up all known records for Ryker Grier?"

Chasem presses his lips together. "No, Fiona, that won't be necessary. I know who Ryker is." His fist slams down hard on the desk, causing everything on it to jump. He pulls out his phone and starts dialing, listening for a few minutes before speaking. "Hey, Brice, this is Chase. Listen, call me as soon as you get this, okay? This is urgent. Make sure you're alone when you call. Thanks." When he hangs up, he glances to me.

"This is bad," Chasem utters. "We need to find him."

He gets up. "Fiona, we are going to head out to Amherst Ridge. Please monitor for any type of activity on the internet anywhere for either Hartlyn or Ryker. Please send it to my phone."

"Yes, sir," she replies. "Safe journey."

It's a three-hour drive to Amherst Ridge. All three of us are on pins and needles, and time seems like an enemy. Conversation is quick and choppy, like talking more than a few words would somehow curse the trip. Chasem and I both check our phones a million times for a reply from Brice, but we find nothing.

Chasem has the car up to a hundred miles an hour at times. His Audi A8 moves fluidly in out of traffic, the speed hardly noticeable. His headlights cut through the black night with just enough time to see the blur of a vehicle, which, as soon as we see it, gets left in our wake. We have to find Brice. Even though my neurotic, controlling uncle has cameras fixed on the outside of Brice's place, he wants to go there and look around. To smell is probably a better estimation of it.

My shoulder throbs, but I push that out of my mind. Memories of Brice flood my mind almost like I'm trying to prepare myself for the worst. I rub my eyes. No, he's not hurt. He's okay. We will find him. But it's still difficult to reassure myself.

Nick's hands rub my neck from the back seat. "Try not to think about it. We're going to find him and things are going to be okay," he says.

My phone rings and I almost can't get to it quick enough. I look at the screen and see that it's Missi. Crap. I consider not answering it but decide at the last minute to go ahead and do it.

"Hello?"

"Hey, Scarlett, are you okay? You never made it to school. Last I heard from you, you wanted me to let them know you were going to be late, but you never showed." Her voice is hesitant and laced with concern.

"Oh God, I'm sorry, Missi. I actually dislocated my shoulder trying to get off of the stuck train and Chasem had to take me to the hospital. My arm's in a sling."

"No way. You have been so clumsy lately. What's that about?"

I laugh. "Well, my uncle says it's growing pains. It makes all teenagers clumsy, apparently."

"You more than others. Well, I have your homework assignments. I'll email them to you, okay?"

"Thank you, Missi. I appreciate it."

"Well, I won't keep you. Call me tomorrow, okay?" she asks, hopeful.

"I will. See ya."

"See ya," she says and I end the call.

"Good cover," Chasem says as he swings past a corvette that looks like it's crawling in comparison to our speed.

"I just realized I probably need to pull out of school, don't I? I mean, if I go to the Alabaster City? I really wanted to graduate," I say with an air of petulance.

"Maybe you still can. But for this year, yeah, maybe you finish out homeschooled through Excelsior. You too, Nick," Chasem says, glancing back into the rear view mirror.

"I am graduating this year," Nick reminds him.

"Oh," Chasem acknowledges. "Well, we'll figure it out. I don't want you to miss doing that."

"My mom doesn't, either. She'd throw a blood clot if I don't graduate. She agreed to let me stay with you and transfer, but she won't agree to me not finishing school this year."

Chasem nods thoughtfully. "I'm not sure how we do this. I've never had a helot this young, but don't you worry. There's an answer for this."

"Okay," Nick says in surrender.

The rest of the trip is quiet. I send three more texts to Brice in the hope that he'll see how worried I am and will answer.

Daddy, please be okay. Please.

He's always reassured me that he'll protect me, and I've never even considered the fact that he would need protection, too. My human world and revenant world are colliding in ways I never thought possible.

We pull up into the driveway of the cabin and the singular light illuminates the porch, but the interior is black. The car is hardly stopped when I bolt out. "Scarlett, wait!" Chasem yells, but I ignore him and dash up the stairs. I try the door and it's locked. I search for the spare key under the ugly ceramic frog I made when I was seven, then unlock the door. I start to rush in when I feel an arm pull me back.

"Dammit, wait!" Chasem says angrily in my ear. He pushes me back and pulls out a gun from a holster under the back of his shirt. He looks in, then disappears into the darkness. It's the longest moment waiting for him to search the small cabin. Chasem returns and turns on the interior light. "Empty," he pronounces.

When we go in, it's like I've been transported in time. My bed rests over to the left, still made with a purple comforter and my childhood stuffed animal, a well-worn donkey, resting spread-eagle on it. My father's bed to the right is neatly made. I look around, then walk to the bathroom just past his bed and turn on the light. He's nowhere to be seen.

The air is hot and still, like no one's been there for a while. The air conditioner hasn't been turned on, which he would definitely have used if he'd been here recently at all.

Chasem lifts a piece of paper off the front table and reads it silently.

"What is that?" Nick asks, and I rush over to look around Chasem.

It's a note scribbled in a rough hand.

'Hello, my Captain. How far we have moved on from those former relations. Are you feeling nostalgic? Yeah, neither am I. If you're reading this, it means I failed to get Scarlett Bramstall. She is very illusive. Kudos to you for training her so well. But make no mistake, I will get her.

As you can gather from this little missive, I've got the human she actually calls father. We're taking him to the capital, and if you want to see him alive again, you will bring Scarlett there. Do not test my resolve. I will kill him if you do not obey.

If you're reading this, Scarlett, I suggest you have your uncle bring you. I would hate to send you your human's head in a box. If you want to confirm he's alive, call this number.'

A number is listed beneath the text. I start to dial when Chasem stops me. "Let me."

"But Chase—"

"Stop! Let me," he demands. My heart feels like it wants to jump out of my chest. Chasem dials the number and then puts it on speaker.

It rings for a few moments, and then Ryker answers. "Well, well, Captain Black. Nice to hear from you."

"Put him on," Chasem demands with no preamble.

"Hello to you, too. Do you have Apollo's daughter with you?"

"Yes," I interject, and Chasem motions for me to be quiet.

"Nice move you pulled earlier. That's twice you've eluded me and thinned out my helot population. You really need to be nicer to them. It's so hard to find good help these days."

"Put Brice Ellis on the phone," Chasem barks.

"What? No please? I'd reconsider your manners if I were you," Ryker growls and I hear Brice scream.

"Daddy!" I shout.

"Come on, Chasem. You know how to ask nicely. Don't make me hurt him again," Ryker threatens.

"Please," Chasem grinds out.

"Thank you. Here you go." I can hear the smile in his voice.

"Scarlett?" Brice painfully asks.

"I'm here, Daddy," I cry.

"Are you okay, Brice?" Chasem asks.

"Yes. In a little pain, but not permanently hurt—"

His voice is cut off by Ryker. "That will change if you do not bring Scarlett to the Alabaster City and the royal court. Do I make myself clear?"

"Don't do it!" Brice yells, and I hear someone hit him.

Chasem paces. "Damn you, Ryker. Damn you to hell."

Ryker laughs a throaty laugh and replies, "You first." And the line goes dead. Chasem stands there with his fists drawn in tight, his face a crimson burn.

I collapse on the bed and start to cry. I feel Nick's hand on my back. "He's alive, Scarlett. Don't give up hope. We'll get him. We will."

I hold onto my midsection. My insides feel like they're going to completely fall out if I don't. In that moment, I have a flash of a younger Brice staring down at me, holding a bloody baby. I see hands reach up for the baby and then I can feel a slight prick of pain as the baby bites me. Then I hear my own strangled words say, "I love you, Scarlett."

I sit back and stare at Chasem. I don't know how to make sense of it, and a part of me pushes it out of my head because we have bigger things to worry about.

We need to find Brice, and soon.

TWENTY-NINE
OFF TO THE MOTHERLAND

CHASEM IS A BLUR OF ACTIVITY THE NEXT COUPLE OF days, securing a plane for us and setting up things for the Neville Treatment center and all his holdings. I don't pretend to understand it all. He's able to get forged passports for Nick and me. When he brings them to us, I'm angry.

"Nick can't go," I scream at Chasem. The idea of him around a whole city of revenants is scary. Not all who live in the city are pale; some are most assuredly dark.

"Haven't we had this conversation before? He's going. If I try to keep him from going, he'll figure out a way to make it there and that won't be good. So drop it."

I almost fall on my knees before Chasem. "Please. I couldn't take it if another person I loved was in danger because of me. Can you order him as a ceannard? Have him kidnapped? Something. Please, I'm begging you."

Chasem's face softens. "I wish I could say that any of that would work. I'm sorry, Scarlett. The best thing we can do is to make sure he we keep an eye on him."

I swallow hard as a lump forms in my throat. "If any harm comes to him..."

Chasem pulls me into a hug. "Have some faith in me, Scar. I'll do my best to keep him safe." I hold tightly to him and fight to keep from crying. So much is on the line here. Brice's life,

Chasem's, Nick's, and finally, mine.

We pull apart and Chasem goes down to the ninth floor to talk to Fiona. I stare at my fake passport. I am now Arabella Prince and Nick is Brian Jones. It looks very official. Chasem's traveling name is Charles Prince.

Nick arrives a short time later with a duffel bag full of clothes. He sees me sitting at the bar and comes to sit beside me.

I glance at him and try to smile. "Hey," I say weakly.

"Hey, yourself. I don't like how worried you look. We're going to get to Brice, and everything is going to be okay. Trust me."

I stare down at my hands. "You have no idea what we're about to walk in on. The Alabaster City is the capital for revenants. I've never been myself, but I can't imagine having a human among them is a safe thing."

"I'm a helot, so, from my understanding, that means I have some sort of rights or protections there. I think you're worrying for nothing. Trust me." Nick rubs my arms. "Come here," he breathes and pulls me off the chair and into his arms. I go willingly. I wrap my arms around him and press my hands against his strong back. My head rests against his chest and I close my eyes, inhaling his perfectly succulent scent.

My muscles begin to relax as I hold him. He is my talisman against everything wrong in my life.

Bite.

The word comes unbidden to my mind and I jump back and stare into his confused face. "I'm sorry. I just...I don't know."

"It's okay," he whispers and leans in to press a soft, endearing kiss on my lips. "We're going to get through this, you'll see."

I nod and hope he's right.

Emma arrives at Chasem's apartment before we leave. She

hugs me hard and smiles. "Don't worry about anything. Everything is going to be fine," she tries to reaffirm.

"I hope so." We look at each other for a few minutes.

Chasem hands her some credit cards and notes. "If you need anything, here you go. Fiona's number is on there too, if you can't reach me. She's very resourceful for an A.I." Chasem looks very intense as he gazes at Emma. She takes what he offers and nods stoically.

"So, she's staying here at your place?" I ask Chasem, a little confused. He gazes at Emma and then back to me with a nod.

"I want someone here while I'm gone," he confirms.

"What about Eddie?" I ask as he moves around the apartment, getting us ready to depart.

"He eats all my food," Chasem says with a half-smile, and Emma nods like it's a fact.

She hugs me again and, to my surprise, she hugs Nick. Nick is surprised too and awkwardly pats her on the back.

I stare out the jet's window as we fly through the dark night. My insides are jittery and unsettled. I worry about Brice. If they've hurt him, I will shed my pale revenant vow and kill them all, slowly and painfully. Tears threaten to come, and I push them back with every bit of will I have.

"Here," Nick says as he sits beside me. He places a glass of blood in a concave cup holder on the table in front of me. "Chasem says you need to drink this."

"Thanks," I say weakly. I know I need to keep myself fully fed, but nothing sounds good. "Where is he?"

"Up talking to the pilot. Pretty sweet ride, huh? I've never been on a private jet before." Nick glances around, wide-eyed. "Just how much money does Chasem have?"

I shrug. "No idea. I know that the Neville Treatment Center is just one of his various companies. He owns a lot of them."

"Sweet," Nick says appreciatively. "He said this jet belongs to his company, but he didn't really get into details."

I reach out and take the glass of blood. I take a sip and it has an odd taste. Not bad, just odd. I take a couple big drinks and then set it back down.

"Chasem says there are bunks towards the back if we wanted to sleep. We still have a few hours to go."

"I'm not sleepy." I turn to look back out the window. I wonder what's happening to Brice right now. I can't lose my father. I just can't.

Nick takes my hand and gives it a squeeze. "Neither am I."

I turn to look at him and his concerned eyes. I want to say something meaningful, but I have no words. Glancing back to the dark night, I watch the clouds go by beneath us like specters in the night.

We arrive at the Kolyu Ganchevo airport in Bulgaria. "Airport" is actually a euphemist term for it. It's a stark place, set out in the middle of nowhere. It consists of one large building and a few smaller hangers. Soldiers are scattered around, guarding the larger building with several doors working as "terminals". Surprisingly, they do have a customs processing area, and we make it through without a hitch. I suspect it's because Chasem paid off everyone who came to mind. The airport reminds me of a ghost town. A car waits for us, and we take off driving towards the Alabaster City.

I opt to sit in the back with Nick as Chasem drives. He puts his arm around me and we both look out the dark windows as the landscape furiously speeds by. We've left the windows down, and the cool air of evening rushes in and caress our faces. It feels refreshing, and even though I'm exhausted from the long flight, I have no desire to close my eyes.

Almost three hours later, we drive up a rocky dirt road and Chasem navigates slowly, the headlights bouncing around like someone running with a flashlight. Eventually, we make it up the road and arrive at what appears to be a deserted, rustic cabin.

"Stay here," Chasem orders as he gets out. He stands outside the car, holds out his hands, and turns. After a few moments, someone appears beside him with a weapon drawn. I lean down to take in the sight of the man. He's bald and has strangely designed tattoos in an odd arrangement on his head. His neck reveals a Dawning mark in crimson. He looks Chasem over like he's trying to decide where to begin. If he wants to disarm Chasem, good luck. He'll be at it all night.

Eventually, another man walks into the light. He's older, with long salt-and-pepper-colored hair and an unruly beard of the same color. His cheeks are round and rosy, and his eyes are so pale blue they almost look devoid of color. When he gets to the bald man, he gently forces him to lower the gun, then walks to Chasem and hugs him. Chasem slaps him hard on the back a few times and then turns to face us, motioning for us to get out.

I make it around the car and walk towards Chasem. The two men drop to their knees in front of me. Confused, I look at my uncle.

"Dietrich, no need to bow. You're making her uncomfortable."

Dietrich glances up my way. "It's an honor, Princess. My apologies. I didn't recognize you at first. Please accept my humble apologies. Truly," Dietrich says in a deeply accented voice.

"My name is Scarlett and I'm not a princess," I clarify. Dietrich looks to Chasem for guidance.

He shrugs as he helps Dietrich to stand. "If she doesn't want you to bow, take that as an order," he says. Dietrich nods, then reaches over to the bald man. "Stand up, you fool. Did you not hear her?"

"Princess, huh?" Nick asks with a chuckle.

"No, I'm not. Can you tell them, Chasem?" I frown at Chasem

and watch him shake his head.

"Come, Dietrich, do you have any of the aged scotch we could break into?"

Dietrich's lined face smiles wide. "Of course I do. Come in, come in!"

We follow Dietrich toward the cabin, but the bald man disappears into the wooded area around us. He must be a guard of some sort.

The old wood of the cabin protests as we walk up and into the door. The cabin looks like it was once a small barn but at the last moment was converted into house. Still, even that conversion was done poorly. Some of the wood is cracked and dirty, and old newspaper lines a few of the windows.

Dietrich ushers us in and the inside surprises me. It's cozy and much more decorated than Brice would have ever done with his own place. One of the walls houses a large bookshelf with hundreds of old books, marked in an odd language on the spines. A fireplace rests to the right, a small kitchen area in the back corner. The carpet is a deep crimson and, married with the dark wood of the walls, it feels as if the very light is being sucked out by it.

"Please sit, Captain," Dietrich says as he motions around.

"I'm not a captain anymore, Dietrich." Chasem sits down in one of the plush chairs in front of the fireplace, indicating we should take the couch.

"Princess? Would you allow me to serve you coffee?" His question is so genuine that I have to nod. "Very good." He sets about preparing the coffee, occasionally glancing our way. A few times he swears in what I can only guess is Russian.

I glance at Nick, who watches Dietrich in slight amusement. Chasem sits and looks around the cabin, then offers me a quick grin.

Dietrich returns with a tray of cups and a coffee pot. He pours the coffee and hands us each one with a smile. "I do not entertain much, so I hope the coffee is to your liking," he says as he sits down. "I like mine a little stouter than most."

I doctor up a steaming cup with cream and sugar, and after blowing on it, I take a tentative sip. It's the strongest coffee I've ever had. I imagine the spoon being able to stand up on its own. I force a smile and nod to Dietrich. "It's fine, thank you."

Nick takes one sip and places his cup back on the table. When I look at him, he shakes his head once with a furrowed brow.

"So, I do not expect this is a social call, Chasem. What can I help you with?" Dietrich asks as he takes a big gulp of his coffee.

"No, not a social call. I need to get into the Alabaster City. Undetected. I was hoping you could assist with that." Chasem takes a sip of his own coffee and then adds, "Where's the scotch?"

Dietrich looks as if he's remembered something and rushes up to the little kitchen. He pulls out a bottle that reads "The Glenlivet XXV" with a couple of glasses and returns. Pouring the drinks, he raises his glass to Chasem and us, saying, "Tvoye zdorovye!" Nick and I raise our rancid coffees in response.

"Tvoye zdorovye," Chasem repeats and throws it back with a smile.

"So, you want to get back into the capital," Dietrich begins slowly. "How soon?"

Chasem pours himself another drink. "As soon as possible. Can you make it happen?" He leans back and stares into Dietrich's eyes.

"I can. But as I recall, you told me it would be a cold day in hell before you returned there. Do you not remember that the King wants you dead?" Dietrich stares plainly at Chasem's face.

"I want him dead, too," Chasem admits.

"That is treason, Chasem. If I aid you in getting into the city, I'll be an accomplice to that very thing. You'd see me under a death sentence? Or worse, part of the evil king's experiments?"

Chasem laughs. "Dietrich, we both know you've done many more things before now that are far worthier of a death sentence. This would only be one more thing of many."

"Details, details," Dietrich says and chuckles. "But nothing has ever been proven."

"Look, Dietrich, I wouldn't be here if it wasn't important. We have to get into that city undetected. I have my own contact once I get inside."

"Does she know you still live?" Dietrich asks quietly.

Chasem nods once.

"Who?" I find myself asking. Dietrich and Chasem both glance at me.

"Valentina," Dietrich says.

At the same time Chasem says, "No one."

"Who's Valentina?" I demand and lean forward in my chair.

Chasem shoots Dietrich a hateful look, then turns back to me. "She was just an old friend of mine," he says quickly.

"More than a friend, if I recall correctly," Dietrich offers.

"Shut up about that, or I will pull your tongue out through your ass. Do you understand?"

Dietrich smiles and raises his hands in surrender. "Fine. But if she is your contact inside, you better hope she is not married. Otherwise, her new husband will certainly kill you."

"She's not married," Chase says too quickly, then adds, "Besides, that isn't the issue at hand. Can you get me inside?"

Dietrich studies Chase for a moment, then leans up on his knees and grins. "There hasn't been a city that has ever been able to keep me out."

THIRTY

THE SOKOLOVS

THE NIGHT AIR IS COOL AND TASTES OF PINE AND mint. The crickets sing rhythmically to each other and the world seems unperturbed by my current situation. I lean against Nick as we sit on the top stair of the porch and stare up into the clear, starry sky.

"I wonder if he's okay," I say absently, letting my fingers trace his arm.

"I'm sure he is. They need him alive, Scarlett. It's their only bargaining chip. So they won't kill him." Nick pulls me a little closer. His hand is warm against the bare skin of my arm. We can hear Chasem and Dietrich laughing inside over something.

"What do you make of Dietrich?" Nick asks.

I shrug. "I don't know. Chasem seems to know him pretty well."

"I wonder why he keeps calling you Princess. The bowing thing was a little weird, too," Nick offers.

I turn over in my head how to begin this conversation. "Well, maybe because it's true."

Nick studies me for a minute. "What's true?"

"That I'm sort of royalty," I say quickly. I've never considered myself that. I never meant to go into the revenant world, let alone its capital, regardless of who my father is. So, to me, I'm not a princess. I'm just Scarlett Ellis, daughter to

Jasmine Black and Brice Ellis.

"What do you mean? As in, like, a real princess?" Nick asks incredulously and shifts to get a better look at me.

"My blood father, Apollo, well, he's the King of the revenants. So, in essence, I'm a princess."

"No flipping way," Nick says under his breath. "But I thought you said he wanted to kill you."

"Just because he's a King doesn't mean he's good," I clarify.

Nick nods and stares out into the darkness. "Still, I think it's pretty cool that you are. I mean, how many girls can say they're a bona fide princess?" He smiles at me.

"Oh, shut it, would you?" I say, pushing him away gently. He laughs and kisses my temple. "So, are you scared? I mean, about going into the capital and facing him?"

"A little," I admit. "I don't know what to expect. I've prepared my entire life for being Undawned, so I've planned on fighting renegades. Never in a million years would I have expected to go to the Alabaster City. I don't want to meet Apollo."

"You don't have long 'til you Dawn, either. What are the chances Apollo would change his mind and just let you? Why is he so afraid of that?"

"Because I'll be stronger than him. Revenant parents take a subservient role to the child once they've Dawned. It doesn't always turn out bad, but Apollo never wanted me. It's why my mother ran away in the first place. He could have killed me up to a week after my birth and it would have been legal under revenant law."

Nick's eyebrows raise. "Then how can he kill you now? Isn't it still against the law?"

"Yes," I admit. "But I don't think Apollo is concerned about the law."

"But you're his own daughter, his own flesh and blood. He can't be that uncaring for you, can he?"

"Like your father, you mean?" I counter and immediately regret it. Nick looks away and down at his feet. "I'm sorry, that was a cruel thing to say."

"Yeah, well, my father was...I don't know." His voice is laced with pain.

I wrap my arms fully around him and kiss his cheek. "Let's not think about it, okay?" I whisper against his sweet skin.

"Okay," he concedes, and he turns to me with mournful eyes. I reach up and kiss him deeply, feeling his arms tighten around my body. Heat spreads all through me and I want more of him. His hands caress my back and I find myself climbing into his lap in response. Nick's hands are eager and his mouth hungry. I feel his tongue push into my mouth and I let it. God, I want to feel his skin against mine in the most profound way.

Bite.

I stop kissing him and look at him. He's panting hard and searching my eyes.

"What?" he asks. "Is something wrong?"

I shake my head and try to loosen the fog starting to settle in my head. But it's not fog, exactly; it's like looking through different eyes. Much like when my eyes change, but instead it's like something else is taking over. It occurs to me that it's similar to what happened when I killed Cal.

Suddenly, I try to get out of his lap and find myself tumbling down the stairs. Nick scurries to catch me but can't reach me quick enough. Before he can actually get to me, the bald man hovers over me, eyes changed and fangs fully exposed. He extends his arm over me protectively, holding a blade and hissing towards Nick. Where did he come from?

Nick shrinks back right as Chasem and Dietrich appear at the door. "Lev!" Dietrich says.

"Scarlett!" Chasem yells at the same time.

Lev stands protectively over me like he'll kill Nick at any moment.

"What are you doing, Lev?" Dietrich asks.

"The princess was pushed down the stairs. The human was going after her," he spits in a low voice, accented exactly like Dietrich's.

"I fell, that's all!" I protest. "Nick didn't do anything." I try to get up, but Lev has me essentially pinned down.

Everyone stands still for a moment, frozen in a mask of horror. "Let her up!" Dietrich demands at the same time as Chasem reaches me and lifts me to standing.

"Are you okay?" he asks, and I nod.

"Yes. Where did he come from?" I incline my head towards Lev, who still leers at Nick.

"Lev guards the place. He feels more comfortable out in the woods than I do. He is a good son. He meant no harm," Dietrich attempts to explain.

Lev looks unconvinced that there's no danger but finally puts his blade away. He bows to me, then, in a flash, he's gone.

"My apologies for my son," Dietrich says. "He means well."

Nick looks unappeased but comes to stand beside me. "She fell from the porch. I didn't push her and I was only trying to help her."

Chasem pats him on the back. "You don't have to explain. No one here thinks you were."

"Well, he did," Nick shouts as he points to the woods.

"It was a mistake," Chasem says. "Let it go."

Nick nods once and I see the same look of surrendered determination that he had when I watched his dad beat him. I want to pull him into my arms and offer some sort of comfort, but I can't.

"Come in. I've prepared a meal. I'm sure you are hungry. I have blood as well. It's deer mixed with some groundhog, but still good. Come." Dietrich motions for us to go inside.

I feel Nick's hand wrap around mine and we go up into the cabin.

The meal is an odd mix of Chasem and Dietrich discussing the Alabaster City and Nick and me sitting in stoic silence. I listen as they discuss Apollo in such intimate terms, and it's oddly fascinating. Even though I want nothing to do with Apollo, I have to admit I'm mildly curious about him. After all, I do have his DNA.

Dietrich has unspoken ease with Chasem, their years of knowing each other apparent. Chasem actually seems different with Dietrich than he ever has been with me. I begin to see him as more of a man and less as my uncle. Not that I didn't see him as a man before, but it's like with Brice. When you grow up with someone, you see them for how they relate to you as a child, and can't fathom who they really are. But when you start to see them as the individuals they are, it turns your idea of them on its head. I look at Chasem and realize that's exactly what I see now. Chasem the man is pretty cool. I'm proud to be his niece.

After a time, Dietrich turns to me. "You must be tired, Scarlett. Would you like to lay down for a bit? I only have the one bedroom, but you are welcome to use it." His clear eyes bore into mine.

I realize I am tired, and to close my eyes for a moment would be good. "Sure. Thank you."

Dietrich stands up and looks at Nick. "Young man, you are welcome to a pallet on the floor as well. You look rather worn out."

"Thanks, that sounds good." Nick offers a weak smile.

At that, Dietrich disappears into the bedroom to prepare it.

I glance at Chasem. "So, when do we go to the Alabaster City?"

"In a few days. Dietrich has to set it up, so we'll stay here until it's safe."

"But what about Brice?" I beg. "We have to get there as soon as we can."

Chasem leans up on elbows. "We are going to the Alabaster City and we will find and save Brice, but no one is going to know you're there just yet."

"When then? Won't they kill him if I don't show?"

Chasem shakes his head. "No. Not yet, anyway." I feel tears coming to my eyes. Chasem stands and walks toward me. "Honey, I promise you, they won't kill Brice. I have people all over the city who are still loyal to me. I will know when they get there with him and where they hold him. His rescue will be a piece of cake, but it has to be a surprise. If they know you're there before it's time, they'll kill him for sure and tear the city apart to get to you. Understand?"

I begrudgingly nod. I don't want to get it but, sadly, I do.

"Good girl. Trust me. I promise we'll get him out." Chasem pulls me in for a hug and kisses my forehead. "Now go get some rest." He directs me towards the bedroom door where Dietrich waits.

Dietrich shows Nick and me the accommodations and we step inside and shut the door. We hear Dietrich question, "Is it okay for the human to be alone with the princess?"

I hear Chasem laugh. "Perfectly okay."

Nick looks at me and we both stifle laughter. He pulls me to him. "He thinks I mean to deflower you."

"Deflower? I think that's an ancient term." I grin at him.

"It was the nicest way to put it. Anyway, go lay down and get some rest." He motions towards the bed and takes off his shoes to lay down on the pallet at the foot of the bed. I stop him and pull him toward me.

"Sleep with me, please," I beg and stare into his eyes.

His eyebrows lift in a question. "Um, sleep. Right."

"Only sleep," I affirm strongly. "I'd just feel better if you were with me. Please?"

Nick thinks about it for a few moments and then consents. I slip off my shoes and lay down on the bed. My heart thrums in anticipation. He lays beside me, spooning my body against his.

The last thing I hear before I drift off to sleep is Nick as he whispers, "I love you, Scarlett."

†HIRTY-ONE

PREPARING

A MAN IS KISSING MY HANDS, HIS EYES WET WITH *tears. His face is apologetic and scared. "I'm so sorry, love. I thought it would last longer. I never meant to hurt you." He continues to press kisses to the spot on my hand that bears an ugly burn. His own arms bear burn marks, but he seems largely unconcerned with them.*

"Please say you forgive me, please," he pleads desperately. But I feel suspicious of the apology. He has done this to me before, and apologized profusely when it failed again. He's never going to find the cure to that part of our genetic defect, not for a lack of trying on his part, but it just isn't going to happen.

His hand reaches up and caresses my cheek lovingly. "Darling, please say something," he breathes. His pale green eyes seem cold in spite of what he says. I know if I do not say I forgive him, he will pout and make my life hell until I 'see things his way'.

I force my face to look accepting and I smile. "Of course, my husband. Think nothing more of it. I know you'd no more hurt me than you would hurt yourself." I place my hand gently over his and he brings it up to his lips and presses a soft kiss to it. I want to run away, but I force myself to sit calmly before him.

"Good. I have a gift for you," he whispers and eagerly gets up to walk to a cabinet. Pulling out a small, black, satin box, he

returns to me and lays it in my hand. "I hope you like it."

I open the box to stare at the most exquisite gold necklace. The pendant is a triangle with a raven and a hawk, each grasping a two-headed snake in their talons. Even with the odd subject matter, it is rather beautiful.

"That is my family's seal. I thought it might be something you would like to wear, now that you belong to the Bramstall family." He grins expectantly, waiting for me to stay something.

"It's lovely. Thank you," I add as excitedly as I am able.

"Let me see it on you," he says as he takes it out of the box and places it around my neck. When he comes back to stand before me, he looks rather pleased. "It looks perfect around your neck."

He leans in to kiss me and I realize I'm repulsed by his touch.

I wake up with a jerk and look around the dark room for the man. He's nowhere to be seen, but I do reach to the necklace around my neck. It's still there; the same one in my dream. My heart hammers in my chest and the thoughts swirl around in my head. I can almost smell the man who had kissed my hand.

I glance over to Nick, who's sound asleep, his arm thrown over his eyes and his legs in a tangle. Relief washes over me that I haven't woken him up. I slip out of bed and walk out to the front room. Chasem and Dietrich aren't there.

The windows are completely covered, so the sun must be up. But where did they go? And, more importantly, where does Lev hide in the woods to protect himself from the sun?

I walk around the room, looking at the various books on one of the bookshelves. Most have dark leather covers and are written in a language I don't immediately recognize. I pull one out and turn it over, realizing it's written in revenick—an odd, flowery version of the revenants' written language.

I sit down at the table, staring at the title and the imprint of a large red cross emblazoned on the front. It takes me a few moments to decipher the title, but I eventually make it out— *Bastille and the Knights Templar.* As I thumb through the pages, I make out words like 'helot' and 'revenant' and 'ceannard'. Somehow, this Bastille was related to the revenant world.

A noise from the floor startles me. A portion of the floor opens like a hatch, and Chasem's head bursts through from a space below. I quickly put the book back on the shelf just in time to see Dietrich appear behind Chasem.

"Did you rest?" Chasem asks as he walks closer to me. I look beyond him to see Lev coming up the stairs behind his father. I involuntarily shrink back.

Lev sees my reaction and bows with his palms up. "My apologies, princess. My sole desire was only to protect you as your loyal servant." His voice is deep and smooth. He waits, unmoving.

Chasem whispers to me, "You best touch his palm to tell him he is forgiven, or he'll stay like that."

I swallow hard. I have to touch him. I force my feet to move and I touch his palm. I quickly back away, not stopping until I bang into Chasem.

Lev looks up and smiles. He seems supremely happy.

"Well, now that that's over, can we move onto something else?" Chasem says with an air of irritability.

"No," I counter and look at Lev. "You should understand something about Nick. He's my boyfriend and Chasem's helot. He would never hurt me, and you are never, *ever* to attempt to hurt him again. Do I make myself clear?" I don't know why, but I feel incredibly bold. Like maybe I'm buying into the whole princess thing for a moment.

Lev pales as much as that bald wonder can, and he nods. His baritone voice says, "Understood. I will not hurt the helot. You have my pledges, my princess."

I feel my shoulders relax. "Thank you."

"Sit. I'll make you something to eat." Dietrich indicates the table as he walks to the small stove and makeshift counter.

"It's okay, really. I'm not that hungry," I protest, but Chasem looks towards me and shakes his head slightly. "But okay, that's fine," I amend.

"I was contacted by Ryker this morning. He wanted me to know that Brice is still alive, but that our time is running short."

"Oh, God," I whisper. "Do you think they hurt him more?"

Chasem shakes his head. "No, they let me speak to Brice for two seconds. He sounds about the same. He's holding on."

I let my weight drop in the chair. Chasem sits beside me, and I'm relieved to see Lev hovering across the room, close to his father. He's nowhere near me, with his arms crossed, regarding me with a very intense look.

I lean over to Chasem and whisper, "Is he always that scary?"

He glances at Lev, then back at me. "He sees his primary mission in life as being a protector of his father, and now of you, apparently."

"It isn't necessary. Does he know you're a fully ascended warrior and that nothing's going to get through you?"

Chasem nods. "Yep. But Lev has a profound sense of honor. You're going to find that sentiment in certain pockets of the revenant world that still believe we're inherently good. They still have a healthy respect for the aristocracy."

"So, others aren't so...honorable?"

"No. They adhere to the law so they aren't executed, but other than that, they don't really believe in anything beyond themselves...and blood. That's why our society fractured into pale and dark. But there are still more of us than them."

I ponder that. Lev means well, but I can't relax around him. I mean, I could probably hold my own in a fight against him, but still. His muscles are corded and lean, the very air around him menacing. Put that with the intricate tattoo on his bald head and, well, I'm not sure I'll ever be able to warm up to him.

"Hey," a voice says from the doorway of the bedroom. Nick stands there, reaching up to stretch, showing his pale belly and a small patch of hair below his navel.

I quickly look away, slightly embarrassed. Why did I look there? I hope no one saw me.

He sits down beside me. "You been up long?" He reaches over and grabs my hand and gently squeezes it. My eyes flicker to Lev, who visibly stiffens but does nothing.

I look at Nick. "No, just a few minutes."

He nods. "Wow, Dietrich, whatever you're making smells great."

Dietrich's voice floats over. "You must have a good zavtrak to start the day."

"Zavtrak?" Nick says, a little less gracefully than Dietrich had with his Russian accent.

"Forgive me. Breakfast."

Nick nods. Glancing at his watch, he seems to make a mental calculation. "It's 5:00 here, so 10:00 back home. Think it's okay to call my mom?" Nick asks Chasem. "She wanted me to keep her updated."

Chasem nods. "But keep it quick."

Nick gets up and heads back to the bedroom to call his mom. When I hear the door shut, I look at Chasem. "Hannah must be beside herself, having just lost her husband, and now her son's off in a foreign country."

He picks up his phone and looks at it momentarily. "She's doing okay."

"You keeping in touch with her?" I ask suspiciously.

"Of course. I told her I would." Chasem has a wistful look on his face.

"What's wrong?" I ask.

He shakes his head. "Nothing. She's just a good human

woman who's had too much on her shoulders. I wish I could relieve her a bit. So much I want to do..." His voice trails off and then he looks up at me. "Just my own sense of honor coming out, I suppose. But no worries." He places his phone on the table. "We need to talk about our journey into the Alabaster City. We're going tomorrow."

My heart jumps. Tomorrow? I'm not ready. "You have a way in?" My voice sounds remarkably small.

Dietrich puts a plate in front of me loaded with a bowl of what looks like oatmeal, surrounded by eggs and bacon. "We do. It took me reaching out to my contacts to get you in." Dietrich puts a plate in front of Chasem. "It's going to be dangerous, to be sure."

"Agreed," Chasem says as he takes a bite of food. Dietrich returns with two more plates, putting one at Nick's spot and one that I can only guess is for himself. Lev makes his own plate and stands at the counter, not saying a word.

A glass of blood is put in front of me. "Bear," Dietrich says by way of explanation. "Captured by Lev here." Lev nods. Dietrich sits and glances at us. "You'll have to leave at the first sign of dark tomorrow evening. Everything is in place."

I eat my breakfast and wonder just how in place everything really is.

THIRTY-TWO
BREACHING THE WALLS

WE STAND ON THE PORCH THE NEXT NIGHT, SAYING our goodbyes to Dietrich and Lev. Although both seem to want to go, it's an impossible task. Dietrich can't make it, and Lev would never leave his father.

Dietrich kisses my hand and bows. "To you, Scarlett. You have my undying loyalty. I wish you great success in your endeavors within the city, and with both your fathers." He speaks gently.

"I only have one father," I correct. "Brice Ellis. Apollo was just a sperm donor." Dietrich's eyes widen, but he doesn't counter my statement, only nodding.

Lev comes forward and bows before me. "Be safe, princess. I wish I could come along to assist you, but I am needed here. Safe travels." He turns to Nick. "My apologies to you again. Please protect the princess," Lev implores.

Nick's lips tighten. "With my life."

My breath catches. The thought of Nick giving his life for me sends terror through me. I will never let him close to anything that will put him in danger. I feel like correcting Lev to tell him I'll protect Nick, but that seems pointless. Still, I will make sure Nick is safe.

Lev smiles appreciatively, and the effect transforms his face. He no longer looks like a menace but much more friendly.

"Let's hope it does not come to that." He extends his hand to Nick and Nick takes it.

"Agreed."

Lev steps back and Chasem hugs Dietrich tightly. "I owe you, Dietrich. Truly."

As they pull apart, Dietrich's pale eyes smile. "No, my captain. I have owed you more than I could ever repay. This was just a small drop in that rather large well."

"We're even," Chasem pronounces and steps back. "Let's go," he says to Nick and me, and we pick up a bag with supplies. The plan is to drive as close as we can without detection and then hike to the outskirts of town. From there, someone will sneak us into the city.

Chasem shakes Lev's hand appreciatively and we head out to the car. I watch Dietrich's and Lev's silhouettes on the porch for as long as I can, and then I feel a sense of sadness at leaving.

"Will they be okay?" I ask Chasem as we start to make our way down the bumpy road.

"Yes. Dietrich has been hidden in the woods for many years now. If anyone knows how to stay concealed, he does." Chasem's eyes glance forward, concentrating hard on holding the steering wheel as it tries to moves of its own accord. Even though the night is dark, it's easy for Chasem and me to see, but I wonder just how hard it is for Nick.

We drive for a couple hours in silence. I notice that Chasem grips the wheel tightly on occasion but says nothing. Is he wondering about Brice and how he's fairing with the revenants? God, they could so easily break him. My heart races in my chest.

I think about when I was little, and Brice tried to explain the differences between him and me; that he was a human and I was a revenant. I didn't get it at first, but when I did, I remember crying because I loved my father and I wanted to be just like him. Brice held me close and told me it didn't matter. But to a small child, it did. He just rocked me and told me all the ways I was like him—intellectual, thoughtful, kind—and those characteristics were more important than any turn of a nose or biology itself.

After a time, Chasem pulls along a dirt road and then completely off the roadway, as far into the woods as the car will go before he has to eventually stop. We get out of the car in the dense woods and try to camouflage it as much as possible with fallen branches and leaves. Strapping on our backpacks, we make our way through the forest underneath a full moon and cloudless sky. The crickets mask any noise we make as we walk along the floor covered in pine needles.

Chasem leads the way along the narrow path. "So, are you going to tell me who Valentina Arcieri is?" I ask him.

He almost stumbles but catches himself before completely face-planting it on the hard ground. "She's...an old friend."

"Uh-huh. I heard you say that before, but there was a tone. Who is she really?"

Chasem doesn't face me. "I don't think there was a tone," he says with disdain.

"Oh, yes, there was. Come on, who was she? Old girlfriend? A wannabe wife? What was she to you?" I push, and he just continues walking like I haven't spoken. I hear Nick chuckle.

"She was someone very dear to me. A very good friend. We were never more," he says solemnly. It's quite an admission. Chasem's never been involved with anyone, as far as I know.

"Was that because of you or her?" I ask, hoping he'll give in and share something about himself beyond the wall he keeps up tight around himself.

"Because of me. I had too many demands on me at the time. I was a new captain and had a lot of responsibility. I didn't want to get married to anyone. But if I had married anyone at the time, it would have been her."

"What about now? Is she still someone you could see yourself marrying?"

Chasem is quiet for a long time, so much so, I'm sure he won't answer. "No, not now," he finally admits.

"It isn't because of me, is it?" I feel a pang of guilt, because he's already given up so much for me. I honestly don't want him to give up a future as well. Especially if she's someone he still loves.

"I'll admit, that's been some of what's kept me from thinking about that. But no, honestly, it's not about you. I just have something different in mind," he admits quietly.

"Oh! Something different, huh?" I exclaim. "Tell me."

"Scarlett, we're not going to sit down, braid each other's hair, paint our nails, and tell each other our deep, dark secrets, okay? So drop this." His voice is sharp, and I realize I should probably let it go. But another part of me can't want to meet Valentina. The fact that Chasem had even slightly been interested in her seems like such a revelation. So, Chasem was more than just a warrior and my protector; he was a man.

After walking through the thick, suffocating brush, Chasem eventually stops us. A clearing is visible through the trees ahead, but I can make out little else. He stops to look at Nick and me.

"I need you both to wait here at the woods' edge, hidden well out of sight, okay?" We both nod mechanically. "I need to go to the west side of the city and see if our contact is there. I'll be back." He strips off his backpack and his jacket, wearing only boots, black jeans, and a black shirt. Then he slips soundlessly into the night.

Nick and I inch up to the edge of the clearing, and I'm floored by what I see. The clearing is at least two miles wide and leads to monolithic white walls, reaching at least fifty stories high and surrounding the city. The walls are so white they almost glow.

The tops of the walls have large canopy netting, like spider webs, suspended over the city with thick metal cables. The netting appears to stretch on for miles and miles. Halfway down the massive walls, an expansive ledge wraps around the entirety of the city. Armed soldiers walk around it, dressed in fatigues and holding automatic weapons. Large turrets like something out of a sci-fi movie rise up at various points, and the weapons inside move about, seemingly perusing the clearing below.

A singular road leads into the city toward large metal gates about five stories high with a smaller gate below. Periodically, cars drive into and out of the city, but it's sporadic movement.

"That's awesome," Nick whispers, gazing at it in awe. "How in the world did they build that?"

"I don't know. How did they build a tower so high it almost reached Heaven in the human Bible? How were the pyramids built? The Great Wall? Men are ingenious and industrious."

"But how are cities like this hidden? I bet you can't find this on satellite imagery."

"From the way Chasem explains it, it's all about payment to various governments. Revenants are largely left alone by the human world, and there are people in power who know we're here. But as long as they're paid off, they don't care. It keeps the cities off the mapping satellites and things like that."

We wait for an hour, watching the soldiers walk along the walls. I start to get antsy and wonder where Chasem is. I find myself pacing, hoping that something hasn't happened to him. The crickets are too loud and the woods feel like they're going to choke me.

Nick catches my arm as I walk by him. "He'll be here." He pulls me into his arms, and as much as I love that spot, I'm too wired to remain there.

I pull back to say something when Chasem appears. "Oh,

thank God!" I say. "What took you so long?"

Chasem shoots me an irritated look. "Come on. They're waiting for us."

We follow along the periphery of the woods, taking care not to get too close to the edge of the clearing. Our circuitous route takes us along the west wall of the city. Chasem pauses by the edge and watches. We stand there for about twenty minutes, and then a pen light flashes three times at the top of the soldiers' wall.

"Come on," Chasem demands, and we run quickly toward the wall. I'm almost there when I realize Chasem and I run much faster than Nick, so I double back to make sure he's okay. He runs hard and fast for a human, but still slower than us. It takes forever before we eventually make it.

Three repelling ropes hang over the edge of the wall. We tie the ropes around our waists, and as soon as we're affixed, Chasem makes a signal and we're hoisted up at breakneck speed. We're pulled over the top of the wall by two women and a man.

The dark-haired man slaps Chasem on the back. "Captain Black. Good to see you."

Chasem smiles. "I'd like to talk more, but we really need to move."

"I agree," the man says. "Follow me." We rush across the top of the wall, which is so wide it could allow for two lanes of traffic. We eventually make it to a door and are pushed inside. We stand at the top of a metal stairwell, which winds down twenty stories. One of the women with short, spiky hair leads us down the stairs with her guns drawn.

"This is the most dangerous spot. We really need to get down these flights as soon as possible," she warns, almost running down the stairs. I keep glancing behind me to make sure Nick's keeping up. Chasem stays right with him, but I never hear Chasem utter a word of complaint at Nick's speed.

Our footsteps echo off the concrete walls like drumbeats. We eventually make it to the bottom and the woman with short hair tells us to wait. She approaches a large door and inches it open, a beam of light shining on her face. She makes a signal and then closes the door.

Beside the door is a pile of clothing, and she thrusts caps and jackets into our hands. "I'm sorry, My Lady, at being so abrupt, but we have to hurry before the enforcers know you've breached the city walls." She awkwardly bows.

"It's okay," I say, stuffing my hair under a cap. Chasem and Nick also cover themselves.

The second woman with tightly braided hair leans in. "Go out the door when she says, and stay to the left. You'll be at a guard's station, and there'll be a diversion to the right to keep everyone distracted. Once out, Marcus will take you to the safe house. Understand?"

We all nod. The man, Marcus, waits behind the spiky-haired woman. She watches for a moment, then opens the door. "Now!" she commands, and we dash behind Marcus as he runs by her.

The door opens into the lobby of a small building, with a large counter to our right and a set of doors to our left. Armed guards face away from us, arguing with a white-haired woman dressed in long, flowing robes. She makes lots of noise, and all eyes are on her. Marcus leads us along the wall until we reach the door and come out onto the street.

It's almost like New York City, full of vehicles and noise and people walking along the sidewalk. They seem largely unconcerned with us as Marcus walks fast. We eventually make it to a car, and Marcus jumps into the driver seat.

"The guards' standards have fallen since Ryker took over," Marcus quips as he starts the car. "My Lady, my name is Marcus Potter, and I am forever at your service." He inclines his head towards the rear view mirror. It's then that I get a better look at him. He looks like the older revenant version of Nick. His hair is so dark it's almost black, clipped short in a military style, and he's so tall he seems almost folded into the driver's seat.

"Can you just drive the car and quit trying to butter her up?" Chasem shoots at Marcus.

"Still as even-tempered as always." Marcus laughs. "When Dietrich sent me the message, I had such hard time believing you'd set foot in this city again. It was rumored you were dead."

"Reports of my death have been greatly exaggerated," Chasem says, looking out the window. "But I never had intentions of returning here. Ryker just made it impossible to stay away."

I watch the various buildings go by; some have the word 'Bourse' on them. "What are those?" I ask.

"The Bourse? Those are blood markets. You can get just about anything you want there, including human blood. People say they slaughter humans at some of the markets run by dark revenants, but it's just rumor." Marcus studies my face in the rear view mirror, then turns to Chasem. "Have you not educated her on the city at all?"

"It wasn't like I had intentions of bringing her here," Chasem says, not turning to Marcus.

"You were just going to run with her forever? A rogue? Hunted like an animal by renegades?" Marcus asks, the judgement in his tone more than apparent.

Chasem's head whips around. "It's none of your business," he shouts, so loud my eardrums feel like they're going to burst.

"Fine. I'm sorry. It just seems like, since she's the heir and all..." His voice trails off.

"Yeah, and Apollo is so willing to submit. Sounds like him, doesn't it?" Chasem spits.

"Guys," I interrupt, "can we talk about this later?"

Nick shakes his head in amazement, but just stares out the window. Chasem rubs his face and breathes hard.

Marcus shrugs with a look of apology. "No problem, My Lady," he says, and stays silent the rest of the drive.

THIRTY-THREE

CLAIMING

WE DRIVE DOWN A NARROW SIDE STREET AND STOP at a small building that can only be compared to a brownstone. Stairs lead up to the entrance, and Marcus waits for us to get out. He awkwardly reaches across the seat and gives Chasem a side-hug.

"Look, man, I'm sorry for what I said back there," he begins.

"No problem. Thanks for helping me out," Chasem says and pats Marcus on the shoulder.

I get out of the car, and Marcus yells to me, "Good luck, My Lady."

I lean down and look at him. "Thanks."

Marcus eyes Chasem as he gets out. "Good luck to you, too. You're certainly going to need it with what's waiting for you."

"Why does everyone keep telling me that?" Chasem's voice is sharp and frustrated.

Marcus shrugs. "Friendly warnings? Trying to help a revenant out? I don't know, but anyway, I wish you well. You're going to need it with the vixen in there." He smiles, then speeds off.

The three of us stand staring up at the building. Chasem takes in a deep breath, seemingly preparing himself mentally, and then he takes the steps up to the entrance with Nick and me following close behind. He raps on the door and waits.

The door opens and before us stands a mesmerizing, beautiful woman. Her long, thick blond hair is braided down her back, her skin fair and smooth. Her eyes are clear blue, like the Jamaican ocean, and her face reminds me somewhat of a bird, but in a perfectly formed, dainty way.

"Hello, Valen," Chasem says softly.

She regards us for a moment, and her eyes linger on Chasem. "I see you've finally made it," she offers. "Come in quickly before someone sees you." She closes the door behind us. Then she turns to me and extends her hand. "I'm Valentina Arcieri. But you can call me Valen."

I take her hand. "I'm Scarlett Ellis, and this is Nick Lightener."

She shakes his hand and then turns back to me. "Ellis?"

Chasem interrupts. "Brice Ellis. He's the human who raised her, the one we're here to rescue."

"Ah," she says with a knowing look. Obviously, they've already spoken to some degree. I don't like that, because I want to know what Chasem has said.

Valen's home is exquisitely decorated. To our right is the living room, warmly accented in earthy browns and tans. To our left is a stairwell to the second floor, and the kitchen sits ahead of us. Valen leads us into the living room and indicates we should sit. Nick and I sit together in a love seat, our hands intertwined.

Valen's eyes flicker down to that and she smiles, offering no comment. She doesn't sit. "Do you guys want anything to drink?"

"Yes," I say at the same time as Nick.

She smiles. "I'll be right back." Chasem awkwardly stands and follows her back to the kitchen.

I would love to be a fly on the wall during that conversation. Instead, I drop my head onto Nick's shoulder and close my eyes. "I can't believe I'm here," I whisper, breathing in Nick's scent.

I feel his lips on my forehead. "I know, right? The great revenant capital. Now we just need to find Brice."

I desperately hope that Brice is still unharmed. I'm not sure how Chasem thinks we'll ever be able to find him. But he's assured me he has people in the city who have been his eyes and ears. The last update, apparently, was that Brice is alive and mostly unharmed. I silently pray to whatever deity might exist that they will protect Brice until we can reach him.

Valen and Chasem return ten minutes later. She carries a tray with some soft drinks, bottled water, and various snacks on it. Laying it down on the coffee table in front of us, she offers a polite smile. I notice her eyes are red, like she's been crying. "I wasn't sure what you'd like, so I brought a couple choices," she offers apologetically.

Chasem sits down in a high-backed chair, facing us. He rubs his eyes and lets out a heavy sigh. Valen sits down in the opposite chair and plays with a bottle of water. I hesitantly reach up for a soft drink. Nick grabs a water.

We sit there in pregnant silence. Valen stares at me, and when I glance at her, she smiles. "You do look so much like your mother. Same beautiful eyes and face. If only she could see you now." Her voice is sad and thoughtful.

"Thank you," I reply. "You knew Jasmine well?"

She looks wistful. "Very well indeed." She looks at her hands for a moment. "So, Nick, Chasem tells me you're his helot," Valen comments. I shoot Chasem a dirty look.

Nick starts to answer, but I interrupt him. "He's my boyfriend." Valen's eyebrows shoot up and she looks a bit embarrassed, then glances at Chasem.

"Well, there is that," he offers dryly.

"I'm sorry, Nick and Scarlett. I meant no disrespect." Valen gets up. "Will you excuse me for a moment?" She walks back to the kitchen. Chasem waits for a moment, then follows her again.

"Wonder what that's about," Nick says quietly.

"I'm not sure. They have a history, apparently."

"God, Chasem, do you have no regard for anyone else's feelings?" Valetina's voice drifts from the kitchen.

"Of course I do. I just didn't want to tell you that detail unless she wanted to. I'm trying to be respectful," he shoots back angrily.

I lean up on my knees. I wish I could fly away, but at the same time I'm curious about them. Like watching a train wreck.

"No, what you want is to act like relationships and love don't exist. You're incredibly good at that," she accuses, and her voice cracks.

"Valen," Chasem begins. "I'm sorry. I'm sorry I hurt you, and I'm sorry you've waited for me. I was never going to claim you. I made that clear from the beginning."

"Liar. You lied by being with me, loving me, leading me on to believe you wanted more. Words mean nothing when your actions tell me you love me." Valen is almost crying by now. "Try to tell me you didn't love me."

Chasem's voice softens. "I can't, because I did love you at the time. But I...I just couldn't be what you needed. I'm sorry I hurt you. I never made you any promises, and I always tried to be clear about my intentions."

Their voices get softer for a few more seconds and then Valen walks by us, her eyes full of unshed tears. She says shakily, "Nick, Scarlett, you can stay in either one of the rooms at the top of the stairs on the right. I hope you'll excuse me. Help yourself to whatever you need in the kitchen." She offers a sloppy bow and almost runs up the stairs.

Nick chuckles. "Well, that wasn't awkward at all."

I look at my hands. This is painful, even for me. Part of me aches for Valen. I can't imagine how much it hurt her to wait for Chasem and then hear from his own lips that it wasn't to be.

Chasem eventually walks in and sits down in the chair.

"So, do you want to sit down and braid each other's hair now?" I offer to lighten the mood, but Chasem just gives me a sideways look. I throw up my hands. "Just kidding."

"You kids go get cleaned up and maybe get some rest. It'll be a few hours before we meet up with a few folks to help. They think they know where Brice is, so we're going to make a strategic plan to rescue him."

Please hold on, Daddy. We're coming.

The house is quiet and dark when I open my eyes. I'm restless and can't sleep. Nick lays across the bed, having tossed the covers off himself. I look him over before I leave. He's so beautiful. Even his bare feet are perfect. Sleeping, his face takes on a carefree look, all the worries wiped away. I resist the urge to lean down and kiss his cheek.

I slip out of the room and down the stairs as soundlessly as I can. I pass by the living room and try to keep quiet so as to not wake Chasem. He opted to sleep on the couch instead of one of the beds upstairs. I make it to the kitchen and turn on the light. It's spotless and neat, decorated in happy yellows and pale blues. Modern appliances are everywhere on the counter. Valen must like to cook.

Opening the refrigerator, I grab a cold bottle of water then make my way to the table in the small nook, surrounded by windows. All the shades are drawn.

I pick at the bottle's label as I think about Brice, and finally allow myself to cry. The warm tears trail down my face and land in puddles on the table. I can't lose him. I can't. He and Chasem have been my anchors my entire life. Everything I am I owe to both of them, but more specifically to Brice. He taught me how to walk, how to count, and how to read. He was both mother and father to me, nursing me if I got sick and standing his ground when I was being a complete brat about something. His resilience to the knowledge that my mother was different, and adapting to that, was amazing. He found ways to get me blood, ways I'm not even sure about now, and helped me to thrive. I owe him so much. Now, he's being held by men who want to hurt me. If it takes me turning myself over to them in exchange for his safety, so be it. I'd willingly make that trade.

A hand appears beside me with a tissue. I jump when I realized someone's there.

Valen stands in front of the table, staring sympathetically down at me. "I'm sorry. I didn't mean to scare you. Are you okay?"

I accept the tissue and wipe my face. "I will be once we find Brice."

Valen wears a flowery nightgown and robe, resembling an elegant runway model. Her blond hair is free and flows down in lush waves across her shoulders. She's almost too stunning to look at for long. I can see why Chasem had fallen in love with her, if that was what it was.

"Brice. He's the human who was taken?"

"Yes. He's my father. He raised me after Jasmine died. By the way, thank you for not treating me like I'm, like, super royalty or something," I say, then blow my nose.

She smiles gently. "Well, except for the hair, you look so much like your mother. It's like I'm speaking to her. When she was a princess, she never put on airs. She was always just Jasmine to me." Her face takes on a sad look. "I miss her every day."

"You were close?" Suddenly, I want to know all the details of who my mother was, beyond what Chasem's told me as her brother.

"Yes, she and I were best friends. When she came here to visit Chasem, I worked at the royal court, and we became fast friends. I even stood up for her in her wedding."

"Really? Are revenant weddings like human weddings?" I lean up on the table and sniffle, trying to focus on what she's saying. I try to imagine what my mother might have looked like, a grown woman dressed in a white gown and walking with a bouquet of flowers, rushing forward to meet her groom. I've seen only one photo of her from Chasem, and it was of the two of them caught in a laughing moment together, pre-Dawning. They were probably sixteen and looked so much like each other.

"They're similar only in that they're a ceremony. But we have our own traditions and vows to take."

I nod. "There's so much about the revenant culture I don't know. I know all about Dawning, about what you say and do, but beyond that I feel pretty stupid."

"Well, what do you want to know?" Valen offers.

I clear my throat. "Well, I heard Chasem say he didn't claim you, but I thought claiming meant...killing."

Her face flashes pain for a moment, and then it's gone. A small smirk flits across her lips. "Yes, well, Chasem didn't claim me, that's true. But claiming isn't killing. What made you think that?"

I shift uncomfortably in my chair. How do I begin? I'm not even sure I can get the words out. "When I'm with Nick, and we're kissing, sometimes I want to...well, what I mean to say is..."

"Bite him?" she finishes for me. "You have a desire to bite him, right?"

"Yes, but I've only bitten one human before and I drained him dry. So I thought they were the same."

Valen leans up on her elbows, a slight grin on her face. "Chasem never explained any of this to you?" I shake my head and a look of realization appears on her face. "Of course he didn't. Typical, scared man."

The heat spreads up my neck and into my face. "He only

said it was about the birds and the bees, and he didn't want to have to explain it."

"Okay, then. When you felt compelled to bite Nick, did you feel possessive, like you wanted to almost *mark* him, for lack of a better word?"

"Yes," I admit.

"But not in a way to feed from him. There's a subtle difference when we feed and when we claim. When you drank from a human, did it feel the same as wanting to bite Nick?"

I think about it. With Cal, I wanted to feed; I needed his blood. It felt like he was prey. "I'm not sure, but I think it was a little different. I hadn't eaten anything for nine days, and something in me took over. When I bit the human man, Cal, I couldn't stop, or didn't want to stop. I'm not sure which. And when I'm with Nick and we're....you know...kissing, sometimes I want to bite him, but I don't want to hurt him."

"You won't," she assures with a soft smile. "You saw the human as food, and with Nick, your revenant side wants to 'claim' him. That's a very different thing than feeding, although they do feel similar in the initial physiological response. But you won't hurt him. You can't. If you truly claim him, your very nature won't allow you to kill him in those moments. It's an instinctual thing. You biting him leaves your mark on him in a way that other revenants will recognize, and you'll be connected to him for life. It would take a lot to break that bond. To claim someone is to commit yourself to them. Usually your desire to claim someone doesn't kick in until after you've Dawned, so I'm surprised you're feeling those desires now."

"I just get afraid that I'll hurt Nick. That I'll lose control and kill him," I admit very quietly.

Valen reaches across the table and takes my hand. "You won't. The fact that you love him will keep you from doing that. The dark part of the revenant nature can't overrule your desire to claim. And it does feel strong, almost like a sex drive.

It's compelling, compulsive, and feels a little wild. Just trust that you don't want to hurt him."

"But I killed Cal," I say, and I start crying again. "I went against the one thing making me a pale revenant."

Valen gets up and comes to me, holding me very maternally. "If you couldn't control it, that tells me you were beyond starving. You were dying. Your drive to live took over. No one can hold that against you."

I let Valen caress my hair and hold me. For a fleeting moment, I pretend she's my mother. She lets me cry, and I consider everything she's said, that I was dying and my drive to survive was what controlled me, pushing me to kill Cal. And that drive is different from when I want to bite Nick.

"So, you don't think I'll hurt Nick? Kill him, I mean?" I sniffle.

"No, I don't. You love him, right?" she asks softly.

"Yes."

"Then I think you want to claim him only, and I think there's nothing in the world that would push you to take his life." She gazes down at me with reassuring eyes. I nod at her and she pulls back. "Would you like some herbal tea? It might help you sleep."

"Sure," I concede, and I hear the repeated click of her turning on the gas stove. Before long, we both have tea and sit at the table in comfortable silence. Once I'm finished, I start to walk my cup over to the sink to wash it when she stops me.

"I'll get that. Go on to bed, now." She smiles at me.

"Thanks, Valen. Thank you for all of that."

Her smile gets bigger. "Any time, Scarlett. I hope you can consider me something like an aunt, and if you have any more female questions, let me know."

I answer her smile with my own. "I will. Good night."

"Good night."

†HIRTY-FOUR

PLANNING

"**Y**OU WILL NOT ALLOW YOURSELF TO GET PREGNANT, *do you understand?*" he yells, his breath hot on my face. He holds my arm so tightly it hurts.

"Let me go," I plead. I try to jerk my arm free, but can't. The man with pale green eyes glares at me and his grip tightens. "You're hurting me!" I protest.

"I don't care. You will do as I say and make sure this never happens. Do you understand? I will not allow any pregnancy, so you will take steps to prevent it. Do I make myself clear?"

I stare at his red face, and before I can answer, he backhands me hard, sending me tumbling to my hands and knees, taking the contents of my dresser with me. I taste blood in my mouth. When I look up at him, his eyes glow and his fangs have dropped. I try to get away from him, but he kicks me hard in the stomach. I can't breathe. I can't even will my lungs to pull in air, there's so much pain. I roll to my back and grasp onto my stomach. Fear churns through me for my small occupant. He has no idea I'm already pregnant, and he must never find out.

He kneels down beside me as my stomach muscles finally relax enough for me to breathe. "Do. I. Make. Myself. Clear," he demands, leaning in close to me. It's not a question anymore.

"Yes," I whisper. "No babies. I understand."

"Good," he says, calmer now, then stands to his full height. "If *you want to raise a child, maybe you could volunteer at the governmental pods to help take care of the unwanted ones." He looks around. "I'll make sure the palace doctor gets you what you need. Now, clean up this mess."*

He disappears through our bedroom door, leaving me there in a puddle. I shake so badly I can hardly get up. I eventually make it to the bed and rub my lower belly. It feels okay, so maybe he didn't hurt the baby. I will have this child, with or without his help.

I jerk awake and realize that light pours in from the window. I involuntarily yell, scaring Nick in the process. He shoots up out of bed, searching for the hidden foe.

"What?" he asks, looking around in a panic.

"Pull down the shades," I say, scurrying out into the hallway. Nick jumps up and looks for shades beyond the curtains.

"There aren't any!" he yells.

"What? Why not?" I'm pressed against the hallway wall when Valen and Chasem rush up the stairs to see me huddled there.

"How can you not have shades on your windows?" I scream at her. "Sunlight!"

She comes to stand beside me. "Scarlett, it isn't real sunlight. The city is protected by special shading, so no sun ever makes it in. That light you see is artificial. Watch," she orders and walks into the room toward the window. She holds her arm directly into the light. Nothing happens. No burning or pain. "See? Nothing to be afraid of. Come see for yourself."

Nick helps me up and I see Chasem standing at the top of his stairs, dressed in a black tank top with his arms folded. He smiles and indicates I should go to her.

I walk in slowly, unsure as to what I'm seeing. Valen stands there with her arm directly in what looks like sunlight. She urges me toward her. "I promise it's okay," she reassures. She offers her hand, and I take it. I let her pull me closer to the window, then hesitantly step into the light. I extend my arm to mirror hers, and the light rests comfortably there. It has no temperature whatsoever. I smile at Valentina.

"Cool," I admit, turning my arm over to look at it.

Valen returns the smile, then turns to walk out. Nick stares at me with something unfathomable in his eyes. As he steps closer to me, he seems somewhat pleased.

"What?" I ask him.

"You look really beautiful in that light." He smiles and trails his knuckles down my face. Before I know it, he presses a soft kiss to my lips. An explosion lights up my insides and I want him so much closer to me.

Bite.

My heart pounds as I hear the word, and I consider what Valen told me. Claiming is not killing, and I won't hurt him. I tell myself to calm down and not to pull away. I won't hurt him.

What about Cal? I didn't want to hurt him, either.

I consider that for a few seconds. It wasn't me that had a hold of me in the moment I bit Cal. And if I really think about it, I even saw him differently. He was food. Nick is something different to my nature. He's mine.

I kiss Nick's neck and linger over the spot I want to bite. It takes all my will power not to do it. We're not alone in a room where no one can see. The door is wide open, and Chasem was just at the top of the stairs.

Nick is the first to pull back this time, and I feel triumphant. I made it through without running away. He gazes down at me with a question. "What are you thinking about? You have the funniest grin on your face. Is it the light?"

I shake my head as I feel my smile growing. "No, not the light."

Chasem interrupts. Dang, was he there the entire time?

"We're going to have company in a few moments. Scarlett, I'd like you to meet them." He stands just inside the doorway.

I glance over at him, a little embarrassed. "Okay. When?"

"In about half an hour. Come down and get a bite to eat first." With that, Chasem ducks through the door and heads off down the stairs.

"Sometimes he can be a little abrupt," Nick observes as he looks back down at me.

"And his timing is bad," I add. Nick pulls me against him in a warm hug. I press my hands against his strong back, thankful this human boy is mine. All mine. I think about what Valen said about claiming, and how it's a deep bond, hard to break. Do I really want to claim Nick? I know my primal self does, but logically, can I think about that now, at sixteen, facing my Dawning? Chasem's words echo in my head; he tried to explain I was too young.

Well, whether or not I want to think about that, the issue is here. I have to consider it. I know I love Nick; I know I want to kill any other girl who ever gets close to him, and I know I never want to be away from him. So maybe, on some level, I do want to claim him.

Nick kisses my forehead. "Come on, let's go get something to eat before that company arrives."

An hour later, there's a knock on the front door. Valen answers it and steps aside to let our company in—two men and a woman. One of the men I know, Marcus. The others I don't. The woman is tall and muscular, with fiery red hair plaited to her head in tight, small braids. She wears all black leather, weapons visibly strapped on at various points on her body. The man with her is large, with skin the color of chocolate. His eyes are a deep brown color, and he has a neatly groomed goatee. He's dressed in a long, flowing overcoat, everything also all black.

Chasem greets them all with a hug.

"I heard the rumors but didn't want to believe it," the woman begins. "Chasem Black, it has been a long time."

"Well, you know me. I hear there's a good party in the capital and I couldn't resist. How have you been, Paige?"

"Not bad. It's been rather boring here without you around to stir up trouble." She grins at him.

Chasem turns to the other man. "And you, Holden?"

"I'm well. I agree with Paige. It's been much too quiet without you around." His voice is rich and deep, almost causing everything around him to vibrate.

"I'd like to introduce you both to my niece Scarlett," Chasem says proudly as he turns to me.

Paige and Holden stare at me. "As in Bramstall?" Paige asks quietly and glances at Chasem. He nods, and as soon as he does, the three of them drop to their knees before me.

I stare at them for a moment. "I prefer Ellis, if you don't mind. Please get up. I'm not anything special, okay?"

Paige looks up, confused. "You're our princess, next to rule. You sure are something, and I mean no disrespect by pointing that out."

"Good Lord! I command you to get up and treat me normally, and if any of you call me princess, I'll cut your throat!" I shout. It feels good to shout at them.

They get up and Paige says contritely, "Maybe not a Bramstall after all. Your father would have had us executed for not immediately bowing."

"He's not my father. I might share some genes with him, but beyond that, he's nothing to me. Understand?" I say hotly.

Paige nods, smiling. Holden starts to chuckle as he turns to Chasem. "I see she has inherited your bad attitude."

"Zip it," Chasem says with no ire whatsoever. "Let's go into the kitchen and lay out our plan for tonight."

I rush to Chasem and grab his arm. "You're going to get Brice tonight?" My heart races with the possibility.

"Yes, we are. Brice is going to be safe soon. I promise." He turns to the others, stepping into the kitchen.

Nick and I follow behind them and watch as Marcus unrolls a map of a building. Everyone leans over to look at it.

Marcus begins. "From what we were told, they're holding him at the edge of the city in a medical lab of some sort."

"Labs?" Chasem asks. "Kind of an odd place to keep him, don't you think?"

"Yeah, well, you wanted to know where he was, not what they were thinking. Sorry, my mind-reading is broken today," Marcus replies smartly. Chasem gives him a rude sign, to which Marcus smiles. "Right back at ya, Cap."

"I know you've been gone a long time, Chasem, but there are a lot of rumors that some bad stuff happens in that lab. Undawned who have tried to live in peace here have turned up missing, and some people think they've been taken to that lab. It's random gossip and conjecture. Why he would take your human friend there, I don't know." Paige stands up with a dismissive wave of her hands.

"People are disappearing in the city and nothing's being done about it?" Chasem stands straighter.

"Only the Undawned, maybe some rumored renegades. But given our current ruler, life here has been miserable. There's nothing left from Lucian's rule." Holden's voice lowers to almost a whisper. "There's talk of rebellion." His eyes flicker to me for a moment and then back to Chasem.

"Look, as much as I hate Apollo, I'm here to save Brice. That's my goal, okay? So don't give me talk of rebellion or anything along those lines. I can't worry about that right now." Chasem's face is stern and drawn. He looks them over and says, "Can we just concentrate on saving the human?"

Everyone glances around at each other. "Absolutely," Paige finally answers. They look over the map again and finalize how they're going to get into the labs to rescue Brice. Just a few more hours and Brice will be safe.

After a long time of planning, Marcus, Paige, and Holden leave. Nick stops Chasem in the hallway. "Why didn't you include me in any of that planning?"

Chasem pats him on the shoulder. "Because you're not going."

Nick's face flushes red. "But why? I can hold my own," he protests.

"Listen to me, Nick. I'm going to be gone, and Scarlett will be here with Valen. I need you to stay here and watch over them for me. Okay?" Chasem sounds almost paternal.

Nick considers it, then nods. "Okay." When he turns to walk towards me, Chasem offers me a wink and walks up into the living room.

"Why do I feel like I've just been had?" Nick asks me as he pulls me into a hug.

"You haven't. Chasem just has the verbal finesse of a bowling ball," I say, laughing against him.

"Well, at least I'll be useful here," he observes, and I feel a pang of guilt at not telling him I made sure he would be nowhere near the danger.

†HIRTY-FIVE
THE RESCUE

IT'S DARK IN THE CITY. THE LIGHTS DIM LIKE THE setting of the sun, then eventually turn to night. With the coming darkness, Marcus, Paige, and Holden return to the house. They stand awkwardly in the foyer, dressed like a swat team. They're heavily armed and have mics strapped to their throats.

When they first arrive, they all start to bow, but I wag a finger in warning to them. That succeeds in breaking them from the urge. Chasem comes down the stairs, dressed exactly as they are. He nods to them.

"We have twenty with us," Paige announces. "All loyal to you and the cause."

"And when you say 'cause', I hope you mean the rescue of Brice Ellis," Chasem growls.

Paige shifts uncomfortably. "No, but they're committed to that as well."

"Good," Chasem says, picking up some weapons from the table. "Because that's the only thing going down tonight. Understood?"

"Loud and clear," Holden answers before Paige can speak.

"We'll be waiting outside," Paige says, and they turn to step out. Chasem looks at Valen, Nick, and me. "Remember, keep them safe," he says to Nick, and hands him a Glock.

Nick weighs it in his hand, then nods. "You can count on me," he reassures, standing tall.

Chasem turns to Valen. "If I don't return, get her to New York City." He hands her a phone. "Call the first number on this. It's Fiona, and she'll tell you everything you'll need to do."

Valen nods stoically. "Just make sure you come back."

"Believe me, that's the plan." He grabs her hand and squeezes it with a weak smile, then turns to me. He pulls me into a hug. "I love you, Scarlett. When I come back, I'll have Brice with me, okay?"

"Okay," I say, trying to sound confident. Chasem kisses my forehead. "I love you, Chasem," I add. "Come back safe."

"When have I ever let you down?" he says with a smile. "And that time I wouldn't play dolls with you doesn't count." He laughs.

"Yeah, right. Whatever. Just come back and I'll forget all about it," I try to say lightly. But I know I'm failing.

He kisses my forehead again, then steps towards the door. He looks at the three of us one last time and is gone. I run to the window and watch as he gets into a dark van, then it pulls away.

Throughout the rest of the night, I find myself pacing, walking through the small living room and staring at the clock. Time moves at a snail's pace. Nick wraps me in his arms at different times, trying to reassure me that everything will be fine.

My heart feels weak at the thought of losing them both. What if something goes wrong? What if Ryker kills them both? What if, what if, what if?

We sit around the kitchen table when I eventually jump up. I can't take it any longer. I want to get out of the house, out of this place, but I've got nowhere to go. I'm trapped like an animal, hoping and praying. I look towards the front door and decide to go out.

Valen calls to me before I make it. "Do you want to see photos of your mother?"

I spin around. "You have some? Of course I would. Chasem only had the one of them, because Apollo destroyed everything else of his." He even killed my grandparents, I think sadly. When my mother disappeared, Apollo went crazy looking for her and killed them when they couldn't tell him anything. He turned them out into the sun to burn, then razed their house to the ground, bringing portraits, family heirlooms, and every-thing else with it down in flames.

Valen stands and smiles. "Come with me."

"I'm going to stand guard down here. You go on," Nick reassures me with a small smile.

I follow Valen as she gracefully scales the stairs, leading me to her room. It's completely organized, the bed made so neatly I'm sure a quarter could bounce off it. She goes into a walk-in closet and pulls out a large box.

She sets it on the bed like a prize. "I'm not sure how I kept these safe, but somehow, Apollo's men didn't think they were important when they searched for her. Pictures are harmless, I suppose." Her voice is sad.

"How did he not hurt you when she left?" I ask while she touches the top of the box.

Her face lifts and she hesitates. "I didn't come out un-scathed. I just made it out alive." I see the tears forming in her eyes. "He thought I knew something, but I didn't. Your mother kept her plans to herself when she fled the city. Smart girl. It took months of imprisonment, then two more of house arrest before he finally realized I knew nothing."

"But he didn't hurt you?" I find myself asking.

"He did, but I'd rather not speak about it, if you don't mind." She quickly brushes a tear away, then opens the box and tries to sound happier. "Now, here's all I have left of Jasmine. All my memories of her packed into one, singular box." She pauses, letting her hand rest over it.

When she removes the lid, a blush-colored tissue lays neatly folded over the contents. She gently pulls it back, exposing a crown of dried flowers. She brushes it aside and tugs at the corner of a picture underneath.

"This is Jasmine." She lays the photo in my hand, and I gaze down at a laughing woman. Her dark hair is twisted into a braid laying on her chest. Her eyes are the same color as Chasem's, and she's so beautiful. She sits in a chair, laughing like someone just told her a joke. This was my mother. She was so young, so radiant and alive. I can't help staring at it until Valen pulls out another one.

The next photo is of both Valen and my mother, wearing shorts and running tops. "Your mother was trying her hand at running about then. We both sort of sucked at it." She laughs, then the sadness returns to her face.

She hands me another picture of my mother sitting at Valen's kitchen table. She wears jeans and a nice top, forcing a grin. "This was shortly after she got married. She lost something after that. I'm not sure what. Your mother became very secretive and slowly quit coming to see me."

I pull out a picture of her and Chasem wearing fake mustaches. This makes me burst out laughing. "Oh, that was a fun evening," Valen says. "We danced all night. I think that was the night I realized I was in love with your uncle," she whispers, lovingly brushing the photo with her fingers.

I don't know what to say. I know Valen loves him, and her pain is almost a presence in the room. "You never married, did you?" I ask sadly.

"No. I never found anyone who meant anything close to what I felt for Chase." I reach out, take her hand in mine, and squeeze. She looks up at me with tears in her eyes. "Thank you, Scarlett. I don't mean for you to hear all that. Truly, I don't. But your mother and uncle have been such a big part of my life." A tear escapes down her cheek and she brushes it away.

Seeing the flower crown, she picks it up and turns it over in her hand. "Your mother had me wear this when she married your father. Wait, I have a picture of what we looked like." She digs around and slides a photo from the bottom. It's an eight by ten, and I make out four people in the photo. When I get a closer look, my heart stops.

I know the man standing by Jasmine. His pale green eyes have greeted me in my dreams for more nights than I can remember. He smiles in the picture, dressed in some sort of royal attire and holding Jasmine close to him. Beside him stands Chasem, dressed in a leather military uniform.

I shrink back so quickly I fall off the bed. Valen tries to catch me but is unsuccessful. "What's wrong?" she asks. I find myself backing away from the bed like there's a wild animal there, ready to attack.

"Scarlett, what's wrong?" Valen squats in front of me and takes my hand. "You're scaring me."

"That's Apollo?" I stammer.

Her eyebrows raise in question. "Yes. Why? Have you never seen pictures of him?" I shake my head slowly. "I'm sorry. I should have thought about the fact that you didn't have a photo of him. Why do you look so scared?"

"Valen, I need to know something," I begin, searching her face. "You don't inherit your lineage memories and history until you Dawn, right?"

"Right," she begins slowly. "Why?"

I shake my head. I'm not sure how to explain it to her. I feel like something's really wrong. How can I be dreaming about a man I've never met, unless... It hits me like a ton of bricks. I have her memories. Somehow, those dreams are my mother's memories.

"Give me a minute, please," I say, trying to force myself to breathe. When he kicked me in my dream, he was kicking Jasmine. I know he didn't want Jasmine to have me, but the fact that he was physically abusive to her sends shutters through me.

"Okay. Do you want me to get you something to drink?" She rubs my arm comfortingly.

"Yes, that would be great," I affirm.

"Be right back," she says and stands. She disappears through the door, and I'm left wondering how this happened. How did I get Jasmine's memories? It doesn't make sense. She's dead. Something is seriously wrong here, and I can't put my finger on it.

I rub my face and stand up to look through the box. Then suddenly I hear Valen scream, "Scarlett!"

I rush out the door and down the stairs. Before I reach the bottom, I see two men carrying Brice. Chasem is behind them, assisted by Marcus.

They place an unconscious and beaten Brice on the couch, and Marcus helps Chasem into a chair. Chasem holds his side, blood gushing out between his fingers. I'm torn between who to help first.

Nick pushes me towards Brice. "Valen and I will take care of Chasem. You go to Brice."

I kneel before Brice as Paige leans down to help. "He was out when we got there and hasn't woken up once." His face is battered, one eye completely swollen shut. There's dried blood on his neck, where it looks like it bled out of his ear, and I see bruises everywhere.

"Daddy! It's Scarlett. You're safe. Wake up. Please wake up," I beg while they start working on him. Paige cuts open his shirt and I want to faint. They've cut him up and down his chest, and there are bite marks all over him. "Oh, God," I breathe.

Then Brice stops breathing. Paige pushes me out of the way and feels for a pulse. "His heart stopped," she yells and begins

CPR. I drop to my knees and watch as she breathes into his mouth, pushing on his chest. One, two, three, four, five, six, seven, breath, breath, breath, and then again. On her fourth time through the cycle, he takes in a sharp breath.

"Daddy!" I say again, and he coughs violently but never opens his eyes.

Paige patches up his cuts and gives him an injection of something. "Antibiotics," she explains, then sews up some of his deeper gashes. He doesn't move, and I take his hand.

"Daddy, I love you. Please don't leave me," I whisper in his ear, and I feel him squeeze my hand. "Can you hear me?" He squeezes my hand again but doesn't open his eyes. A profound sense of relief washes over me.

Looking toward Chasem, I see they have his shirt off too, and Valen's working on sewing the gash closed. Blood pours out of it, saturating the high-backed chair. Chasem grips the arm of the chair as she works, and he gives me a reassuring nod.

Marcus stands off in the corner with Holden and a few more men. "They're doing some sort of experiments in that place," Holden's deep voice begins. "We let as many of the Undawned go as we had time for—which wasn't a lot, but we got to as many as we could."

"Why did they want Undawned?" Valen asks as she works on Chasem.

"No clue. But there had to be about fifty in cages," Marcus comments over Holden.

Chasem looks at me. "They had Brice strung up. It looks like they've tortured him. We wore masks when we rescued him, but I'm afraid they'll know we're in the city now. Who else would want to rescue some captured human?"

"Do we need to move?" I plead. "Should we go now?"

Chasem winces. "Sorry," Valen says as she pulls another stitch through.

"Yes, we need to move soon," he agrees.

"I know of a safe house," Paige says while she works. "It's a few miles from here, but well off the grid. It's in dark revenant territory."

"Is that safe?" Nick asks.

Paige glances at him. "Guaranteed. No one would look for us there."

"But won't that put Nick and Brice in danger?" I say, and Paige glances at me.

"They won't even know you're there, so I think it's a good bet." Paige finishes with Brice and covers him up with a blanket. "He's pretty beat up, and he's lost a lot of blood. He should eat something when he's awake," she offers. "There's plenty of food for him when we get to the safe house. How you coming along, Cap?" Paige asks Chasem, her hands on her hips.

"He'll live," Valen answers before Chasem can say a word. He looks down at her, then to Paige, and nods.

I reach down to kiss Brice's hand, and I feel him squeeze it. I have my father with me again.

†HIRTY-SIX

SAFE HOUSE

BRICE FINALLY OPENS HIS ONE GOOD EYE AS HE'S carried into the rear of the safe house. It's a three-story brick building that looks like it had originally been some sort of clothing store at some point. There are mannequins everywhere on the first floor. We make our way to the second floor, which houses two large flats.

Holden places Brice on a bed in one of the rooms, and Paige sets about making sure he's comfortable. I watch closely for any sign of distress from him, but he keeps his eyes closed most of the time.

Once Paige has him settled, she goes to get him something to eat. Brice reaches out his hand to me and I take it.

Nick smiles and says, "I'll give you guys some space. I'll be in here." He walks into what could be considered the living room, although it only has a few cots, a large table, and some chairs.

"Hey, baby. You're looking way too sad," Brice's raspy voice whispers between his split lips.

I kiss his hand and lean down to touch it to my forehead. "I was so scared, Daddy. I thought for sure they were going to kill you."

"I'm fine. Hey, quit crying. You're getting my hand wet," he complains. He releases my hand and caresses my face. "Have you slept? Your eyes are pretty dark."

"No, but I will," I affirm.

"Is Chasem okay? I heard someone say he was hurt."

"He'll be okay. It's just a deep cut. But Valen got him sewed up," I say, wiping my tears away and sniffling. I will myself to stop crying.

"Valen?"

"She was mom's best friend," I answer.

"I would like to meet her if she knew your mother," he pushes out.

"Okay, maybe later. Just try to rest right now."

His eyebrows come down slightly. "I wish you weren't here in this city. You're too close to Apollo. You should get out of here. Take Nick and go. I'll get out of here as soon as I'm able to get my legs to work."

"I'm not going anywhere," I reply sternly. "We'll leave together when it's time." Actually, what I really mean is 'after I've Dawned', but I know Brice will be opposed to that.

"But you need to get away, baby. You're in danger." He tries to sit up right as Paige comes in.

"Do not try to get out of that bed!" she warns, setting down the tray of food. She's an odd sort of incongruous image, dressed like a swat officer and carrying a tray of food like a maid. She gently pushes Brice down, and I do the same. It doesn't take much; he has nothing left in him to fight.

"Go on, let me get some food in him," Paige whispers to me.

I lean in and kiss Brice's sweaty forehead. "I'll be back."

Paige takes my place beside him on the bed and begins to feed him.

Walking out to the living room, I see a group huddled around the large table, eating. Nick stares out one of the windows, and Chasem lays on a cot with one hand covering his wound and one arm slung over his eyes to sleep. Valen sits at the table and turns to look at him while I pass. She gives me a quick nod.

I come up behind Nick and wrap my arms around him, laying my cheek flat against this back. I feel his hand come up and caress my arm.

"How's Brice?" he asks

"Alive," I say. "They roughed him pretty good. But I have my dad back."

Nick turns around and holds me. "I know how it feels to have someone you love violently hurt by someone you're related to. It's...painful. You feel completely powerless."

"I'm so sorry, Nick. I've been completely selfish. You just lost your dad. Has your mom heard anything about the investigation?"

He shakes his head. "No, but apparently that isn't unusual." He pulls my chin up and kisses me softly. "Don't worry about my stuff. Whatever's going to happen is going to happen. I have no control over any of it. I know Chasem has made sure my mom and sister are being looked after, so you only worry about your dad and uncle. Okay?"

"Okay," I concede. We stand there, holding each other in the dim living room corner while the group at the table quietly talks strategy against Apollo. They're taking action now that they know what he's doing in the labs. "Do you want to eat?" I ask Nick, and he shakes his head. "Well, I do," I say and pull him to the table with me.

I make a small plate and head toward a couple cots not far from Chasem. Nick sits beside me, making small circles on my back with his hand as I eat. I watch our motley crew of men at the table. I've never been around so many revenants in my life, and it's weirdly comforting. I'm typically the minority, but not here in the Alabaster City.

After eating, I convince Nick that I'm tired, but it's so he'll lay down, too. We push the cots side by side so we can hold hands. Nick lays the gun Chasem gave him beside his cot. My plan backfires, and I fall asleep.

His hands are around my neck and his face is strained with fury. I can feel my feet dangling and I believe this is the end. He'll kill me after all.

Apollo seems to realize that I'm about to die, because he releases me into a puddle. I cough air out and heave it in. I lay on the floor, rolling to the side to try to make it easier to breathe. He looms over me, furious.

"You did look at him, did you not?" he accuses. "Hmm? Tell me you didn't."

"Not like you think," I try to explain. "I just glanced his way when he came in. It was completely innocent. Stop being so insane."

He raises his hand and hits me hard. "You do not talk to me that way. I am your husband and your sovereign. You will show me some respect!"

"I'm sorry. I'm sorry." I try to tame him. He can't hit me again. It's not for me I worry, but for my passenger. I will myself not to cover my stomach and alert him to the fact that there's a third party with us. He'll kill me for sure, then.

He stands and straightens his clothing. "Apology accepted. Now, I'd like you to come down to the lab at sunrise. I want to try another version on you. I'm fairly certain I've had a breakthrough."

I nod absently and try to smile. He leans down to me. "Why do you make me hurt you? You know I don't want to mark you. Don't you want to please me? Shouldn't a wife want her husband to be happy?"

"Yes, you're right. I'll try harder."

My eyes open slowly and I'm gazing up at an unfamiliar face as she leans over me. It takes me a moment to recognize Paige. She motions to me to be quiet, as Nick's still sleeping. I gently swing my legs over the cot and get up. She pulls me along.

"I'm going out for a short time and wanted to let you know in case you want to sit with him," she says quietly.

"Of course. How is he?" I ask, glancing into Brice's room.

"He's better. Resting. I won't lie, he's lost a lot of blood, both from bites and from the deep cuts. But I think he'll be okay. I have a feeling he won't like it, but he needs to be nursed for a while." She shakes her head in amazement. "Your dad is a strong man and looks like he fought them hard. I admire the hell of him. One kickass human."

"Thank you," I say.

She squeezes my shoulder in support. "I'll try to be back as soon as possible." She turns and goes out the door.

I glance over to where Chasem has been resting, but he's not there. Instead, one of the other men sleeps on the cot. I look around and realize I don't know where he is, and Valen's missing too. Light pours through the windows, so it's daytime. The light is still a wonder. I've been so used to sleeping during the day and being awake at night.

I walk over to a window and gaze out. People mill around just like in New York City. Cars drive by and people sit out on the stairs of their building. Across the way is a Bourse. I shudder to think that there might actually be a human in there being drained dry.

I turn away and step into Brice's room. I lean in and kiss his head, then stop to look him over. There isn't much of him that isn't marked. I want to kill Ryker and Sarah Boll—or rather, Hartlyn McKee. If I get a hold of her, I'll tear her throat out with my teeth.

I sit in the chair and think about my dreams and how they're really memories. How is it that I'm having these now? My Dawning is in a few days. Days. Not months or weeks, days. Everything is bearing down on me fast, everything I never imagined would happen.

I grew up with Chasem making me memorize my lineage, and I know that's part of the ceremony. But when I asked him later why he'd have me do that and know what makes up the oaths, he admitted it was only to make sure the knowledge of our lineage wasn't lost, even if I didn't get the history and familial memories with it.

The memories part is odd. We inherit them, but we can't recall most of them unless they're chemically induced for the scribes for any settling of disputes or to prove who you are. The blood cannot lie. Knowing that, how is it that I'm remembering Jasmine's life? I never drank her blood and I haven't Dawned. Something is really bizarre here. My life is spinning out of control.

"Scarlett!" Brice calls out and thrashes. I leap from my chair and realize he's still asleep. I shake him gently to wake him. Suddenly, Nick's in the doorway with his gun drawn, followed by two other revenant men.

I raise my hand to them. "He's just having a bad dream. It's okay. Nick, put the gun away." I shoot him a look and then turn back to my dad. "Dad, wake up. I'm okay, I'm right here."

His good eye opens in a panic and he looks around. His body relaxes and he sighs hard. "I was dreaming?"

"Yes. Breathe. I'm okay and you're okay."

His breathing slows, but he still grips the blankets in his fists. I reach out and peel his fingers back to hold his hand, brushing my fingers back and forth over the back of his hand until I hear his heart rate slowing back to normal.

After a few moments, he whispers, "I dreamed you were dead."

"But I'm not, and dreams don't mean anything, okay?" I reach up and brush back his hair.

He turns to face me. "They talked about you all the time, the men who were holding me. They want to find you in a very bad way." He jerks his head and hand away angrily. "You shouldn't have come here. You should have run away and let me die. Because of me, you're in danger. I'm letting your mother down."

I grab his hand back and use my revenant strength to keep it there. "No you aren't! You have protected me my entire life!"

"You shouldn't have risked your life for mine. Instead, you're here in this city, in danger, because you had to save me. This is all my fault." His voice rises in anger and volume.

"Stop this!" I shout, and it feels good to yell. "This is not your fault. This is Apollo's fault. And you are my father, my only father. You're worth the risk to my life and everyone else's. Why can't you see that?"

A tear escapes his eye. "Because I don't want to see you die and stand by helpless as it happens. I love you, and I would gladly die in your place so you can live."

I turn his face toward mine. "You can't control everything, Daddy. You can't. And it's not your job to keep me safe from everything. Sooner or later, you need to let me grow up and face this." I feel a tear slipping down my own cheek. "It's going to be okay. I promise you." I hope.

I lean over and wrap my arms around his neck, leaning into him as gently as I can. I feel his tears hitting my head as they run down his cheeks.

"I can't lose you, baby. You're all I have in this world. To think, I endangered you by putting you around that woman—"

I pull back and feel my eyes change. "She's the one who endangered you and me both. She deceived you and works for Ryker and Apollo. None of this was your fault."

"But if I had only been able to see through her—"

"No! She lied to you. You were just being the good, trusting man you are. Let yourself off the hook, okay?"

He nods and closes his eye. His hand searches mine out again and I take it.

"I love you, beaner." Beaner. He hasn't used that name since

I was about eight. That was his nickname for me when I was little. I push down the tears wanting to come. I'm not going to cry.

"Love you too, Dad. Now, quit taking responsibility for all of this and get some rest. I'll be right here."

"Okay," he says, and I pat his hand. It doesn't take long before his breathing slows and deepens.

THIRTY-SEVEN
REVELATIONS

CHASEM AND VALEN RETURN, FLANKED BY A FEW MEN and women carrying bags of groceries. One of the bags has packets of blood, packaged like they were pulled off a store shelf. It's really odd to see. Nick and I get up when they enter.

"How's Brice?" Chasem asks as he walks into the makeshift kitchen area and puts the food in the refrigerator.

"He's okay. He's asleep right now," I say. Nick starts to help with whatever he can to put the food away. One of the women smile at him and he smiles back. I want to tell her to back off. Instead, I come up beside him and rub his back and smile at her. She rolls her eyes and continues putting stuff away.

"This is a lot of food," Nick remarks.

"Yeah, well, we're going to be here for a few days, so we just wanted to make sure we had what we needed," Chasem clarifies. "Oh, Nick, your mother wants you to call, so as soon as it's morning back home, hit her up." Nick nods.

We hear the door open again and see Paige slip in, carrying a long box. She nods to everyone and heads back to Brice's room. I follow to see what she's doing. She lays the box by his bed and checks his bandages. When she catches sight of me, she steps out of the room. "How has he been?" she asks and her eyes bore into mine. She looks like she's waiting for the worst news ever.

"He's been sleeping mostly. He woke up for a while but went right back to sleep."

Paige nods thoughtfully. "Did he eat?"

"No, not yet."

"I'll make him something," she announces and walks toward the kitchen.

I stop her, nodding toward the room. "What's in the box?"

She gives a small smile. "Satellite radio. I thought maybe he'd like that." She gives me a shrug and proceeds to the kitchen area.

Nick comes up behind me. "I think she has a crush on him," he says in a low voice.

I playfully punch him. "No she doesn't. She's just being nice."

"Uh-huh. Very nice. A little too nice," Nick says and dodges my next punch.

"Shut up," I say, playfully batting at him.

Chasem walks toward me. "Scarlett, we need to talk about your Dawning."

I stop playing with Nick. "Okay," I begin slowly. "Now?"

"Now is as good a time as any," he remarks and leads me out of the apartment to a space across the hall.

The room is filthy. It's strewn with newspapers and trash, and the air smells stale. There's a lone living room chair there, almost stripped bare of its upholstery, and a singular metal kitchen chair. Chasem drags the kitchen chair across the room right as Nick falls in behind me. Chasem sees him and shakes his head, but he doesn't ask him to leave.

I sit in the skinless chair and stare at Chasem. He turns the kitchen chair backwards, leaning against the backrest with his arms dangling over it. "So, you Dawn in less than a week," he begins.

"Uh, yep. Nothing new there," I confirm.

"Pipe down on the attitude," he says, irritated. "I've been

talking to Marcus and Holden, and we think we have a plan."

"They're going to help?" I ask suspiciously. "Why would they agree to do that? I'm nothing to them."

"You are their hope," Chasem counters.

"Hope? I don't understand," I say weakly.

"It's my fault, really. All your life I've prepared you to fight against renegades, to keep yourself under the radar. I never in a million years thought you'd be here in the city on the verge of your Dawning." He rubs his eyes. "You've never prepared yourself for the possibility of taking the throne."

"What?" I almost shout. "I'm not taking the throne. I'm... I'm...I'm a high school student who lives in New York City. I eat gummy worms. I'm not royal," I protest. "I'm not what they need to rule them. I can't even rule myself."

"But you're in line for the throne. Once you Dawn, you'll be stronger than Apollo, and the next in line to succeed him."

"There are just two problems here," Nick finally says. "From what I know of Apollo, he won't let her Dawn. And secondly, he won't let her have the throne. So how do you propose to overcome all that?"

"Well, technically you only need to drink his blood at some point on the day of your Dawning. That's really all that's needed to Dawn, and a scribe to bring the blood of the origin. Then the ceremony will be official."

"Apollo isn't going to just let me drink his blood," I protest. I get up and pace across the dirty room. "And it's not like he's concerned with the law. He's trying to kill me now, or have you forgotten?"

Chasem stares up at me with his whiskey-colored eyes. "I haven't forgotten. But he won't have a choice. The plan is to get you in and take the King prisoner. He won't have a choice but to let you have his blood."

"So you think you'll just be able to get me in there? Just like that? And Apollo will just gladly let you take him hostage?"

"He won't have a choice." Chasem confirms. "I know the royal mansion like the back of my hand. I have people still loyal to me, and now there's a threat of a civil war because of what he's doing to the Undawned."

"And what is that?" I fold my arms and sit back down.

"We aren't sure, but we've heard that he's turning them out into the sun to burn. Pale revenants can't let that stand. I don't know why he'd willingly kill them, but Apollo is a sick bastard." Chasem's face rests in a stern frown.

It hits me like a lightning bolt—all the memories I have of Jasmine's. "I think I know what he's doing," I say in a small voice.

Chasem's eyebrows come down. "Oh yeah? And how is it you think you know?"

"I have Jasmine's memories," I blurt out and watch all the blood drain out of Chasem's face.

"Wait, that's not possible. You haven't Dawned," Nick says. "Do I understand that right? Don't you have to Dawn to get all of that?"

Chasem still says nothing and we stare at each other. Finally, he breaks my gaze and gets up to walk around.

"Come on, someone say something," Nick begs.

"You understood it right," I confirm and watch Chasem pace. "Chase, whose blood have I been drinking these last few months?" He keeps walking like he hasn't heard me. I shout, "Whose Chasem? Whose?"

He turns to me. "Jasmine's, all right?" he shouts, and it bounces all over the room.

"Am I missing something here?" Nick asks.

"I've been giving you Jasmine's blood," Chasem says with his hands on his hips. Then he drops back down into the chair again. "I should probably start from the beginning."

I force myself to remember to breathe. "Yeah, maybe you should."

"When your mother found out she was pregnant, she came to me and told me enough to help me understand that she needed to get away from Apollo. She also told me that he would likely kill her if he found out she was pregnant, or the baby when it was born. She had heard of revenants storing blood for their children on the off-chance that they would perish before the child had Dawned. A few revenant doctors had discovered a way to keep blood, much like embryos and sperm are kept for humans. So, she started harvesting her own blood, and we had it shipped away from the Alabaster City."

"To the Neville treatment center," I say.

"Yes. As soon as she told me what she wanted to do, I set up the corporation and stored it for her. It took months. When she started to show her pregnancy, she fled the city, as did I. We made it a point for me to not know where she was, but she continued to send her blood to be stored. It came from places all over the world, and under different names."

"She never expected to live, did she?" I ask in a small voice. Why else would she send her blood like that?"

"I'm not sure. She didn't tell me everything. I wished she would have. I would have done anything to keep her safe."

"So, why start giving me the blood a couple months ago? If I need to Dawn before I get the family memories and strength, why give it to me early?" I push.

"Your mother and I had a revenant doctor friend who had been experimenting with a lot of different things—our blood, how it relays and carries memories, and why dawning occurs at the seventeenth birthday. He theorized that if a revenant is saturated enough with their parents' blood ahead of time, their Dawning will take to them even stronger than normal. This would make the child even more powerful."

I find I need to move. Nick's hand drops off my shoulder as I get up. "Did you know I'd start getting her memories even before I Dawned?"

"No, I had no idea," Chasem admits. "I only wanted you to be strong. My only goal was that, when you came of age to Dawn, you'd have your mother's strength. That was all I wanted. But I could never be sure I would get you to a scribe for the Dawning ceremony, so your lineage would be uncertified and you'd be hunted. But stronger than you would have been otherwise. Your mother wanted you to have every chance you could."

"But now you want me to Dawn. With the blood of both mother and father," I demand.

"As it should be," Chasem says. "I have a scribe loyal to the cause against Apollo. He will be there to perform the ceremony. Once your blood is mixed with the origin and you drink it along with Apollo's and Jasmine's, you'll be fully Dawned and safe."

"What's the origin?" Nick asks. I wonder the same thing. Chasem's never explained that part of the ceremony. In fact, he's told me very little about it at all. The realization that I'm going to Dawn is both thrilling and terrifying.

"It's the blood from the first of our kind. The scribes keep it somehow in their holy city, somewhere far north of here. I'm not even sure how they do it, considering we've been around for thousands of years. The origin blood is very old, but once that blood is mixed with parent's blood, it's far more than potent. That's what causes the Dawning."

"I'm in the twilight zone," Nick utters. "Or the revenant zone, as it were."

"Why did you never tell me?" I demand hotly. "All this time, and you never told me about Jasmine's blood and how to Dawn. Why?"

Chasem gets up, walks toward me, and takes me by the arms so I have to look at him. "You are all I have left in this world. I would move heaven and earth to make sure you were protected. Anything. I didn't know how to tell you, and I wasn't sure I needed to tell you. I figured when you hit seventeen and didn't Dawn, we'd move when we needed to and fight when it was necessary. But I'm committed to making sure you'll always be safe."

"Safe now includes Dawning?" I challenge.

"Yes, now it does. Trust me, Scar, I thought this over a million different ways. If we can get you Dawned, you won't be hunted, and you can actually stop what Apollo's doing to so many innocent lives."

"You didn't know about that before we came here. The innocent lives, that is," I say.

He shakes his head. "No, I didn't. When I originally thought I might be able to get you before Apollo and Dawned, that was my only goal. Then Brice was taken, you were attacked twice, and it just solidified what needed to be done."

We stare hard at each other and he rubs my arms as he waits. I let my head drop against his shoulder and I close my eyes. It's all too much to take in.

"Now, do you want to tell me what you think Apollo is doing? What exactly do you see through Jasmine's memories?"

"Brace yourself," I whisper as I lift my head and look at him. "He's trying to find a cure to burning in the sun."

THIRTY-EIGHT

VOWS

I **SPEND THE NEXT COUPLE HOURS TALKING OVER WHAT I** saw in my memories from Jasmine. The women burning, the injections from Apollo, and the multiple times out in the sun. Chasem looks very thoughtful as I explain it all to him.

"We can't tell anyone about what he's actually doing," Chasem warns. "We need to keep it a secret."

"And why?" Nick asks before I get a chance.

"It's complicated. But if he actually is on the verge of finding a cure, some might actually be sympathetic to what he's doing and won't move against him. The killing will continue unabated." Chasem's face is resolved.

"You mean they would let people just be killed? Like revenant lab rats?" Nick's voice is sharp. "What about pale revenants and the philosophy that all life is precious?" he demands as he stands.

"You'd be surprised by how much of a temptation it would be to be able to walk in the sunlight. Revenants have been relegated to the dark for our entire existence. Can't you see how much of an incendiary device that would be in the middle of our society if Apollo did find a way to withstand the sunlight?" Chasem leans into me. "We need to keep this secret. Promise me you understand that." His eyes search mine for a reply.

I nod. "Yeah, okay. I'll keep it quiet."

"Good," he says and leans in to kiss my forehead. "Let's go back and start the plan to get you into the royal residence when it's time. Okay?"

"All right," I agree and watch him go out the door to the other apartment. I take Nick's hand and he shakes his head at me. It's only later that I realize we didn't talk about how the Dawning ceremony happens. I just hope that, when the time comes, he'll be able to get me through it.

Over the next few days, in order to get away from the constant planning and talking, I sit with Brice, but honestly it becomes a competition with Paige. She's very attentive to him and kind. I watch a few times to see them interact, and Brice laughs and talks, but he's guarded. Part of me wonders if Sarah aka Hartlyn didn't just ruin him for life.

When I catch Paige gone for a break, I walk in to sit beside him.

"Hey, honey, how are the plans to storm the castle going?" he says with a laugh. The swelling in his eye is down and he can use it, although it's hard to look at it when the sclera that once was white is filled with blood.

I wave my hand. "I don't know. They keep talking about how to go in and how many to go in with them. Chasem leaves the apartment constantly to talk to *sources* and how to keep me safe. It's a little bit tiring, but Nick seems pretty interested."

"That's good, I guess. He isn't going, is he?" I shake my head no. Brice tries to sit up but winces. I rush to him and adjust his pillows, pulling him up so he can sit. "Thanks," he whispers through gritted teeth. "I'm so sick of being in this bed. I'm actually glad when I have to go to the bathroom, although I'm not fond of having Chasem help me."

I laugh at the quick mental image and try hard to push it out of my head. Paige walks in with some food and sets it on the table beside Brice. She smiles at him and he returns it, then she ducks out of the room.

"She seems...nice," I say hesitantly as I watch him gently reach for the bowl. I help put it in his hand.

"She's really good company and has helped me out a lot. Honestly, I couldn't be better taken care of, considering the circumstances." He takes a bite of the stew and moans in appreciation. "This is really good."

I watch him eat and thank God he seems to be healing. I hear someone bust into the door in a panic, handing something to Chasem. Standing, I walk to the open door of the room.

Marcus holds a sheet of paper. "I got this as an alert on my phone, too. They're looking for you and Brice, although they don't mention Scarlett. I'm not sure why."

Chasem studies the paper and looks up at Marcus. "Anyone see you come in here?"

Marcus wipes his head with his arm and shakes his head. "I don't think so. I was pretty careful not to attract attention."

I walk over to the group huddled around Chasem, forcing them aside to look at the paper. It's a regular-looking piece of paper with hologram pictures of Brice and Chasem. The images turned to allow you to see all sides of them. The sheet reads "Wanted for High Treason" in bold red letters.

"Damn, they're going to be all over this place," Holden says in his booming voice. "We need to move."

"We should be safe here. I promise you, this place is well off the radar." Paige's firm body stands defiant, her hands folded across her chest. "No one would even know to look here."

"But people have to see us coming and going," Marcus accuses. "You can't think no one has noticed us here."

"Look, I don't want to put any of you bozos in danger any more than I want to be. Believe me, I've used this place multiple times, and no one has ever reported anything to the enforcers."

Everyone looks at each other and then at Chasem, obviously

waiting for his assessment. He turns to me and gives me a studied look, then gazes back down to the image. "I'll have to be careful going in and out the next couple of days, and after that...it won't matter. Everything should be done. But Paige?" He gives her an intense look. Her shoulders stiffen. "We need an alternate plan immediately, and a way to get out of here as quick as we can."

She nods. "There's an escape route through the basement. We'll get out, no problem."

There's some mumbling among the rest of the group while Chasem thinks. "Okay. We'll stay, for now." He glances at the rest of the group, his body taut and commanding. "Everyone needs to be on alert. We need to move in and out of this place as if your life depends upon it, because believe me, it will."

The men and women with us all nod in agreement. Chasem stares at Paige and she nods, too. Then she turns and heads into Brice's room. I watch her explain to Brice in hushed tones what's going on. Brice's fearful eyes shoot up to mine and meet my gaze.

"It's okay," I mouth to him, and his eyes flicker. He closes them in surrender and nods, but he looks unconvinced.

I take Nick's hand and ease out the door to the neighboring apartment. My feet slide along the dusty floor and I shut the door behind us. Before he can get any word out, I throw myself in his arms. He holds me and kisses my head.

"Hey, now, what's this?" he asks gently.

"I needed to be alone with you. I can't take any more of that talk." Nick's heartbeat is strong and steady. I'd know it among a million heartbeats; it's unique and as individual as he is. I know it like I know his face. I lean into him, holding him close, attempting to focus on its rhythm.

He pulls me harder against him, locking me in an iron embrace. I close my eyes and inhale his scent and the aroma of his sweet blood. Desperation bleeds into me like I'm drowning.

All my years of training were meant to help me survive when I became a rogue. Now, I'm going to be face-to-face with a man I've only seen in my dreams, to possibly be killed and never see Nick again, or my father, or Chasem. If everything goes wrong, we all die.

My heart constricts and I can hardly breathe. Why do I have to be who I am? I can't take the weight of responsibility bearing down on me like a guillotine. My life could be over in two days. Two days.

Bite.

I hear the compulsion in my head and I don't react. I'm not as afraid of it as I once was, but I'm not sure what to do with it. I'm too young to claim Nick, it's true. Do I want to be connected to him for life? I consider it and realize the answer before I even finish the question—yes. Yes, I want to be his for life, too young or not. I want only him.

His hand rubs small circles on my back, his heart speeding up just slightly, and his breathing quickens. "I love you, Scarlett. I've never ever felt like this for anyone in my life. I just want you to know I'm all yours, forever." His voice is husky and low at my ear. I turn my face up to his and gaze into his gray eyes.

"I love you, too. And it's forever for me, too. Even though that might only be two more days, but I only ever want you."

His lips are on mine in a rush, hungry and needing. The butterflies rumble in my stomach like they're made of iron, and a buzz builds in my ears. His hands roam all over me, reaching under my shirt and stroking my back. I trail my hands up his abs and his breath catches at my touch. I smile triumphantly against his lips and let my hands continue up to his chest.

Nick's heart pounds hard as he kisses me deeply, his tongue desperately exploring my mouth. I want more. As if he could read my mind, he takes off his shirt and urges me to take off mine. I lift it off in a fluid move and let it drop to the floor. Our stomachs touch, skin on skin, and it's intoxicating. Nick's lips trail down my neck as he presses kisses against me. I hear myself moan.

Bite!

I feel my fangs drop and my eyes change. I'm panting, wanting, needing. Every part of me wants to respond to that command. But I push Nick away.

He's breathing heavy too as he stands looking at me, his lips swollen and red. He is glorious, standing there before me, shirtless. Every line of him is perfect, and I want to kiss every inch of him.

"I...have to explain something to you, Nick," I begin.

He attempts to catch his breath. "Okay," he says. "What?"

"I want to bite you and—"

"I can see that," he interrupts. "Your eyes are glowing and your fangs are down. I told you already, you can bite me if you want to. So go ahead." He urges me to come closer.

I take a step back. "About that. I want to claim you with that bite."

Nick's eyebrows come down a little. "Okay," he says slowly. "What does that mean, exactly?"

"For my kind, it means I will be bound to you for life. There'll be no going back for me. If I claim you, the bite will heal, but will be visible for anyone to see. Everyone will see it, and if they know anything about my world, they'll know you were claimed by a revenant."

His eyes grow intense. "Like being married? Or is it like the revenant equivalent of losing your virginity?"

"Well...yes," I admit. "Both are probably the closest thing to it in the human world. Valen says the bond can be broken, but that it's hard to do. Sometimes death can't even do it. But if I give into it and bite you, there'll be no going back. Do you understand what I'm saying?"

His chest moves up and down like he has run a race. His eyes bore into mine as he nods. "Yes. And I say bite me, claim me, take me. Hell, I don't care. I'm already yours anyway, body and soul." He steps towards me and I step back again. I have to make sure he understands.

"You're sure?" I ask, my heartbeat thrumming in my ears.

"Yes," he says without hesitation. "I told you, I only want you."

I think about it for a moment and take in where we are. The apartment is dirty and strewn with garbage. I think about the fact that this will be where I claim him, and I don't like it. I want it to be special, planned, better than this.

"I don't want to do it here," I say. "If I claim you, I want it to be somewhere special, or at least better than this place." I will my eyes to change back and I breathe slowly to claim down my insides.

"Okay," he concedes and looks slightly disappointed. He reaches down and grabs our shirts from the floor. We put them back on, and his arms come around me.

"But I love you, Scarlett. I meant it when I said forever. There's no one in this world I will ever want more than you."

"I love you, too. Forever." His lips come down softly on mine.

THIRTY-NINE
INFILTRATION

THE NIGHT ARRIVES TO HEAD TO THE ROYAL MAN-
sion. I haven't been able to sleep, and neither has Nick. It
isn't the light that keeps us awake; it's the palpable tension
radiating around the apartment. Revenants come and go as
plans are finalized and talked over ad nauseam. Chasem
largely keeps me out of the discussions, telling me that my
only goal is to make it in front of Apollo with him, and the rest
will just happen. He assures me a scribe will be there, and
Apollo will have no choice but to let me Dawn.

Dawning. The time is here. I have the span of one sunset to
another before I Dawn. Twenty-four agonizing hours. I wonder
if Apollo can feel me, so near. If I don't Dawn, I'll have to fight
renegades my entire life. That was the plan all along, but with
the possibility of Dawning in front of me, I have to admit, I'd
rather do that than spend my life fighting. I just wonder how
high the price is going to be.

Paige has announced that she won't be going with us. She
and a few others are going to stay back at the safe house to
protect Brice. I'm not totally surprised. When she gazes at
Brice, there's something there more than kindness. I won't
allow myself to entertain exactly what it is. Well, maybe I'm
just in denial, but I'm not going to think about it. I just don't
have the mental space for it right now.

I sit on the edge of the bed with Brice. I hold his hand in mine and trace the lines on it, then bring it up to my lips in a gesture of thanks. I feel like I may never see him again. Gazing up into his blue eyes, I force a smile. I can feel my throat closing up and my chest squeezing tight.

Brice looks at me, his blond hair a mess. Even though he has a beard from lack of shaving, and new lines have formed around his eyes, he looks like the Daddy who raised me. He brings his other hand up to my face and strokes it. "It's going to be okay. You're going to go in there, confront Apollo, and Dawn. Then you'll be free to live your life, no longer in danger."

I lean my cheek into his hand, wanting to remember every second of this moment. To remember what he smells like and feels like, and to cherish every minute he's given me in my life.

"Do you remember teaching me to ride a bike when I was six?" I ask.

His hand leaves my cheek and he chuckles. "Of course I do. It took me two days to string lights along the path to my cabin so I could help you learn. You were determined to get it. You fell down so many times and I can't even think about how many scrapes and cuts you had."

I smile. "I was just a little stubborn."

"A little?" he says with eyebrows raised. "You didn't stop until you were able to ride the entire path without falling. That took, what, hours? You were more than a little stubborn."

"But I got it, and you ran beside me the entire time I tried." I gaze down at his hand in mine. I remember how, once I had mastered the path, he pulled me off the bike and tossed me up in the air in celebration. Each time he threw me up, I felt as if I was flying. His arms were so large around my small body.

"It was hard to watch you try to learn. Each fall was painful. But I had to let you. You were never going to learn by not falling." His voice is slightly sad.

"You've been the best daddy a girl could have ever wanted. I'm proud to call myself your daughter." I feel a tear roll out of my eye.

Brice's hand comes up and wipes the tear away. "And you are the light of my life. Nothing means more to me than you." He coaxes me into a hug and I go willingly, curling myself gently against his chest.

"Dad, if I don't come back, know that I love you and that I want you to be happy." The tears come faster now. They roll down my nose and spread across his shirt as they land.

"Stop with that talk. You will come back, and we'll go home, and things will be like they were. Okay?" I nod more in appeasement of him and less in any type of belief that I will make it back. I rise up and brush my face off while Brice helps. "Just be careful and listen to Chasem. He knows what he's doing."

I smile at him and will myself to remember every line of his face. "I will," I say and smile.

"Good girl. Now, go on and get this done once and for all," Brice says. I lean in and kiss his cheek, and he kisses mine. "I love you, beaner."

"I love you too, Daddy." I squeeze his hand and stay for a moment, then finally make myself turn to walk out. As I do, I see Paige lingering by the door. She tries to be discreet by standing back, but I'm sure she heard everything. Somehow, I don't feel offended by it.

Stopping in front of her, I gently nudge her a few feet from the doorway and whisper, "If anything happens to me, get him out of the city and home. Promise me you'll keep him safe."

Paige stares blankly for a moment. "Yes, My Lady. I'll keep him safe, you have my vow." She bows her head and touches my hand to her forehead. "I vow upon my life to keep Brice Ellis safe from all harm. If I should fail to do so, may my own life be forfeit." She lifts her head and looks at me as she releases my hand.

All righty, then. I'm not sure what that just was, but it sounded pretty serious. "Thank you, Paige. He means more to me than my own life."

"Understood. And as for you, I pray your Dawning happens and you claim your right as heir to the throne. Godspeed, My Lady." Paige smiles, then disappears into the room with Brice.

I let out a heavy sigh and turn to the noise of the chattering men and women, arming themselves and talking through the finalized plans. Nick stands among them, dressed in the same leather gear as they are.

"What do you think you're doing?" I ask Nick. His gray eyes shoot up in confusion. Then he glances around at gathered revenants and Chasem.

"Preparing?" he says. Everyone falls silent as they look between us.

"Scarlett," Chasem begins.

"No! You told me you'd keep him out of this," I charge. My eyes have changed and I don't care. I glare at him.

"He's in it, Scarlett. Whether you want to admit it or not, he's as deep in this as you and I, and he will go." Chasem's body is stiff and unrelenting.

"But it's too dangerous for him. He's a human!" I protest.

"He's armed, he's got us to watch his back, and he's going," Chasem pronounces sternly. No one moves.

Nick crosses his arms in response, almost daring me to say no.

"What if I order you?" I say to Chasem. "As the princess of the revenants?" I lift my chin in a challenge.

Chasem laughs. Actually laughs. "Well then, I think the fact that I'm your uncle somewhat trumps that. If you want to try to enforce that little order with me, go right ahead, but you'll just end up being very frustrated, because there's no way in hell I'm going to obey that."

I gaze around to each person there. They all look down at their feet like they're the most interesting things in the world. Only Nick and Chasem glare at me.

"Are you done throwing a tantrum?" Chasem asks me, and the blood rushes up into my face.

"I just want him safe," I protest. "It wasn't a tantrum."

Chasem's face softens. "And we'll keep him safe, along with everyone else here." His face is stone-serious, his lips pressed tightly together. "Now, can we get ready to go?"

I look around for some sort of support, but there is none. Nick is determined, and Chasem...well, he's just being Chasem, and I have no recourse. I can't order him, and the only alternative is if I shoot Nick myself to keep him here. I consider it for a split second and then realize I can't make him stay.

"Yes," I say somewhat petulantly.

The group of revenants seems to visibly relax, and they finish up the plans to get us inside the royal mansion. I feel a hand take mine and I glance down to see it's Nick. I want to be mad at him, but the reality is I'm sick with worry. He could get killed during all this.

Finally, Chasem addresses everyone at once. "Let's go." In a flurry of activity, everyone moves toward the door. I peek in on Brice one last time and smile. He gives me a smile and a wave.

Chasem pauses and hugs Valen, who stands by the door. "Thank you...for everything," he says softly.

She smiles sadly. "You're welcome. Just make Jasmine proud."

He nods once and disappears. She hugs me before I step out. "Be careful, honey. Come back stronger."

"That's the plan," I whisper. "Thanks, Valen."

She grins. "Hurry on now, before they leave you." And she chuckles like she made a big joke. I rush out the door to follow the rest of the group.

It's dark outside now, and we make our way to the back of the building and a black van. Marcus takes the driver's seat and Holden sits in the passenger seat. I climb in and stare into Chasem's face. He's breathing in slowly, and every part of him seems coiled to strike. Nick sits beside me and takes my hand.

"This is a Hail Mary, if you ask me," a blond female revenant says, sitting beside Chasem.

"Yeah, it is. But we do this right. Whatever the scientists in those mad labs are doing will stop, and Scarlett will Dawn."

"Like I said, a Hail Mary."

Chasem says nothing more as we drive through the streets of the Alabaster City. The quick movement of the van with no windows leaves me feeling claustrophobic as we twist and turn. I remind myself to breathe through my nose and out my mouth. It seems to help. I reach up to my necklace and close my eyes, thinking about my mother. I would like to think that if she were here, she would be proud of me. I think of all the birthdays she missed, all the moments of my growing up where she wasn't there. All because of one man—Apollo.

I'm coming for you, Apollo.

The van dips down into a parking garage of an unoccupied building. We corkscrew down until we're at the bottom floor, then drive to a back corner where a group of about twenty revenants wait. They're all armed, standing silently. When we pull up, they turn to us. Marcus and Holden get out first, and the door to the van slides open.

The air of the parking garage is cool and musky. Everyone files out before Nick and me, but when I emerge, the new group of revenants drops to a knee with bowed heads. They all have a hand turned up to me, raised above their heads. It reminds me of the same stance Lev took when he wanted my acknowledgment. I glance at Chasem, and he motions me forward. This is probably easier than yelling at them to stop. I have a feeling this is going to be the standard response to my presence.

I walk slowly between them and allow my hands to skim the tops of their hands. When I do, they each stand and wait. Once at the end, I see we're at a large iron door. Everyone turns to face Chasem.

Holden begins, his voice a strong, deep rumble. "This tunnel will take us to the basement of the royal house. The tunnel may be guarded, so once we disengage the lock, expect resistance. Once they're dispatched, we move forward to the right at the fork, which will lead to the royal chambers. The chambers should be empty, and Apollo should be in the throne room. From there, we're going to have to make our way as quickly as possible to the throne room. Protect the princess at all costs. *All* costs." He glances around, and each revenant nods in response.

"In we go," Holden pronounces, pulling out a huge key and unlocking the large iron door to the tunnel. When it opens, rats scurry out in a panic.

A revenant man with black, inky hair and slanted eyes jumps up. "Ugh! I hate rats. Anything but rats!"

"Suck it up, Eric. There are going to be plenty down this tunnel," Marcus says as he bumps him.

Eric flips him off. Marcus laughs, steps into the darkness, and disappears. The revenants go in one by one, swallowed up by the blackness. I take Nick's hand and go in with him. Chasem and three other revenants come in behind us, and the door slams with an explosive boom.

FORTY
THE BELLY OF THE BEAST

THE SQUEAKING OF THE RATS MAKES ME WANT TO scream, but I force myself to focus and keep moving. I allow my eyes to change and see the heat signatures all around us. I shudder. In the hundreds, rats move about here and there, steadfastly trying to keep out of our way. We move as quickly as possible, and a few times rats get in the way, screaming out as they're stomped on by running revenants.

I hear Nick cuss under his breath a few times as we move. "How many do you think are in this tunnel?" he asks, breathless.

"Not many," I lie.

"Good," he says and keeps moving behind me. "They really weird me out."

Before long, we reach a lit section of tunnel, devoid of the masses of rats in the dark section. Not far from that point is where the tunnel forks. Marcus stops, his assault rifle pointed out like a compass needle. He squats down and motions to Holden about moving forward toward the right while he and a few others guard the left. Holden nods and creeps forward to the right, his gun drawn as he moves.

Marcus motions for us to move. We fall in line behind Holden and the others. I glance to Marcus as we pass him, and he winks at me. I give him a quick nod, then continue forward.

The tunnel is lit with this sickly yellow glow from the lights above, casting strange shadows beneath us.

We come to a metal spiral staircase leading up to a door. My heart pounds so hard that I'm sure the others can hear it. Chasem turns to me and takes my hand. "Stay close to me. Whatever happens, stay close. Understand?"

"Yes," I whisper.

Chasem nods to Holden. Holden's large body begins the assent, his gun pointing upward toward anyone who might come through the door. We follow behind him like he's the Pied Piper. He disengages the lock with a soft click, then slowly opens the door. A bar of light shines down his body as he peers through the opening. After gazing in a moment, he steps inside. The woman behind him slips through with her gun drawn as well. We all wait for what seems like the longest minute. Finally, Holden's head peeks back through and he motions for us to follow.

The stairs creak as we slowly follow behind. There's no sound as each one breaks through the threshold and into the room. I'm so anxious and scared at the same time that I want to push them through faster so I can be in the room and see what everyone else does.

When I finally make it, I'm standing in the middle of a huge room with floor-to-ceiling windows covered in white sheets. The walls are covered in white fabric wallpaper with gold accents. A king-sized bed sits to the left with an immense canopy overtop, draped in gold fabric. To the right is a set of couches and a chaise, embroidered with the seal I wear around my neck in pendant form. Above the furniture on the far wall is a massive photograph of my mother. She stares, doe-eyed, into the camera, her elegant hand resting on her bare shoulder. She gives only a faint hint of a smile, as if she holds a secret. I stare at it in awe. She's the most beautiful woman I've ever seen.

Chasem's voice sounds beside me. "Lovely, wasn't she?"

"Yes," I whisper without looking at him. I think about how Brice told me that when he saw her the first time, rain-drenched and in pain, he immediately fell in love with her. Their time together was only to deliver me, but he couldn't help loving her. Looking at her ethereal beauty, I feel the same sort of overwhelming pull. She must have been mesmerizing.

"For all her external beauty, she was that and more on the inside. She loved with the same sort of purity," he says sadly. I glance at him and see his forlorn expression. I reach over and give him a compulsive hug.

"My Lady, Chasem, we must keep moving. We must find the king," Holden commands. This succeeds in breaking the moment and we tear ourselves away, turning toward the door to the interior of the residence.

My heart is in my throat as we ease into the hallway. No guards are anywhere in sight. We move slowly and I instinctively keep my hand on the gun strapped to my thigh. Chasem has commanded me not to use it unless I absolutely need to, but it's a comfort to have it there along with my other weapon. It's a little scary to think about the fact that I might meet revenants of Chasem's level. But I just have to trust my training will kick in, when it's all said and done.

I hear Nick breathing beside me. I hope even more that we can keep him safe.

We reach a corner of the hallway toward the throne room. Holden steps around the corner first, I hear a scuffle, and then it's quiet. He reappears and motions for us to follow. We head down the long hallway, passing empty room after empty room. Holden stops at another turn in the hall and uses a small device to see around that sharp edge. He indicates that there are two ahead of us and readies his gun. Diving low to the ground, he squeezes off two quiet shots—snap, snap. I hear weight hit the ground and he moves us forward.

Something in me like a voice echoes in my head. *Scarlett,* it calls—foreign, weird. Almost like when a renegade zones in on me, but instead of millions of voices, it's a singular, soft, male voice, beckoning me.

We turn the corner and I see light flooding from an opening to the right of the hallway ahead, the room's guards lying dead beyond the view of the opening. "Throne room," Chasem whispers. Holden moves ahead past the first body and uses the tool to look inside. He signals that it's empty.

Going through the doorway is like entering a cross between the British royal throne room and a medieval church. Even though it's well-lit, there's an oppressive darkness to it. The room is large, a huge throne sitting at the back. The way to that throne is lined by what appears to be gold statues of men and women. Some hold poses of anguish, some frozen with gaping mouths.

"What the..." one of the revenant men with us whispers.

"I heard rumors of this. But hearing it and seeing it are two entirely different things." Holden gazes at the grotesque statues.

"Strange art to be in a throne room, don't you think?" Nick replies as he stops in front of a woman holding onto herself with a silent cry. "It looks so...real."

"That's because it is," a female revenant says. "There are stories that if you oppose the king, this will happen to you. You'll be dipped alive in gold."

I immediately shrink back in fear. I'm standing in a room of corpses. What kind of monster is Apollo?

The room explodes with soldiers breaking in from all sides with guns drawn. They completely overwhelm our small group and wrangle us all into the center with our hands up and not one shot squeezed off.

They grab us quickly. One takes a hold of me by the neck, threatening to squeeze my airway shut. I look at Nick, who's on his knees with a gun held to his head. Chasem is being held by two soldiers, and the others have been forced to their knees as well.

"Well," a male voice says beyond the throng. I struggle to see him, but only his dark head is just visible above the crowd of soldiers. They part in time for me to see Apollo, dressed casually like he's heading out for a bite to eat. He looks around until his eyes rest on me, his mouth twisting into a wry smile, but he doesn't approach. Instead, he walks to Chasem, Ryker smugly behind him.

"Hello, my brother-in-law. I knew you'd show up sooner or later. I've been waiting for you." He punches Chasem in the mouth. Chasem's head swings back, then jerks up again. His lip is split, and without warning, he spits blood into Apollo's face. One of the soldiers slams the butt of his gun on the back of Chasem's neck and he falls to his knees.

Apollo slowly walks towards me, without a care in the world, as he pulls a handkerchief from his pocket and wipes his face. He stops in front of me, just inches from my face, then reaches out to grasp my chin.

"Leave her alone!" Nick screams and is rewarded with a punch to his face from one of Apollo's men.

I feel it happen without warning, my eyes glowing green and my teeth dropping of their own volition. I growl and glare at Apollo. "Do not strike him! Or I will kill you."

Apollo smiles, then he chuckles. "Fond of the human? Is he your own helot? You haven't even Dawned and already you have one? How *cute.*" He sneers the last word, looking at me and turning my face side to side in his hand. He sighs regretfully. "You look so much like your mother. Tell me, how is Jasmine? I half expected her to turn up here with you."

"Dead," Chasem replies through gritted teeth. "Much like you'll be soon enough."

Apollo's face pales and he takes a step back from me. "What happened?" he asks patiently. No one says anything. His face turns a bright red. "What happened?" he roars, so loud my ears hurt.

"She died in child birth," I strain to say, the hand on my neck about cutting off my air. "Her body gave out because she had to run from you!"

I didn't even see it coming, but Apollo strikes me so hard my head snaps back. This sets off a flurry of struggling from the group, and it takes a few moments for the soldiers to get the prisoners under control. I can see Chasem, face-down on the ground with Ryker's boot on his head. Three others help hold him down.

"It's going to be so fun to kill you, my captain," Ryker says, glaring down to a struggling Chasem.

"Kiss my ass," Chasem grits out. A kick launches toward his face, and Chasem quits moving. I silently pray that he isn't dead.

Apollo's face is suddenly close to mine again, his hot breath on my cheek. "You killed her. I never wanted her to have a child, and this is entirely your fault. Well, no matter, my little murderer. I'll have you as a statue here soon enough, if you make it through. Guards!" Apollo pronounces, and I see a flash of syringes placed in everyone's necks.

The light recedes quickly.

FORTY-ONE

SUNLIGHT

I **FEEL LIKE I'M STANDING, BUT I CAN'T MOVE. MY ARMS** and legs have been strapped down to something. I will my eyes to open, but they won't do what I say. There is an odd buzzing in my ears and I feel heavy, unable to move. It takes a few tries, but eventually I get my eyes open to a sliver.

The room is dark and expansive, with cages stacked three stories high, filled with revenants. There's a tank to my right holding a chained, naked man. He has a breathing apparatus on and his body is covered in burns. I turn my head around as much as I can and try to yell for Chasem and Nick, but something's in my mouth. All that comes out are incoherent noises. I don't see them and can only hope they're all right.

I look down and see I'm attached to a standing gurney. Men mill around, looking into microscopes and at computers. One of the men turns around and I realize it's Apollo. He walks towards me, taking a clipboard from one of the men with him and reading it as he approaches.

"Glad to see you're awake, Scarlett. How are you feeling?" he asks genteelly. I want so badly to hit him, but I'm effectively neutralized. "Tsk, tsk, Scarlett. Your eyes tell me you're losing your temper. We have to be able to talk civilly if we're to get through the next few things together. Hmm?" He moves around me like he's examining an art exhibit. "You are so much like Jasmine. Except for that hair of yours. If that were not so, I would almost mistake you for her."

My heart pounds and my face feels hot. I struggle to break free from the bonds holding me. I want to rip his heart out, and I make an internal vow that I will.

"You're probably wondering where you are. Well," he begins with a wave of his hands. "This is my workshop, the place where I create masterpieces. What do you think? Too dark? Too cliché? I understand."

He moves to stand in front of me. "You're probably wondering where your friends are right about now, and that pesky uncle of yours. Soon, I'll have them as my trophies. I'm very anxious to see Chasem with gold skin." He sighs heavily, as if the conversation is a burden. "For now, they're being safely kept to insure your participation. So, what do you say?" He stares at me with his eyebrows raised. "Oh, right." He reaches up and pulls the gag from my mouth.

"You monster!" I scream with a gravelly voice. He backhands me and smiles.

"Uh-uh," he cautions. "If you want me to kill your friends quickly and not torture them first, you'll be a little more polite."

I'm breathing heavy, and the rage thrums through me like electricity. I imagine a million different ways I could end his life, and I feel absolutely no remorse for the thought.

"Do I make myself clear, Scarlett?" he asks, leaning in.

My lips are tightly drawn, but I force them open and say, "Yes."

Apollo leans back triumphantly. "So glad we got that settled. As I was saying before," he resumes his walking, "this is my workshop, my studio for creating. I've been working at this a very long time. Would you care to see some of my work?"

My eyes are big and I don't answer. What can I say?

"I'll take that as a yes." Apollo grabs a remote and points it up to a screen hanging above a set of cages. A clock ticks down the minutes at the bottom and the lens focuses on a grassy field bathed in sunlight. My brain recognizes it immediately from Jasmine's memories. It's the same place Apollo had urged her out into the sun. In this recording, an image of a revenant man dressed only in a pair of shorts is thrust out of a door and into the sunlight.

As he lands, he screams, but not because he burns. He screams in fear, shielding his eyes, then looks at his hands and realizes he's still alive. Overjoyed, he spreads out his arms to embrace the sun. The man almost jumps up and down, dancing in the sunlight. He eventually lays down in the field, spreading his arms again, as if he's sunbathing with a profound look of happiness.

"Keep watching," Apollo says close to my ear, but I don't face him. I'm glued to the image on the screen like a bad reality TV show.

After a few minutes, the man sits up in a rush. A small tendril of smoke emanates from his shoulder, and he jumps up to rush towards the door through which he'd exited. Before he can make it, he erupts into a pile of ash, his scream abruptly cut off.

"Four minutes. The longest we've ever had. We're pretty close to solving this little mystery, but still it eludes me. I will crack the genetic sequence that causes our kind to burn, and when I do, I will rule more than just this world. Humans will never again have power." He sighs as if a weight's just been lifted. Walking toward me, he smiles. "Would you like to know what it feels to be in the sun?" He taps the clipboard in his hand and looks curiously at me.

"I already know," I whisper.

"And how would you know? Hmm? You aren't burned up." His voice is patronizing, and he sets the clipboard down, folding his arms.

"I saw it in Jasmine's memories," I say exultantly.

Apollo's eyes grow wide and the smirk leaves his face. "What did you say?"

"You heard me, you piece of dung. I have her memories. I saw what you did to her. How you shot her up time and time again and pushed her out into the sun like some sort of lab rat. Some wonderful husband you were," I spit.

His lips tighten and his face bursts in shades of red. "Liar!" he screams as he slaps me.

The explosion in my sight does nothing to dampen my anger. "Yep, just like that," I shoot back, and he hits me again. It hurts less this time, but it does still make me see white. I jerk my head back and see his green, glowing eyes. Good. I'm getting under his skin. "Come on! Is that all you got?" I scream back at him as he rears back to punch me.

One of his assistants stops him. "My Lord!" His yelling succeeds in stopping Apollo from completely beating me. I feel a trickle of something warm running down my face, no doubt blood. There's more in my mouth, too. I lean over, spit, and smile back at him. "Temper, temper," I mock.

He pulls out a knife, coming at me again, but the same assistant holds him back. "You can't, My Lord. Not if you want to use her."

Apollo's eyes fix on mine like lasers. He blinks for a moment as if coming out of a dream. Then he glances at his assistant and in a fluid movement buries the blade in the man's shoulder. "Never touch me! Do you understand?" he shouts as the man slowly crumples to the floor. His assistant pants, his eyes glowing green, most likely from the pain.

He nods. "Yes, My Lord," he grinds out.

Apollo sweeps the clipboard off the counter and it lands with a clatter at the assistant's feet. "Get her ready to send her out."

"Yes, My Lord." The man gets up and almost crawls away.

Apollo approaches me and adjusts his clothing. "So sorry to disappoint you in your quest to Dawn. I have no need for a successor, and I certainly don't need you to rule me." He leans in close, his jaw twitching and his nostrils flaring. "You. Were. Never. Wanted."

A small pain lances through me at those words. It lasts for a moment before I gather myself, unwilling to let my mask of defiance break. "Your loss," I say. "But I honestly don't care. I had a father who's ten times the man you'll ever be." I lift my chin proudly.

Apollo's jaw still twitches, but he forces a smile that does not touch his eyes. "Ah, Brice Ellis. Yes, well, that human did taste good. Clean blood. He must take extraordinarily good care of himself, eating right and all that. His screams were music to my ears. But make no mistake, after I dispatch you and your friends, he will die a slow, painful death at my hands. I will drink him dry."

I totally lose my control and scream as wildly as I can. I struggle hard against the bindings, feeling them cutting into my wrists and legs, but I don't care. I want to hurt Apollo, hurt him worse than anything for what he did to Brice. Something in me tells me to calm. Think. I hear Brice telling me to use my brain and not my brawn. My brawn will not win in this situation.

It's hard to comprehend that the revenant in front of me is my genetic father, that at some point, my mother desperately loved him. She had cared for him in spite of the abuse and might have remained had I not happened. How could someone as truly wonderful as my mother have ever loved him? I realize I have to not think of him as my father and only think of him as a sperm donor. My father is back at the safe house, healing. The man in front of me is nothing to me except a means to an end.

"Prepare her," Apollo commands as he turns his back to me. "You will die knowing you helped further my cause. I think I finally have the genetic cure for being in the sunlight."

Before I know what's happening, someone walks up to me and injects me with an orange liquid. It burns through my veins like molten lava. My body shakes, and I can't control it. The shutters start at my feet and inch their way through every part of me. I can't stop it. Color and noise fill my mind and I see images of Jasmine and Brice floating in and out. I hear Chasem's voice in my head, telling me to stay strong. It feels like years go by, and then mere seconds. Time bends and my vision goes haywire.

Apollo's distorted face is close to mine. "Give her a few minutes and then we'll send her out." I want to reply, but I'm lost in a maelstrom.

My eyes jerk open. Everything is very clear but I can't hear anything. People move around me, wheeling me towards a door. The stabbed assistant talks to me, but I only know that because his lips are moving. As if someone suddenly turns up the volume, I make out his voice.

"...wait until the first door is closed and then the second will open," he explains, like we're getting ready to do something benign, never mind that he casually explains how I will die. I'm going to burn up in the sun and never see Brice, Chasem, or Nick again. I wonder if they'll ever know what happened to me. I want to cry at the thought of never seeing them again, but I won't let my body mourn. I won't. I will not go to my death in tears. I will go down defiantly until the very end.

They unstrap me and I see I'm surrounded by men wearing full body suits, complete with masks. A few hold guns and a few more have cattle prods.

"Those don't really hurt all that much," I offer to one of them near me. The weapon lowers for a second as I smile and then, as if he's reconsidering it, the man jerks it up in response. I laugh. "Wimp."

The assistant enters some numbers on a panel and then the iron door engages with a loud bang, lifting slowly. Once it's fully up, I'm forcefully pushed out into a chamber. I stand there facing another iron door. The noise of the door behind me closing pounds like a detonation.

I stand there with three of the men in suits. Two have guns trained on me, the other one hits me with a cattle prod. The shock goes through me like being stabbed, but I allow myself only to wince. I won't give them the pleasure of having hurt me. I walk forward to the second door and it slides open.

Before me is a shadowed alcove, and beyond that a meadow of grass surrounded by a high wall. The same meadow in which the video of the man was taken. I hesitate, staring at it.

"Death by gunshot or death by sunlight. You pick," one of the men says to me, muffled by the mask covering his mouth.

I feel another jolt of electricity from the cattle prod, so I walk.

My feet feel heavy, like lead, but I keep moving forward into the shadow. I glance down to the line where sunlight and shadow meet, then take a deep breath and inch my feet into the sun. Apparently, it's not quick enough, and someone pushes me forcefully into the brightness.

The first thing I think is *warm*, not burn. The sunlight feels so good on my skin, and I realize how white I am. I gaze up to the sun and it hurts my eyes. I can't look at it, but it seems an indistinct ball with no defined, sharp edges. It bears down on me like the enemy it has been my entire life.

I wait calmly on the grass, sitting on my heels with my hands resting calmly on my thighs. If I'm going to die here, I will die meditating on my life. I'm moments away from becoming ash, and the only thing I can think of is Nick—how I love him and should have claimed him. I close my eyes and try to send him a mental message of love. I think about how I first saw him in the coffee shop and how I wanted to kill his father for beating him.

I see his gray eyes as they twinkle when he looks at me. I think about how his dark, curly hair flops in his eyes sometimes. My revenant side tells me I *did* claim him, regardless of not having bitten him. I'll die knowing I belong to him, and him to me.

I think about sushi and our first kiss. I can still remember his heartbeat speeding up and how he pulled back, clearly affected by the kiss as much as I had been.

Nick, I love you.

Next, I think of Chasem. I think about the few times he had a full-on laugh, which was rare. I remember Brice introducing me to him at four, telling me he was my uncle and he was like me—allergic to the sun. Chasem was so large and had to bend himself into a smaller form to talk to me. I thought he had a friendly face and asked him why his skin was drawn on and what it said. Chasem patiently explained every tattoo.

Brice was my rock, the one constant in my life. I remember how he taught me math when I was two and let me read to him, although he had to hold the books for me because my stubby fingers just couldn't. He would tuck me in when it was light and tell me all kinds of fantastic stories of things I would accomplish when I got older.

Then a weird memory of Jasmine's floats into my mind. She gazes down at her large belly while a tube runs from her arm to a bag suspended beside her. She squeezes a rolled-up towel. "Be happy, my little passenger. I can't wait to meet you, to know if you're a boy or a girl. Just be happy and live your life on your terms, not on what others expect of you. I love you so much." I feel the swell of her tummy and then a quick kick from an unseen party. Jasmine laughs, and it's like music. "Well, now," she chuckles, "I see you hear me, little Scarlett or little Michael. Just know you're going to have a blessed life."

I run the faces and names through my head because I want them to be the last thing I think about when I leave this earth. After a time, I just whisper over and over again, "I love you, Nick. I love you, Nick."

FORTY-TWO
BATTLE

MY BODY FEELS STIFF, AND I REALIZE I HAVEN'T moved in quite some time. I open my eyes and find I'm still sitting in the sun. How long have I been here? Why haven't I burned up? I glance down at my arms and everything looks right—no hint of ash at all. Have I died and just don't know it? Does your spirit hang around when your body's gone?

Well, Father Jamison down the street was right. You do have a soul that goes on without the body.

I hear the door to my left slide open with a clatter. A revenant man is pushed out into the sunlight just as I had been. He shakes and pleads with his captors, wearing a sweat-stained tank top and torn dress pants.

"Please don't do this. Please. I don't want to die," he begs and tries to push back in through the door. The men in protective suits don't relent as they stab at him with the cattle prod, forcing him out again. The balding man is roughly shoved into the sunlight and he looks for a place to retreat, but they stand there, guarding the shade.

The man rushes to me and takes my arm, his eyes wide with panic. "Please tell them I hurt no one. I keep to myself and I haven't hunted anyone for food. Please. Tell them to let me back in."

Realization hits him and he stops, glancing up at the sun.

Confusion crosses his face. "I'm not burning," he says slowly. He turns his hand over and over in the sun. "Why am I alive?" he asks me, like I'm the expert.

"They gave you something. A cure maybe," I say, attempting to calm him. His unshaven face is blank for a moment. Then a switch of relief flips inside him.

"A cure? For burning in the sun?" He sounds so hopeful. "I won't die?" I hear his heartbeat slowing, and a wide grin spreads across his face. "I'll be able to walk in the sun like a human?"

"I think so," I say with an air of hope. After all, I've definitely exceeded the four-minute limit, still here and exposed. Apollo must have found the cure. Without meaning to, I glance down at my arms just to confirm they're still unsinged.

The man lets out a heavy breath and takes my hand to shake it. "I'm Salvatore Calderon. I'm a rogue, but I still consider myself a pale revenant," he says proudly, lifting his head.

"I'm Scarlett Ellis," I answer awkwardly.

He shakes my hand a little too roughly. "I have been in a cage for months. They wouldn't talk to me. I was scared at first, but then it just turned to incredible loneliness. They don't let us talk. It's so good to talk to another person." He smiles and walks in a small circle. "The man inside is King Apollo, right?"

"Yes," I affirm bitterly. I don't want to concede anything good about him. Is being King good? Somehow in my mind, it should be.

The man laughs and holds out his arms. "Walking. In the sun. Amazing, no?"

"Yes. Very." I try to smile.

"Maybe I no longer have to hide from the renegades. Maybe..." His voice trails off as he looks down at his skin. A small ash spot has formed. I want to cover him with something, but I have nothing, and the men in the shadows hold their guns out to keep us from running there.

"Help him!" I scream to them, but they remain unmoving.

His panicked eyes look up at me and tears fill them. He reaches out to me. "I never hurt anyone. Why do this to me?" He reaches my arm and grabs it just as his entire body goes up in a quick burst, the word "please" reverberating around the meadow. The sweet smell of his burning body fills the air. Just like that, Salvatore is gone.

I instinctively rush back away from the pyre as far as I can, pushing myself against the stone wall. My heart hammers and I want to get the image out of my head—the anguished look on his face as he died. Whatever's in my stomach makes a quick exit and lands on the grass, a white mess stark against the green blades of grass. I drop to my knees, closing my eyes and covering my ears so I won't hear the dying man's plea. This is different than Cal dying. With Cal, my bite made him euphoric and he died without pain. Salvatore felt every bit of his death. At least it was quick.

Rough arms grab a hold of me. The men's touch sparks the angry revenant side of me and I kick one solidly in the groin. He falls down, and as he does, I jerk off his protective cap. I hear him screaming in pain as he burns, and the sweet scent drifts up from his remains.

I'm already on the next one with the gun. I spin him around and fall behind his body, forcing his arm up and shooing the one with the cattle prod. He goes down in a heap. I rip the cover off the one in my grasp, who ashes immediately. I pick up his gun and put it in my waistband.

My revenant mind tells me none of these men had Dawning marks on their necks. They must be renegades. It wasn't surprising, considering how Apollo operates. The one I shot lays face-down, but I rip off his cover, take his gun, and keep walking towards the door as I hear him burn.

I'm angry. I want vengeance. My vision goes into heat-sensor mode and I feel my fangs drop. This day may have been the day I would have Dawned, but it *will* be the day Apollo is punished for everything he's done.

The exterior door is open, and I walk into the interior before the last door. I push buttons on the keypad next to it to get it to open, but nothing happens. I see the camera in the corner and glare at it.

"Let me in!" I demand hotly, pounding on the door with my fists. Even though it bends at my emotional power, it doesn't open. Pulling out one of the guns, I shoot the panel several times and the door behind me drops as this one opens. I'm completely unprepared for what I see.

Fighting's broken out on the main section of the floor between revenants and lab workers, cages flung open on all three levels. Prisoners rush in a flood to get out as quickly as possible.

I want to engage, but I can't differentiate the good guys from the bad. One person catches my eye—Holden. If he's here, maybe Chasem and Nick are as well. A renegade comes rushing at me with a blade drawn, and I level the gun and shoot him between the eyes. It makes a neat hole on the front of his head, and as he crumples, I see the rather large hole on the back.

Another springs at me, and before I can level my gun at him, he tackles me to the ground, dislodging my weapon. He rains down blow after blow to my face, screaming while he punches. "You will taste so sweet." He smiles and pulls back while he bares his fangs, yelling up to the sky and preparing to strike.

I push my hands hard under his legs and manage to feel the tip of one of my blades. I wiggle my fingers until I can wrap them around the weapon, then I jerk it out. As he comes down to bite me, his head's momentum meets my blade. It goes up through the soft tissue of his chin and into his head. He collapses to the side in a heap. I push him off, pulling out my blade and search for Apollo, but I can't see him in the melee. Something along the wall gets my attention; it's Marcus, holding onto a wound in his stomach that gushes blood.

I run to him. "Marcus!" I yell, looking for something to put pressure on the wound. I grab a white jacket and wad it up, pushing it into his hands. "You're going to be okay. Just keep pressure on it," I command.

"Watch out!" he yells, and I instinctively turn to pull the last gun from my waistband. I shoot another renegade before he reaches us, and he crumples quickly. "Good shot, My Lady. Chasem taught you well," Marcus says weakly. "He was here, but I think he went after Apollo with your helot, Nick. They went thought the door to the left before things really got going. I don't believe they knew you were here."

My eyes shoot up to the doorway, and I consider what to do next.

Marcus must have seen my hesitation. "Go, My Lady. Go. I'll be okay. Go Dawn."

I stare at him and he motions me ahead. I nod and stand. When I do, Holden sees me. He whistles loudly as the fighting seems to ebb. There are more of us left than there are of any workers or renegades. The remaining lab workers have surrendered and sit on their knees, guarded by a female revenant.

I move towards the door and realize I'm being followed by several of our men and women. I hear someone say, "For the honor of the princess!" to which a battle yell of agreement rises. I want to turn and thank them or say something significant, but there just isn't time. We rush down a tunnel lit by sickly pale light. Holden catches up to me and pulls me down a path to the right. Chasem's and Nick's scents are fresh in the air.

We come to an epic iron door standing open just a crack. I

barrel through with Holden yelling a warning in my ear and attempting to hold me back. I ignore him and push him away, bursting into the throne room.

The first thing I see is Chasem. He holds Apollo against him, a knife at his captive's throat. He's surrounded by five soldiers and Ryker, all with guns drawn. No one moves. Chasem pushes the blade so hard against Apollo's neck, a small bead of blood runs down the king's throat.

"You're trapped, Cap. Let him go," Ryker commands.

Beyond them, I see a body crumpled in a pile, unmoving, and a strangely dressed man hovers over the body in a protective stance. The man wears an odd hat and long robe. His face isn't human but shaped into what can only be described as rat-like. He has a long, narrow snout and dark-set eyes, his large mouth protruding with long fangs. At his side stands an immense man, more muscular than anyone I've ever seen, including Chasem. He's shirtless, and leather straps overlap each other across the expanse of his chest. A leather mask covers his entire face, leaving only eyes visible. They stand behind Chasem, but they don't appear to be foes. Chasem himself seems unconcerned about them.

I look back at the crumpled body and realize why it seemed so familiar. It's Nick.

I start to run to him, but Holden holds me back.

"Stay back or I'll cut his throat!" Chasem warns Ryker. I hear heavy footfalls behind me as more of Chasem's men rush through the opening and flood the throne room.

"No, you won't," Ryker challenges. "If you kill him, your precious Scarlett can't Dawn and won't be in line for the throne. So, I don't think you're going to hurt him." Ryker inches forward.

The blade goes into Apollo's neck but not enough to cause serious damage. Blood runs in rivers down Apollo's shirt.

"Stay back, you fool!" Apollo yells to Ryker and his men.

Everyone freezes, unsure of what to do. "Do as he says." More of Chasem's men flood in with guns drawn. Chasem's fighters advance against Apollo's men, and the guards lower their weapons and drop them to the ground in surrender.

Chasem looks victorious but doesn't release the king. I consider this my opportunity and run to Nick. The two men with him part to let me touch him. I turn him over, seeing blood trickling from his ears and mouth.

"Nick! Oh, no. Please, Nick, don't be dead," I pray, pulling him into my arms.

"He is not dead, princess, but he needs medical assistance," the robed man says.

"Someone, please! Get me some help!" I command, feeling the tears rolling from my eyes. A few of Chasem's fighters near us and look Nick over. I step back to let them work. One must have had some medical training because she looks into his eyes and examines his head, searching for reflex. I bite my nails as she works.

Slowly turning, I fix my gaze and rage upon Apollo. Chasem still holds him with a knife to his throat. I rise up, my vision going heat-signature.

"Oh, too bad. Did I break your little helot?" Apollo sneers at me. Ryker snickers at the comment. I slowly walk towards him and let my full revenant side wake up. I will hurt him for all the pain he's caused me.

"It's all come to this, Apollo. Jasmine's daughter will Dawn and she will have the throne. There's absolutely nothing you can do about it," Chasem jeers into Apollo's ear.

Apollo's face burns bright with fury. In a fluid move, he pulls a dagger from a hidden pocket and buries it into Chasem's gut. The room explodes into fighting again.

FORTY-THREE
DAWNING

I **SCREAM AS CHASEM CRUMBLES TO THE FLOOR, THEN I** rush forward with the other fighters. Before I can reach him, Apollo lands a hard punch to my face, sending me skittering to the ground. Fights break out all around us, but Apollo's men are overtaken quickly and Ryker disappears in the melee.

I search quickly for Apollo, hoping he hasn't escaped, and find that Chasem's men have descended upon him. I stand up defiantly and say, "Let him go. He's mine." I pull my blades out as they obey and step back from him.

Apollo pulls out a blade from the back of his belt and weighs it in his hands, smiling at me. "Do you think you could win against me in a fight? Really, Scarlett, are you that stupid?"

"Come see," I say and watch his movements. He's right-handed, so his weaker side will be his left. Even though he's a ruler, he moves with the confidence of someone accustomed to hand-to-hand combat.

"Scarlett, no," Chasem grinds out.

A circle forms around Apollo and me as we size each other up. He's the first to lunge forward, like a leopard, quick and sure on his feet. I dodge the lunge and he just misses what would have left me with a huge knife slash.

He laughs and mocks me as he turns. "Well, you're a little faster than I'd planned. I'm afraid not fast enough." Apollo rushes me again, but this time he shifts at the last minute and changes direction, moving the blade from his right hand to his left. He catches my right arm and I drop my blade. He spins to bury his blade into me, but I parry away just in time.

The blood gushes down my arm. Apollo sniffs the air in a show. "Mmm, you smell delicious. I wonder how that will taste spilling out of your dying body." He laughs and comes at me again, but I crouch low and tackle him, grabbing him around the middle. The collision flings the blade from his grip, and he lands hard on his back. I succeed in getting in solid punches to his face, but they have little effect. Before I know it, he spins me over and wraps his hands around my neck. Then he squeezes.

I twist my hips and force his weight to shift, finally knocking him off my body. I get to my feet and attempt to kick him, but he rolls out the way just in time. He gets to his feet and laughs.

We circle each other in a deadly dance. He gazes at me with an odd mix of hatred and bitterness. Why can't he love me? I was just an innocent child, *his* child. It's a lucky thing that I wasn't raised in his house. Providence could have made it so I didn't grow up bitter and power-hungry, as Apollo seems to be. How did my mother ever love him?

I rush at Apollo, leading with my knife, and realize too late that I was too close to him. He easily kicks the blade from my hand and it skitters loudly across the hard floor. I turn in time to dodge a thrust at my stomach. Seeing an opportunity, I jump on his back and wrap my arms tightly around his neck. He lets go of his blade to instinctively grab for my arms.

Everyone seems oddly quiet as we struggle, and before I know what's happening, Apollo slams my back into something I can't see and the force of it pushes all the air out of my lungs. I can't help but release him. He turns to come down on me with a blow, but I scramble under a table, hearing his strike land uselessly above me. I burst out and reach my blade right as I hear him reach his. When I get to my feet, he rushes towards me, stabbing. My blade catches him in the thigh, and he bellows a strong curse.

"Come on, Apollo. You wanted my death so badly, deliver it, already," I taunt, hoping to incite him. He turns and smiles at me. In a series of moves, we each land a cut on each other, but neither one of us falls.

After a few more attempts to kill one another, we're both panting. Circling, I know we're each looking for an opening to dispatch our opponent. Apollo rushes at me, and I turn to notice a table against the wall. I shove it at him with everything I have. He reaches out to shield himself from the heavy furniture and drops his knife. That's my opening—I hurl my blade at his head, but it misses and embeds itself into the wall behind him.

Apollo stands upright and smiles at me. "You will not win, and you will not Dawn. You will die at my hands, just like your little helot over there in the corner." He looks beyond me to Nick. "Kill him," he commands, and I turn to see who's there. Have his men gotten free and I just didn't see it? Nick lies in the corner, protected as ever with none of Apollo's men around. But my glance is just enough to distract me from my fight.

I turn in time to see Apollo reaching out to put his hands around my neck again, and he pounds me into the wall, holding me up like an insect on display. All the air is knocked out of me and my feet are no longer on the ground. He leverages all his weight against me, holding me high up on the wall. I struggle to get his hands off, but his grip is sure. It occurs to me I might actually die. No air moves through my lungs and my sight dims quickly. No matter how I struggle, I can't get lose.

I hear Chasem's words in my head. *Fight! You have to keep*

fighting, no matter what. Do you understand? It will be a matter of life or death. Never surrender, do you understand?

I will myself to stay conscious and bring my knee up hard into Apollo's chin. The blow forces him back, and he releases his grip on me. I heave in air, struggling to breathe. Apollo sees the blade on the ground just as I do, and we both lunge for it. We reach it at the same time, and he tackles me.

Then he freezes, his breathing suddenly labored. I push his weight off me to see the blade impaled in his chest. His eyes are wide and his mouth moves, as if to speak, but all that comes out is a river of blood. I lean in to hear what he's trying to say, but there's nothing.

I close my eyes and can hear something heavy scraping along the ground. Whatever it is, I know it's responding to me, but I cannot put into any coherent words what I'm feeling.

"The statues..." someone whispers, disbelieving.

"Scarlett, quickly. Before he dies. His blood," Chasem shouts, and it succeeds in pulling me out of the moment.

The robed rat man in the corner approaches with a dish and a blade, then pulls out Apollo's arm and slashes it. Placing the dish under his arm, he collects a large amount of blood. When he's satisfied, he steps back and motions to me.

"Princess, are you ready to Dawn?"

I glance at the carnage all around me. Nick lays unconscious, now attended to, and Chasem's face is pale from blood loss. Apollo's dying right before me. Some small part of me thinks that someone should be trying to save Apollo, but no one makes a move towards him.

Reaching over, I find a jacket and put it into Apollo's hands and push it towards the wound. "Keep pressure on it. With any luck, you won't die," I say bitterly.

I start to get up when I feel Apollo's hand grab mine. I turn to see him as he struggles to speak, but all I hear are gurgles. Something in me snaps, and I grab his collar and shake him.

"Why did it have to be like this? Why? My mother loved you. Things did not have to be this way."

He just stares at me. I'm not sure if he understands what I've said. He nods and then, very slowly, his eyes go blank. Apollo's hand drops from my arm, and I stand to look down at him. He's dead, and it was by my hand. Seeing him now, with all the bravado gone, I can see what my mother saw. Apollo looks innocent, handsome, not the monster he became. I remember how she felt gazing at him and how she did once love him. I'm surprised by the flood of sadness that hits me. I have never had any feelings for him other than fear. Now, I feel only grief over what he's done.

I take in a deep breath and look around the room. Everyone who had been standing suddenly falls to their knees in salute.

"All hail the queen," the robed man says. The entire room echoes those words in a loud reaffirmation. The robed man steps closer. "Quickly, My Queen, before the blood dies. Please, sit here."

He sits me down on the stairs leading up to the throne, then places the dish of blood beside me and turns to retrieve what resembles a cooler. From inside, he retrieves a vile of blood and smiles. "Queen Jasmine's. Captain Black had forwarded this on for this ceremony."

I watch him pour the vile into a new bowl and mix it with Apollo's blood. Reaching into a bag affixed to the belt around his robe, he produces a packet of powder and lays it to the side. From that same belt he retrieves another vile of blood, which moves and undulates like it's trying to escape its confines.

"Blood of the origin. Holy. Living," the scribe says. When he pours it into the dish and mixes it with my parents' blood, the color shifts into the deepest crimson I've ever seen. It's almost black. Heat emanates from it while it shifts in the bowl on its own. The scribe dips a small cup into the bowl and hands both the cup and the powder to his large assistant in the mask. Taking the rest of the mixed blood, he turns to me, holding the dish reverently in his hand.

"Queen Scarlett, please present yourself before the blood of your parents and of Derakus, father to us all." He waits patiently, gazing gently into my eyes. Then he leans in. "You need to kneel," he reveals in a whisper.

"Oh, sorry." I drop to my knees before the scribe. He dips his thumb into the dish and brings it up to my forehead to draw a symbol there. As he does, the blood burns, like it's burrowing into my skin. A whisper sounds in my mind; I hear it calling my name. I blink a few times, trying to focus.

"Recite your lineage," the scribe declares, and I look to Chasem. Still panting to catch his breath, he gives a nod. I look back at the scribe and recite from four generations back. Chasem made me learn the lineages and vows from the time I was little, not for Dawning but just so I'd know who I am. I wonder now if he'd ever hoped that somehow this day might actually arrive and I'd be prepared.

When I finish, the scribe's rat-like eyes glimmer in approval. "Now, repeat the vows after me."

He speaks slowly, and I repeat the vows, one after another. Vowing to be true to the revenant people, to uphold the laws instituted by the scribes, and to protect our culture at all costs. The vows are long and the words cumbersome, but I succeed in getting through it without stumbling.

The scribe smiles. "Your vows are accepted and your lineage is true. You are sealed and accepted, Scarlett Bramstall," he says.

"Ellis," I correct. "Scarlett Bramstall Ellis, adopted daughter of Brice Ellis. I want that entered as part of my lineage," I demand. "He is my father and should have a place of honor in my line."

The scribe looks surprised. "Very well. It will be entered in the annals. Now... You are sealed and accepted, Scarlett Bramstall Ellis." He hands the dish of blood to me.

I hesitate, looking at it. The swirling of the blood is almost hypnotic. I bring the dish to my lips and drink until nothing is left. It burns down my throat and into the pit of my stomach. The effect is immediate. My body seizes and I fall back on the ground. Everything in me begins to shift, like the very code in my cells is breaking apart and reassembling. I can't stop my legs and arms from moving as they spasm.

All I see is light above me, and then my body rises from the ground. A voice emanates from the light. "Scarlett Bramstall Ellis, firstborn of the light. I am Derakus."

I want to reply but my lips won't move. Instead, images rush by me like a warped movie screen—memories of my ancestors, of births and deaths, flashing by at the speed of light. Bits of conversations blend together, all of it seeping into my very soul.

The voice continues. "I find you worthy. Lead the revenant race with care." I feel an overwhelming surge of strength enter the mark on my head and rush down into my bones. My body feels as if it's growing, expanding, saturated with a glorious power. The light retreats quickly.

The room comes back into view and I'm flat on my back, staring into the eyes of the scribe. He smiles and extends a hand to me. I stand up and look at everyone still on their knees. The scribe pulls me to a chair beside a small table and the large man with the mask. In the masked man's hand is a tattoo gun and the blood that had been mixed with the powder. He motions for me to sit.

The large man rips my shirt at the collar and tattoos the Dawning mark on my neck—the crimson warning to any who would try to kill me. My body now carries the familial memories and histories of both my lines. I try to sit still, but it burns as he works, feeling more like a brand and less like the bee stings I was told a tattoo would be.

I force myself to remain still while he works, watching as Chasem and Nick are lifted out of the room. At some point, I guess, Chasem passed out, looking completely white. I see Holden start to leave and I stop him. "Please let me know how they're doing as soon as you find out."

"Yes, My Queen," he says with a bow and turns to walk out. I want to correct him and tell him to call me Scarlett, but it's rather moot and I don't have the energy. I don't want to be queen. I only want to be me, to go home to New York.

I scan the throne room while the tattoo gun buzzes in my ear. I look at the horrible statues lining this hall and the bodies of the dead strewn throughout, including Apollo's.

"Scribe," I say, and he stands before me. It's odd to look into the face of someone who looks so much like an animal.

"Yes, My Lady?"

"Can someone come in and clear the bodies from the room? What are typically done with them?"

"Well, there is a ceremony, and usually they are placed outside in the sun before dawn. The day is almost over, My Lady, so it would not happen today."

I consider this. "Can they be placed elsewhere until tomorrow?"

"I'm sure they can." He snaps to a servant and instructs him to remove the bodies.

"Just one thing," I add. "I will deal with Apollo's body. Please make sure they know this." He nods and walks away to speak to the others. "Also," I call for everyone to hear, "have all these statues removed and inventoried. I want to know who they were and to what family line they belonged." The men and women bow in acknowledgment. "I want them properly buried since they cannot be burned." They bow again.

I sit there patiently with the buzzing in my ear and close my eyes. I can call up any memory of anyone in my family line. I think of Lucian, my paternal grandfather, and try to recall anything about his death. Instead of getting the memory of it through his eyes, I am given Apollo's memory. I force myself not to jerk as I watch him poison Lucien's food. So, Apollo killed his father.

Much like I did.

Then again, maybe not. I acted in self-defense. He murdered.

The buzzing stops and I feel a cloth wiped down my neck. The large man stands in front of me and bows low, his hand lifted palm up in supplication. I touch it and he rises.

The scribe steps beside him and bows. "My Lady, we will take our leave now. I will return in three days' time for the official coronation, although you are the Queen as of right now. Is there anything more of me you need?"

How would I know? But I shake my head and he smiles politely. At least, I think it was a smile. He and the large man walk out of the long room, dodging men and women as they remove bodies and statues.

I stand and try to get my head around all that's just happened. It's overwhelming and more than a little unbelievable. I turn to face the massive throne behind me like it's an obstacle to overcome. I don't want it. I don't want to rule or anything related to it.

I grab a servant girl by the arm and she jumps. "Yes, my Queen?"

"Can you take me to where Chasem and the human Nick are held? Please?"

She nods. "All the injured were taken to the medical section of the mansion. Would you like to follow me?"

"Please," I reply, and she leads me out of the large room.

FORTY-FOUR
HURT

WHEN I ARRIVE AT THE MEDICAL WING OF THE mansion, I lose my breath at the sight of the ended battle and the ensuing carnage. Bodies fill the beds, attached to various wires and tubes. A few beds have bodies with sheets pulled up over them. My heart thuds hard in my chest and I look around in a panic.

A woman approaches. "My Lady, your uncle and helot are this way." She points to the far right where they lay side by side. Nick doesn't move, his eyes drawn tightly shut. Chasem's awake but in fierce pain, monitors marking time by his heartbeat.

I stand between the beds, not knowing what to do first.

"He's hasn't woken up yet," Chasem grits out through an oxygen mask. I glance at him and back to Nick, then brush Nick's hair back and kiss his head. "I'm here. I'm here and I won't leave you." I take his hand and give it a squeeze, but I get nothing in return.

I turn to Chasem. "How are you feeling?"

"Like I just had a leisurely massage. How do you think I'm feeling?" he asks with a scowl.

"Jerk," I respond. But I'm really relieved he's awake and talking. A doctor joins us and bows to me. "How are they?" I demand, and he looks up at me through his glasses with a startled look. Maybe I'd used too sharp a tone.

"Well, your helot has sustained a concussion. The swelling is not enough to put him into an induced coma, but it's borderline. The brain is resilient, and every case is different. For now, we're simply monitoring him. Otherwise, his vitals look good."

I stutter, "O-okay. What about Chasem?"

"Mr. Black has had his liver perforated and lost a lot of blood. We gave him two units of blood, both intravenously and orally. We just need to keep an eye on him. His body is traumatized."

"Don't talk about me like I'm not here," Chasem says angrily. His heavy breathing fogs the mask.

"My apologies, Mr. Black," the doctor stammers.

"Quit being difficult," I chide Chasem. I turn to the doctor to reassure him. "He's fine. No need to apologize to him."

"Very good. If you need anything more, I'll be right over here." The doctor indicates the other beds with a wave of his hand and almost runs away.

I sit down on the side of Nick's bed and stare at him, willing him to wake up and look at me. But he remains still.

"We lost Marcus," Chasem says, and I turn my head to face him, feeling like my heart isn't beating.

Everything in me sinks as the loss hits me. I cover my mouth and want to cry. I didn't know him very well, but he risked his life for me and paid the ultimate price. "I'm sorry, Chase. God, I'm so sorry." I bite my lip to keep from sobbing, but I feel tears running down my face anyways.

"He was a good man." Chasem's voice cracks at the end but he doesn't look at me.

"Was he married?" I ask in a small voice.

"Yes. Her name was Teresa. No children."

Teresa Potter. I make sure to commit the name to my memory. I want to face her and try to find the words to express how much I feel the loss and how much what he did saved my life.

Alarms sound by Chasem, and his eyes flutter closed. People scramble around me and push me away from him. I yell at them, but they steadfastly ignore me as they bring a crash cart toward him. I watch in horror as they try to bring a dead Chasem back to life.

I send a message to Valen to come to the Mansion. She arrives with an escort and rushes past the guards at the front of the hallway, short of breath and suspicious of everyone until she sees me.

She embraces me and examines the Dawning mark on my neck. "Thank God." She squeezes me again, then pulls back with tears in her eyes. "I was so worried. Where's Chasem?"

I pull her quickly with me to the medical room. People bow as we pass them, but I ignore them as much as I can. In his bed, Chasem doesn't move, connected to machines. The tattoos on his bare chest show in proud revenant language, and he still wears the oxygen mask.

"He coded, but they brought him back. Nick hasn't woken up, either. The doctors don't know why. Something about trauma to the head and that it takes time for the brain to repair itself. It's a waiting game for both of them."

Valen leans over Chasem and kisses his forehead. I see the tears roll down her nose and onto his skin. "Rest, Chasem. I won't let anything happen to you," she whispers.

Chasem's head moves but his eyes remain closed. He softly utters a name. "Hannah?"

What?

I see the shock register on Valen's face. She stands a little straighter and looks at me. "Who's Hannah?"

"Nick's mom. Nick is Chasem's helot, not mine. He's been keeping her updated on what's been going on. He probably just wants to tell her about Nick," I try to reassure, but honestly I'm as shocked as she is by his utterance.

Valen nods tightly and sits down in the chair beside his bed, taking his hand. "I'm here," she whispers, but it seems like a reaffirmation to herself and less like she's trying to convince him.

I sit down on Nick's bed and take his hand. There's nothing I can do, nowhere I can go, and no way to fix this. The doctor reassured me he's stable but that head injuries are hard to pinpoint to predict how a person will respond. Everyone is different.

I kiss his hand and press it to my face. "I love you, Nick. I love you so much. Please wake up. Open your eyes for me." He just lays still. I move to the chair beside his bed and think about how Valen and I mirror each other's tense waiting. I don't want to leave until they're both okay.

The staff leave us alone for the most part as we sit there. People come in and take out the bodies of the dead a little at a time. I know they'll be readying them to be placed in the sun to burn. I've never seen a revenant funeral. I'm not even sure that's what you call it, but still.

The thought of the sun has me considering the time I spent out in it. I didn't burn, not even a little. Whatever Apollo did to me, it succeeded in giving me the ability to withstand the sun—for how long, I'm still not sure. Even Derakus called me the firstborn of the light. Am I the first to actually be able to do this? Is that what he meant?

I consider what Chasem had warned me about a few days ago, about how revenants would not want to overthrow Apollo if they knew he was actually on the cusp of finding a cure for the sunlight issue. Apollo's rule is a moot point now, but the sunlight issue most certainly is not.

A hand on my shoulder startles me awake. Above me stands a girl a little older than me, with silky brown hair pulled back into a ponytail. Her warm, sable eyes regard me. "I didn't mean to startle you, My Lady." She bows. "My name is Selena, and this is Titus." She points to a boy behind her with hair so blond it's almost white, cropped close to his head. "We are your assistants."

I sit up in the chair and realize my body aches from my awkward sleeping position. I move slowly, testing out the muscles and what hurts. "Assistants?" I ask and finally manage to sit up straight. I look at Nick, and there's still no change. Then I glance at Valen, who only gives me a faint smile.

"Yes, ma'am. The scribe sent us to you. He said you might need some help. You have a coronation to prepare for and the counsel needs to meet you. You also had some plans for the body of King Bramstall, we were told. We are just in need of direction." She stares at me with the most unbeguiling eyes. They both seem poised for some sort of orders. To be given by me. Oh, boy.

"Okay," I say and stand. Nick's hand falls limply from mine. I'm torn about what to do and look at Valen again, like she can give me the answers. But her face is blank. I stare hard at both of my would-be assistants. "I'm not leaving this spot. So we'll go over everything here, okay?"

They both bow, and it takes very little time for them to bombard me with information and questions about things I'm not even sure I know how to approach. Thank God for Valen. She softly offers suggestions when she sees me struggle in any way.

I'm not meant for this. I don't want this. I want to run away more than anything—just to be home, in my own apartment, watching TV and eating cereal for dinner. I want to play chess with Brice. I don't want to be here, telling a whole world what they need to do and to listen to my orders. For God's sake, I'm a barrista, not a sovereign. They'll realize this soon enough, and I wonder what will happen to me then. Can they unnominate me? No. I realize that's impossible. As with everything in the revenant world, this is all about blood.

FORTY-FIVE
SHIFTING

I SOON DISCOVER MOST OF THE REVENANT WORLD WAS not aware Apollo even had a child, so my appearance on the scene confuses a lot of them. In my defense, the scribe confirms who I am and that I'd been in hiding from the former king. On a lot of levels, this makes sense. Those who knew Apollo knew he was a tyrant and had no intentions of sharing his throne or lineage with anyone. Plus, many in the revenant world view children much the same way he had—unwanted and feared. And here I am, like a bomb thrown right into a power vacuum. I don't feel welcome; I feel like an intruder.

When Selena had told me the counsel needed to meet me, what she really meant to say was they needed to get their mind around the unexpected shift in power with my Dawning and Apollo's death. Now, the council hears the story of my fight with Apollo and that I'd killed him in self-defense. They have no option but to accept me and my presence here.

They insist I have a bodyguard as well, and since I don't really feel like I know or trust anyone else, I choose Holden to take on the role. He gladly accepts.

Two things need to be done, and they both require me to leave Nick and Chasem. I have to speak with Teresa Potter, and I want to be the one to oversee the funerals—or whatever they call it—for those who died in the fighting.

I'm dozing in my chair, holding Nick's hand, when I heard a familiar voice. "Scarlett?"

I jerk my head up to see Chasem staring at me. I scurry up as quickly as I can to reach him. Valen smiles at me. I reach down and take Chasem's strong hand in mine.

"You big jerk. You scared the crap out of me. Don't do that again, do you understand?" I snarl.

"I'll see what I can do about not getting stabbed in the future. Sorry to inconvenience you by almost dying," he shoots back. His eyes go to the side of my neck and he reaches up, his fingertips lightly tracing the tattoo. Chasem smiles. "It looks good on you. Really good."

I take his hand, bring it to my lips, and kiss it. "Yeah, well, you thought I needed you before. Now I really need you. So hurry up, get off your butt, and get better."

"Yes, ma'am," he says with a roll of his eyes. He turns to Valen and smiles. "Could I have some water?"

"Sure," she says and checks the container by his bed to find it's empty. "I'll go get some more. I'll be right back." She gives a small smile and walks away.

"Has she been here long?" Chasem asks with a slight frown.

"Almost the entire time. She won't leave your side," I say and glance down at his troubled face. He seems like he wants to say something but holds back. "You know, you called her Hannah," I reveal, and he looks at me in shock.

"Geez. Did I really?"

"Yeah. Care to tell me why you'd be asking for Hannah?"

"Not really." He turns his head to see Nick laying in the bed beside his. "She's probably worried sick about him. How's he doing?"

"No change," I say as my throat threatens to close. "The doctor says he'll wake up when his brain is well enough. But he couldn't say when."

Chasem nods. "I need to call Hannah. I just...I just don't

know what I'll say about him." Chasem struggles to sit up and Holden joins me to help him. Chasem stares with an amused look at Holden. "Still hanging around?"

Holden holds up an arm with a wrist plate on it, engraved with the royal symbol. He shakes it around. "Hey, lookie-lookie at who's the new queenie bodyguard."

Chasem rolls his eyes. "So I saved Scarlett only to let her die because of an incompetent bodyguard."

"Hey, now. Don't make me stab one of your other vital organs," Holden shoots back playfully. He adjusts Chasem's pillows right as Valen returns with a container of water.

Behind her, a man appears and bows before me. "My Lady, a Teresa Potter is here to see you. She's waiting right outside."

"Thank you. I'll be right there," I try to reassure the man. He bows and disappears.

Chasem takes my hand. "Are you going to tell her about Marcus?"

I nod thoughtfully. I might hate my new role, but I think she needs to know her husband died for me. I almost can't get air into my lungs at the thought of talking to her. "It seems like the right thing to do. She should hear it from me."

Chasem tightens his lips and nods. "He died with honor. She should know he was a true hero."

I take a deep breath and squeeze Chasem's hand. Letting go, I walk with Holden to break the news of Marcus' death to his widow.

I sit leaning against the wall with my legs drawn up to my chest, sobbing. Holden stands in front of me, trying to protect me from any stares leveled my way. I can still feel Teresa's arms around me as she all but collapsed at the news of Marcus' death. I tried to explain to her that he died valiantly and that he would be given every honor afforded in his presentation to the sun.

She had spoken through broken words about how they

hadn't been married all that long and that they were planning to relocate to a revenant city in Canada within the next couple of months. They wanted to build a new life together. Now, nothing was left but shards of a broken dream.

I had taken her to the Daystar temple to assist with the preparation of his body. It had taken all I had to stand there while she wept over him. Eventually, it was too much and I ran from the room to find this secluded spot.

I force myself to stand and wipe my eyes with my sleeves. Holden never looks at me but respects that I'd just needed that moment to myself as much as I was allowed.

When we make it back to the mansion and medical area, Chasem angrily endures a liquid meal. He's surly and complains about everything on his plate. Even the bottle of blood isn't to his liking. His impatience tells me he's not one to convalesce; he wants to be up and around.

"Scarlett!" a voice exclaims from the doorway of the room. Paige pushes Brice in a wheelchair, his smile so big I think his face might break. I jump up and run to him, falling into his lap.

"Daddy, I'm so glad you're here!" I wrap my arms around him.

"Hey, hey, a little easier." He laughs and lifts my head, then pulls my face to his and kisses my cheek. "My baby girl. I hear it's all over and you're going to be safe now."

I nod. "It seems so."

He smiles and I glance up at Paige. "Thanks for taking care of him."

"No problem," she offers.

I call Selena over. "Can you set him up somewhere comfortable and get him a few guards and all that? For Paige as well?"

Selena nods quickly. "Yes, ma'am. Helot quarters?"

"No. This is my father. I want him treated like royalty, understood?"

Her face blanches and she splutters, "Of course, of course!"

Brice smirks and shifts in his seat. "Royalty, huh?"

"Absolutely. You're the king of my heart." His answering smile warms me.

The next hours we spend planning out the Daystar ceremony, in which the dead will be turned out to the sun and allowed to burn. The scribes usually oversee it, but I make sure they understand I want to be a part of it, too.

FORTY-SIX

GOODBYE

THE DEAD HAVE BEEN MOVED TO A BUILDING AT THE edge of town, which has access to the area directly exposed to the sun. It's a building inlaid with gold and jewels, nothing like the funeral home in which Nick's dad's funeral was held. It looks more like a small palace. Revenants' experience of death is extremely sacred, apparently.

There's no sitting room or parlors for anyone to pay their respects. The building is broken into two sections—the west side for preparing the bodies and the other section on the east side for viewing the courtyard in which the bodies are placed. A dark, tempered window allows anyone to watch, should they want to see their loved ones turn to ash.

When I walk into the west room, my nose catches the sweet scents of spices wafting in the air. More rat-like men dressed in robes clean each body, stitching up wounds and massaging in the spices. The bodies lay in neat rows, covered in black sheets.

The walls are all black stone and a little oppressive, much like the labs in which Apollo's experiments had been performed. I stand at the entrance of the room and look around until I see the dead king's body. When the scribes take notice of me standing there, all activity abruptly stops and everyone bows.

"Please, keep doing what you were doing," I say. They slowly stand and return to their previous ministrations. I walk forward towards Apollo's body. Two scribes stand there and don't move.

His dark hair is wet and brushed back from his forehead, his face pale. I stare at him with completely different eyes. When I'd looked at him before, it had been with anger or in the midst of fighting. Now, he isn't a threat. He looks like just a man. I find myself picking up his hand and examining it. It's just a normal hand, nothing to indicate the evil he'd brought into the world. His fingernails are manicured and his skin is soft.

I gaze down at his face. He looks like he's sleeping, all the anger and fury drained out like bathwater from a tub. I can almost see him though my mother's eyes, feeling the love she'd had for him at one point—a love that eventually turned to profound fear. But as he lays here, he almost seems innocent.

I'm not sure why, but a part of me wants to cry. Things could have been so different, so completely and utterly different. Why couldn't he have loved my mother enough to allow my birth and maybe, as a result, love me too? I could have been raised knowing who I am as a revenant and Dawned like my mother and uncle had, with love and reverence. We could have been a family. Instead, we're a tragedy.

A ball of pain wells up inside my chest. I feel the loss of what I never had with Apollo. Even though Brice is a wonderful father, it still feels like I've lost something, knowing Apollo just wanted to destroy me. I feel like I'm betraying Brice just by feeling the pain of this realization, but I can't help how this cut slowly draws across my heart. It probably has more to do with my mother's early memories of him and the love that had once been there. And as limited as that love had been, Apollo had loved Jasmine in as much of a way as he could.

I look up to see a scribe staring at me. I try to blink away the unshed tears settling in my eyes and focus on him. "Can we take him out last?"

The scribe nods. "Yes, My Lady."

When the bodies are ready, the scribes roll them out in front of the families, one by one, to view one final time. The families and friends kiss the dead, speaking soft words to them, and then the scribes wheel the bodies out into the Daystar courtyard. They line the bodies up and lay over each a gold sash with revenant writing.

I decide to roll Apollo out myself. As I walk by the mourners gathered there to say goodbye, they all bow. There's no one to say anything to him besides me. I purse my lips, determined to keep my head up and do this.

Once in the courtyard, all the scribes retreat to the glass viewing area with the families while the retractable ceiling is pulled back. I watch them go and stand by Apollo's body.

One of the scribes calls to me. "My Lady, the sun. Please come inside."

I shake my head and stand before Apollo's body. I see Holden dash toward me, but I raise my hand. "No. I'll be fine. Please, Holden, stay there."

"Scarlett—".

"It's okay. I promise," I reassure and stand watching the sky. It changes from light gray to a swirl of reds and oranges as the sun makes its appearance. The light breaks over the wall and hits my face. I hear the gasps of the watching crowd as they realize I'm not burning.

The warmth caresses my face and trails down my arms until it hits the bodies around me. A hissing sound fills the air as they fade to gray ash. I look down at Apollo's face, crumbling slowly and breaking away like the tide hitting a sand castle. I don't turn my eyes away until his body is completely washed away.

"Goodbye, Apollo."

I hear the retractable ceiling being pulled back into place as I walk back into the viewing area. Everyone stares in petrified horror at me. A few murmur to each other in disbelief at what they've just witnessed. Even Holden looks apprehensive. Behind him, Selena and Titus stand in shock. No one moves or says anything to me.

I stop and turn to the scribes. "Thank you," is all I manage to get out, and then I turn to leave the Daystar house. I want to run but force myself to walk normally. Before I make it out the door, the scribe who oversaw my Dawning stands by the door. Unlike the others, he smiles at me.

"My Lady," he says genteelly.

I pause and look at him. "You know, I never did get your name."

His black eyes sparkle and his mouth quirks up into a bigger smile. "Dare I say there wasn't time for introductions? My name is Aberon." He inclines his head slightly.

"Nice to meet you, Aberon," I say and extend my hand to shake his. He glances down, then takes my hand. His hand is slender and bony, covered in a very fine grey fur. During my Dawning, I'd just been so consumed with doing what I needed to Dawn that I hadn't even really looked at his oddness.

"You seem to be the only one not exactly surprised at what I just did," I remark under my breath.

He releases my hand. "Do I? Hmm," he replies, then bows and smiles again. I stare at him for a moment, hoping he'll explain, but he doesn't. I look back toward the surprised crowd, then exit the Daystar temple and slip into the car waiting to take me back to the royal mansion.

"My Lady, that was..." Holden begins. "Amazing. No revenant can stand in the sun, yet...you did. You stood in the sunlight and didn't burn. How is that possible?"

As we drive back to the mansion, Titus and Selena stare at me. I don't look at Holden as I watch the buildings rush by.

"Honestly, I'm not sure how. I just know that I can." I trace my fingers over the glass of the window. "Can we just let this drop for now?"

Holden makes a noise of assent and I feel relieved.

It's dark in the hospital ward, and everyone's sleeping. The rest of my day has been filled with Titus and Selena telling me everything I'll have to do for the coronation before the counsel tomorrow. I endure it as much as I can but find myself snapping at them. I just want to forget it all.

The only light in the room is on Nick's side table, and it gives an eerie glow to the rest of the room. Chasem sleeps, and Valen's taken the spare bed next to his. Holden already went outside to guard the room, although I wonder when he's ever going to sleep.

I keep my head down on the edge of Nick's bed as I sit holding his hand. I trace his fingers with my own and whisper to him. "I wish I could talk to you. I miss you. I miss your voice. I...I watched my blood father turn to ash today, which is a revenant version of a funeral." I lean in and kiss his fingertips. "Wake up, love. Please wake up. I need you. I'm just barely getting through this."

I lay my head down on his bed and close my eyes. Chasem had called Nick's mother earlier and told her he was okay but never explained he's still unconscious from a blow to the head. Yeah, that was probably smart. I can't imagine how I would have reacted to that kind of phone call.

I'm startled by a hand on my head and jerk up. Nick stares down at me with amusement in his eyes. "Nick, you're awake! Stay right here," I command.

"I don't think I'm going anywhere." He chuckles hoarsely.

I get the doctor, who examines Nick, looking into his eyes and asking him how he feels. Nick calmly answers all the questions, and after a few minutes, the doctor asks, "Would you like something to eat?"

Nick nods. "Yeah, that would be great, doc."

The doctor gives me a reassuring smile and leaves to get a nurse. I sit down and smother Nick's hand with kisses. "I'm so glad you're awake."

"How long have I been out?" he asks in a small voice.

"Three days." I put his hand on my cheek and gaze up into his beautifully handsome face. "But you're awake, now."

"Where am I?" he asks, looking all around. "Oh, hey, Chasem," he says, and I turn to see Chasem looking over at him through the dark.

"You're in the hospital wing of the mansion."

"Cool." Nick moves his body a bit, readjusting his limbs. "I feel so stiff."

"Well, yeah, you lazy slob. You've been laying around taking it easy while I've been fighting the world. I've missed my wingman," I say playfully.

"Lazy? Huh. I'll show you lazy." He moves to tickle me and immediately grits his teeth and clenches his eyes shut. His hand goes to his head and he lays back down.

"Take it easy," I groan. "You have a concussion, which is saying something considering how hard that head of yours is."

He chuckles. "Okay, no sudden movements. Got it."

The nurse brings him soup and gently lifts him into a sitting position. She puts pain meds into his IV, and he eats slowly, listening as I tell him all of the things that have happened and what's coming tomorrow.

"Coronation, huh?" he asks, taking a bite and then stopping. "Hey, turn your head."

I do so. I know what he wants to see—my Dawning mark.

"Wow. That's a killer tattoo. A little like Chasem's. That's your Dawning mark, right?"

I smile. "Yep. I've actually Dawned, been pissed off, and am now ready to rule. Not," I joke. He laughs and my heart leaps.

I've missed that more than I would miss air.

Nick finishes his soup and slides his body further into the bed, his eyes heavy.

"Go to sleep, babe. I'm here, okay?" I brush back the hair from his head and lean in to kiss him.

He nods. "I love you," he whispers and closes his eyes. For the first time in weeks, I feel like things might actually be okay.

FORTY-SEVEN

CORONATION

I STAND AT THE ENTRANCE TO THE GREAT HALL OF THE revenant king—which I guess, if I think about it, will be for the revenant Queen. I've been dressed in tight, leather fighting gear and not what I expected as the proper attire for ascending to a throne. I'm armed like I'm heading to a fight, too. Serena assures me it's what royalty wears during a coronation.

I stand there, flanked by Holden, Titus, and Selena, staring around at the spectacle. The hall is dark with black brick walls and long black sheets of fabric billowing in waves on the ceiling. My path is lined by men and women revenants, and even some humans, all dressed in black and silver. I feel like I'm going to my funeral, and it sends a shiver down my spine.

At the end of the hall stands Aberon next to what appears to be a christening stand, although a line of smoke rises from it. He smiles as he holds a large book. Sitting to the side of that group are Nick and Brice. Chasem stands, bracing his side but defiantly not using a cane or any other means of support. I shake my head. Stubborn fool.

"My Lady," Titus says and motions me forward.

I walk as calmly as I can towards Aberon, who's surrounded by a host of other scribes and revenants. The crowd watches me go and I hear their murmurs.

"...walks in the light..."

"...killed Apollo..."

"...abomination..."

That one stops me for a second. Abomination. I look around in an attempt to find the person who said it, but everyone's lips are closed, all eyes on me.

Titus signals to keep moving, so I start again. A few men and women standing beside him look angry—or constipated. I can't really tell which.

When I reach Aberon, he smiles, leans in, and says quietly, "My Lady, we meet again."

"Indeed we do," I agree.

Aberon turns to the crowd. "This evening, we accept as our sovereign Scarlett Bramstall Ellis, rightful heir to the Bramstall throne. Her lineage has been accepted through the rite of Dawning, taking into herself the history of the Black and Bramstall lines. Through the act of an outlaw, Apollo Bramstall attempted to take the life of his daughter. By the mercy of Derakus, she defended herself from such attack and now is the sole heir to the revenant throne." He pauses and glances around the room. "Further, she has been given the title by Derakus himself: Firstborn of the Light." The collective gasp is so loud for a second it's like the room itself made the noise. People look afraid, angry, or confused. No one seems to welcome me or the fact that I now rule them.

Aberon turns to me. "Give me your hand," he commands. I comply, and he produces a long, gleaming blade. My heart thuds and I want to run away again, but I force myself to remain still. I glance beyond Aberon to see Chasem nodding in assurance. Aberon pulls my hand over the stand with hot, burning coals. With a quick slash, he cuts my hand, and blood drips onto the coals. The smoke immediately changes from gray to white.

I see Chasem smile. This must be good, but I have no idea why. Aberon pulls me away from the stand and another scribe binds my hand. A third motions for me to kneel.

I look up at Aberon, who then opens his book and pulls out a small silver crown hidden inside. "You are accepted as a pure revenant ruler. Rule with care," Aberon says and he places the crown on my head. Even though it's small and wiry, it feels immensely heavy. He reaches down to help me up.

We turn toward the silent crowd. No one moves. From the side, I hear Chasem clapping, and then the rest of the crowd reluctantly joins in, somehow. Before I know it, the entire crowd is cheering for me. Oddly enough, none of it feels like a celebration; it feels like a witch hunt.

Back at the mansion, several council members arrive to meet me, along with the dignitaries who had been at the coronation. Other contacts are made via video conference, and I have to sit and act like I know what I'm doing. It's tiring, but Chasem and Holden stand beside me the entire time. Selena and Titus lean in to tell me who each person is as they approach me.

After a few hours, I'm done. I ask Selena and Titus if they can ask everyone else to just come back tomorrow. Do I really have to meet the entire council and government leaders from all over the globe at once? Really?

I need to rest and get away, and my assistants lead me to a series of apartments on the upper level of the mansion, directly above what had been Apollo's room. The apartments are smaller but opulent, and all join to a central living area. I take a room with Nick, which makes Chasem raise his eyebrows. Brice mirrors his expression, but neither of them say a word.

I shut the door to our room and watch Nick lay down. Before I can even talk to him, he's asleep. I don't begrudge him the rest; he's still healing from the concussion. But I'm not ready to sleep yet.

I walk through a set of French doors leading out to a

balcony. Light fades into the Alabaster City's version of a sunset. I lean over the railing and gaze down at the courtyard below. People flood out of the mansion, getting into heavily shaded cars to leave the city. No one notices me watching.

Suddenly, I recognize Ryker standing by the gates, his arms folded like he doesn't have a care in the world. He smiles at me and drags a finger across his throat. Then he laughs. I stiffen immediately, wanting to yell for the guards below, but I lose sight of him in the crowd.

I rush back into the other room and alert Holden. He's up in a flash and heads outside our suites to alert the guards. I step back onto the balcony and watch as the ceremonial guards look everywhere outside the gate. They don't find anything. Of course not. Ryker is gone, and with him any feeling I may have had of security. He'll eventually find me. I just hope I'm ready. I'm not now, though, and the terror makes me sick.

I get to the bathroom in time to lose whatever's in my stomach. I'm heaving when I hear a knock at the door.

"Scar, you okay?" Nick asks.

"I'm fine. Go away. The last thing I want is for you to hear me puke."

"Too late. Do you want me to go get someone?"

"No, I'm okay. Give me a minute and I'll be out."

"Okay." He doesn't sound convinced.

I lean back against the cool porcelain of the bathroom sink and draw my knees up to my chest. I'm so tired and overwhelmed. If they don't find Ryker, what will that mean for me?

When I step out of the bathroom, Nick's there sitting by the door. He glances up at me with a look of relief, then stands and pulls me close, looking me over. "You okay?"

"Yes. It must have been just all the stress today."

"They're all talking about Ryker out there. Did you see him?" His gray eyes hold a storm of trouble.

I reach up and caress his face. "I did, but he got away." I

walk to the bed and Nick follows me.

"He's alive and out there?" He starts to put on his shoes but I stop him.

"They've got it under control, Nick. They do. Holden knows about it, and so do the guards. They'll find him. Just rest, okay?" I let my hand rest over his shoelaces.

He lets out a heavy sigh. "Okay," he says reluctantly, then lays back on the bed.

I kick off my socks and shoes, unbuckle the tight leather fighting jacket I've been wearing, and wrap myself around him. "I love you, Nicholas Lightener," I breathe.

"I love you, Scarlett Ellis." He rests his arm on mine, wrapped around his body as I lay behind him.

In the quiet room, I listen to Nick breathe softly and realize he's gone back to sleep. My poor Nick. I know it'll just take time for him to be back to normal, but it's painful to see him and Chasem injured. They're okay and healing, I remind myself.

I gently disengage myself from Nick and sit by the window again, grabbing my cell phone. I turn it over and over again in my hand, then finally send a text to Missi.

She immediately responds. *Hey! How have you been? How's the vacation?*

Oh, you know, relaxing. How's school?

Same ol', same ol'. When you coming home?

When? Yeah, that's the question.

I'll be home soon, I write. *Can't wait to see you.*

Details! I want all the details, okay? Maybe we can go get dinner or something when you get back. Hit me up.

Absolutely. Talk to you later!

Ciao!

I finally know what I want to do. More importantly, I know who I really am, and this isn't it. I'm not sure how it'll go over, but I don't want to be here. I'm not anything but me, and I want to graduate high school and sleep in my own bed. I no longer have to be afraid of renegades, or even the sun. So what can life be for me now? I certainly don't want to be cloistered like a princess locked up in a high tower.

I lay back down on the bed and nuzzle into Nick. He shifts a little and puts his arm around me but doesn't open his eyes. My nose rests right next to his neck and I inhale. It's the best smell on the face of the earth, and I let myself drift off to sleep.

FORTY-EIGHT
GOING HOME

"**W**HAT DO YOU MEAN?" BRICE ASKS, CONFUSED AS he takes a bite of food. We're all sitting around a large table in the bright dining room of the royal apartments. A servant makes sure to fill his cup before walking away. Several other servants stand back, awaiting any order I might give. Ugh.

"Just what I said. I'm going home." I look at my plate and take a bite I really don't want, but it helps to burn off the nervous energy. I feel all the eyes on me and I want to squirm. But I'm sure of what I want to do, and I will go home.

"But you can't. You're the queen, now," Nick observes and looks around the table at everyone.

"*Because* I'm the queen, I can do whatever I want." I look at Chasem and meet his eyes. His face is stern but he says nothing, just takes a drink of his wine and continues to watch me.

"They won't just let you go, will they? I mean, don't you have to stay?" Brice holds his fork and knife in his hand, poised to stab the innocent chicken cacciatore on his plate.

"I'm not a prisoner, am I?" I ask, looking directly at Chasem.

He rubs his lip with his finger as if to consider what I've asked. He shakes his head. "No, you're not a prisoner."

"Then I'm going home," I say again to make sure everyone

understands. I'm not going to stay here. "I want to go back to school and graduate. I want to think about college, and life, and whatever else I want to do. It might involve coming back here, but right now I just want to think about finishing high school. End of discussion." I take another bite of my food but I don't taste it. Somehow this talk has killed my taste buds.

"What will happen here?" Valen asks quietly. "How will the government run? I mean, you have to make all the final decisions, of course. Who will do it if you're not here? Or are you abdicating?" Valen's eyes are wide with fear.

"If I have to, I will," I say and my voice shakes.

"You can't. You absolutely can't. Too many people died to get you were you are," Holden breaks in. "Think about Marcus, if nothing else. You owe it to everyone to try to run this government the way it was supposed to be run, not in Apollo's brutal fashion, or the way any of the would-be successors to your family line would want. If you don't rule, there will be anarchy and probably a civil war, especially now that everyone knows the atrocities performed in that lab of his."

Everyone talks at once, throwing out ideas of who would be the next in line to rule if I should, say, be killed. I consider that. What can I do? I don't want to be the cause of the final downfall of the house of Bramstall. I put my head in my hands for a moment and feel Nick caressing my back.

"Could someone be her representative here?" Brice asks, and everyone quiets as if it's actually possible. "I mean, she could still rule but live back in New York and return here when she's needed. Someone could stand in her place, making sure everything gets done."

I feel a twinge of hope and glance at my father. He gives me a reassuring wink. "Could I do that?" I ask. "I mean, is that possible?" I can't keep the hope out of my voice.

"Well, I don't see why not. Apollo and his father left the capital all the time with a minister behind in their place,"

Chasem says and takes a sip of his wine. His face has relaxed a little, which bolsters me even more.

"But who could do it?" Holden asks. No one says anything for a moment.

"What about Valen?" Chasem offers. Everyone looks at her and her mouth falls open.

"Me? Why me?" She pushes back from the table.

"Because your father was on Lucian's counsel for years. You grew up watching and learning from him. His lineage is trusted by the revenant world. You'd be a perfect choice. Plus, I'm sure he could still give you any kind of advice you need. Hell, even Dietrich could be convinced to help out if you needed him. He was also on the counsel before Apollo took power." Chasem drinks the rest of his wine and puts down the glass. When the servant approaches to refill it, he covers it and shakes his head.

Valen looks a little pale, then shifts her gaze toward me.

I smile at her. "Would you? For me? For my mother? Would you be my minster here?"

"Scarlett, this is such...I mean. Wow. I'm not sure I could," she protests, raising her arms.

"You could, and you'd probably do this whole gig better than I would. I haven't been raised to be queen, but here I am. So, what do you say?"

Valen bites her lip. She glances around at the whole table and, to my surprise, everyone seems to accept the idea. "Okay." She nods slowly, and then with more confidence. "Yes, I will."

The last thing I do before we leave the Alabaster City is sit in Apollo's room and gaze up at the large photograph of my mother hanging there. She was a beautiful woman, graceful. Her warm eyes seem to almost regard me like she knows I'm here.

I feel a hand on my shoulder and turn to see Valen. She sits on the armrest of my chair. "Your mother was otherworldly," she says. "Even though she was quiet and unassuming, she was the strongest person I knew."

I nod. "I wish I'd known her," I say longingly.

"You do. She's inside you. All her memories, all her feelings. Go somewhere quiet and think about her. She'll come to you. It takes practice and discipline to recall things cleanly without a scribe's help, but it will happen." Valen strokes my hair. "She'd be really proud of you if she were here."

God, I hope so. I want her to be. I want everything that happened here to be for something meaningful and a move towards progress for the revenants.

"I remember when this photo was taken," Valen offers as she looks up at it.

"You do?"

"Yes. Your father had just asked her to marry him in front of the entire court. She was just about ready to say yes when they caught that shot. I never saw her look so happy." Valen kisses my head and stands. "You better hurry. The car's ready to go." I see unshed tears in her eyes.

I nod and take one last look at the picture, then I turn and wrap my arms around Valen. "If my mother were here, she'd tell you thank you for helping her daughter and that she loves you."

"She's always here," she whispers and hugs me tighter. "Now, you better hurry before Chasem throws a fit."

Our goodbyes take a long time. Many revenants come out to see us off, and with all the extra people in our entourage, three cars scream off towards the airport in the dead of the Bulgarian night. The counsel has begrudgingly accepted Valen as my minister, and will keep in very close contact with me through her.

Of everyone leaving with us, Holden is the most nervous, having never lived outside a revenant city. He's not sure what to expect from the human world. Chasem assures him it'll all be fine and that he may actually like it more than the revenant cities.

My body finally starts to relax at the thought of going home, of seeing Missi, Trevor, and especially Emma. I can't wait to be in my own world, although I do have to concede to Chasem that I'll move into his building permanently. No more apartment. I'm still going to keep the lease, but I agree not to live there for the time being. At least I'll be in New York.

I consider the fact that I'm no longer limited by the sunlight. No one has asked me about it yet besides Holden the day it happened, but I'm sure the questions will come my way eventually. I'll let them know what I remember from Jasmine's memories in time, although I'm not exactly sure how to explain how any of it works. I don't leave out the possibility that all the injections Jasmine was subjected to had something to do with me being the first able to withstand the sun.

FORTY-NINE
HOME

"**F**IONA, ONLINE," CHASEM COMMANDS INTO HIS PHONE as we walk into his building.

"Welcome back, sir," Fiona echoes through the first floor. "I see you have returned with Nick, Scarlett, and Brice, and you have others with you as well, sir. Shall I add them to my database as friends?"

Chasem chuckles as he looks at Holden, Selena, and Paige, plus the three new revenant guards. "Yes, all present are residents, Fiona. Please add their bio signatures to your database for access to the building."

"Very good, sir," Fiona replies.

"Not me," Brice counters. "I'm going to head home in a few days." He moves slowly to sit on the couch. The trip home had been long and hard on his body. Paige stays close beside him.

"Sarah's still out there, and Ryker," I remind him. "You need to consider moving in here."

Brice looks up in pain. "Yeah, well, no one's keeping me from my house. End of discussion."

"Look, Brice—" Chasem begins.

"No! No, I'm going home when I feel up to the drive. If they really want to kill me, they'll find a way whether I'm here or in my own home. I'm not going to run and hide like some mouse. I'm going to go home."

"I'll go with him," Paige offers. "I won't let anything happen to him."

Brice looks up at her with a tiny trace of annoyance on his face. "I don't need a babysitter. I've lived up there for years by myself and with Scarlett. I don't need to be looked after." His voice sounds tight coming out.

"I'm not going to be there to babysit you," Paige protests. "You've become my friend and I came along to help my Queen's family, you included. So, either you accept my presence in your life outright, or I'll just figure out a way to live around you without your consent." She folds her arms.

He looks at her, then at me, I fold my arms, too. Inside, I'm surprisingly pleased. I already know why Paige has returned with us. It's as plain as the look of affection she gives Brice now, but he seems completely unaware of her regard for him. Maybe that's good. I'm glad it doesn't bother me like the whole Sarah/Hartlyn thing.

"You do have that extra bed, Dad. It might be good for you to have some company," I say, trying not to smile because I can see he knows he's being unreasonable.

"Fine," he says. "But it is my place. My rules. My life," he adds petulantly.

Paige offers a small, victorious smile. "Yes, sir."

"They said it was because of his gambling. They arrested a man by the name of Simon Hawks, who worked for some bookie on the east side." Hannah sets cookies on the table in front of Chasem, Nick, and me. Abby is almost laying on her brother, she's so happy to see him. Holden's found a place to wait outside.

"Why didn't you tell me about that?" Nick demands. "I mean, I had my phone. You could have texted me or something."

Hannah smiles gently. "Well, I wanted your celebratory vacation with Chasem and Scarlett to be free of stress. Telling you that wouldn't have changed anything. I knew you'd find out as soon as you got home. The evidence against him is pretty compelling." She brushes her chestnut-colored ponytail back from her shoulder, then waves to the plate. "Eat." She smiles shyly. "I'm glad you guys are back and had a nice vacation to celebrate your birthday. Did you have fun?"

We look at each other and smile. "Yes, Mrs. Lightener. We had a great time."

"Oh, you got a tattoo!" Abby announces as she leans over to point at my neck. I tilt my head to the side and lift my shoulder in an attempt to hide it. .

"A tattoo?" Hannah asks with her eyebrows raised.

"Yeah, just a small act of rebellion," Chasem adds quietly.

Hannah leans forward and her fingertips lightly touch my neck. "Wow, that's pretty. All in red, even. You don't see many tattoos like that. And it's similar to yours, Chasem." She looks down at me. "Were you trying to be like your Uncle?"

"Well, yeah. I've loved his for such a long time, I thought if I ever got one, I'd get one like his." I offer a smile to add to the tale.

"It certainly is unique. What kind of design is that?" she asks as she sits back down in her chair.

"Just a random tribal design I like." I smile and wish I can cover up my neck.

Hannah nods. "All the kids have those now." She glances at Nick. "Tell me you didn't get one, too." With a sheepish smile, she shrugs at me. "Not that yours is bad, Scarlett, it's just—"

I raise my hand. "It's okay, Mrs. Lightener. No offense taken."

Nick smiles at his mom and shakes his head. "Nope, Scarlett's rebellion was enough for both of us." He looks at me with mock disapproval.

I fake a shrug. "Chasem yelled at me for hours. But what can he do? I'm seventeen."

Hannah jumps up. "Oh, that reminds me." She retrieves a

small package from the kitchen, handing it to me as she sits down. "Happy belated birthday. I hope you like it." She fidgets as I unwrap the present.

Inside is a small gold bracelet with a heart charm. Hannah smiles.

"I helped pick it out," Abby adds.

"It's beautiful. Thank you," I tell her. I reach up to hug Abby then across for Hannah. When I do, I notice a spicy, repellent scent to her skin. It makes me want to pull away quickly, but I force myself to complete the hug.

"I'm glad you like it, dear," Hannah says. She grabs a cookie.

We say goodbye to Hannah and Abby, and Nick explains he wants to stay the night with his mom. I know he's missed her and his sister, and they need the time together. I think it's a good thing.

I stand on the top of the stairs outside with Chasem gazing down at the car as the door closes behind us. "So," I say as we just stand there. "Hannah's sick." Something in me eventually worked out the scent as I'd sat there with her. Poor Hannah.

Chasem nods but doesn't look at me. "Yep." His face is hard and troubled. Then he takes in a deep breath and lets it out.

"Cancer?" I ask.

Chasem nods again. "She doesn't know yet. I've got to figure out a way to get her to a doctor and treated. But, yeah, I think cancer. I may be able to help her treatment through Neville and my connections there."

I turn back toward the house and see the light on in Abby's bedroom. "You've known for a while, haven't you?"

"Yep. Since before Tim was killed."

"Nick doesn't know, does he?" My heart aches over what this will mean for him. God, can he never get away from loss?

"No," he says quietly. "He will, though, soon enough. She needs to get to a doctor first. I'm going to try to take care of her, if she'll let me."

Tears sting my eyes. I feel Chasem's arm wrap around me. "Come on. Let's go home."

FIFTY
CLAIMED

Six months later

I'M GLAD YOUR MOM WAS ABLE TO COME TO YOUR graduation," I say to Nick as we sit on the roof of Chasem's building. Part of it has been converted to a garden, full of lush trees and flowers of every kind. Chasem had it built for Hannah. He brings her up every moment he can in her wheelchair. She never seems to mind that it's always in the evening after the sun has gone down.

"Me too. I like the new wig she got. It's more like her natural color than anything else she's worn. It made her look like the old her."

"I think so, too. She seems to be getting through the treatments okay." I play with his hands.

He takes a moment to think, gazing out at the multiple building window lights, so much like stars in the sky. "Yeah, she does. I just wish she didn't have to be pushed around in that damned wheelchair."

"At least she's living here with us. I think my revenant guard have a soft spot for her and Abby." I smile and watch Nick's eyes.

His lips move but he seems to struggle for words. Then he forces a swallow, and I realize he is close to tears.

"Hey," I say. "It's okay." I hold his head close to my chest and brush my finger through his dark curls.

"I can't lose her," he says. "Abby needs her, too. What girl wants to grow up without a mother?"

What girl indeed.

He raises his head. "Oh, I'm sorry. I really am. I didn't mean to say that."

I stroke the side of his face. "I know. It's okay. But you're right. No girl wants to grow up without her mother. And Abby won't be without hers. You'll see. Your mom's going to beat this."

Nick's gray eyes regard me tenderly for a long time, full of unshed tears. Before I know it, he presses a kiss to my lips. His are soft and full, and I close my eyes to take in the taste of him. "Claim me," he says against my mouth in a soft whisper.

I pull back and look into his eyes. "You're not thinking clearly. Ever since your mom got sick—"

"I *am* thinking clearly. Holden told me just how sacred it is and so has your guard. I wanted to ask Chasem about it originally, but now I'm glad I didn't, considering..." His eyes flick away, just for a second.

I stand up and walk to the silk tree, touching its smooth bark. My heart thrums excitedly in my chest. I remember our conversation in the Alabaster City and how I was going to claim him there but it didn't feel right.

His voice is at my ear. "I mean it, Scarlett. With my father dead and my mom on the verge of dying, I know what I want and what's important to me. Life is too short. I want you forever. I would do whatever I could to never be away from you, ever. Don't you understand? My feelings for you are as irrevocable as claiming me is for you. You're it for me." He turns me to face him, the intensity of his feelings bleeding out of him. "I want you to claim me, if you'll have me." His lips are pulled tight as he waits.

Well, if he wants me, why not?

I gently push him back against the wall beside the silk tree and let my face linger at the vein in his neck. "Are you sure, Nick? If I do this, I can't ever go back. I'll be connected to you forever. Claiming is an almost permanent thing."

His heart hammers like it's about to break free of his chest. His rubs his hands slowly down my arms and pulls me close. "I don't ever want anyone but you. Do it. Claim me," he begs, his breath warm on my face.

I let my fangs drop and gently turn his head. I kiss his neck softly, then lick it, tasting the salt on his skin. "I love you, Nicholas Lightener. I claim you as my own."

Bite, my mind says, and for once, I obey.

Under the silk tree, in the cool of the night and the most intoxicating fragrance from the flowers, I claim Nick. My fangs puncture the soft veil of his skin, sinking down to the vein pulsing like a beacon. His blood pools in my mouth, but I don't suck to drink. I let it fill my mouth and trickle down my throat like a fine wine. My instinct tells me this is less about feeding and more about bonding with him.

His blood is unlike anything I've ever tasted—sweet, quenching, perfect, almost as if it were made for me. I feel my body trap him against the wall beneath the leaves of the silk tree in an unbreakable embrace. But Nick doesn't struggle. A hum sounds so loudly in my head. I'm alive and hot and my revenant side lights up.

"Oh, God," Nick breathes. His hand rushes up under my shirt and caresses my bare back, his heart pounding a million miles a minute. All I can feel is who he is in every part of who I am, like I've been broken into a million pieces and his blood brings everything together. Though we're two people, we're now one whole.

I hold him in place and feel my energy shifting the trees around us, bending them back in surrender to my power. My soul feels as if it's fragmenting, and a part of me binds to Nick.

He moans softly, and I feel the deepest need for him. He is mine, and I am his. I will never part from him.

I release him from my bite and watch with curiosity as the puncture marks heal on their own, remaining visible on his neck. Before I can think more about it, Nick's lips are on mine, hungry with need. His hands are like flames on my bare skin.

"I want you, Scarlett. All of you," he breathes against my cheek.

"You have me, forever," I whisper and realize there are tears running down my face.

"Forever." His lips find mine once more.

THE END

Acknowledgements

Thank you God. I cannot move, or breathe or exist except by your good favor. I am thankful for all the gifts and blessing you have brought my way. May I always keep you first in all that I am and all that I do.

I'd like to thank Kat Hutson for all your support in this project. Not only did you do a great job with the editing, but you were just an overall cheerleader and good friend. I think your overall enthusiasm helped propel me to the place where I am with this story. I couldn't have done this without you and our long email rants back and forth. I am very grateful I met you and feel like I have a true kindred soul in you.

GL Skye, thanks so much for your beta reading and support. I'm glad we are friends. I'm going to be looking for that compound when all hell breaks lose.

Gabby Matlock, thank you for expending all your time to beta read this and for being a strong supporter of my writing and me. You are a wonder!

Jerome Sayers, you are just an awesome dude! Your artwork blows me away and nothing makes a day like a few funny texts back and forth. How you translated a scribbled sketch into the beautiful work it is, I have no idea, but you exceeded my expectation.

Courtney Houston, I'm so glad we met and became the good writing friends we are. I've never knew so much energy and creativity could be in packed into such a small package. You wow me my friend!

Heather Snodgrass, thank you for all your support and finding those sneaky typos that get past everyone.

Kevin Jackson, I'm so grateful that we have become critique partners and friends. Your love of this story with all my crazy story twists is awesome! Thanks again.

Lorie Langdon, I thank God the day he allowed us to become friends. You have shared joys with me and tears with me. You are a blessing to me and I adore you! Plus your writing blows my socks off. True story.

Carey Corp, thanks for your friendship and support. You are full of knowledge and advice and I am so very fortunate that God allowed our paths to cross.

Kierdan, thank you for being the beautiful representation of Scarlett for this project. You are beautiful and wonderful and my life has been so blessed from the moment I felt you kick in your mother's belly and when I help deliver you. It was through thankful tears that I gazed down at you in my arms that wonderful day in January. I love you.

Billy, Kayleigh, Landon and Aiden, I love you.

Rebecca Andriot and Rachel Olney, thank you for listening to me ramble on endlessly about this project and never telling me stop. Our weekly meet ups are like a shelter from the storm!

And finally to Bill, what can I say that would even measure up to your love and support? There are no words that are even articulate enough to express it. I have no doubts that God sent you into my life to heal me, bless me and teach me. You are considerate, kind and more patient that anyone I have ever known. Why you love me I'll never know, but I'm glad you do. A lifetime with you is just not enough. "God Rules".

ABOUT THE AUTHOR

After working in the legal and technical fields for many years, Jennifer Osborn took the plunge into full time writing in 2015. She is the award-winning author of The Shilund Saga and The Sentinel's Insurgency. When not writing, she listens to a different muse and creates paintings and collages of all sorts.

She lives in the Cincinnati area with her husband, three dogs and two cats.

YOU CAN FIND OUT MORE ABOUT HER AT

www.jenniferosborn.org

ALSO BY JENNIFER

The Sentinel's Insurgency

The Veiled, The Expanded Edition

CPSIA information can be obtained
at www.ICGtesting.com
Printed in the USA
LVHW021840280120
645066LV00018B/1516